SEASON

OF THE

DRAGON

BOOK ONE OF
DRAGOS PRIMERI

NATALIE WRIGHT

MENARIS
BOOKS

TUCSON

For FF & JRF

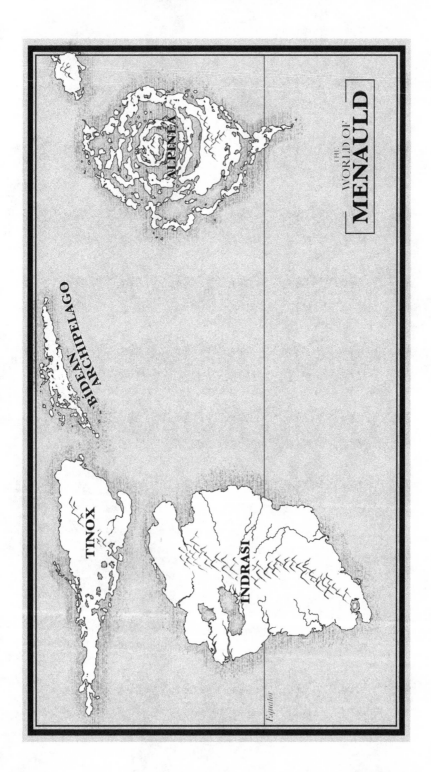

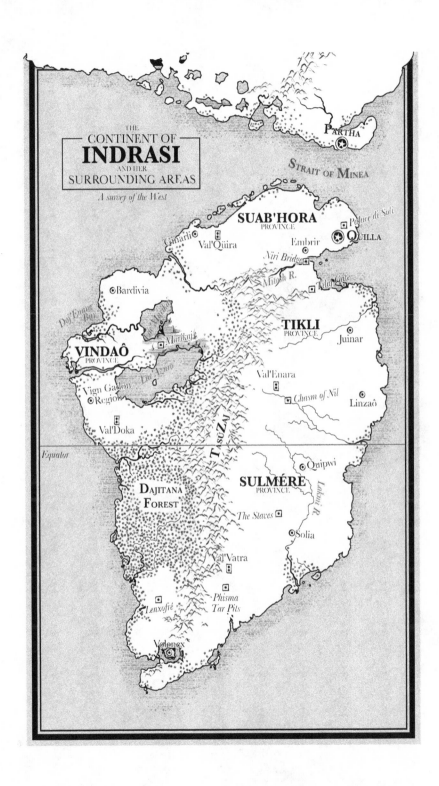

CONTENTS

PART I

SONG OF NIYADI

Wake wee Niyadi, wake!
Escape the Shadow's dream.
Your love awaits,
Her light you seek.
Embrace Indrasi's shore, ho!

Ride brave Niyadi, ride!
Across the starry sky.
Erase the night,
Hero to all.
Banish the Shadow's call, ho!

Dance glad Niyadi, dance!
Rejoice in Lumine's arms.
Win her sweet kiss,
The Queen o'Night.
Fight to deserve her hand, ho!

Stay friend Niyadi, stay!
Empty your cup o'drink.
Bring honeyed ale,
And bosoms pale.
Sing 'til your brother wakes, ho!

–Song of Niyadi, Sulmére Drinking Song, c. 1380, 3rd Era, Kovan Dynasty

CHAPTER I

Quen's two hearts drummed an uneven rhythm, matching the thunder of the approaching herd. The people of Solia crowded the wide dirt boulevard, whooping and ringing bells to welcome the first returning herdclan of the season. Quen wanted to join the excitement, but she dared get no closer than Fano's smithing tent set a row back from the main road. *I don't want a repeat of last year.* The galloping herd entered Solia's gates, and the ground quaked. Quen's shadow heartbeat, normally a phantom quiver, thrummed.

A head taller than most people from Sulmére Province, Quen easily peered over others and spotted the first riders through the gate. To her surprise, her brother, Rhoji, led Pijwar Herdclan into town. *I wondered where he'd gotten off to this morning.* Rhoji's kopek, Gambol, trotted proudly, his freshly oiled, leathery skin glistening in the midday light of the two suns. Rising winds fluttered

Rhoji's blue feather earring and rippled Pijwar Clan's orange banners.

Despite his morning ride into the Sulmére's shifting sands, Rhoji's bone-white linen tunic and riding pants remained pristine. *How does he manage that?* Ubiquitous Sulmére dust caked Quen's sand-colored linen tunic and wide-legged pants.

"Hika, Rhoji!" Quen called.

The crowd's cheers swelled, welcoming their favorite local son as if he'd been gone on a year-long quest. Rhoji was merely the second son of a clanless Solia merchant, but neither Rhoji nor his adoring fans seemed to know that.

"He'd look like a Sulmére prince if he wasn't riding a damned kopek." Fano, Quen's friend and a traveling blacksmith originally from the capital province, thrust a wheel loop into the quench, steam rising and quickly dissipating in the dry air. "Kopeks look like something dead, buried, and brought back to life." Fano wiped copious sweat from his broad forehead with a dusty, oil-stained cloth.

He's not wrong. Gambol's hairless skin, taut across his keg-shaped skeletal ribcage, gleamed like aged leather, his long legs spindly but agile. Quen called again and waved to Rhoji. He gave her a head bob and veered toward her just as the lead riders of Pijwar Clan galloped, their thukna herd now barreling into the gates behind them.

Gambol got within a few feet of Fano's smithing tent and jerked away, his eyes showing the whites. Rhoji pulled at the lead, trying to get close enough to talk without shouting. Like all animals Quen encountered, Gambol didn't want to get near Quen. *My damned curse.* Not even Dini, the town Bruxia—healer and wise

12

woman—could explain Quen's curse with animals. But whatever the reason, Quen's oddity meant she was unfit for binding with a herdclan. In the Sulmére, a person without a herdclan or honorable profession was *pesha*— no one.

Quen sighed and wrapped a strand of her keffla around her nose and mouth to keep out the dust. She tried to console herself. At nearly twenty, Quen was the last of her peers without a herdclan. *I probably wouldn't enjoy being a herdwife, anyway.* Studying at a Pillar was her only hope for an honorable future. Or at least one her father, Pahpi, considered proper. They impatiently awaited an emissary from the Pillar of the Way of Water, Val'Enara, to advise whether the Archon would admit Quen. She had no magical ability—no innate understanding of Menaris. *But they train in the Orrokan arts of war. Maybe that will be my path.*

The pungent odor of thukna musk filled the air, and Quen wrinkled her nose. The ground rumbled as the herd sprinted through Solia, intent on the life-giving waters of the Lakmi River at the eastern edge of town. *I didn't scare them this time.* It was reason enough for celebration after the debacle the prior spring. Quen twirled, the ends of her keffla catching the breeze, her tunic's billowy sleeves like wings.

Rhoji stared down at her and said, "You look like a lopsided cart without a driver."

Her rare moment of joy repelled his brotherly barb the way her presence repelled even the most docile woolly drey. *Allow me some peace, Rhoji.*

The bony protrusion on the back of her neck tingled, and she rubbed it and then chastised herself. *You can't will it away. Stop, or you'll only draw attention.* Quen removed her hand from the prominence that had grown under her skin a few weeks ago. It was a sign that she was losing her lifelong battle to suppress the shadow soul within—the soul of a changeling known as a Nixan. Quen was determined not to let the Nixan have its first Promena—metamorphosis. Though most Nixan morphed from human to beast form and back again with ease, some Nixan remained in animal form after their first Promena. *I'll be keeping my skin, Nixan.*

But even Still Waters, the relaxation technique Pahpi had taught her, barely worked any longer to calm the wild second spirit within. Quen breathed deeply and repeated her Still Waters mantra. *I won't let you win, Nixan.* The pounding of the shadow heart calmed, and Quen sighed with gratitude that she'd regained control. *For now.*

The last of Pijwar Clan's thukna passed, and now drey, horned sheep-like animals ready for shearing, waddled through the merchant square. The air was thick with dust kicked up by the herd. Pijwar Clan's children brought up the rear of the small but proud herdclan. They rode on the rounded shellbacks of juvenile ranju, waving. Their eyes, the only part of their face visible amidst the wrap of their kefflas, were bright and twinkling. *I bet they're smiling.* The crowd cheered even louder, their bells clanging. Rhoji clapped, though his red leather riding gloves muffled it. Fano put two fingers in his mouth and whistled.

Quen clapped politely, but she dared not allow herself to join in the revelry wholeheartedly. The internal battle to restrain her wild second soul took great concentration, and just being near the excitement was risky enough.

14

Pijwar Clan gathered now on the Lakmi River's banks. Rhoji clicked his tongue and steered Gambol into the street. "Join me at the tanning bay before Niyadi is past zenith. I have a new dye to try out before Jima Clan arrives."

Quen rolled her eyes. *Thinks he can lord over me.* "Who died and made you First Kin?"

"Do what you will, but if Pahpi catches you at Yulina's drinking instead of in the tanning bay, he'll have your hide." Rhoji trotted toward the town center, leaving Quen in a soured mood.

Please, Lumine, send Val'Enara's messenger soon. Though Quen had doubts about finding happiness sequestered in a remote sanctuary, she'd at least be free of working hides and Rhoji's haughty attitude.

Skins can wait. Quen pulled her bone-hilted dagger from her waist scabbard and began sharpening it on Fano's whetstone.

"Didn't you sharpen it yesterday?" Fano's paunchy belly jiggled as he laughed. "Whad'ya do? Cut leather with it?"

Quen stroked the blade across the stone. She retorted, "Keeping it sharp enough to shear the rocks off a fella who doesn't know when to leave off the ribbing."

Fano laughed harder. "Remind me to keep my stones away from your blade, then."

Quen joined in his laughter. The repetitive stroking of the blade against the stone calmed her spirits. The Nixan's phantom heartbeat was now silent, and Quen let out a sigh of relief.

Her respite was short-lived. As Quen stowed her freshly honed dagger, the ridges on the back of her neck zinged like a taut rope snapping. Her neck deformity burned, and queasiness washed over her.

Through the still-dusty air, Quen squinted at a hulking figure entering Solia's western gates. Two fiery-orange eyes of a kopek-sized black wolf pierced the sandy haze. Riding the strange beast was a woman dressed in black robes.

Kentaros, monks and masters of the Pillars, wore such robes. Deep-crimson embroidery edged this Kentaro's robes. The black-and-crimson combination didn't match any of the four Pillars. The woman's long, flowing hair was as black as the wolf's and contrasted with her pale skin.

A symbol etched in red ink emblazoned the stranger's forehead. Kentaros bore the Trinity's symbol inked in red—a blazing sun, inside of which was a crescent moon cradling a miniature sun. But the stranger's mark was not the Trinity. Instead, she bore the mark of a fiery red dragon inside a radiant sun. *Where is the Sister, Lumine, and Niyadi, the little brother sun? A Kentaro not bearing the Trinity mark? That's odd.*

Quen rubbed her neck. The bony prominence had never burned like this before. It felt like her spine was breaking through her skin. She feared the nubby ridges had finally poked through. Quen wasn't sure if excitement or an ill omen caused the novel sensation. Though the Brothers, the sun gods, were blazing as ever, she was now cold. *Run, stupid. Run from this stranger.* But Quen's feet remained planted like a koiyu tree.

Hairs on Quen's neck stood on end, and rivulets of sweat ran down her sides. Apparently unaware of Quen staring like an awestruck child, the woman paid her no heed. She kept her eyes on the horizon but wore a wide, serene smile. It was the sort of smile reserved for family or good friends, not outsiders.

Most animals, when approaching Quen, got wide-eyed, flared their nostrils, let off the acrid odor of fear, and jerked away. But the approaching wolf displayed none of the usual signals of wariness. *If this creature isn't afraid of me, maybe animals outside the Sulmére won't fear me, either.*

The odd Kentaro kept her eyes on the horizon as she rode through town. Quen wanted to stop her. *Why didn't her wolf react as animals normally do around me?* But she was as mute as a stone, unusual for Quen.

Merchants exited their tent stalls to watch the newcomer pass. Spring waters in the Lakmi brought new people to Solia. The town was filling with seasonal merchants and entertainers. Though Kentaros from the Pillars sometimes stopped to resupply in Solia, it was rare. Rarer still was a stranger riding a wolf.

Rhoji apparently hadn't gotten far, and he approached. The stranger pulled on thin leather reins, and her giant wolf stopped.

"I bid you welcome, Mast—I mean Mistress—er, esteemed…." Rhoji stammered. He bowed his head.

Quen chuckled at Rhoji's stumbled introduction.

"You may address me as Kentaro Nevara." The woman had a smooth, reassuring voice. If Rhoji had offended the Kentaro, she didn't show it. "And with whom do I have the honor of speaking?"

I feel pulled to this stranger like iron filings to a lodestone. Her phantom heart tharumped, and Quen closed her eyes and sought Still Waters. *It's like trying to corral a wild bull kopek.* After several repetitions of the mantra, the Nixan soul was again silent.

Rhoji straightened, thrust his chin out, and said, "Rhoji Tomo Santu di Sulmére."

Kentaro Nevara's eyes widened, but only for an instant. Her smile grew broader. "Ah, how fortuitous." She bowed her head and murmured, "Hiyadi provides." When she raised her head, the smile faded. "I came many leagues to speak with your Pahpi and Madi. Please take me to them."

Rhoji blanched, but soon his color returned. "I am afraid I can only meet half of your request, Kentaro Nevara, as my Madi, Suliam, has gone to the arms of the Sister." To his credit, Rhoji kept his voice even and his gaze unaffected.

Around Quen, Rhoji never maintained composure when speaking of their mother. If Quen spoke their mother's name, Rhoji would rage or storm away. Though Suliam hadn't died in childbirth, she went to Lumine's arms when Quen was barely one year. For reasons Quen never understood, Rhoji blamed her for their Madi's death.

The Kentaro touched her fingertips to her chest, her mouth, and last, put the pad of her right thumb to the symbol on her forehead. She whispered, "May the Sister embrace her."

Rhoji kissed his fingers, put his thumb to his forehead, and gave the required reply, "And the Brothers' light welcome her."

Among the Pillars of Vaya di Solis, this ritual prayer for the dead was the only thing all four shared. It was as universal as complaining about taxes levied by the Kovan Dynasty.

"You are here to see Pahpi then," Rhoji said. "I can take you to him should it please you."

Kentaro Nevara gave a favorable nod. "Most gracious."

Anyone in town could have pointed the way to Santu's Stand. With only a hundred permanent residents in Solia, everyone knew everybody else. And since her Pahpi owned Santu's Stand, the largest store for goods and wares in the southern Sulmére, all who visited Solia knew Santu.

Quen followed, but neither Rhoji nor Nevara glanced her direction. Rhoji, always looking for an opportunity to impress someone he considered important, was busy kissing up to the Kentaro. And the Kentaro remained focused on whatever made her ignore everything around her.

As they approached Pahpi's store, Rhoji offered a hand to help the Kentaro off her mount. Any herder's daughter would blush if the tall, dashing Rhoji offered his hand. But Kentaro Nevara was no herder's daughter.

The Kentaro dismounted on the side opposite Rhoji. Rhoji's cheeks colored.

At first wary of the imposing Kentaro, Quen was beginning to like her. *If she can take Rhoji down a few pegs, I hope she stays all spring.*

"This way." Rhoji opened the rickety door covered in flecks of bright yellow, and they entered the round earthen building locally known as "Santu's Stand."

Quen entered behind them, catching the door with her foot so it wouldn't slam.

The Kentaro inspected Santu's indoor market. Her upper lip curled as though she'd smelled something foul. As far as Quen was concerned, Santu's Stand was the finest building in town. Most merchants and traders worked out of tent stalls that sprang up along the main road, tucked between the permanent small mud-brick huts. *If the Kentaro thinks Santu's Stand is beneath her, then whatever Pillar she's from must be something to see.*

Pahpi had pulled back the canvas roof. The bright midday light of the big brother, Hiyadi, and his little brother, Niyadi, flooded the interior of Santu's Stand.

Pahpi had his back to them, talking to a herdwife about a small bottle he held. "This is huson pine oil. I think it's what you need. Our Bruxia, Dini, uses this on squalling babes who tug at their ears."

"How much?" The herdwife opened the small leather purse hanging from the primitively made leather belt at her waist. Worry pinched her brows. She pulled some coins from her pouch.

She was a young woman, likely Quen's age. *And she looks like she'll soon have another babe to worry over.*

I know that young mother. The woman had bound with Waloo Herdclan. Raiders assailed Waloo, a small herdclan, a few years back. Waloo lost most of their herd and their best herdsmen.

Santu pushed the woman's hand gently. "Fah," he said. "It is such a small bottle. Save your dars but promise you will use it. Your babe will be happier—and you and your herdsman, too, I should say." He chuckled and put the bottle in her hand.

The herdwife tucked the small bottle into her leather purse. "Thank you, Santu." She kissed Pahpi's weathered cheek, then turned to make her way out.

She stopped when she saw the three standing inside the door. Santu turned and noticed Kentaro Nevara.

Quen had seen Pahpi angry only a few times in her nineteen years. Once, she and Rhoji tussled over the last slice of cream cake. They'd broken a cask of precious still water. Pahpi made them do chores for Dini an entire month, and neither got to eat the cake. The other time was a few months ago when word of new Kovan Dynasty taxes arrived.

Santu looked angrier now than he had on either of those occasions. Bushy salt-and-pepper brows were knit over eyes like charred coals. His usually jovial smile had turned to a large frown beneath flared nostrils.

His voice was a low growl. "How dare you darken my door!"

Santu drew his belt knife and advanced on Kentaro Nevara. "I told you if I ever saw you again, I'd kill you."

CHAPTER 2

U ndaunted, Nevara faced Pahpi's poised blade. *Either she doesn't consider Pahpi a threat, or she's prepared for death.*

Rhoji thrust his body between Santu's dagger and the stoic Kentaro. "No, Pahpi!"

Santu's steel blade remained at the ready, his face red with rage. If Santu killed a Kentaro, the Jagaru would take his head. The Sulmére's roving bands of vigilante justiciars, Jagaru wouldn't bother carting a Kentaro killer to a Dynasty prison.

Nevara evinced neither anger nor fear. *She doesn't cower while a man intimidates her with a blade. Impressive.* Though Nevara didn't blanch, Pahpi refused to back down.

Fano once told Quen of Kentaro who conjured swords of flame. *For once, Pahpi, heed Rhoji's advice.* Quen moved to his side and put her hand on the wrist holding the knife. "Whatever this stranger has done, you cannot make justice your own." Quen tried to speak calmly, as Pahpi did when Hiyadi's fires rose in her, but her voice quavered. She coughed and continued, using Pahpi's often-used phrase. "Still Waters."

Pahpi looked at her as if he'd just seen her. His lower lip still trembled with anger, but he allowed Quen to lower his arm. She peeled the knife from his fingers and eased it into the scabbard hooked to his belt.

Pahpi wiped the spittle from his lip. "Leave us, you two." His hand shaky, he gestured at Rhoji and Quen. "This 'Kentaro' and I must have words." He emphasized 'Kentaro' as though it was a filthy word, at least when applied to Nevara.

Rhoji hesitated and glanced at Nevara to see if she was okay being left alone with Pahpi. Kentaro Nevara didn't beg him to stay. Rhoji blanched, then bowed and said, "I will take my leave, then." He hurried out, no doubt wanting to escape the Kentaro's dismissive attitude toward him.

Quen acted as though Pahpi hadn't told her to leave. *Why did Nevara travel such a distance to speak with Pahpi?*

"You too, Quen. What we must discuss—"

It might be about me. Quen had no basis for the idea other than the burning neck ridge and the agitated quiver of her shadow heart since Nevara entered Solia's gates. *I must know if this concerns me.* "I'll help you maintain calm waters, Pahpi." She stroked his arm to calm him and prove herself useful.

His brow smoothed, and his voice was even. "This Rajani wants to discuss matters from long ago. It is no business for your ears, Quen." Pahpi chucked her under the chin like he'd done when she was a child. "Put up the sign, so no customers disturb us."

What is a Rajani? Don't dismiss me like a child.

Pahpi's lips were a thin line, and his voice was a low growl. "Go."

Quen had never seen Pahpi so unyielding. She'd always done her best not to defy him. Pahpi unquestioningly accepted her in his home, regardless of her oddities and curse with animals. *I need Pahpi's support, but I must know why the Kentaro came to speak to him.* Sunlight glinting off Nevara's ruby-jeweled hair clip gave Quen an idea. *I'll leave as he commanded, but I'll find the answers I seek.*

Quen bowed dutifully to Pahpi. "As you wish, I will take my leave." Protocol required her to bow respectfully to her elders, so she briefly bowed to Nevara, too, before backing out of Santu's Stand.

I can listen from above. As a child, she'd splayed herself on the roof and "spied" on Pahpi through the opening many times in a game she'd played with Rhoji. *It should work as it did before.*

She moved swiftly to the back of Santu's Stand. Rhoji was nowhere to be seen. *Probably gone to trade skins with the Pijwar or gossip at Yulina's.* Santu's Stand hid her from the view of people milling around the merchant square.

Though a robust climber, Quen wasn't overly fond of high places. Sweat beaded on her brow. She pressed her keffla lightly against her forehead to sop up the perspiration. Light on her feet and nimble, Quen quickly made her way up the side of the mud building. The mixture of stones, reed-filled mud, and sand plaster created natural indentations in the otherwise smooth walls, perfect foot and handholds for climbing.

Quen eased out onto a round wood beam. *It feels smaller than when I was a child.* Her heart raced as Quen shimmied toward the center. The wood beams groaned from her weight. She stopped to rest, her arms trembling. She creeped again, patient and deliberate. The beams were silent. As she neared the edge of the opening, she straddled between two logs, so each had only half her weight. She rested her hands and head on the thick waxed canvas shutters.

Santu hadn't calmed down since she left him. "You are the reason she died, you blighted shadow-spawn bitch."

Quen covered her mouth with a hand to stifle a gasp. She'd never heard Pahpi utter profanities or say an unkind word. And what had he said—"reason she died." *Is he speaking of my Madi?*

Kentaro Nevara didn't recoil at his insult. "You are an intelligent man, Santu. And industrious to create a life— here." She looked around with her lip again curled in apparent disgust. "Yet you are ignorant in the ways of women. There is much that eludes you, Kensai."

Kensai? It was the term applied in the Pillars to someone raised from Rising to Ascended in the study of Vaya di Solis. Quen knew her father had studied at Val'Enara in his youth, but he'd never talked about being full Kensai.

Santu's harsh laugh was ironic. "Don't tell me you came here to teach me about women." His face was dark, his sour mood palpable. "You have no right to speak her name, let alone march into my home and raise a claim to my daughter."

'Claim to my daughter'? What is he talking about? Quen sweated so profusely that a drop fell from her forehead to the floor of Santu's Stand.

While Pahpi didn't notice, Nevara looked up. As quick as the strike of a desert asp, Santu grasped a long, thin, gleaming silver sword from a dusty scabbard hidden beneath sacks on the shelves behind him. He thrust it at Nevara's midsection.

Nevara leaned the upper half of her body back, displaying abnormal speed. *Swiftness like I have. The kind that makes people wary of me.* The woman dodged Santu's attack without leaving the spot where she stood. Nevara sprang backward, feet over head, putting distance between them.

It was a move Quen had used when sparring with Heiji, a younger boy from the Jima Clan. Quen had easily avoided Heiji's practice blade, and he'd suffered a humiliating defeat at the hands of a girl. Heiji had accused her of being a slint, shadowy slithering beasts and the worst type of Nixan known for stealing children in the night. Though Quen never performed the somersaulting move again, word of it spread through the herdclans, and no children would befriend her for several seasons. *Is this woman a slint? Am I one too?* The idea made Quen's chest feel like a band had tightened around it.

As soon as Nevara landed, she pulled her hands toward her chest. Fiery embers engulfed Nevara's torso in a warm glow. She thrust her arms up, and a wide column of fire rose from the dirt floor. Flames licked through the opening in the round ceiling.

Quen pulled away from the hole, barely avoiding being singed by the flames.

"Call your quenching waters now, Kensai Santu," Nevara mocked.

The flames hadn't reached the opening. Quen eased back to the edge. *Extinguish these unnatural flames with Enara's waters, Pahpi.*

Nevara's flames reflected on Pahpi's silver blade. His hands shook so hard the blade quivered, yet he didn't call dousing waters. *Why doesn't he call on the waters of Enara to quell her Vatra fires?*

Pahpi lowered his weapon.

Nevara's smile widened. She lowered her arms, and the column of fire dwindled, then sputtered out. The swirling embers vanished, too. Where the column of fire had risen, the ground was uncharred. If Quen hadn't witnessed the flames, she would never believe a fire had raged in Santu's Stand. *Or maybe it was an illusion.*

Nevara smoothed her hair, though it didn't appear unkempt to Quen. "She is not like others. Surely you have noticed this by now."

Santu wiped the sweat from his brow with a still-shaky hand. "I know she is my child. To me, nothing else matters."

Nevara scoffed. "Loving her won't keep the beast within at bay."

Quen's hearts pounded, and her ears were suddenly hot. The shock made her feel like one of the blacksmith Fano's iron wheel loops tightened around her midsection. *How does this woman know my secret?* Her sweating hands were slippery on the wood, and she nearly fell.

Pahpi's voice held contempt. "You are no Kentaro. Your Dragos Sol'iberi cult caters to fearful and superstitious people—and to those ignorant of the inner heart of Vaya di Solis. Quen's mismatched eyes mean the gods bless her doubly, nothing more."

Nevara said, "You know her bicolored eyes only hint at the truth. She has a neck ridge. I felt it myself when she was a babe."

Quen's innards seized into a tight ball. *I felt it myself when she was a babe.' Who is this woman?* If Nevara had been around at Quen's birth, she must have known Quen's mother, Suliam. Even though Nevara frightened Quen, and Pahpi wanted no part of her, Quen wished to speak with her. *What does she know about my neck ridge? And how did she know Suliam, my Madi?*

Wetness played at Santu's lids, making his eyes twinkle. "The vile magic you used on Suliam may mean Quen was born touched by Vay'Nada's shadow. But I raised her with the teachings of Vaya di Solis. She has the gentle and loving light of Lumine in her heart." Santu kissed his thumb and made a crescent mark on his forehead. "Nearly twenty years, and Quen is still Quen. Lumine protects her."

Does Pahpi know? Quen's fingers trembled as she fingered the bony prominence on her neck.

Nevara ignored Santu's comment. She searched the inner folds of her robes.

Santu raised his sword again, this time in a defensive posture.

Nevara moved slowly to not unnerve him further and produced a rolled scroll. Santu relaxed his posture and lowered his weapon. Nevara untied the yellow silk tie around the scroll and handed it to Santu.

Pahpi used the tip of his sword to push the scroll away. "This changes nothing. Suliam made that promise while under your spell. Such a promise is void, and I'll not honor it."

Quen crawled closer to the edge, trying to read the scroll. She was too far away, and the print was too small to read.

With a finger fitted with a silver claw-shaped cap, Nevara pointed at the scroll. "She was under no spell save for the desperation of any Consular's wife to deliver a third child to complete the Trinity. Suliam promised the child to the Dragos Sol'iberi before she was even conceived. Quen is a child of the fires, Santu, not truly yours. She belongs with my Rajani sisters and me. I came to collect what you owe us."

'Child of the fires?' 'Touched by the shadow' could refer to being Nixan. Most people called Nixan "shadow-spawn" and assumed they were creatures of the shadow's realm, Vay'Nada. *Has Pahpi always known? Has he been trying to prevent my Nixan soul's Promena with Still Waters training?*

"I do not care what Vay'Nada bargain of dark spirit you made with Suliam." Pahpi dashed the scroll to the ground and trampled it into the sandy dirt floor. "Quen is a person, not a sack of flour. You will never take her." He rose to his full height and filled his chest with air, making it larger. Instantly, he appeared younger and more vital.

Nevara shrieked, her cackling laughter like a wounded bird rather than a woman. Her eyes, thickly lined in black kohl, were dark, menacing orbs. "Do not try a glamour with me, Kensai." Her laughter died. "I came to collect what Suliam promised to the Dragos Sol'iberi." She thumped her chest. "I came for what she promised to *me*."

Nevara isn't a Kentaro from a Pillar? Sweat soaked Quen's underclothes and keffla. *Pahpi said Nevara stank of Vay'Nada—the shadow realm. What does that scroll say?*

There was a subtle movement below as Quen pondered the many questions and possibilities racing through her mind. Though she hadn't taken her eyes off them, she still couldn't believe what she saw.

"Meet Corvus, Santu." Nevara closed her eyes, spread her arms wide, and tucked her head. She flapped her arms up, then slammed them down to her sides. By the time her fingertips hit her thighs, she had fingers no more but wings. Before Pahpi stood a giant raven. The raven flapped its mighty wings and sent goods flying off the shelves of Santu's Stand. Its feathers and eyes were as dark as the bubbly tars of the Phisma pits, its yellow talons as sharp as daggers. A woman mere seconds before, Nevara was now a giant raven named Corvus, poised to strike Santu with knife-like claws.

Quen pushed to her feet. She sprang like a snake uncoiling, did a somersault as elegant as a traveling performer, then splatted like a thrown melon between Corvus and Santu. The graceful leap turned ugly entrance knocked the wind from her, but it served the purpose. Quen had thwarted Corvus's attack, at least for a few seconds.

Breathing was painful. Quen felt her side. *Bruised ribs.*

"Quen, for the love of Lumine's teats, what are you doing?" Santu asked.

"No 'thank you'?" Quen let out an indignant breath.

She held up a hand, and Santu helped her to stand. His brows knitted again. The glamour he'd affected of being larger and younger wore off. With his Bardivian height and breadth of shoulders, Santu had always been an imposing figure. But compared to the giant bird Corvus, Pahpi looked small and vulnerable. *Corvus could have struck him down.*

Quen squared her feet and put herself between Corvus and Santu. "I don't know who—or what—you are." Her voice was shrill and sounded forced. Quen coughed and swallowed. "If my First Kin says I'm not to go with you, I'll abide by his law. I embrace Lumine's calm waters, not Hiyadi's chaos of fire." Quen had no natural Vaya di Menaris—the magical arts—ability or training, but she knew how to pray. She said a silent prayer to Lumine, the patron goddess of Enara, and hoped quenching waters would magically appear from her hands. As usual when she called on them, the elemental spirits didn't answer. The air remained dry and still.

Corvus landed with grace. Its beak and feathers melted like a mirage on a blistering hot day. Nevara returned to her original form in less time than it takes to sneeze.

Her black eyes bored into Quen as though she could see through her to the bony ridges on her spine. "We determined your destiny before you were born, girl." Nevara's voice was a low hiss, full of rancor she'd hidden with false sweetness. "Wherever you go, tragedy will follow. Until you face the truth of what you are, you'll lay waste to villages. Kingdoms even." Nevara's attempt to smile came across as a grotesque sneer. "Come with me to

Volenex." She held out a silver-clawed hand. "You belong with the Rajani of the Dragos Sol'iberi. We have the answers you seek." She leaned closer and whispered, "You have seen Corvus, my Nixan soul. I know how to help you through the pain of your first Promena."

Quen had many questions, and she was desperate for answers. *What does it truly mean to be Nixan? And can I banish my Nixan soul completely?* Nevara's invitation tempted.

Before she could blurt out the questions swirling in her mind, the base of her neck tingled again. The hairs on her arms were on end. It was like she was being turned inside out through her navel. Moments ago, she'd been sweating through her underclothes from the midday heat. Now she shivered as the Void of Vay'Nada, the shadow realm, sucked away her heat.

She swayed, and her vision doubled. The sound of licking flames, the crackle of burning wood. Shouts and screams. The odor of burnt hair and flesh. Nausea washed over her, and Quen swallowed hard to keep the bile down. Quen shook her head, trying to clear her clouded mind. She'd never had a vision before. *Nevara is doing this to me. She's drawing power from Vay'Nada to befuddle my mind and scare me.* Nevara tempted her to go to the Volenex place she'd mentioned. But the idea of someone reaching into her mind and manipulating her thoughts made Vatra's fires roil in her gut. "Do not curse me with Vay'Nada."

Nevara's placid smile returned. "It is a prophecy, not a curse."

"Prophecy?" Quen grabbed the scroll Pahpi had smeared into the dirt. The words were illegible, covered in dust. She blew it off, but before she could read it, Pahpi snatched it back.

Pahpi's voice was strained. "This is the Shadow's work, Quen. Old business that concerns us no longer." He thrust the scroll to Nevara. "Take your dark words from my house and never return. We walk in Lumine's light."

Before Quen could tear the scroll back from Pahpi, Nevara seized it. "Have it your way, Kensai Santu." Nevara rolled the scroll and tucked it inside her black robes.

Dammit. I wanted to read what that infernal scroll says.

Nevara gestured around them. "This is your home, after all. Such as it is." Her expression reflected her distaste. "If I am unwelcome, I shall take my leave."

"But—" Quen couldn't let Nevara leave. She wanted to face Nevara and pepper her with the jumble of questions buzzing her mind like a hive of angry bees. Quen's mother, Suliam, had made a dark contract with Nevara. A contract for *her. Mother, why? Dini once said only curses and plagues come from bargains made with shadow-spawn. Is that why I'm cursed, why the shadow sucks at me? Why would you make such a vile bargain?*

But Pahpi would hear no more. His voice was firm and filled with anger and disdain. "Leave, vile creature, before I cut you down."

Nevara bowed, though she kept her eyes on Quen and Santu. "The sands beckon me home." She rose, graceful and composed, her dark eyes like two black beads. "Mark well, Quen Tomo Santu, what you witnessed here today. You can run from destiny, but it will find you. Is it not better to embrace the truth than commit your loved ones to the flame?"

Quen wasn't sure what Nevara meant and was still puzzling over how to answer, but Pahpi spoke low through gritted teeth. "Get out."

Nevara's surly glare disappeared, and she once again wore an amiable smile. "When you tire of living in the chaos you cause, you will find me at Volenex." She flourished her robes as she turned, flashing their dark-red edges. Nevara called back on her way out, "I look forward to our next meeting, Quen Tomo Santu, child of Volenex."

Quen began to run after Nevara, but Pahpi's wiry arm held her back. He spoke through gritted teeth. "I said no. For the love of the Three, Quen, when will you learn to leave things be?" Pahpi never said harsh words to her or struck her in anger. Pahpi's vehement reaction both surprised and worried her. *I don't want to fight Pahpi.* Though he was strong and virile, especially for a man in his middle years, Quen's strength had grown in recent months. *If we have an altercation, I might hurt him.*

The door banged shut behind Nevara, and they were alone. Nevara's exit left a void pregnant with unanswered questions.

Why does this Nixan come to Santu's Stand? And how does she know my secret? What promise did my mother make? And what are Rajani and this Dragos Sol'iberi Nevara mentioned? Destiny. Prophecy. Flame. *What does all this mean?*

Nevara might have departed, but questions remained. And Pahpi had answers.

Quen shook with anger, rage, and fear. Hot tears welled. She'd never raised her voice to Pahpi, but she couldn't contain the cauldron of emotion. "You told me Volenex was mythical. A place from stories like *The Saga of Ilkay*. But Nevara said she'd be there. What is the truth of this, Pahpi?"

Pahpi pinched the skin on the bridge of his nose. "Volenex belongs to Vay'Nada spawn, not decent folks walking in the light of the Three."

Quen groaned. "That's not an answer."

Pahpi's eyes were wide with anger and shone black. "Volenex is home to the Dragos Sol'iberi, a splinter faction of Val'Vatra Pillar. The Dragos Sol'iberi worship dragons and other Vay'Nada spawn. Eons ago, Vatra Pillar banished them. It's a cult of the Shadow, Quen. Full of Rajani Nixans and evil." As if expecting her next question, he added, "It is no place for you. Or anyone who prays to the Three."

One question down, many remained. Quen pressed further. "Tell me what Suliam promised. What does that scroll say?"

Pahpi shook with rage, his voice raised and full of contempt. "Nevara's words are ghosts of whispers. The past does not control us." He turned away, as though ignoring her would make her questions disappear.

Fear of the Nixan overtaking her and fused with growing rage that Pahpi withheld knowledge she needed. Quen pulled at his arm, her voice loud and angry. "Look at me, dammit!"

Pahpi turned, his eyes dark with anger. "Quen, I suggest—"

"No!" Quen screamed. "See me, Pahpi. Tell me the truth. Name what I am!"

Pahpi winced, his eyes rimmed in red and wet with tears. *Is that fear?* Worried she'd hurt Pahpi, the bubbling cauldron of anger burned now at a simmer. "I'm sorry—I didn't mean—"

Pahpi's eyes glistened. "Name you?" His lower lip quivered. "You are Quen Tomo Santu. My daughter. You walk in Lumine's light."

"Stop lying to me!" Quen ripped the keffla from her face. "Look at me. Say it aloud. Name me true."

Pahpi turned away. "I cannot …"

Tears made tracks on Quen's dusty face, and her voice was a dry croak. "You've lied to me. My whole life." Quen abandoned any attempt to stave off tears. She hiccupped with great sobs. "You lied to me, Pahpi."

His wary expression was gone. Pahpi's eyes were soft and brimming with tears. "Please, Quen. Do not dredge up the bones of my past. You are my child. You live in Lumine's light. I have told you this your whole life. It is not a lie." His eyes pleading, Pahpi reached for Quen's hand.

Quen shook with anger and sadness like she'd never known. She stared down at Pahpi's outstretched hand, and through bleary eyes, she barely recognized it. It was no longer the hand of her beloved Pahpi but of a stranger who'd chosen to ignore the bits of her he disliked. He'd loved her, but only the part he approved of. "How can you say you love me when you won't see the truth of me?" She wiped her nose on her sleeve and ran from Santu's Stand, leaving Pahpi's hand hanging, waiting for the reprieve from guilt she was unwilling to give.

He called out to her, "Quen!" But she ignored him, and the door to Santu's Stand banged shut behind her.

CHAPTER 3

E avesdropping hadn't answered Quen's questions and had left her with tenfold more. The fervent need for answers drove away care about what people might think of her. *I'll never belong to a herdclan, anyway. Not now.* She opened her stride wide and allowed herself to move with the inborn speed rather than concealing her abilities. Juka, patron spirit of sky and æther, blew her usual afternoon wind. Quen donned her keffla and covered her nose and mouth as she ran from the only home she'd ever known.

Tears streamed down her face, still hot with anger. Her tears dried nearly instantly in the dry air. Pahpi had always been the tether that grounded her to Menauld, keeping her from flying off into Juka's vast sky. With Pahpi's faith, Quen had been hopeful she could conquer the Nixan with whom she shared a skin.

How can I trust love built on a lie? Pahpi had known, if not that she was Nixan, then at least that a powerful curse touched her. *If I can't rely on Pahpi's love, how will I keep the Quen part of me from being consumed by the Shadow?* Her world was splintering.

Hoping to catch Nevara before she left, Quen sprinted to the town's stables. An ancient wooden pole structure that looked like a strong wind would knock it down, the stables housed kopeks sheltering from the heat. Several of them screeched, and a few reared up as she passed.

Quen yelled over her shoulder, "Yeah, well, I'm none too fond of you either." She tried to ignore the squawking kopeks as she scanned the interior to see if Nevara's giant wolf was resting inside, but it wasn't there.

At the far end, Rhoji rubbed Gambol's leathery skin with huson pine oil, the piney scent masking Gambol's unpleasant musky odor. Rhoji had removed his keffla, and his long locks blew behind him like a black flag, the single blue feather in his left ear whipping about his neck in the breeze. "Where are you going in such a hurry? I will need help with evening meal soon."

"To—help Dini with something," she lied. Fortunately, Rhoji was far enough away to not see her facial expressions. Her eyes often got wide when she lied, a dead giveaway to anyone who knew her, and Rhoji knew her very well.

Rhoji crossed his arms and narrowed his eyes at her. "Dini's quarters are the other direction."

Quen pretended not to hear him. She picked up speed again as she headed to the center of town. She needed answers, and only Nevara would give them.

Quen ran past merchants, busy helping folks from the newly arrived Pijwar Clan as she headed toward the western gates of Solia. There was no sign of Nevara or the black wolf.

The odor of sulfur assaulted Quen as she passed Fano's smithing tent. Though he'd arrived a week ago, Fano's smelter burned white-hot by day and orange by night.

Quen had known Fano most of her life. When she was only five, Fano had placed a blade in her hand and taught her how to throw. She got lessons from him each spring until she out-threw him in her sixteenth year. Fano had good-naturedly told her he was done teaching and gifted her the bone-hilted steel throwing dagger she wore.

She fingered the polished bone hilt of the dagger, her most cherished possession. She'd fashioned a belt and scabbard from light-grey drey hide and had rarely taken it off since.

Fano yelled, "Hika!" He waved his hammer in the air, gesturing for her to come over.

Quen waved and walked backward as she spoke. "Can't talk now. Looking for the Kentaro. Did you see her leaving town?"

Fano thrust the wheel loop he'd been hammering into the fire. His laugh sounded like someone had pushed it through a giant bellows. "You mean the pretty one?" He pantomimed a well-endowed chest.

"Lumine's teats, Fano. I'm serious. I need to speak with her."

Fano chuckled. "Better not let your Pahpi hear you talk like that. He'll know where you learned it." He took the loop from the fire and continued hammering it. "Sorry, Quen. I didn't see her pass. And I'd remember a beautiful woman riding a wolf."

Dammit. How did Nevara exit Solia without Fano seeing her? But Fano became a single-minded smithing machine when he worked. *Maybe he just didn't notice her.*

He called out as Quen resumed running toward Solia's gates. "Come to Yulina's later. I'll buy you a drink."

"Maybe later," she called back. Fano had been from one end of the Sulmére to the other and was always a great one for stories. Having been no farther than Quipwi, the next town north along the Lakmi, all Quen knew about the world she'd learned from Fano and other travelers. And unlike Solia's superstitious and wary people, Quen's peculiarities didn't bother Fano. Between his days as a sailor and ranging the vast expanse of the Sulmére Province, Fano had likely seen stranger things than Quen's unusual curse with animals.

Fano hammered the red-hot iron into a curve to match up with the loop he'd already beaten out of the thin, straight metal line. "Stay out of trouble," he shouted.

Not likely.

Now at the western gates, Quen paused. Chasing after someone in the desert was a bad idea. Even if she knew the direction Nevara had gone, Juka's afternoon winds would erase her tracks within minutes.

Juka's breath was only one of many reasons she should remain in Solia and not chase after Nevara. *But I must know what's on that scroll.* There was no time to coax a kopek with sweet jishni root to allow her to mount, so she pressed forward on foot. A pair of dogs tugging at a bone gave up their game and ran at the sight of her.

"Cowards," she called over her shoulder.

As soon as she was beyond the western gates of Solia, Quen opened her stride and sprinted without restraint. Moving this way was freeing. She tapped into reserves of strength from deep within, choosing to ignore the fact that the power likely came from the Nixan soul she despised.

Sulmére dust colored the horizon the same hue as the sand, making it difficult to distinguish ground from sky. Quen's favorite story, *The Saga of Ilkay*, described Volenex as an 'angry mountain.' The only mountains visible in the haze were the ones to the south, so she went in that direction. *I hope I've chosen correctly.*

Juka's afternoon breeze blustered. Quen double-wrapped her keffla and covered her vision in a gauzy layer of linen to keep the swirling sands from scouring her eyes. Running at full speed, Quen practically skimmed the sand's surface as gusts slapped her tunic against her thighs.

No longer a typical afternoon breeze, Juka was threatening a haboob. Sands whipped, and dehydration swelled Quen's tongue. Juka's thirsty winds lapped the sweat from her skin.

Standing still and squinting at the horizon, she saw something moving ahead, far in the distance. A dark figure. *Nevara?*

Quen summoned more speed than she'd ever tried before. At first, her hips and knees protested. She ignored the discomfort, and after a few minutes, her joints loosened. Through the shimmering haze of blazing late-afternoon heat, a black blob wavered on the horizon.

She called out, "Nevara!"

Quen concentrated, but the only sound was the whistle of sand skimming the dunes. *Juka's breath.*

She yelled again. "Nevara—it's Quen Tomo Santu. Please stop, so we might speak." Though Quen screamed, the dunes swallowed her voice. She didn't know if Nevara—or whoever rode ahead—heard her.

A faint crackle amongst the whistling wind. *Is that a call back?* Quen continued running at top speed, practically hovering over the dunes.

The dark figure was closer, but still difficult to discern through the wavering heat rising from the sands. As Quen neared the figure, she realized it wasn't a rider.

Quen called again. This time the response was clear. "Brock-brock," it croaked. It was a raven's call. *Corvus.*

The giant black bird spread its wings wide, creating a dark shadow on the sands. Its great beak opened, and it let out a loud croak. It sounded like the bird said, "Come."

Quen ran toward Corvus and away from Solia.

Winds lashed her tunic, and sand swirled. Juka threatened a massive sandstorm. The kind that separated drey from their herd and killed herdspeople not wise enough to find shelter. *I should turn back.* Yet Quen couldn't make herself turn away from answers.

Ahead, a flash of black. Juka's breath carried a call. The raven croak was like a crooked finger beckoning her onward.

Drawing on reserves of strength she had only recently realized she had, Quen railed against the gale. It was like trying to move a mud-brick wall. No longer skimming the dunes, her feet sank into the sand. Her legs, mired in the dune, shook with effort as she tried to pull them out for another step. *I'm no match for Juka's mighty breath.*

Ahead, Corvus flew like a seed husk bandied about by a strong wind. *Juka hinders Corvus as well.*

The air, now more sand than æther, made breathing perilous. Quen could barely see her hand stretched out before her. She lost sight of Corvus and called with all the force she could muster. "Corvus!"

The gale roared, drowning out everything but the eerie sound of sand whisking along the dunes. She called to Corvus again and again until her throat was raw. There was no response.

With each step, Quen sank deeper into the dune. As she walked, the winds deposited fresh, unpacked sand in front of her. Corvus was no longer visible on the horizon. Juka had stymied her quest for answers. Her longing for answers would have to wait. *I just hope I live to see tomorrow.*

Quen rarely prayed to the lesser gods and spirits for aid. But she prayed now to the only deity that could get her out of the mess she'd put herself in. She stood knee-deep in a dune and spoke silently to the guardian spirit of the wind, air, and æther. *Juka, please gentle your winds so I can find my way home.*

Why didn't I bring food, water, and a staff to help me push up out of the dunes? Quen cursed herself for being so rash, running off like a newborn drey, blind and searching for its mother's teat. If she survived the day, her father and brothers would give her the rough side of their tongues, and she'd deserve it. Her father would never forgive her for disobeying him and chasing after a woman he'd said was the spawn of the Shadow.

Is this my punishment? She asked it of the Trinity—Hiyadi, Niyadi, and Lumine—and half expected an answer.

She stood still as stone, waiting for the winds to subside. Her breath was ragged, heart pounding so hard blood rushed in her ears. The Nixan phantom heartbeat, usually a vague flutter, now thundered and panicked her further.

A voice. Sometimes, from deep within, she "heard" the voice of her Nixan soul. Like cheese curds rising to the surface of milk, ideas sometimes came from her deepest self. Thoughts that weren't her own. *Is this voice the Nixan taunting me?* Quen held her breath, remaining as still as possible, trying to determine if the voice was from inside or out.

Again, a voice, and it was not from within. But it wasn't Corvus either. The voice was human.

"Nevara?" Quen sounded like the crackle of husks in a thrasher. She tried to wet her tongue, but her mouth was as dry as baked linen. *That isn't a good sign.*

There it was again. It wasn't the trickster spirit's jape. Someone called her name.

"Quen!"

Rhoji? Quen pulled a foot from the sand, her heart racing with renewed hope. She managed less of a croak and more of a call this time. "Rho-ji?"

A kopek brayed and coughed. A man yelled, "Quen?"

It is Rhoji. The winds still thrashed but had gone from tempest to mere windstorm. She said a silent thank-you to Juka and the Three for answering her prayers. Rhoji wasn't her first choice of aid. He'd tease her about how she got lost in a haboob until the day she died, but as

Pahpi always said, a person dying of thirst doesn't refuse a drink.

"Rho-ji!" *Keep calling so I can follow your voice.*

They called back and forth to each other, each round getting louder and louder as they followed the sound to find one another. Before long, he was a dark blur on the horizon, the sands pink and orange behind him. From somewhere deep within, Quen found the strength to run. Gone was her preternatural speed. She moved with the loping clumsiness of someone nearly desiccated by Juka's torrent of hot air.

At last, he was close enough she saw Gambol's dark eyes squinted nearly closed, protected by two layers of thick lashes. Rhoji's keffla covered his entire face, but his bone-white tunic was visible against the black of Gambol's skin. She stopped, her legs quivering beneath her, and waited for him to come to her.

Gambol swept up to her side. *This is the first time Gambol hasn't been skittish around me.* Rhoji reached down, and she took his hand. She wasn't sure how she got up and behind him, but she rode on a kopek with her brother as if it were normal. *Has the curse that makes animals fear me somehow lifted? Perhaps Juka really has answered my prayer.*

They'd gone less than a mile when Juka decided she hadn't been heard nearly enough for the day. Dust devils formed columns of sand around them, blocking their path toward Solia.

That's what I get for praying.

Rhoji had to yell over the rumble of the lashing wind. "We need to take cover until this storm blows itself out." He pulled on the reins, kicked Gambol's ribs, and called out, "Hika!"

45

Gambol's wide, flat feet and toes were made for running on the sands. He was unperturbed by the thrashing wind and sand. Quen wrapped her arms tightly around Rhoji and bounced hard on Gambol's bony back as he trotted.

"Where are we going?" Quen's voice was still dry as crisp bread.

Rhoji didn't answer, but pointed.

Ahead, barely visible through the haze of dust, stood the towering natural stone sentinels known as the Staves. Like two massive timbers thrust into the ground by giants, the Staves served as a landmark for travelers from Solia north via the Trinity Road to the capital or west to Quipwi. In two days, their brother, Liodhan, would pass the Staves on his way to Solia with his herdwife, Zarate, their new daughter, Lumina, and the whole Jima Clan.

But the Staves were leagues away from Solia. *How far did I run?*

Quen allowed herself to rest against Rhoji's back. Before long, they were in the long, cool shadow cast by the towering twin pillars of stone.

Rhoji pulled her from Gambol and sat her gently at the base of the eastern tower. It blocked most of the strongest winds whipping from the south. Rhoji unwrapped her keffla and opened her mouth, pouring warm water down her gullet. Her throat was so dry she couldn't swallow and nearly choked as she spat it out. He poured again, more slowly this time, and she got a sip down and then another. Soon she had a hand on the water sac and pulled it to her, greedily downing Enara's elixir of life.

"Easy now. You don't want to make yourself sick." His tone was gentle and without reproach.

Missing a chance to chide me? That's unlike him. Her mouth wet again, she could finally speak. "What, no scolding?"

Rhoji unwrapped the keffla from around his eyes. "There will be time for that later. After I'm certain you will not die from this stunt you pulled."

There it is. The judgmental edge in Rhoji's voice Quen was accustomed to. "Why did you risk coming after me, anyway? There are no skins in it for you."

A vein at his temple throbbed, and his lips were in a thin line. "Because if anything happens to you, Pahpi will blame me." His voice held a bitter edge. Rhoji thrust the water sac in her direction.

"And here I thought for a minute that it was because you actually cared." *If he knew the truth about me, even fear of Pahpi's retribution wouldn't be enough to get him to help me.* Quen sipped the water more slowly, savoring the sweet trickle down her parched throat. *Whatever his motive, if Rhoji hadn't searched for me...* She shuddered, thinking of what might have happened.

She handed the sac back, and Rhoji took a long drink and eased down beside her, resting his back against the cool stone. The throbbing vein was gone. "You know it's a fool's errand running into the desert on foot when the sky is the color of sand. What could have possibly made you lose your damned mind?"

Quen considered telling him the truth. After all, she'd given Pahpi a tongue-lashing for lying to her. But she couldn't admit the truth to Rhoji. Shared history, family obligation, and dread of Pahpi's reproaches held their relationship together. But their sibling bond, though fraught with friction, was one of the few relationships she had. She couldn't risk blowing it up entirely, so she withheld the truth.

Instead, she snuggled against his shoulder, wind-blown and weary. All she could say was "The Kentaro."

His shoulder lost some of its tension.

The winds howled, and sand pinged against the stone. Tired from her ordeal in the haboob, Quen nodded off. All too soon, Rhoji gently shook her awake.

"The winds have calmed. Rouse yourself. Niyadi makes his way to slumber, and I want to get back to Solia before Vay'Nada's shadow is full."

She blinked and rubbed the sleep from her eyes. The sky was ablaze with orange as Niyadi, the little brother sun, marched toward the horizon. It was only a few hours until Hiyadi, the larger sun, would rise. But the shadow hours weren't the time to travel in the Sulmére. Though short, full night was cold and black.

And it is only getting longer. As Niyadi made his once-every-three-generation march toward Vay'Nada's realm, nights grew darker and longer. Incremental bit by incremental bit, they were losing ground to the Shadow.

Rhoji lent a hand as she tried to get astride Gambol, but he scampered away. *The gods didn't lift my curse after all. Gambol must have been more worried about Juka's winds than me.* Rhoji pulled sweet jishni root from his belt pouch and calmed Gambol. While he was distracted by the irresistibly sweet snack, Quen leaped onto his back in one lithe move.

The rocking motion of Gambol's gallop lulled her into a waking dream state. She'd lost out on the chance to speak with Nevara, a Nixan as she was. But soon, Liodhan would arrive, and she'd get to meet her new niece,

48

Lumina. She was an aunt, and thinking of spending time with a wee babe to spoil made her smile.

Rhoji broke the silence. "Did you spy on Pahpi and the Kentaro?"

The question pulled Quen from her reverie. She was loath to reveal all she'd heard. *He'll disown me if he learns the truth.* She deflected his question. "Why do you ask? Do you know something about her?"

"About her? No. But it's only a matter of time before Kovathas come asking questions of Pahpi."

She sat up straighter. Kovathas were the long arm of the Dynasty, extending its influence beyond the capital to collect taxes and flex its copious muscle. In years past, Kovatha were rarely seen as far south as Solia. But last season brought a steady flow of Kovatha mages through town. Traveling merchants told disturbing stories of the growing fear invoked by Kovatha mages. People said they'd begun threatening to use magical torture to force people to pay huge levies to avoid being hauled to a Qülla prison. Pahpi complained to anyone who would listen about the Dynasty abusing its power to collect levies to fund its gluttonous appetites.

"Why would Kovathas question Pahpi?"

Rhoji harrumphed. "Do you pay attention to anything? Come on, Quen. It's nearly your twentieth year. It's time you learned more of the world than what lies within the walls of Solia."

Quen couldn't disagree, but it didn't answer her question. "Is Pahpi in trouble?"

Rhoji shrugged. "Maybe not yet, but he soon will be if he doesn't stop speaking ill of the new Dynasty taxes to every herdwife and cheesemonger who will listen. By

Niyadi's ass, it wouldn't surprise me if Pahpi's complaints against the Dynasty have already made their way to the ears of the Exalted in Qülla."

Like a jolt of white-hot lightning splitting a summer-orange sky, the sensation of being pulled inward seized Quen. It was like it had been briefly in Santu's Stand when Nevara issued her prophecy, only this time much stronger. The tang of metal filled her mouth, and her head swam. Acid swirled in her gut, bringing a wave of nausea.

Pain exploded behind her eyes, and she shut them tight. Smoke burned her lungs, and Quen coughed. Voices cried out in pain and horror, but the sound was warbly and distorted like it came from the end of a long tunnel. Fire crackled, and burning timbers popped and hissed. Quen gagged as the odor of burnt hair and flesh filled her nostrils.

Terrified by the horrific vision, Quen cried out.

"What in Hiyadi's name? Quen, what's the matter with you?"

The vision had been as vivid as reality. She'd coughed from the acrid smoke, yet no fires burned around them. There was only her and Rhoji astride Gambol, trudging up a dune.

The vision faded, and the pain receded. She gripped her head on either side and pressed lightly, as though she could push the lingering odor of death from her mind. "We must hurry." She kicked at Gambol's ribs, trying to urge him to run.

"What are you on about?"

She kicked again and shouted, "Hika!"

"Stop, Quen. You'll spook him, and he'll throw us." Rhoji pulled on Gambol's reins and stroked the animal's neck, trying to soothe him.

"It's Pahpi. I fear he's in terrible trouble."

Rhoji said nothing for a few moments, as if contemplating what she'd said. At last, he clicked his tongue and gave Gambol a gentle kick. "What kind of trouble?"

"I fear the worst kind."

CHAPTER 4

Nearing Solia, Rhoji descended over a rise above the town. He pulled Gambol's reins and yelled, "Ho!"

The Lakmi River valley cradled Solia like an emerald shining in the sands. Bright-green shoots of gliniri grass edged the river's banks, overflowing with snowmelt. White-plastered mud houses and Pijwar Herdclan's colorful orange tents dotted the valley. But now, the air over Solia was grey with ash, the sky above the village yellow and thick with dark smoke.

Rhoji pointed to the ashen sky. "Fire in Solia. Yulina's, maybe? With all the spilled ale and the grease-filled trough she never empties, one spark, and it would go." He snapped his fingers.

"Maybe. But the smoke is billowing worst over the eastern flank, not the western." *Santu's Stand anchors the eastern edge of Solia.* A rope of fear pulled tightly across her middle.

Rhoji's muscles tensed under her arms. *He must think the same thing I do.*

Without her urging, Rhoji kicked Gambol hard and shouted, "Hika!" as they took off down the rise.

Quen couldn't take her eyes off the clouds of dark smoke billowing from Solia. The yellow-grey haze was thick and ominous. With all the desiccated wood, any small fire could cause the entire town to burn to the ground.

An immense black shadow hovered over the village. It moved silently and quickly, soon engulfing the town in shadow as if Vay'Nada was about to eat her village.

Juka's winds whipped again, pressing as though intentionally holding them back. Sand scoured their path. Quen rubbed her eyes, sure the shadow she'd seen in the sky was an illusion. *Like seeing shapes in clouds.*

Despite the sand burnishing her face, Quen forced her eyes open. The silhouette remained over Solia, higher in the sky but still cloaked in swirling yellow-grey vapors.

Quen pointed to the sky. "Do you see that?"

"By Hiyadi's light, what is it?"

She had no answer. As Quen gawked at the sky, an immense dark figure emerged from the dense cloud.

The looming specter was an impossible creature. Indrasian the First vanquished the flying demons from Indrasi nearly a thousand years ago. His prize was a dynasty still in power. *It cannot be.*

Impossible, yet there it was. The flying beast was... a dragon. And it soared over her village, covering it in a cloak of shadow.

Purple scales so dark they were nearly black covered the dragon's massive head and body. The scales reflected the last bit of sunlight from the dying day and shimmered deep blue and turquoise. The flying beast stared in their direction, yellow eyes beneath furrowed brows of wispy black tufts of hair. Its eyes, nearly the same color as her amber-yellow one, were huge and glowed in the dim light of twilight. The dragon opened its maw, showing teeth as large as a grown man's hand, long black whiskers protruding from its snout, covered in downy fur.

She tried to get out the words "It's a dragon," but her throat was too tight and dry to speak. Before she could say anything, the creature flapped its enormous wings and turned back to the plume of smoke. *Back toward Solia.*

The dragon opened its mouth wide and spewed blazing fire. The beast roared as it belched flame. Burning timbers popped and hissed, relinquishing their last hoarded moisture.

Though she saw it with her own eyes, Quen tried to convince herself it wasn't real. Dragons existed in stories people told children who needed a fright to keep them from wandering. They were the beasts in heroic legends of men slaying a dragon to win favor.

Dragons didn't circle the sky above her town.

The ridge on her neck throbbed, and she broke into a cold sweat. Her heart fluttered an unusual rhythm, and darkness played at the edges of her mind. She tried to do as Pahpi had taught her—to think of deep, dark water smooth as glass as she breathed deeply. *Still Waters.* With the Still Waters mantra, Quen regained composure. *It grows ever more challenging to keep the Nixan at bay, but I won't lose myself. Not today.*

"By the light of the Three...." Rhoji's voice was a hoarse whisper, barely audible over the howl of the wind.

Urging Gambol with whistles and kicks, he shouted to Quen, "We need to get you to Solia."

Considering the danger looming over Solia, it was odd for him to suggest. "Why?"

Rhoji whipped his reins from side to side. "Because there isn't an animal alive that wants to be within a league of you."

Rhoji was right about Quen's ill rapport with animals, but the circling dragon wasn't likely to spook like a witless kopek. But she kept the thought to herself. She urgently needed to get to Solia. *Pahpi's in trouble. I feel it.* Quen didn't want to admit to herself that the despised Nixan soul aided her instinct.

Still a mile away, the scent of burning wood filled her nostrils. Soot billowed about them as if they were in the yellow-grey cloud of smoke. Her lungs burned, and she coughed and gagged. The air tasted acrid.

The dragon banked and came directly toward them. A part of her wanted to yank the reins from Rhoji and take Gambol in the opposite direction.

Yet she couldn't pull herself away from staring at it. The dragon's purple-scaled nostrils flared, its long white horns peeking out from thick curls of glossy black hair.

Rhoji rode directly toward it. The dragon's massive body swooped, claws outstretched. The beast was coming for them.

Her father's voice came to her. *"Still as calm waters."* She breathed deeply, trying her best to hush her racing hearts. Quen pictured Lumine, the patron goddess of Enara, her visage reflected in a nighttime pool of clear water, and she silently prayed. *Sister, be with me. Bring me peace and stillness while the dragon's heart freezes like the peaks of TasūZaj.*

As Quen concentrated on chilling the dragon's fire, she caught the odor of late summer lightning. Sounds were muffled, yet her hearts stammered, both beating in slow motion.

Quen reached for the sheath on her belt. Her movements were slow, as if she maneuvered through air as thick as honey. An eternity of time stretched between herself and the fire-breathing beast. She undid the loop on her scabbard, aware of the feel of the leather and the odor of burning wood and reeds. She pulled out the dagger Fano had gifted her, reassured by the weight of it. In the state of heightened perception, she felt the normally undetectable whorls in the polished bone handle.

The fiend was so near its hot breath made her face feel like she'd stuck it into Fano's smithing fire. As the beast opened its enormous jaw, Quen hurled the dagger with all her strength, aiming for one of its brilliant amber eyes.

The dragon whipped its head away as it let out a bone-chilling screech. It reared back and turned away. *There—behind the dragon's colossal head. A rider? Yes, a passenger.* Clad entirely in black, the figure blended so well with the dragon's dark scales the rider was barely perceptible, especially in the waning light. The rider's lips moved, apparently speaking, but Quen couldn't be sure whether to themselves or the beast.

The dragon spoke in a voice so deep and low that Quen felt it more than heard it. Its language was an odd mixture of long vowel sounds and clicks, most of its words undecipherable. But one word sounded like a name. *"Ishna!"* The name was familiar, though there was no reason she should know it. *Ishna.*

Quen's head throbbed, and the ridge on her neck burned like someone had stabbed her with a red-hot poker. *This is even worse than when the Rajani woman, Nevara, was in Solia.* The Nixan soul was trying to force its way out. Quen again called on the tranquility of Still Water, and it was enough to suppress her shadow soul for a time, anyway. *I grow tired of playing this game with you, Nixan.*

As soon as the dragon stopped speaking, the air above it shimmered like heat rising from summer sands. The winds, once howling, were silent and still. The rider called out to the dragon in a strange foreign tongue, and the beast turned and flew toward the shimmering pocket of air. As it entered the peculiar bit of sky, thunder pounded, and the air crackled with lightning energy, the odor of sulfur strong.

In an instant, the dragon and rider vanished. The shimmery air returned to normal. Juka's breath became a soft breeze again, the sands still. The clouds over Solia cleared, though thick grey smoke remained.

"Stop. I need to find my dagger." Quen didn't wait for Gambol to stop and leaped from his back.

"Damn the dagger."

Quen ignored Rhoji's suggestion and searched the rocky sand for the dagger, her fingers trembling. *Why didn't the beast kill us? Was it an illusion, like how Pahpi used magic to appear younger and larger when Nevara visited Santu's Stand?*

But the dagger was gone. The Nixan soul within said, "It was no illusion." Quen refused to listen to the Nixan, even when it was right.

The smaller sun, Niyadi, dipped below the horizon. Lumine was a crescent, giving scant light to the night. Vay'Nada's shadow now cloaked Menauld in total darkness. Quen shivered.

"Come," Rhoji said. "We need to check on Pahpi."

Their village glowed orange on the horizon. A lump in her throat ached with tightness. The closer they got, the thicker the smoke. She wrapped her keffla yet again, another layer to keep out the stench of burnt hair.

The flames had turned traveling merchants' tents into piles of ash. Her stomach roiled. Quen hoped people made it away from the market square before it burnt.

Quen came first to where Fano's smithing tent had been. His great stone fire ring still glowed bright orange. Wood handles meant for axes and hammers were piles of white ash. Only blobs of melted iron and steel remained.

Frozen in place like a man-sized cinder, Fano's fingers still clutched melted and twisted smithing tongs. His charred-black neck craned as though he'd been looking to the skies when he died.

Quen tore off her keffla and retched in the ash-covered dirt. Rhoji dismounted and stood behind her, a hand on her shoulder.

"I am sorry. May the Sister welcome him into her arms."

Quen couldn't form the words for the reply. She'd never realized what little solace perfunctory condolences provided. When she spoke, her voice cracked. "Pahpi."

As she ran, her town's glowing embers and smoldering ruins were a blur. Her chest was in a vise, her vision bleary. She didn't want to see what lay ahead, yet she couldn't help hurtling toward Santu's Stand. "Pahpi!" she called.

The crackle and hiss of still-smoldering embers were the only answer to her call.

"Pahpi!" she screamed. At least she tried to call, but the tightness in her throat made her voice a strangled cry.

Santu's Stand was a pile of glowing embers. The fire had also destroyed the packed earthen buildings behind the store. Her quarters—Rhoji and Liodhan's—and the stalls where she and Rhoji had tanned and dyed hides. Dragon fire had obliterated everything they had.

She leaped over the rubble, ignoring the heat of smoldering coals. Her sight, always keen even in the dark, scanned the remains of Santu's Stand. The place she'd spent most of her waking hours. A gleam of silver caught her eye.

A lump of black cinder in the shape of a hand still held the silver blade Pahpi had brandished at Nevara. Dragon fire had reduced her beloved Pahpi to a man-sized charred coal. The only recognizable piece of him left was the amber pendant he always wore around his neck.

Her wobbly legs gave out, and Quen fell. Hands shaking, she grabbed the pendant, but it was still hot. She let it remain on the cinder that used to be her Pahpi. Darkness played at the edges of her vision, her stomach queasy.

"Quen?" Rhoji called.

"Rhoji," she croaked.

He fell to his knees beside her. Rhoji made a sound like an animal ensnared in a trap. Quen put her arms around him, and to her surprise, Rhoji wrapped his arms around her, too. Their mutual grief obliterated the petty obstacles between them, at least for a time. They held each other tightly as though they'd spin off into the heavens if they didn't. They said nothing. The only sounds were the crackle of embers and the occasional sniffle. Her head on Rhoji's chest, she heard his heart thumping wildly. They sat frozen like memories of forgotten things and stared at what used to be their everything.

Black soot smeared Rhoji's once-immaculate tunic. Ash covered his dark hair. Rhoji's fingers trembled as he grasped the pendant made of amber from the forests of the Vindaô Province where they'd been born. Through watery eyes, Rhoji stared at the lock of their mother's hair encased in smooth amber. Despite Vaya di Soli scripture making it taboo to keep any part of the dead, such pendants were common. Pahpi had worn this pendant inside his clothing, never visible but always close.

Rhoji was about to put it around his neck but hesitated. He placed it on the rubble that had been Santu Inzo Dakon di Sulmére. Their Pahpi.

"He loved her. It should stay with him." Fresh tears played at Rhoji's lashes. "Why here? Why him?"

Those weren't the questions Quen had. *How can a dragon, known only in stories, fly over my village and murder my father? Why did this happen the same day a Nixan fought with Pahpi and claimed my mother promised me to Volenex?* She kept her questions to herself and proffered no answers to Rhoji's. Discussing it would require her to reveal more about herself than she wanted.

60

Instead, she said, "Do you think Dini and the rest survived?" Her voice cracked. "Otara—"

Rhoji wiped his face with the dirty sleeve of his tunic. "It's stone. Maybe—"

Quen rose and wiped her backside. She had no stomach to stare at her father's scorched flesh. "I have to go check on her."

"You're leaving him? Do you not care at all that he's..."

Quen's first instinct was to quarrel. He was accusing her of being heartless. *Like the slint I fear I'm becoming.* But her urge to leave the charred remains of their father wasn't out of lack of grief but because she feared to remain. *The longer I linger by his body, the more I want to bury myself in the sand beside him until I'm nothing but bleached bone.*

"I have no stomach to stare at his scorched flesh or to argue with you. Not today. Handle grief as you will, Rhoji, and allow me to handle mine as I will."

Rhoji wiped his eyes, smearing ash across his face. Finally, he said, "You are right." He sniffled. "Go find Dini. She may have injured to care for."

Quen turned to go, but Rhoji caught the leg of her pants. Tears welled, and his lip trembled. "Do you—think he suffered?"

Rhoji had never asked her opinion about anything. She put a hand on his shoulder and squeezed gently. "It was quick. I don't think he suffered." She gently kicked the sword with her toe. "And he went down fighting. An honorable end to the life of a Kensai."

The sword reflected the orange light of fires still burning. Rhoji's voice cracked. "Do you think Lio will mind—do you think I can keep it?"

Their older brother, Liodhan, was now First Kin. By rights, all Pahpi owned was now his. But Jiniro, the father of Lio's herdwife, Zarate, was Lio's father now. *Rhoji needs scraps from Pahpi more than Lio.* "Keep it, Rhoji. I think you'll have more use of it than Lio."

He plucked the sword from the sand and wiped tears from his cheeks with his sleeve. Rhoji held it reverently with both hands. "This is a finely crafted sword. Not something common in the Sulmére. I didn't know Pahpi owned such a blade. I wonder where he got it?"

And why he kept it hidden. "We didn't know he was full Kensai until yesterday." *Was that only a day ago?*

"We can find comfort in knowing he didn't suffer long." Quen's throat tightened. "And he has joined Lumine the Sister and bathes now in her eternal waters. He's at peace."

Rhoji nodded. "He once again stands at our mother's side. Thank you, Quen. Your words comfort me."

After what I witnessed between Nevara and Pahpi, I wonder if Pahpi wants to stand by our mother's side any longer? But thoughts of their parents reunited comforted Rhoji, so Quen held her tongue. *Let him remain at peace in his ignorance of our parents' eternal secrets.* "Are you sure you don't want me to stay?" *Please say no. It's all I can do not to race from my soot-covered life.*

Rhoji wiped the dust from Pahpi's sword on his tunic. "No, go. Check on our Bruxia. I will be along later."

Quen sped away from the charred remnants of their home. Rhoji wanted to stay and pay respects to Pahpi.

That is Rhoji's way, but I can't bear sitting with the horrid odor of his burnt flesh.

She could run from his burnt remains, but Quen couldn't escape her guilt. Her last words with Pahpi had been harsh ones. *I refused his hand. I should throw myself on the pyre for penance.* She wiped her face on her sleeve, smearing tears and snot onto her cheeks.

Grief made her legs leaden and her feet thick. Otara anchored the southeastern edge of Solia, but it might as well have been ten leagues away. Built in a prior era, Otara was a honeycomb of apartments and food storage caches carved into the sandy beige stone of a weathered mountain shouldering the shores of the Lakmi River. Through watery eyes, the stony edifice was a bleary smudge on the horizon.

Pijwar Clan's orange tents already colored the banks of the Lakmi. Soon more herdclans would arrive and erect tents, each group claiming a different color so that the verdant banks of the Lakmi would become a rainbow. Lio's herdclan, Yima, claimed regal purple, and the thought of Lio and his new babe raised her spirits. *I'm relieved the fire didn't harm Pijwar, but it makes no sense. Why would a dragon burn a village but leave a thukna herd untouched?*

The conversations with Rhoji about Pahpi and the Dynasty flooded her mind. *Did the Kovan Dynasty send the dragon as a warning to the people of the Sulmére?* It was a wild, fanciful thought, but she would have said that about dragons less than a day ago.

Quen called to Dini as she wove through the maze of small apartments and halls of Otara. An elderly woman told Quen to look for Dini in the eastern apartments. "And stop shouting," she hollered as Quen scurried away.

Quen found Dini where the woman had said she would. The Bruxia knelt on the smooth stone floor, her gnarled hands shaking as she wrapped a charred arm loosely with a cloth.

Quen didn't speak. She, too, knelt on the other side of Dini's patient.

The severely scorched body barely resembled a person. Fire had burnt off the hair and seared the clothes into the flesh in a few places. Ugly red and black wounds marred the face. *The dragon's fire permanently disfigured this person.*

Dini handed a small bowl of a gooey substance to Quen. "Apply this to her arm. Gently." She'd only just handed it to Quen when she added, "Hurry now. I've given her the nys't, but she won't sleep long. She'll awaken with twofold agony, such is the Vay'Nada bargain of the nys't."

Quen used the small wooden paddle spoon in the bowl to apply a thick layer of the medicine. "Who is this?"

Dini glanced across her patient and gave Quen an even stare. "Yulina."

The world spun like a child's top at the edge of a precipice. *Would Yulina have preferred to die rather than endure this?* While Quen wouldn't call Yulina a friend, the barkeeper had at least always been civil to Quen. Of course, Yulina welcomed all to her establishment so long as they had the pits and dars to buy drinks. But Quen appreciated having at least one place besides Santu's Stand where they treated her with dignity rather than wariness. *By Lumine's pale light, you didn't deserve this fate, Yulina.* Quen sniffled.

Quen applied the ointment while Dini deftly wrapped Yulina's wounds. All the while, Quen fought back nausea. She tried to focus on her task. She prayed to the Sister to give Yulina the peace of Still Waters. Aiding Yulina was the only thing keeping her from curling into a wailing ball of grief and despair.

Yulina escaped the sleep of the nys't once, her voice a raspy but desperate whisper. "Please."

Maybe Yulina was asking for more nys't. *Or maybe she's asking Dini to put an end to her misery.*

Dini held a small vial to Yulina's lips and poured in more than a few drops of the precious nys't, a potent painkiller made from the night flowers of the nystrem plant. Tears rolled from Yulina's eyes toward her ears, and she yowled in pain when the salty liquid came upon freshly flayed skin.

After Dini had loosely wrapped Yulina's burns, she used strips of cloth to bind Yulina's hands. Before Quen could answer the question, Dini said, "So she doesn't scratch herself or pull off the wraps."

Or grab your scissors and shove them into her own heart.

When they'd finished tending to Yulina, Quen asked, "What more can we do for her?"

Dini wiped sweat from her brow. "You? Nothing. I'll watch her through the night, giving her more nys't as she needs it."

"I'll tend her." Quen was about to stroke Yulina's temple, but pulled her hand back. *My touch would irritate Yulina's raw skin rather than soothe her.*

The Bruxia gave Quen a small, tired smile and took her hand. "Thank you, sol'dishi, but you have enough to do. Though you make a fine assistant, this is Bruxia work. I will perform the O'Dishi chants. Loving prayers are powerful medicine."

Quen wanted to request chants to raise Pahpi from the dead, but she knew it was impossible. Not even the most powerful Bruxia or mage had such magic. As she stared at Yulina's scorched face, Quen was grateful fate spared Pahpi this misery. *He wouldn't have wanted to be maimed like Yulina.* Fresh tears welled.

I am surely in a dream. Pahpi — this cannot be. She rubbed her eyes and blinked. It did nothing to remove the feeling she'd fallen into Vay'Nada, the Shadow sucking air from her lungs.

Dini filled a kettle with water from a large jug and put it on the hot stones by the small fire. "I forgot to ask. Did you need something, or did you run out here just to help old Dini?" She sat down heavily on a wobbly wooden stool made dark with age.

As there was only one seat in the tiny apartment, Quen knelt across from Dini so their eyes met. She wiped her nose with the back of her hand. Dini welcomed Quen as she did everyone in Solia. Quen had always appreciated how Dini made her feel like a part of the community when most didn't.

Assisting Dini had distracted Quen from the grief welling like raging waters behind a levee. Dini wrapped Quen in warm arms, and the dam gave way.

Her grief came out in a torrent of long, wailing sobs. She soaked Dini's tunic with tears and snot. The clamps of pent-up emotion that had held Quen's chest in a tight grip released. Silent and patient, Dini gently stroked Quen's hair, taking Quen's grief onto her resilient Bruxia shoulders.

Quen's voice quavered. "I'm an awful person." She hiccupped. "By the Three, when my time comes to travel the River, Lumine will not welcome me into her arms."

Dini pressed Quen away from her so she could look at her face. "What are you talking about? Awful person?" Dini tsked and gestured toward Yulina with her head. "You helped me give relief to our barkeep here. And I've never seen you refuse to help a person in need, Quen. Not even people who—well, never did you any favors."

Yulina's brow furrowed. Even in the deep sleep of the nys't, her body knew pain.

Quen snuffled, and her words came out in stilted hiccups. "My last words to him...." Her ragged breaths halted her words, and fresh tears welled. "I gave him the rough side of my tongue. And I refused the hand of love and kinship when he offered it." The constriction of guilt bound her chest again.

Dini's eyes softened. "Ah, the suffering of regret." She rubbed Quen's back. "Shh, sol'dishi, calm your mind."

"That's the thing, Dini. I can't. I'll always...." Her breaths were ragged hiccups.

"Breathe, child. That's it. Still Waters, as your Pahpi taught you."

She tried to do as Dini said, but thinking of Still Waters reminded her of her spat with Pahpi, her last memory of him. The ridge on her neck throbbed. *I wish I could wrest the damned Nixan heart from my body and dash it against Otara's stone. To be done with the shadow soul once and for all.* Quen breathed deeply as Dini told her, releasing a quavering breath, then another. Finally, she could speak again and voice the worst of her fears. "What if Lumine will never welcome the likes of me to her arms?" *A Nixan shadow-spawn like me.* Fresh tears welled. "Then I'll never see Pahpi again."

Dini sighed and kissed the top of Quen's head. "Lumine is forgiving, not vengeful. She will not deny her grace because of a few harsh words said in anger. And Pahpi carried Lumine's light in his heart more than anyone I knew. He knew you loved him and wouldn't hold a disagreement against you."

Quen wiped her nose. "Do you really think so?"

Dini tucked a stray tendril of hair behind Quen's ear. "I know so." She cupped Quen's chin in her plump hand. "You question the wisdom of your Bruxia?"

Quen knew better than to question Dini. She shook her head and exhaled, her tears momentarily quelled.

Dini put herb bundles in cups and poured hot water over them while eyeing Quen warily. "I know your grief is fresh, but I urge you to fulfill your Pahpi's wish. Study at Val'Enara Pillar. The Ascended Masters will teach you how to release the pain that darkens your heart, sol'dishi. You'll see." She handed a warm earthen cup to Quen.

I can't think of a future without Pahpi. She raised the cup to her mouth, and her lip quivered.

"Oh, sol'dishi. I didn't mean to—"

Quen wiped her eyes and waved off Dini's apology. "It's all right. I just..." She sipped the tea and willed the empty pit in her stomach to be calm. Finally, she said, "I can't go to Val'Enara now. Lio and Rhoji need me." Quen's voice quavered. "And... without a guide, I'll never make it across the Chasm of Nil."

"We'll find a way, sol'dishi. It is what Pahpi wanted for you."

But it's not what I ever wanted for myself. However, today was not the day to spar with Dini over her future path. The Way of Water was Pahpi's answer to all troubles. But Quen couldn't think about her future. Not so soon after the shock of losing Pahpi. *My future smolders, reeking of burnt flesh and dragon's breath.*

That dragon murdered my dearest Pahpi and robbed me of my future. The fires of vengeance roiled in Quen's belly, filling the void of loss with a molten core of anger. Quen drank the tea, but it did little to soothe her rankled mind. *How can I lock myself away in a Pillar while that Vay'Nada spawn lives?* A fervent monk's prayers wouldn't protect her loved ones from the murderous dragon's fire.

Quen eyed the pulpy herbs at the bottom of her cup, considering how she could ask Dini the many questions swirling in her mind. But she was tired and unable to focus. *If I talk about Nevara, Rajani, dragons, and Volenex, I'll probably reveal too much.*

She drained her remaining tea in one gulp, handed the cup to Dini, and kissed her wrinkled cheek. "Thank the Three you...." Quen wrapped Dini in a crushing hug.

Dini said, "Go, sol'dishi. Help Rhoji and those in need." She sniffled.

Quen left Dini to her work and, once in the hall, pressed her back against the cool stone wall and closed her eyes. She breathed deeply, searching within for stillness. It was no good.

Quen didn't want placid water or smooth sand. *If I think about Still Waters, I'll remember Pahpi's infectious laugh.*

I'll long for our conversation as we tanned skins by the light of the Brothers.

She pressed her heels into her eyes and willed herself not to cry. Vatra's fires churned in her core like a molten mass. *A force I barely glimpsed and don't understand took Pahpi from me.* Deep inside, something stirred, but was beyond her grasp. It was like an itch she couldn't reach, pestering until the sweet relief of scratching. Quen longed to bring the murderous dragon to justice nearly as much as she ached to exterminate the Nixan part of herself. *I don't know how I'll rid myself of the pesky Nixan, but I'll make that dragon pay for all it took from me. I vow this to you, Pahpi. I will avenge your death if it's the last thing I do.*

Pahpi had counseled that revenge exacted a price too high to pay. *But who's to say what price is too high to avenge the death of a person's most beloved?*

Quen made her way through Otara's maze, glad to see the first deep purple of Hiyadi's light on the horizon, banishing Vay'Nada's shadow. A cloud of dust hung in the air to the west toward the Staves. The ground vibrated with a low rumble. *Riders.*

Though Yima Clan wasn't due to arrive for nearly two days, Quen's heart soared, hoping her brother Liodhan was among the new arrivals. She ran toward the still-lingering darkness of night and the rumbling hooves of the newcomers.

CHAPTER 5

I mpelled by the dust cloud near the western gates, Quen hastened toward it, hoping to greet Liodhan. When she reached the center of her charred village, her hopes of seeing Lio were dashed. The newcomers rode in a small column of only five riders. *Not a herdclan, after all.* The last rider bore a banner emblazoned with the Jagaru emblem—the Trinity over crossed falcata.

Beyond Solia's gates, the desert was orangey-pink, swirling dust hovering in the air behind the riders. The only sounds were the Jagaru flag as it rippled in the breeze and the occasional pops of smoldering embers. Quen wished the Jagaru had arrived sooner. *If they'd been here, maybe they could have stopped the murderous dragon from killing Pahpi.*

The lead rider was an older man built like a merchant's cart. Breezes lashed the loose strands of his keffla. He had a facial scar so red and deep his face looked split in two on a diagonal. The scarred man steered his

71

kopek through the gates and held up a fist, calling for the tiny column he led to halt. "Lumine's teats...." Something—or someone—had mangled his upper lip into a cleft, causing him to lisp when he spoke.

The short, boxy man hoisted himself off his small, dusty kopek and groaned with effort. The kopek eyed Quen warily and backed away. He might have once been a man of average height by Sulmére standards, but years of riding had bowed his legs. He hobbled toward Quen.

Behind him, a woman gracefully dismounted her sleekly oiled black kopek. Her long pale-gold split-front riding tunic flourished as she dismounted, exposing well-muscled legs clad in tight-fitting dark-blue pants. She'd tucked her pants into well-crafted riding boots ending slightly above her knee. She wore her tunic belted at the waist but open above, revealing her torso save for a sliver of blue silk underclothing covering her breasts. With sunbaked skin nearly as dark as her kopek's, close-cropped hair as white as bleached bone, and eyes the color of fresh shoots in spring, she was the most striking woman Quen had ever seen. Even the silver scar slicing from cheek to brow enhanced rather than diminished her features.

"What happened here?" Before Quen could answer, the woman peppered her with more questions. "Raiders. Which way did they go? Was it Gauru Clan? We'll find 'em. Tell us which way they went."

A third rider brought his mount between the first two, laughing a deep, melodious laugh. "Mishny, give her a chance to answer one question before you ask another."

This rider sat atop a stocky dappled horse, a rarity in the Sulmére, where kopeks were the standard mount. He was tall, even atop his horse. When he dismounted, it took Quen's breath away. His legs came to Mishny's waist. He was taller even than Lio. The man tore the keffla from his head, allowing a cascade of sandy-blond hair to fall below his shoulders in loose waves. The rider's skin was pale but reddened by the sun, a sprinkle of freckles across the bridge of his straight nose, and a close-cropped beard of golden hair.

Fano had told Quen about the towering, fair-haired people from the north across the Orju Sea. She had never seen one, though. She tried not to gawk.

The tall northerner fixed his steel-blue gaze on Quen. The look was nearly intimate and made Quen feel squirmy. She didn't dislike it.

"Stuff it, Aldewin," Mishny said.

Aldewin. I wonder what he looks like beneath that tunic? Red heat bloomed on Quen's cheeks.

"Shove your harsh tongue, Mishny," the older man said.

As Mishny and the older man traded barbs, Aldewin's eyes remained fixed on Quen as he stowed riding gloves at his weapon belt. A long, thin steel blade like Pahpi's hung from his belt in a black scabbard tooled with unfamiliar symbols. On his right, he wore a shorter, kukri-style blade, perfect for tight fights. He also carried a staff strapped across his back, a weapon rarely seen in Solia, and under it a sheathed broadsword. *Is he adept at wielding all these weapons? He doesn't look like a typical Jagaru.*

The last two riders, including the flag bearer for the small Jagaru pod, finally arrived and dismounted their kopeks. A woman called out, "Hi-ho!" from behind a keffla-wrapped face.

The voice was familiar, but Quen didn't recognize her. The woman strode toward Quen, took off her keffla, and shook out a mass of tightly worked dark braids.

"Shel!" Quen called. "Where have you been? I expected you last season, but you didn't come." Shel traveled the Sulmére with her brother, Eira, and their father, Nathisen. Nathisen was a cordwain who serviced the nomadic herdclans. It had been two springs since Quen last saw her friend.

They embraced, Shel smelling of huson pine and desert sand. It was a comforting aroma. *Her arms are more muscular, and she's taller, too.* Shel was now about the average height of an adult Indrasian woman, but she was still nearly a head smaller than Quen.

Shel stepped back and looked beyond Quen to the carnage of Solia. Her smile gave way to a furrowed brow. "I wish we'd gotten here sooner."

Eira, Shel's twin brother, sidled up next to her and gave Quen a brief hug of greeting as well. "Where is Rhoji?" His question contained an air of panic.

"He's fine. He's…" Quen kicked the dirt with her toe. Her throat was tight, her voice about to crack. She didn't want to cry in front of the newcomers, especially Aldewin. She finally managed, "At Santu's Stand."

Relief flooded Eira's face. He was already on his way, but Quen caught his arm. Hot tears burned her eyes, and she no longer held them back. "Pahpi—" It was all she could get out before her breaths became hiccups, her lower lip trembling.

Eira's brown eyes glistened with tears, and he wrapped his arms around Quen. His tears wet her shoulder. Shel wrapped an arm around her, too.

Eira wiped his face, and his voice quavered. "He might like some company. I must go to him."

Shel said, "I'm so sorry. I know how you must feel."

Quen doubted that. *How could she know the pain of losing my whole life? Of the growing struggle to keep the Nixan from stealing my skin?* Shel and Eira were her only friends, and having thought she'd lost them, she didn't want to sour their reunion. Quen didn't raise an argument and instead embraced her friend.

She smoothed Quen's hair and rubbed her back. "We lost our da too. Bandits on the Trinity Road south of Enarili." Shel wiped her eyes with the back of her hand.

"I am so sorry, Shel. I didn't know." Quen pressed her fingers to her heart, lips, and third eye as she said the words. "May he find comfort in the Sister's embrace."

Druvna and Aldewin responded, "And be warmed by the fire of the Brothers."

Mishny interrupted the mourning of the two young women who'd lost their fathers. "Cry later. Now we hunt the raiders who did this to your da."

Before Quen could set Mishny straight, Aldewin said, "It was no raid."

"Suda! To Vay'Nada with your Northman rune-reading crap, Aldewin." Mishny's green eyes sparkled with anger.

The older man exploring the merchant tents spoke up. "You don't need runes or be a Juka-jod to see the truth. Use your eyes, woman. This town was no'a burned with torches. Something scorched this village." He plucked a clump of what looked like glass from the sand beside a stall that used to be the cheesemonger's. "This here damage is from a rain of fire. From above." His forehead crinkled, and he looked to the sky as he held up the odd blob of glass.

Mishny took the glass from the older man's hand. "What are you on about, Druvna?" She snickered as she looked at the strange item. Mishny examined the sandy glass blob and scrunched her face. She waved it at Quen and demanded, "What is this?"

She's interrogating me like I caused this destruction.

Aldewin whistled from what used to be Fano's stall. Mishny dropped the glass blob and released Quen from her intense gaze. Quen followed Mishny, Druvna, and Shel to where Aldewin stood.

"By the Three, the fire fused the unfortunate man's hand to his war ax." Aldewin referred to Fano, who still stood, a molten man statue, his eyes to the sky, his ax ready for a battle that never came.

Mishny's voice was a barely audible whisper. "Like we saw further south." She exchanged a look with Druvna.

Aldewin's voice was deep, with a Northman's sonorous accent. "What happened here?"

All eyes were again on Quen.

"You won't believe the truth," she said.

Druvna took a long pipe from his belt, stuffed it with tarry-looking tobacco, and lit it using the smoldering embers of Fano's smithing fire. "We've ranged all the way to the southern border of Indrasi and back, girl." Smoke floated above his square head. "Seen things people ain't 'sposed to see." He fixed his eyes on her. "So try us."

The four circled Quen. They stared at her as though they were waiting for Lumine herself to bless them. Quen sought Shel's face, and her friend nodded reassurance.

"It was no raid," Quen said. "It was a dragon attack."

Not one of them flinched, laughed, or called her a liar. Quen wished they had. Their lack of shocked disbelief in her outlandish claim made the hairs on her arms stand on end again.

"Did it have purple scales so dark they looked nearly black?" Druvna asked.

Quen felt like someone had taken her air. She hadn't expected that the Jagaru would have seen the damned thing before. Unable to form words, she nodded.

Shaking his head, Druvna dashed his keffla to the dirt. "Ilkay's bones, but this is a disaster."

"You've seen this dragon before?" None of them spoke, but their lack of denial was answer enough. "And you didn't warn anyone? You didn't—" Hot tears of anger and frustration shored up by her primordial need to blame someone for her misfortune welled. "If you'd warned us, maybe we'd—"

"Be just as dead as these folks already are." Mishny's stern tone was gone, but her words held no comfort.

Shel said, "We were on our way here. To warn Santu. To let him know what was coming so he could prepare. Set up watchtowers. Get people to Otara at the first sighting." She shook her head. "But we were too late." She wiped her nose with her sleeve. "I'm sorry, Quen."

Quen shook with anger and wanted to take it out on the only people around to blame. *But it's not their fault. Hell, if the Jagaru had arrived two days ago, I doubt anyone would believe them if they spouted about a dragon attack. I wouldn't have, and neither would Pahpi. Even if Pahpi hadn't thought they were curd brains, how could we combat fire raining from the sky?* War axes, Kensai swords, and blades were useless against a flying enemy. *We'll need something more. We'll need Pillar-trained mages to counter dragon fire.*

"What will you do about the dragon now? Be too late to warn other villages or herdclans?" She hadn't intended her voice to contain such an edge, but she didn't regret it either.

Tendrils of grey smoke escaped through the split in Druvna's upper lip as he spoke, holding his pipe with his tobacco-stained teeth. "We aim to hunt the bastard down and kill it." He spoke calmly, like a person telling what he'd eaten for midday meal.

A jolt like sky-fire zinged Quen from head to toe. Her Nixan heart tharumped, its beat off-kilter from hers. For an instant, time moved for Quen as if she lived in a world caught in amber. And in that instant, Quen knew the path she must take.

I can join my friends and fulfill my vow to bring Pahpi's killer to justice. The Pillar will have to wait, Dini.

"It seems we have the same goal, Druvna. How do I become a Jagaru and join your hunt?"

Druvna held out a stubby hand. "Welcome to my Jagaru pod."

That was easier than I expected. Quen grasped Aldewin's wrist, and he took hers. His forearms were tight ropes of muscle.

"Seems we got a new moss-brained squib to join you other youngins." Druvna wiped his forehead with a dusty cloth. Instead of removing his sweat, it merely smeared it into a muddy smudge. "I'm probably going to regret this."

Mishny crossed her arms and scowled. *Either she doesn't like me, or she gives that attitude to everyone. Time will tell which is true.*

Shel hugged Quen. "It'll be nice to have another woman on the road to talk to." She whispered into Quen's ear. "And someone to gossip with about Aldewin."

Mishny rolled her eyes at them.

Aldewin held out an arm to her and smiled, though it didn't reach his eyes. "I guess you'll be riding with us now. What do we call you?"

"My name is Quen Tomo Santu. But you can call me Quen." She took his wrist as he took hers, and her loins tightened while a quiver ran through her. A new but not unwelcome sensation.

She craned her neck to look into Aldewin's soft-blue eyes. He stared first at her sky-blue eye, then gazed deeply into her amber-yellow one.

"Quen."

His hand was warm, his grasp firm. It was suddenly warmer, and Quen wished for a breeze.

"Your eyes..."

That's what you get for allowing yourself to be attracted. Quen attempted to pull her hand away, but Aldewin held onto it.

"Please excuse that I stare. It's just that I never... Well, to see eyes so clearly of two schools. Filled with the fire of Vatra, but also the Still Waters of Enara. They're— beautiful to behold."

Quen's neck burned, her cheeks hot. Aldewin noticed her reaction, coughed, and released her hand. *Beautiful to behold?* No one had ever told Quen any part of her was beautiful. *Well, except Pahpi, and a parent telling their child they're attractive doesn't count.* Quen's true heart drummed wildly, and she looked at the dirt and twirled a toe in the ashy sand.

"I wonder, Quen the Twice Blessed, do you see the world in two ways? Are you truly a woman of both Enara and Vatra?"

If he knew me, I don't think he'd consider me blessed once, let alone twice. "I've seen little of the world beyond Solia." She glanced around them, the still-smoldering embers and acrid, smoky odor bringing her back to the grim reality of her homelessness. "But I care little for Vatra's chaos and destruction." She turned her attention back to him. "I prefer the calm of Still Waters."

Aldewin smiled and gave her a nod. "The world is vast and brimming with wonder. Come with the Jagaru pod, and you'll see more of it soon." He turned and followed Druvna as they made their way toward the river to make camp.

Quen whispered to Shel, "Tell me everything you know about him."

• • •

Santu Inzo Dakon di Sulmére lay on a bed of bone-dry gliniri reeds. He was about to be set afire.

Dini had helped Quen dress Pahpi in his best red linen tunic, the amber pendant on his chest. Dini had carefully wrapped his charred face with a keffla. Save for his bare hands, he looked like a man in repose.

It's a waste of precious wood to burn bodies already scorched beyond recognition. Yet here Santu lay, along with at least a dozen others, ready to be made into ash, their vapors whisked away on Juka's breath. Pahpi had once told her they burned bodies because nothing is wasted in the Sulmére. "A hungry hyena doesn't care what a man achieved in life. The hyena knows only that he needs to fill his belly," Pahpi had said.

Pahpi, the informally recognized leader of Solia, lay on a pyre, ready to drift on the Great River until he found his way to Lumine's arms. *It's better than ending up in the belly of a scavenger, but that doesn't mean I like it.*

Lio, his herdwife, Zarate, and their infant daughter, Lumina, had arrived with Jima Clan the day prior. The cloud of grief overshadowed the expected joy of meeting her new niece. Lio had taken the news of Pahpi's death hard and retreated into the solitude of his tent. There would be no drunken reunion at Yulina's, partly because none were in the mood and partly because Yulina's was now a pile of ash.

Quen stood between her brothers, her back to the gathering of recently arrived herdclans and Druvna's small Jagaru pod. She swore she felt Aldewin staring at her from behind, but she dared not glance back to check. If he wasn't looking at her, she'd feel disappointed. If he was, she'd color crimson and embarrass herself.

They'd begun the Nilva rites for the dead in the morning, and it was now past midday. Musicians from the herdclans had taken turns drumming and chanting throughout the morning. There had been breaks for flatbread, briny olives, cheese, dried jiri fruit, drinks from water skins, and even sips of firewater from personal stashes.

The crowd had ebbed and flowed, but now nearly everyone was back to hear Dini say the customary Nilva prayers to send a soul to the Corner he claimed in life. For Santu, that meant prayers to Lumine and wishes for his boat to find the calm waters of Enara.

There were few dry eyes during Dini's talk about Santu. All in the Sulmére knew him well, and few among them could have found harsh words to say about Santu, even if they'd tried.

Quen expected to be an emotional mess, but the fires of justice raging in her chest burned away her tears.

As Solia was small, Nilva rites were uncommon. Usually, it had fallen to Santu to speak the Nilva. *He was always quick about it, as was fitting. It's not right to linger in public while saying goodbyes to a loved one.* The pyre was expedience, not sentiment, at least as far as Quen was concerned. *The sooner this is over, the sooner I can stop thinking about how hollow I feel without him.*

Dini droned far too long for Quen's taste. She spoke of Santu being free of the burden of the shell he'd carried in life like a lumbering ranju, slowed by having to always take his house with him. "And may Santu follow the eternal river to find peace within the waiting arms of the sister, Lumine, the goddess of many faces and keeper of Enara, the Waters of Life."

It was exactly where the Nilva should end, yet Dini continued. Quen's patience was at an end. She sighed and crossed her arms.

Liodhan, immersed in his grief, sent no chastisement her way. But Rhoji jabbed her in the ribs. Quen shot him a glare, but his eyes sparkled wet in the bright light of the two suns. Rhoji's tears unexpectedly moved her. She redoubled her effort to be still and prayed to Lumine for the patience to listen to Dini until the end.

Dini asked a question, and Liodhan nodded. A man from Jima Clan, Lio's herdclan, came forward and handed a lit torch to Liodhan. Lio touched it to the dry grass at the edge of the pyre. The reeds caught quickly, and sparks flew. The flames licked at the grasses, as dry as the sands from the summer's heat. Within seconds the fire danced at Santu's unmoving feet while drummers pounded a steady beat.

A child cried out, and his mother pulled the young one's hands from his eyes as Santu had once done to Quen. She recalled him whispering in her ear, "Watch, Quen. The flame releases us. Our spirits travel with the smoke to join the river's Dark Waters. We must then make the ultimate choice of our lives. Will we become Vatra's flame and sit at the side of Hiyadi? Or become as ethereal as the wind and dance for eternity with Juka? Some choose to sink deep and become one with Menauld, nourishing the growth of new lives as soil."

Quen had asked her Pahpi what he would choose.

"Ah, all parts are required for the whole of everything, to be sure, but I hope to become rain and river and flood. To nourish the land and at long last find the loving arms of the Sister."

As the flames licked at Santu's unmoving feet, his words echoed in her mind. "Death—the flames—are not to be feared, Quen. Our bodies return to the sands, and our spirits to the Great Sea when it is our time."

But it wasn't Pahpi's time. That dragon stole his time. The thought slithered inside her skull like a clutch of newly hatched rock snakes. Still vibrant, Pahpi wasn't yet elderly. She still had much to learn from him. *I never got to say goodbye. I didn't get to say… I'm sorry.* Quen blinked back tears of grief, but the anguish of guilt was too much. Her sobs were quiet, and the heat of the pyre dried her tears as quickly as they fell.

The flickering firelight made the amber pendant around Santu's neck shimmer. The bit of yellow-gold hardened sap contained the last remnants of the woman who had birthed her but who Quen had never known.

A woman who had apparently made a bargain with Vay'Nada to birth a third child. In Bardivia, the city-state of Quen's birth, the Consular was supposed to emulate the Trinity in all things. They considered it an ill omen for a Consular's wife to have only two children. Quen could understand her mother's desperation for a fertile womb. *But to promise a child to the Shadow…*

Her mind was a vortex of unanswered questions and disquiet. The drums beat in time with the crackling of the fire, the flames rendering the man she loved into a pile of faceless ash. He would become just another bit of dust she'd sweep from her room in the endless battle against the Sulmére's sands.

She'd stared fixedly at the amber, winking at her like an eye. The pendant was the last remnant of the only person who had answers to her raging questions.

Quen leaped forward through the flames. Her fingers grasped the round pendant and clutched it with all her strength. It was hot but not yet melted, and she clasped it as though letting go would end her.

Strong hands tugged at her waist, and screams pierced the air.

Heat scorched Quen from thighs to waist. Someone tackled her and rolled her like a barrel of ale.

Lio's voice was harsh. "What were you thinking? Throwing yourself onto the flame won't bring him back."

She rolled over to face him. A single tear dangled at the corner of her eye, but an impish smile played at her lips. Quen held up the pendant triumphantly.

Lio took the pendant and inspected it. A soft sigh escaped his lips. "Oh, Quen." Fresh tears twinkled in his deep-brown eyes.

Her lips were set in a thin line. "I'll get justice for him, Lio. Justice for them all."

He put out a beefy hand to help her up. Quen's outer tunic was gone below the hips, and the fire singed her split skirt, but the calf-leather apron had saved her from severe burns.

Lio didn't let her statement go unanswered. "As Vas O'Nai said, 'Do not think yourself more powerful than the gods. Let the Great Father exact vengeance, not our hand.' Vaya di Solis has its own way, Quen. And time. No one escapes the judgment of Hiyadi. Not even a dragon." He handed the pendant back to her.

She took the small bit of amber, its leather cord now singed, and thrust it into the small pouch at her waist. She'd never been a fan of advice from long-dead prophets. They had a way of leaving words to support every side of an argument, making them useless at resolving human quandaries. Quen could cite verse too. "Didn't Vas O'Nai also say, 'Mere humans cannot divine a god's design, so we must not deign to determine their path'?"

Lio sighed but nodded his agreement.

"What if *I* am the way Hiyadi will bring justice?"

Lio's jaw tightened. "Your mind thinks loudly. Do you plan to chase after a dragon, throw dirt in its face, and kick it like you did Rhoji when you were children?"

Quen attempted to protest, but Lio cut her off. "You are a woman now, Quen, and it is time you take your place in the order of things, as we all must do." Lio wiped a tear from her cheek, his hands roughened by work. "Pahpi's death is a pain we all suffer. But for Hiyadi's sake, Quen, I'll not allow you to waste your life on a path of vengeance."

Quen knew where this conversation would lead. Lio was First Kin, and as she was not bound to a herdclan, she must abide by the 'law of the house'—Lio's law. And since he was a devout follower of Vaya di Solis and especially of Vatra Pillar, he saw clanbinding as the only viable path for Quen to live an honorable life.

Quen sniffed and wiped her face on the billowy sleeve of her tunic. "I'm going to become Jagaru, Lio. I will hunt the murderous dragon and bring justice to the people of Solia." Her voice was low and without a hint of a question.

Liodhan pinched the top of his nose as their Pahpi had often done when tired of a conversation he wanted to end. "By Sulmére law, I'm now your First Kin, and you must do as I command, and—"

"Command? Listen to yourself, Lio. That's Jiniro speaking, not you." She huffed. "Think about what Pahpi would say—on what he would do. You may be First Kin now, but you don't rule me. I have every right to become Jagaru."

"It is not an honorable life." Lio's voice had risen enough that the small band of Jagaru standing a few paces behind them likely heard. He looked momentarily flustered by his outburst and lowered his voice to a whisper. "I'm looking out for you. You are young and do not fully see the consequences of your choice."

Red-faced, Quen faced him with fists on her hips. "And what herdclan would have me? It may not be the life you would choose, but Jagaru are not pesha, Lio. I'll have purpose."

Lio smiled and held her gently by the shoulders. "You are well-loved by us, sister. Zarate spoke with my Clan Father, and he has agreed to take you into the Jima Clan. You will join in binding by the end of spring and ride with the herd and your mate this fall for the winter grounds. Then we will be family always." He looked at her kindly, unaware she would be unhappy with this proclamation.

"I thought we already were family forever." Hot tears sprang to her eyes, and her throat burned with anger. "I'll never accept Jiniro's authority over me." Everyone knew Jiniro adhered to old ways, and to customs leaving women little freedom once they birthed their first child. *He'll never allow me to hunt a dragon.*

Lio released her, his eyes now like two smoldering coals. "You would shame Zarate. Shame me. We worked hard on your behalf to make this arrangement. It wasn't easy to convince Jiniro to take a chance on you, what with your issue with animals. And he remembered your barbed tongue at my biding ceremony last year. It also displeased him that you spend more time drinking at Yulina's and in knife-throwing contests than learning how to be a proper herdwife."

Even more reason to not join your herdclan. "Pahpi would not want this for me." *I'd rather take vows at Val'Enara than submit to Jiniro ruling my life.*

Lio closed his eyes and shook his head. "Pahpi indulged you, Quen. He lived in a fantasy world sometimes, ignoring the Dynasty edicts when he felt like it, not working harder on arranging a proper binding for you."

Quen wanted to smack Lio, and her hand twitched with the desire. Years of Pahpi's training in the ways of Still Water had conditioned her to search for inner peace when Vatra's fires raged in her. Quen stayed her hand. The drumming had ceased, and though she didn't strike out at Lio, her thundering heart still simmered below the surface. Their disagreement forged a chasm between them, and Quen worried they could never repair it.

Dini pressed her soft hand to Quen's arm and placed the other on Liodhan. "Come, you two, end your quarrel. Death brings us closer to life," she said.

Quen wasn't in the mood for mystic words. "Death is death," she said. She thrust her chin out and drew herself up, facing Liodhan. "You can separate me from the herd, even whip me."

Lio's eyes softened. "I'd never—"

Quen held up her hand. "You can try to force me to obey, but I'm no kopek or drey. I'm not one of the herd, Lio, and I never will be. That is something neither of us can change, no matter how much we may want to. I appreciate what you and Zarate have done for me. But I'll never fit into Jima Clan. We both know this."

Lio swept his hand up and unwound his keffla. "I know no two rivers are identical. But do you truly want to become Jagaru—to never have a family?"

Rhoji had been quiet, engrossed in the flames, his siblings forgotten. He removed his keffla too, his cheeks wet with tear tracks making their way through the ever-present Sulmére dust. "She will be with family." He glanced over his shoulder at Eira. "I'll not leave the work of avenging Pahpi's death solely on Quen's shoulders. By rights, it is the First Kin's task."

Lio began to protest, his eyes dark with rising anger.

Rhoji shook his head and put up a hand. "We know you cannot take up the task. You have a new family to watch over." Rhoji's eyes were red and glistening. "Pahpi would want you to watch over Lumina, not chase after a dragon." He gently squeezed Lumina's tiny foot sticking out from the edge of the sling Zarate carried her in. "I must take up the burden, since you are unable."

Lio's eyes were now filled with tears. "What are you saying, brother?"

"I am saying Quen will not be alone because I, too, will join the Jagaru. We will hunt Pahpi's murderer together."

Rhoji cast another glance back at Eira and smiled.

First Kin duties, my ass. He wants to be with Eira! In an instant, so much about Rhoji that had puzzled Quen now made perfect sense. All the offers for binding he'd denied. His indifference toward women who practically threw themselves at him.

It seems we both have secrets to keep, Rhoji. Quen would keep his secret safe along with her own. *He has as much reason as I for ranging beyond the confines of the Sulmére.* In the Sulmére, though it was common for herdswomen to love one another even if bound to a man, it was unthinkable to form a binding between two men. But she'd heard that in Qülla, it wasn't uncommon for people to join in family with people of the same sex.

Rhoji caught her staring at him, and he blanched, but only for a second. He quickly averted his gaze and turned his attention to Zarate and Lumina. *Act the part of First Kin if you like, Rhoji. So long as you don't stand between that dragon and me.*

CHAPTER 6

S alvaging what they could from Santu's Stand took less than a day. Since throwing herself on Pahpi's pyre ruined Quen's leathers, she was relieved to find an unburned leather riding girdle under a pile of charred wood. She also found the remnants of her favorite book, *The Saga of Ilkay*. The book had been her mother's when she was a girl. As the only possession left to her by her deceased Madi and the only bound book she owned, Quen had cherished it. Quen pressed it to her chest and whispered her favorite passage.

> *"Fear not the beast's fires, Ilkay, for Lumine blessed you with the Waters of Life. Carry them in your heart always, for the Shadow feeds on chaos and fears nothing more than the glassy stillness of calm waters."*

She sniffled and wiped ashes from the singed cover. Though she'd learned enough about Stillness to keep her shadow soul hidden, she'd never felt like the Waters of Life filled her heart. Not like Ilkay. *I have two hearts, and both pull me toward chaos.* She dropped the ruined book in the rubble.

Quen wanted to leave Solia immediately after the Nilva, but Rhoji asked Druvna to stay and help the Solia people who'd lost their homes to settle into Otara. Druvna agreed, though it likely had nothing to do with aid to Solia. He needed time to track the dragon. Without a Juka-jod, people gifted with tracking abilities aided by magic, Druvna's pod relied on intuition and gossip from arriving merchants and herdclans for tracking. Helping survivors was noble, but staring at black-coal reminders of Solia's people tortured Quen. With each passing hour, her itch to hunt the dragon grew. *The sooner we leave Solia, the better.*

Jima camped at the western end of the swollen Lakmi river. Rhoji, Quen, Shel, and Eira camped outside Liodhan and Zarate's tent. A benefit of staying a few days was the opportunity to help tend to Lumina, Lio and Zarate's baby. The babe was bright and her giggle infectious. Quen had spent little time with babies. Finding delight in Lumina's company surprised her.

Yet Nevara's haunting words overshadowed the joy she experienced holding Lumina's tiny hand. *"Wherever you go, tragedy will follow."* Whatever Quen was becoming, she had no place around the helpless babe. *I must get far away from Lumina. I don't think I can survive losing her, especially if I'm to blame.*

The second evening after the fire, they shared a family meal with Liodhan, Zarate, and little Lumina. It was the best meal they were likely to have for weeks. Rhoji and Eira made a spicy stew of smoked fish Zarate brought from Quipwi, served with fresh jiri fruit, leavened bread, and drey-milk cheese. Quen patted her full belly. *I'm like a plump Qülla noble.*

Quen hadn't seen Aldewin since the Nilva. She'd begun thinking he'd moved on without them. But he showed up after the meal and joined smoking a communal pipe. Liodhan had fresh heja tobacco he'd traded for in Quipwi. Aldewin offered to add a 'medicinal herb' that he said calmed the nerves.

After a few rounds of smoking, they were relaxing by the fire. Druvna waddled into camp, Mishny at his side. Both virtually crackled with excited energy, especially compared to the drowsy lot with an herb-induced calm.

Druvna's green eyes were wide with excitement. "Enjoy the comforts as you can now, 'cause tomorrow we ride. Our pod is goin' back on the road." His boisterous voice broke the after-supper stillness of the tent camp.

"What're you on about, Druvna?" Shel's voice was languid from the tobacco and herbs, her eyes narrow slits.

Druvna opened his mouth to answer, but Mishny cut in before he could get a word out. "They sighted a dragon northeast of here. We're heading toward Juinar at Hiyadi's first light." Her expression hovered between a child eating her first cream cake and a young hunter bagging her first kill.

Quen had been lounging on a plump cushion, her head resting on her arm and nearly asleep, but she was on her feet in an instant. "Is it the same dragon with purple scales? Who told you?"

Mishny regarded her coolly, still maybe deciding whether she liked Quen. "There are refugees on the Trinity Road, heading south. They spoke of more dragon fire to the north, toward Juinar."

"Why are they heading south?" Eira asked.

Druvna sat heavily on a pouf. He pulled out his own pipe, lit it, and took a long draw. Smoke tendriled into the twilight sky, and he shook his head. "Say they goin' to Volenex to join some fool dragon cult. Say that they baptize 'em with fire down there so they're immune from dragon fire." He chuckled a raspy laugh. "Some people's got curds for brains."

Rhoji, Eira, and Shel laughed along with Druvna while Aldewin lay back on his elbows, his eyes closed. *What does he think of all this? And why is he so silent? It's infuriating!*

While the others chortled about the foolish things some people believe, Quen couldn't stop thinking about Nevara. Nevara had said Quen belonged to Volenex. Now Druvna was talking about the mysterious home of the Dragos Sol'iberi, the dragon cult Nevara had mentioned. Quen's gut seized into a knot, and her neck bumps tingled. An idea bubbled from deep within. *I should go to Volenex.* The shadow heart quivered, and Quen concentrated on Still Waters. *The Nixan is trying again to steer me. But I'll hold tightly to my skin and go with the Jagaru as planned.* Quen didn't enjoy having to argue with herself.

"Right, Quen?" Rhoji kicked her foot.

"Sure." Wrapped tightly in thought, she didn't know what she'd agreed to.

Druvna stretched his arms overhead, his long pipe still between his teeth. "To Juinar, at first light. The Jagaru wait for no one, so if you whelps aren't mounted and ready, we'll be leaving your sorry arses here in the ruins." He glared at them as if to show he was serious.

"There's no initiation or anything? We just ride with you?" Rhoji asked.

Mishny narrowed her eyes at him. Druvna chortled. "Oh, you get your 'nitiation on the road."

Rhoji stood and dusted the sand from his bottom. "But aren't there vows or oaths?"

Druvna craned his neck and glared up at Rhoji. "You want an oath, do you?" He spat tobacco juice through the slit in his lip. "Okay, here's one for you. Swear you'll have my back and let nuthin'—not even a Kovatha—knife me 'cause if you don't protect your pod, those of us left'll string your skinny arse up and leave your bones for scavengers to pick clean. What say you to that?"

Rhoji swallowed hard. "Yes, well, okay then," he stammered.

Druvna glowered and hawked tobacco juice again. "'Stead of worrying about fancy oaths and such, you best be thinking about your beds 'cause this pod's leaving at Hiyadi's first light with or without you sacks of thukna turds." Druvna waddled away hastily on his deeply bowed legs. Mishny glared at them one last time, then followed Druvna.

Quen hadn't asked for an oath or vow, though she would have gladly sworn one. She was glad to have the pod at her back and eager to prove her worth.

Her sleep was fitful. When Quen drifted off, she dreamed of Pahpi's charred hand still clutching his sword and the dragon's glowing yellow eyes. When Hiyadi's first rays shooed Vay'Nada's darkness away, she was already awake. She'd cleaned her mouth, taken her morning relief, and rolled her bed before anyone else woke.

All except Aldewin. He'd bedded down outside Liodhan's tent with the rest, but was already gone when Quen rose. She didn't want to notice him or ponder his every move. But other than thinking about the dragon, Aldewin occupied the rest of her mind.

True to his word, Druvna and Mishny rode up to Liodhan and Zarate's tent shortly after Quen had rolled her bed. Druvna had donned a dented steel helmet with frayed red and gold plumes and a finely worked red riding girdle over a well-worn deep-gold tunic and pants.

As always, Mishny was with Druvna. She had changed into crimson riding pants pegged by knee-high brown leather boots. A gold tunic, split below the waist, fluttered in the morning breeze. Though she wore no helmet, Mishny had also donned armor. Over her tunic, she wore worn leather-plate mail and an azure riding girdle on the bottom.

Each wore a sheathed blade on both hips, and Mishny had daggers stowed at her belt too. The pair looked like they were riding into battle.

Their battle-ready gear made Quen fully realize what she was signing up for. The harbinger of battle settled in Quen's gullet, where it met a lump of uncertainty. She had no weapon save for the nicked and drab curved blade Druvna had lent her. Quen wore her only remaining set of clothes and the brown riding girdle she'd salvaged from Santu's Stand. Tucked beneath her tunic on its singed leather cord was Pahpi's amber pendant.

"As I expected, Mishny, this pile of lazy moss-brained squib ain't ready to ride. What say you? Shall we leave 'em here in the ashes?" Druvna asked.

Mishny glared down from atop her kopek, Boy. "We can leave this lot of kopek dung behind, but what about your pal Aldewin?"

As though he'd planned for the right moment for an entrance, Aldewin emerged from behind a nearby tent on his brown-and-white dappled horse. Mishny looked disappointed.

Liodhan and Aldewin approached, leading a freshly oiled dark-brown kopek. *I thought Lio was still in his tent.* Lio held out the reins. "This is for you, Quen." The kopek jerked its head but didn't rear up or prance away.

"It's too generous a gift," Quen said. It was a polite thing people said without meaning it. In this case, though, Quen was sincere. She and Lio disagreed about her life's path, but Lio owed her nothing. Lio was true to his beliefs and feelings, as was Quen. Neither of them would ever be anything other than themselves.

"It isn't from me," Lio said. Zarate popped her head from the tent opening and, seeing Lio, came out with tiny Lumina in a sling at her chest. Lio put his arm around Zarate. "Remember, I own nothing. Nabu is a gift from my dear herdwife."

Zarate offered her lips up to Lio for a kiss. "Nabu is the most self-assured kopek in our stables." Zarate petted Nabu's velvety nose. "You need a mount with fire to match yours, not a docile animal afraid of its shadow."

Rhoji laughed as he swung himself onto Gambol's back. "Lumine's teats, Zarate. Are you talking about someone for Quen to bed or an animal to ride?"

Quen's cheeks colored. *I hope Aldewin doesn't notice.*

Liodhan held the reins while Quen hoisted herself up. It was more difficult than she'd expected. Nabu was at least a hand taller than any kopek she'd ever ridden.

Zarate talked sweetly to Nabu while Quen got herself settled. As she pulled Nabu away, Liodhan stood with Zarate, their sweet babe snuggled against Zarate's chest. Quen committed the vision to memory, and her throat tightened. *I might never see them again.*

She trotted to catch up with Druvna and called over her shoulder, "May you find peace in Lumine's arms."

Lio responded, "And may the Brothers light your way, dearest sister."

There was a catch in her throat, but she pressed onward and denied herself one last look at what used to be her home. Charred cinders lay behind. A vast sea of dunes lay ahead. And in her heart, Quen vowed to put a blade through the core of the damned fire-breathing beast before it took someone else she loved.

●　　●　　●

Druvna rode like he was more comfortable in a saddle than walking on land. When he stopped, it was for the animals.

By the second day, Quen's backside was already getting calloused. Quen tried to walk normally when they stopped for meals, but her tight back, hips, and thighs made her hobble. Her only solace was watching Rhoji wince when he sat for midday meal. *At least he won't make fun of me for having a tender arse.*

"It will take a few weeks, but you will get used to it." Aldewin sat down gracefully next to her and offered her a wine sac.

She raised an eyebrow. "Bit early for that, isn't it? Besides, Druvna said no drinking wine or firewater for us 'moss-brained squibs.'"

Aldewin laughed. His chuckle was warm and melodic, as though it was part of a song. *I wish he laughed more and that he'd ride by my side rather than guarding the rear of our pod.* His absence from conversation only made her ponder him more.

"He'll not notice a sip or two. It will take the edge off your pain."

Quen tittered, and her voice went pitchy. "I'm in no pain."

Aldewin gave her a sidelong glance. "If your back and legs don't feel like they've been beaten, then you're a stronger rider than I was when I first joined the Jagaru." He took a long swallow from the wine sac.

Quen ate her ration of bread and a bit of cheese and then took the sac from him. The wine was smooth and tasted of plum and honey. *Better than the jiri wine at Yulina's.* A pleasant warmth spread from her throat to her belly. She handed the wine back. "Thank you."

Aldewin fixed his gaze on her mouth. "You've got—" He wiped a dribble of wine from her lower lip.

The touch had lasted only a second, but it caused a cascade of reactions within her. Her loins tightened, and heat rose from her neck to her ears. Her heart quickened, and it double-thumped. Most disconcertingly, the back of her neck grew hot and tingled where the bone protrusion lay beneath the skin.

As if sensing what his touch had done to her, Aldewin pulled his hand away and averted his gaze. He took a long pull on the wine sac. "I apologize—I should not have...." He cleared his throat. "I'll leave you to your meal."

Quen wanted to protest. To tell him she didn't want him to leave. *I want him to touch my face again, and to feel his...* Merely thinking about his touch made her neck ridge tingle. She feared his kiss would distract her from guarding against the Nixan trying to push its way to the fore. Instead of asking him to stay, she nodded, afraid if she spoke, her voice would reveal how his slightest touch had stoked desire within her.

Aldewin rose in one fluid movement, bowed, and said, "I hope you have a good afternoon of riding."

I can't imagine how it could be now. He'd done nothing more than touch her lip for less time than it takes to shoo a fly, but he'd created a simmering pot of feelings to stew over the rest of the day.

On the road again, Shel and Quen rode behind Mishny and Druvna. After catching up on the happenings in their lives since they'd last seen each other, Quen pressed for information about Aldewin. "So, what's *his* story?" She glanced furtively over her shoulder at the lone rider tall in his saddle at the column's rear.

"He's an odd one, isn't he?"

"I was thinking more attractive than odd," Quen said.

"What?" Shel laughed. "That bean pole? All that sun-reddened skin and pale hair?" Her lip curled in disgust.

Quen's face grew hot. *She doesn't even desire men. She wouldn't know what makes them appealing.* "Forget I said attractive." *Still Waters. Still Waters.* "Tell me what you know about him."

"We camped near Enarili, holding some raiders and waiting for Kovatha to haul 'em to Qülla. Druvna left Mishny in charge—that was fun." Shel rolled her eyes. "Anyways, he came back a week later with the lofty guy. He and Mishny fought about it."

"What did they say?"

Shel shrugged. "We couldn't hear what they said, but everyone within a league heard them argue."

"What's Mishny's beef with Aldewin?" *He rides alone and hardly speaks. How can she find fault with that?*

"You probably noticed that Mishny hates outsiders. If you don't bleed Sulmére sand, she considers you a 'shite eater.'"

"Except for Druvna, none of us were born in the Sulmére," Quen said. While Eira and Shel were originally from Suab'hora, the capital province, Rhoji and Quen had been born in the city-state of Bardivia in the Vindaô Province.

"Exactly. That's why she hates all of us except for Druvna."

A nasty way to live. Hating people just because they were born somewhere else. "So Mishny's sour on everyone. Got it. But what about Aldewin? Why did he join this third-rate pod? No offense."

Shel faked offense. "Third rate? Just because we're small and inexperienced? Our leader a bowed old man, his lieutenant a sour-faced crazy woman?" She laughed.

"I mean, if Aldewin is as handy with all those weapons as he appears—"

"Oh, he is."

"He could make a passel of silver kovars, maybe even gold, as a mercenary. Or join a larger pod with more clout."

Shel shrugged. "I'm just one of the 'moss-brained squib,' Quen. I don't get paid to ask questions about Aldewin. We're Jagaru, and you are too now. All I care is that Aldewin fights better than even Mishny. And there's no one you'd rather have at your back 'cause he'll protect your arse like it was his own. Who cares if he prays to water and shite? So long as he keeps thukna turds off my back in a melee."

Inwardly, Shel had stoked even more curiosity. But outwardly, Quen left the topic alone. They returned to gossip, laughing and chattering.

Mishny glared at them. "By the Three! Those two have more shite runnin' from their mouths than a Qülla sewer." She yelled to them, "Ride at the back, so I have some peace."

"Does she belong to a sect with rules against joy?" They turned and rode farther back, just ahead of Aldewin. They rode past Eira and Rhoji, riding close together and whispering. *I've never seen Rhoji so talkative and quick to smile or laugh. And he hasn't chided me or made a joke at my expense since we left Solia.* His mood was lively despite the long, hot, tiring days of riding. *I wonder if he and Eira....*

Shel and Quen exhausted their gossip in less than a day. They spent two more days speculating about the relationship between Eira and Rhoji, complaining about Mishny's sour attitude, and interpreting Aldewin's every gaze. But Aldewin gave them precious little to speculate about. He ate his meals alone and wandered from camp each evening rather than smoking heja with the others.

102

Curiosity piqued, Quen was going after him. Eira held her back, though. "He needs time alone."

Quen laughed. "He's been alone all day."

"True enough, but he said he needs to stretch. And he's devout, that one. Said he needs time alone to pray to the goddess."

I could do those things with him if he'd let me.

The following night, they made camp along the sandy banks of a desert stream. Though it was likely dry most of the year, recent snowmelt swelled the river.

"Want a feast fit for a Qülla noble?" Shel asked. She dug in the soft sand and retrieved a closed shell. Shel pulled her belt knife and carefully prized the shell open, revealing a freshwater mussel. She made quick work of loosening the tendon, then stabbed the fresh shellfish with her knife and offered it to Quen. "Try this."

Quen scrunched up her face. "Yuck! It's still— wriggly. Don't you cook it?"

Shel gently teased the mussel from her knife, chewed a few times, and swallowed. "Why waste time cooking when it's good raw?"

Encouraged by her grumbly stomach, Quen dug for her own shell. She did as Shel had. The sweetness of the mussel pleasantly surprised her. "Rhoji," she called. "You gotta come try this."

Eira, Shel, Rhoji, and Quen stuffed themselves with fresh mussels, stale flatbreads, and the creamy drey's milk cheese Zarate had gifted them. The others stared dreamily into the fire while Druvna smoked his pipe. But Quen was antsy. *Aldewin can't pray all the time.*

She rose and patted the sand from her backside. "I'm going to find a—private spot." *To spy on Aldewin.*

Rhoji acknowledged her statement with a head bob, and Shel gave her a wave.

Though Hiyadi had set, Niyadi gave enough pale light for Quen to follow the path of desert grasses Aldewin had trampled. Reeds anchored sand in the center of the stream, forming a small island. *I think he's there.*

At the stream's edge, Quen took off her boots and rolled the legs of her riding pants. She waded in the knee-deep water, and as she approached the tiny island, she heard Aldewin.

He sounded like he was talking to someone, but nobody was with him. The gentle babbling of the stream over rocks obscured his voice, making it impossible to understand what he said. *It doesn't sound like a prayer, though. Is he talking to himself?*

Quen stepped deliberately, taking care not to lose her footing on the slippery rocks. When she got to the sandbar, she crouched behind reeds, parted them, and glimpsed Aldewin.

His hands were outstretched, and he held an orb of water aloft. The watery globe shimmered, reflecting the light of Lumine and Niyadi. The water ball was perfectly round, swirling slowly as Aldewin spoke to it in a language she'd never heard.

He's talking to water? What kind of magic is this?

Her feet squished in the soft, sandy soil as she inched closer. Quen pulled her foot out of the sucking sand. It popped, and the sound echoed in the quiet evening.

Aldewin's head whipped in her direction. *Did he see me?* Aldewin spoke more words into the water ball, and a faint blue light emanated from his fingers. The water dispersed into a fine mist, traveled upward, then scattered, and the wind carried it away.

"You're about as stealthy as a herd of thukna," Aldewin said.

Quen pulled her other foot out of the sinking sand and stepped from behind the reed curtain. Aldewin's arms were clasped behind his back, a bemused look on his face.

"I've always been a lousy spy." She closed the gap between them. "What were you doing?"

"Talking."

"To the water?"

"Sure. Have you never seen someone whisper prayers to Lumine?"

"Of course. Just not—magically." *Is he really Jagaru?* "Does the water—talk back?"

Aldewin chuckled. "Not literally." Aldewin swooped his hand downward, flourished his fingers, and drew a swirling ball of water into the air. "The Waters of Life have intelligence." He spun his hand, and the water swirled in a glistening ball.

Quen stepped closer and examined the water. "The Bruxia of my village, Dini, would call this a mummer's trick." Quen sliced through the water with her hand, expecting it to return to the stream. But the water reformed into the tightly bound ball it had been.

"Is this a mummer's farce?" Aldewin's eyes twinkled, his mouth pulled into a mischievous grin. He leaned close to the ball of water and whispered into it. He thrust his arms up, and the water scattered into a mist as before. This time the mist swirled to Quen.

The water droplets reformed into a ball before Quen's eyes. From the sparkling orb, Aldewin's voice emerged. It wavered and gurgled, like he was speaking underwater. "Curious Quen should hope for a cat's nine lives." After the water repeated Aldewin's words, the water fell, and the stream carried it away.

"That was incredible," Quen whispered. *He thinks I'm curious. Is that good or bad?*

Most people with Menaris ability studied at the Pillars, thus making magic in Indrasi something rarely observed. Until she witnessed Nevara raise a column of fire in Pahpi's store, magic was something in stories passed by traders or in books or herbal healing wisdom of Bruxias. But Aldewin's skill with Menaris was wholly new to her. He wasn't using Menaris as a weapon, but for something beautiful. *Once we've brought the dragon down, maybe I should do as Pahpi wished and study Menaris like this at Val'Enara.* "Where did you learn this? At a Pillar?"

Aldewin adjusted the staff across his back and cleared his throat. "At a Pillar? Nah. This is arcane magic, straight from the swamps of Tinox." He chuckled. "Roughian magic, they call it in Partha."

"Where you're from."

He nodded. "Not something most people master anymore."

"But you did."

Aldewin yanked his foot from the mud and returned to the stream.

Quen followed. "This is an odd bit of magic. Why would you—I mean, what purpose does it serve?"

Rinsing off his feet in the stream, he said, "Let's just say my past required much of me, and most of it, I'd rather not recall." His look was harsh; his tone a veritable wall built between them.

Instead of retreating, she moved closer. "I can be a good listener." Quen wasn't usually flirtatious, but her desire to know him made her brazen.

Aldewin feigned a smile, but it didn't reach his eyes. "I would love to talk to you—someday. But we had a long ride, and the energy I used manipulating Menaris for my—prayer—tired me further. Perhaps another night we'll speak."

He began walking back toward camp.

Quen said, "Will there be another night when Lumine shines so brightly? When the waters of Enara lap so gently at our feet?"

He continued walking but backward. "Are you a death siren sent by Vay'Nada to lure me to my end in the waters?" His voice was only half-mocking, containing an edge of grave concern. "I need rest, Quen." He turned and made his way swiftly upstream toward the soft firelight of their camp.

Quen was suddenly aware of how cold and uncomfortable her wet feet were. The thrill of being near him and his magical watery orbs vanished. She was cold, wet, and alone—again—and wished she hadn't made such a fool of herself.

She rejoined the others and plopped down beside Shel.

"What happened with you two?" Shel whispered to Quen.

Her mood soured. She didn't feel like reliving Aldewin's cold rejection. "Nothing happened." Fortunately, Shel didn't press for more details.

Though a dark cloud hung over Quen's mood, the others had already begun passing a pipe of heja and were in good spirits. Eira played a double flute, and Shel drummed on a small hand drum as they sang Sulmére drinking songs. Rhoji's lovely tenor lilted, while Mishny's singing voice was as sour as her general demeanor. Aldewin rifled through his pack, pulled out a small stringed instrument he held on his lap, and strummed along. He kept apologizing for getting notes wrong, as he didn't know all the songs. Quen hadn't noticed an off-key note. The lighthearted songs lifted her dour mood.

Once they'd sung through all the tavern songs they knew, Eira put his flute down. "My lips are tired."

There was a chorus of "No!" and boos, but Eira shook his head.

"Eira, may I?" Aldewin asked.

Eira handed him the flute. "Please do."

Aldewin played a few test notes, checking his fingering. "It's different from the flute I learned on. But I'll give it a go."

Quen had always enjoyed listening to Eira play. He was capable enough to join a traveling entertainer group. But Aldewin's music was bright and clear. *Like Juka playing through him.*

The song Aldewin played was as mournful as it was beautiful. It reminded Quen of the plaintive cry of Nilva pyre songs. By the time he finished, tears had welled in her eyes. Eira wiped his face, and even stoic Rhoji sniffled.

"What's the name of that song?" Eira asked.

"'The Dragon Is Broken,'" Aldewin said. He wiped the mouthpiece and handed it back to Eira.

"A song about defeating a dragon should be a jolly, celebratory song. Or maybe a marching tune," Rhoji said.

Aldewin chuckled. "Perhaps. It's an ancient song from Bídean, the northernmost territory of Tinox. Some say it's the land where dragons were born." His gaze landed on Quen. "Maybe the Bídeans loved dragons. You can recognize the danger, yet still lament that humans broke the majestic creatures and scoured them from the land."

"Maybe the people that wrote the song never had their Pahpi burned alive by dragon fire." Her words were clipped, her voice taut.

Aldewin nodded. "Perhaps not."

"Or perhaps the song recognized the loss on both sides," Druvna said. He'd been transfixed on the dwindling fire during Aldewin's song, and Quen thought he'd nodded off.

"You refer now to dragons?" Rhoji asked. His voice was terse. "They're supposed to be one of the 'sides' you speak of?"

"Of course. Every war has two sides," Druvna said.

Rhoji laughed bitterly. "Are you saying that gnash-fisting bastard of a dragon who killed my father is a *side* in this war worthy of consideration?"

Perhaps wanting to avoid a brawl, Aldewin said, "It's only legend, anyway. Bídeans live in the snow year-round. What else do they have to do but spin fanciful yarns and sing sad songs?" He took a draw of the firewater he'd brought.

Everyone laughed except for Druvna. "What are legends but shadows of history?" He rose and yawned. "My bones need sleep. You moss-brained squibs better be beddin' down soon 'cause I'll no'a wait for you in the morn." He waddled away from the fire.

Soon, the others did the same.

Even though the long day's journey had exhausted Quen, thoughts of Aldewin kept her awake. Quen tossed, and her sleep was fitful. She silently cursed Aldewin for worming into her mind—and for being beyond reach. Everything he said was an enigma. Everything he did made her more curious about him. And like her ill-fated relationship with the gods, every attempt to get closer resulted in being pushed further away.

•   •   •

After a few days of riding, Quen's blisters became calloused, and her rear end, back, and thighs hurt less. Conversations and catching up exhausted, Quen and Shel settled into the meditative silence Mishny, Druvna, and Aldewin preferred. By day five, Quen's racing mind quieted. She focused on the whistling wind and became attuned to how dune shadows marked the passage of time.

Their voyage north was a slow but steady elevation climb and gradual vegetation change. As if stepping through a mystical portal, once across the Béanju River, Tikli Province's rocky hills replaced the undulating sands of the Sulmére. Scrubby bushes and tall, spiky plants Druvna called cactus dotted the slopes.

The odor of salty air was a pleasant and unexpected change. The road skirted a steep drop-off to the vast Zhongdu Sea to the east.

Quen had never seen an ocean before. In his youth, Fano had been a sailor and sailed the Orju Sea and the Straits of Minea to the north, a busy trade route with Tinox. Fano said more than fish filled the Zhongdu Sea.

He said mysterious creatures and unseen forces filled the sea, too. And he'd warned her to never trust someone trying to get her to cross the Zhongdu Sea. "It's home to sea dragons, it is, Quen. They say there are evil changeling women who look beautiful and call to sailors. But when the poor sot jumps in, the woman becomes a hideous darmanitong straight from Vay'Nada and eats him alive," Fano had said.

It was one of the many stories about evil Nixan and their disregard for human life. These tales made Quen maintain her ferocious battle against the Nixan within. *I don't want to steal children like a slint. Or lure a man with song, only to devour him like a darmanitong.* The thought made her shudder.

Like a shimmering turquoise jewel, the sea looked inviting, not like a home for Vay'Nada's spawn, like slints and darmanitongs. "Can we go to the beach for midday meal?" Quen asked.

Rhoji, Eira, and Shel voiced approval of the idea.

But Druvna shook his head. "It's farther away than it looks and a cruel climb back up for the mounts."

Mishny eyed Quen with disapproval for even asking the question. She gave Quen a narrow-eyed catlike smirk when Druvna shot Quen down.

Druvna listened to Aldewin. Quen called back over her shoulder to him. "Aldewin—you'd like to take midday meal by the sea, wouldn't you?"

"Sorry, but I agree with Druvna. The sea is… It will tax the mounts unnecessarily."

His voice had an odd catch. Apprehension? There's something he's not saying. They passed the path down to the Zhongdu, and Quen missed her opportunity for her first taste of the salty sea.

Before long, an acrid smoke odor replaced the sea's pleasant tang. The Jagaru followed the foul odor to the remains of Juinar.

From the looks of the burnt structures, Juinar was slightly larger than Solia. Juinar sat along a wide channel of the Béanju River on its way to the Zhongdu Sea. It was only a day's ride south of the Tilaj Gate, a waypost on the journey to the capital province of Suab'Hora.

The blackened town was empty save for surviving families and opportunists scavenging the ruins. Quen had recently done the same. If Tikli Province people were like Sulmére folks, they'd be mortified to see someone gawking at their grief. *We endure such things in private, not share them with the world.* Quen kept her eyes forward, trying to honor their privacy as she would want them to respect hers.

The small pod of Jagaru didn't go unnoticed. It was Quen's turn to carry the colors, and the flag she bore flapped in the light sea breeze. It was loud in the otherwise silent ruins of the town.

People ceased rummaging, their eyes alight with curiosity about the newcomers. Children ran after the column of riders, their bare feet blackened by running in soot-filled streets.

Unlike in Solia, the dragon fire had spared about a half-dozen of Juinar's structures. *Thank the Three, the tavern still stands.* Druvna marched to the pub, apparently as thirsty and ready for rest as she was.

Mishny tied Boy to the charred remains of a hitching post. "Odd burn patterns."

Druvna didn't stop giving his gaunt old kopek, Dauer, a quick rubdown. "Nothing odd 'bout it. Mindless beast ruled by chaos, that dragon is."

Rhoji patted Gambol's haunches, sending a cloud of dust into the air. "I do not know if the creature is mindless, but I agree with Mishny. Burning the outer ring of the town but sparing the center?"

Mishny nodded and gave Rhoji a rare approving look. "This dragon is no curd brain. Looks to me like it had a plan."

Druvna raised his brows and looked skeptical. "I think you both grasp for something t'aint there. Beasts don't plan."

Quen rubbed Nabu's velvety nose. "Dragons aren't moss-brains like kopeks." She whispered in Nabu's ear, "No offense."

"You an expert on Vay'Nada's spawn, are you?" Druvna squinted at her.

"No. Are you?"

Druvna narrowed his eyes even further at her and spat tobacco juice. He was about to speak when Aldewin interrupted.

"They have a point, Druvna. There is a pattern here." He gestured around them. "The dragon burnt the dwellings but spared the center of town—the commerce. It's as if this dragon, or whoever controls it, wants the people forced out of their homes."

"You think someone controls that thing?" Shel asked.

Rajani control it. Quen watched filthy orphaned children running past houses that were now rubble. *What if I'm a Nixan like Nevara, destined to be a Rajani? Someday I* might be responsible for death and destruction like in Juinar. Her stomach churned.

But Aldewin's point raised another concern. *What if my quarrel isn't only with the damned dragon, but its master?*

Previously quiet, Eira now said what they were likely all thinking. "The beast could have eaten them. Why just burn the town? This makes no sense."

Druvna wiped the back of his neck with a dirty cloth. "Might be what stragglers passing Solia were talking 'bout. They'd been told a dragon cult down in Volenex would do some fire ritual on 'em." Druvna sounded impatient with the entire conversation. "I need firewater in my belly if we keep talking 'bout this dragon shite."

He pushed open the door of the charred but still-standing Juinar Inn. None of them argued against it. Quen looked forward to warm food, drink, and being out of the saddle.

At least that's what Druvna had promised they'd do in Juinar. But as soon as they stepped inside, it was clear they wouldn't have the rest they'd planned.

A woman held the hand of what appeared to be her son, likely sixteen. Her other arm encircled a younger child, a girl of about twelve. "Are you curd brains? I told you, my children aren't for sale. Shove off." She ran her thumb along the side of her nose and then flicked it out to them the way Dini did when telling someone off.

A lanky man with salt-and-pepper hair pressed closer. He towered over the woman and her children. He undid the fastener on his scabbard, and his hand lingered on the hilt of his blade. "You must be mistaken. I wasn't asking. I was telling. Besides, in Qülla, at least your children will have a roof o'er their heads. Two meals a day, most like. My buyer's a top-notch noble from Māja Wix—an old house with prestige. Even servants of Māja Wix are more respected than Tikli trash like you'uns."

Druvna moved with astonishing speed for a man of his years. Before the shady men registered Jagaru had entered, Druvna stood protectively in front of the woman.

"You're not telling nobody nothing," Druvna said.

The other men surrounded Druvna. The three would-be human traffickers pulled their blades, ready to fight.

In one hand, Shel brandished a dagger. In the other, she held a small blacksmith's hammer. Her eyes glistened with excitement, and her mouth set in a smirk. "Time for your true Jagaru initiation."

CHAPTER 7

Ignoble child snatchers circled Druvna, their curved blades drawn. While Quen fumbled with the fob on her scabbard, Aldewin already had his staff in hand. He swung low and wide, knocking the legs out from under one man.

One man called to the salt-and-pepper-haired man, "Do no'a listen to them, Earnôt. I know this one. She no'a proper Jaga—"

Before the man could finish his sentence, Mishny landed a roundhouse kick to his gut. While he reeled, Mishny drew a dagger and slit his throat. The blood gurgling from a gaping wound in his neck swallowed the man's last words.

Earnôt had been standing between Druvna and the woman and children as if defending his prize. When his companion slumped to the floor, Earnôt dropped his blade and stepped back, empty hands in the air. "I want no trouble, Jagaru."

"Dammit to Vay'Nada's cold arse, Mishny. I told you to stop killing them."

Mishny's dark eyes were wide, and her nostrils flared. She was wound tight and ready to pounce. She kicked the dead man's leg with her booted toe. "No one will miss the likes of this scum." She spat in the dead man's general direction.

Aldewin had pulled a cord from his belt pouch and was busy tying the hands of the man he'd knocked unconscious with a staff blow to the head. "According to new edicts from the Dynasty, it's not up to Jagaru to judge his crimes—or his character." His tone clearly showed what he thought of the man's character.

Druvna motioned for Eira to bind Earnôt's hands. "That's the Jagaru creed, right, Mishny? We scour the sands to root out the evils, but it's up to the Dynasty to decide their fate."

"Dynasty. Pha." Mishny said the word 'Dynasty' as though it was a foul-tasting lump of pus in her mouth.

This "creed" Druvna spoke of was new to Quen. *I thought the Jagaru were reeve, Kovatha judge, and royal executioner all in one. That's how they operated when they visited Solia, anyway.*

The mother still had her arm around the girl and held her son's hand. "You can kill the lot of 'em for all I care." She glared at Earnôt and looked ready to spit on him. "Dynasty dungeons are too good for people who'd rip children from their mother for a few kovars."

Mishny kicked the unconscious but bound man. When he didn't rouse, she knelt and slit his throat, too. Her action, swift and defiant, took all by surprise.

Druvna hissed, "Mishny." His face was red, and his eyes blazed with anger. He pulled his hand back, ready to strike her.

She rose and faced him, standing a solid head taller than their bowlegged and age-worn leader. Mishny returned his angry glare with one of her own, daring the old man to strike her. After Druvna withdrew his hand, she said, "Some crimes call for *old* justice. Jagaru justice."

Druvna's face relaxed. A moment of meaning passed between them, and Druvna admonished Mishny no further.

Earnôt, hands bound, shuffled away from them, never taking his eyes off Mishny. He sounded panicked. "You gotta take me to the Tilaj Gate, you do. It's the law. Only Dynasty officials can pass judgment."

Aldewin guffawed. "You're an expert in Dynasty law now, are you?" He cracked his staff across the backs of Earnôt's thighs, dropping him to his knees. Aldewin's nose scrunched up as though he'd caught an offending odor. "You scared the piss right out of him, Mishny."

Aldewin used the tip of his staff to force Earnôt to look into his eyes. "Normally, I'm a by-the-book guy. But this time, I'm with Mishny. Anyone trying to steal children isn't really a person at all." Aldewin's eyes narrowed, his jaw set and twitching. He looked like it took restraint not to pull the broadsword from his back and end Earnôt with one powerful blow. "This woman deserves to see justice served, not wonder if he ever made it into Qülla's dungeons."

Druvna's dented helmet sat askew on his head, and sweat beaded on his upper lip. He drew a stained cloth from his belt and wiped his forehead. "Suda. All I wanted was to get good and pished." Druvna righted his helmet.

"Looks like we got a disagreement 'bout what to do with your sorry arse." He put the cloth back in his belt and gestured toward Shel, Eira, Rhoji, and Quen. "Looks like you squibs get your first Jagaru vote. Sheath your blades, and we carry his arse to the Tilaj Gate, hand him over to the Kovatha, and collect our reward. Raise your blade, and we return his blood to the sands and forfeit the coin."

Shel still held her hammer as though she expected to use it. Without hesitation, she raised it high.

Eira also didn't pause to weigh the options. But he sheathed his blade, breaking ranks with his sister. Rhoji followed Eira's lead. *Is Rhoji respecting Dynasty law or just trying to stay on Eira's good side?* Druvna sheathed his blade while Mishny and Aldewin held their weapons high.

The deciding vote was Quen's. Earnôt's red, watery eyes bored into hers, pleading for his life. Mishny stood tall, arms crossed, glaring at Quen like she was willing Quen's blade to rise.

Pahpi rarely called upon the Jagaru to sort out crimes committed in Solia. He'd preferred the town elders to mete out justice. He said the Jagaru were too much vigilante and too little justice. Quen sighed, thinking about what Pahpi would say if he knew both she and Rhoji had joined the Jagaru. Her chest grew tight.

But Quen couldn't recall Solia ever dealing with men stealing children. *Though Pahpi had no love for the Dynasty, he probably would have handed Earnôt over to Kovatha.* Like Pahpi, most Kovatha were Pillar-trained. *He believed Pillar-educated people could be more fair.*

Before the dragon attack, Quen likely would have agreed with what she imagined Pahpi would decide. But in the weeks since Nevara darkened their door, she'd dramatically increased her knowledge of the world. *I'm uncertain if I agree with your ways of thinking anymore, Pahpi.*

She saw a bit of herself in the young girl still quaking by her mother's side, tightly hugging a soot-covered rag doll. It wasn't long ago that she was a young girl and vulnerable. Quen shuddered to consider what might have happened to the girl if they hadn't happened along.

Quen raised her blade high.

Rhoji looked aghast. Mishny's smirk was likely the closest Quen would come to the woman's approval. Aldewin gave her a single nod, though his lips were a grim line.

Earnôt tried to run, but Shel snatched him by the shirt and pulled him back. She yanked his bound hands and forced him to kneel.

A thin, red-faced woman sprang from behind the bar. "No more blood in my inn! Take your Jagaru business out to what's left of Juinar."

Druvna nodded. "Get him up and out."

Rhoji helped Shel drag Earnôt to his feet, and they marched him out to Juinar's acrid air.

As Quen turned to leave, the mother grabbed at Quen's tunic. Her tired pale-green eyes were red and watery. "You did good business today, young Jagaru. Blessing of the Three to you, and I'll pray the Sister keeps you." She pressed a dar into Quen's hand.

Quen couldn't recall anyone thanking her like this before. Pride swelled her chest. Hot tears stung her eyes. *It'll ruin my image as a brave Jagaru if they see me cry.* Quen nodded once and left, the dar warm in her hand.

•   •   •

Earnôt stood in the center of charred Juinar, awaiting Jagaru justice. Townsfolk, scavengers, and the mother and children gathered to watch as Earnôt tried various arguments in quick succession to wriggle out of his fate.

"I did no'a break the law. You know this, Jagaru. We can sell people in the Capital."

His claim brought a chorus of jeers from the onlookers. One man shouted, "But you no'a can steal a person, you kopek dung." The emboldened crowd cheered even more.

When claiming he was in the right hadn't worked, Earnôt switched gears. "If you kill me, wait and see what happens to you. The childrens was headed to Māja Wix, they was. Mistress Idaya gonna be powerful mad when I no'a bring them for Māja Wix."

His threatening rhetoric didn't dissuade the increasingly large angry mob from jeering and even throwing bits of charred wood at the Jagaru prisoner. The people of Juinar had lost everything. Earnôt hadn't burned their town, but he was there, and the murderous dragon wasn't.

Aldewin whispered into Druvna's ear, and the old Jagaru raised his hand and called for quiet. "Everyone knows what you did was wrong, Earnôt the Evil. And you know it, too. Even in the stinkin' capital, there's no'a captives or enslaved people, only indentured. You wouldn't get past the Tilaj Gate anyhows. This madi deserves justice, and the Jagaru are gonna save the Kovathas the trouble."

Druvna nodded to Mishny, and she forced Earnôt to kneel. He blubbered like a child who lost their toy, showing he hadn't an ounce of self-respect or courage. Eira pushed Earnôt's head to a charred stump, exposing his neck.

Druvna drew his doubled-edge curved blade, but it shook in his hands. He wiped his brow with his forearm.

"What's the matter?" Quen whispered to Shel.

Shel sighed and whispered back. "I think he's afraid he hasn't the strength to do it in one blow."

Without words passing between them, Aldewin pulled the great broadsword from his back and took Earnôt's head from his neck with one mighty stroke. Earnôt's head fell to the ground with a sickening plop. Crimson blood pumped out of the neck before the body, too, fell to the soot-darkened sand.

Silenced replaced the cheers, shouts, and yowls. With a face set like stone, Aldewin wiped Earnôt's blood off his blade. He stowed the broadsword back in its scabbard and walked to the alehouse without a word. People tried to put pits and dars into Aldewin's hand as he passed, but he ignored them and didn't take the money.

Mishny said, "I'll collect your tributes to the Jagaru." She stood amongst the crowd and collected the token coin the survivors of Juinar offered for the justice served.

Shel elbowed Quen. "Come on. Let Mishny gather coin while we get good and pished."

Best idea I've heard since we left Solia.

When they entered the Juinar Inn, Aldewin had already settled at a table in a dark back corner of the place, a mug of ale to his lips. Quen moved to join him, but Shel pulled her toward the bar.

"He needs to be alone," Shel said.

Aldewin hadn't even looked up when they entered. His face was dour, his foul mood palpable from across the room. *Shel's probably right.* Quen followed her friend to the bar in the center of the inn.

Eira, Rhoji, Druvna, and Mishny soon joined them. Druvna ordered ale and plunked down a dar to cover their tab. "Even the moss-brained squibs here get a mug tonight."

One mug became two and then too many. They sang more rounds of "Song of Niyadi" than Quen had ever sung before, each progressively bawdier than the last. Mishny sang lyrics with double meaning, but Shel was not to be outdone.

"Dance strong, Niyadi, dance!" Shel sang, her words garbled with drink but her voice rich and melodious. She added a seductive swivel of her hips to punctuate her lyrics.

When they all cheered and egged her on, she continued.

> "Rise, big ole Niyadi, rise!
> Sink down on bended knee,
> Plant kisses there,
> Tween nether hair.
> Make her swoon and scream, yes,
> yes!"

Shel's verse made even Druvna blush. Quen laughed so hard she snorted ale through her nose. Shel bowed and drained her cup. She leaned to Quen and said, "By the Three, I think my garden needs tending."

Shel had meant to whisper, but her voice carried. Everyone at the bar raised their cups and said, "Hear, hear!"

It didn't embarrass Shel. She laughed with the others, and a farmer across the bar bought her an ale. Not one to pass up a gift cup, she drank every drop.

"Poor guy. He doesn't know Mishny's got more chance of being welcomed in your bed than he has," Quen said. They clinked their mugs, spilling ale on the bar.

"By Niyadi's arse, you know I'm too pished when I think maybe spooning with Mishny is a good idea," Shel said before falling off her stool.

Quen tried to see in Mishny what Shel saw, but even under the influence of ale, she couldn't imagine kindling romance with sour Mishny.

Druvna slid from his chair and nearly fell over. "Get as mush-brained as you want, but remember, the Jagaru won't wait for your sorry arse in the morn. People say they saw smoke farther north, so tomorrow we ride to the Tilaj Gate."

Mishny had drunk as many mugs as the others, but she stood without wobbling. She put several coins on the bar for the barkeep then slung an arm around Druvna and helped him out.

"We should prob'ly—proob'ily—aw, I need sleep," Rhoji said.

Quen had never seen him so drunk. Eira joined arms with him, and they staggered to camp.

The ale and song had taken Quen's mind off the day's events. Relaxed and aroused by the bawdy songs, Quen searched the room for Aldewin, but he was no longer brooding in the corner.

Shel drained her mug. "He left hours ago."

"Who?" Quen's face flushed.

Shel laughed as Quen lent her a hand up off the floor. "By Hiyadi's round ass, Quen, you're terrible at hiding your feelings. You better never play Duple di Marc in Qülla. You'll lose your last skin." Shel tugged at Quen's sleeve and indicated the door with her head. "Let's go. Maybe you can find Aldewin's thighs at camp." She pantomimed humping a man, laughed, and headed for the door.

Quen was going to protest Shel's insinuations, but when she tried to speak, her words were a gurgling mass of vowels. "Ah, piss on it all," she managed, and plunked the single dar she'd received earlier onto the counter. It was all her money, but it was worth every pit to have a few hours away from thinking about dragons, death, and the Nixan soul trying to steal her skin.

She followed Shel to their camp outside the burned town, trying not to stumble. Collecting breezes from the vast Zhongdu Sea, Juinar turned chilly at night. The damp seeped into Quen in a way she had never experienced in Solia. She shivered as she made her way to their small fire.

Druvna was already snoring loudly, his out-breaths whistling through the slit in his upper lip. Rhoji, still wearing boots, had passed out on his bedroll, an arm slung across Eira.

Shel didn't bother carefully smoothing her pallet as usual. She threw it on the ground and practically fell onto it.

The small fire was nearly out and provided little light or heat. Quen stoked it with a long stick, rousing the embers. In the increased light, she noticed Aldewin sitting across the fire. He was so still she'd mistaken him for a large rock in the dim light. Drowsy-looking but awake, Aldewin stared at the flame.

He glanced up at her. "Your first true day as a Jagaru." He drank from his wineskin. "You should get some rest."

Quen unrolled her pallet and sat down. "I'm not tired." She stifled a yawn.

Aldewin smiled and shook his head. "You're not, hey?"

A part of her wanted nothing more than to fall into an ale-induced deep sleep, the prize for the long ass-numbing ride from Solia. But her desire to be in Aldewin's company was greater.

"Tell me, Aldewin di Partha, how you learned to use your stick like that." Her cheeks colored, realizing how he might take what she said after the bawdy singing at the Juinar Inn.

Aldewin's eyes twinkled. He smiled over his wine sac at her, unembarrassed by her question. "Which stick are you referring to?"

"That's not—well, I meant—"

He laughed. "I know what you meant." He took another drink and put the wine down. "Would you like me to show you?"

Quen's heart raced. "Here?" Mishny stirred, and Quen realized her voice had been loud. She whispered, "Now?"

Aldewin gave her a hand up. "Sure. Why not? Come with me."

Her loins tightened, and both hearts beat more rapidly. She'd imagined intertwining with Aldewin for days while riding, but didn't believe it would happen. She followed as he headed away from the warmth and light of the fire. Shivering before, Quen was no longer cold.

Once they were about thirty paces beyond camp, Aldewin pulled the staff from his back. She wasn't sure if he intended to fight her or bed her. Quen stepped back.

He shook his head and chortled. "Don't be afraid. Come." He motioned to her. "I'll show you how to wield a stick, as you call it."

She tried not to show how disappointed she was that he wanted to give her a fighting lesson, not a love lesson. But any closeness with him was preferable to her cold bed, so she moved closer.

"First, you must learn how to grip it." He held the staff out to her. "Come on, don't be shy."

She held the staff gingerly with one hand.

"Come now, it won't bite you." He winked at her. "Take it firmly, in both hands. That's it, but don't squeeze too tightly."

She gripped the staff with both hands and tried to ignore how being close made her want to kiss him.

He stood behind her and put his hands on hers, feeling her grip. His lips were close to her ear, his breath warm on her neck. "Your grip is too tight. Loosen up a bit."

She tried to loosen her grip, but having him so close made her insides quiver. She closed her eyes and tried to concentrate.

Aldewin pushed her feet apart gently with his foot. "You want a shoulder-width stance, but keep your knees slightly bent, not locked. That's it. You want to be ready for anything."

Her voice was low and raspy when she spoke, her desire less than concealed. "I am." She cleared her throat. "Ready for anything."

His whiskers tickled her neck. "Are you?" He guided her hands and swung the staff in a figure eight. "You've got strength, Quen. I can show you how to use it."

Aldewin thrust the staff forward, but Quen wasn't ready for it, still tipsy from drinking. The forward momentum pulled her off-balance, taking Aldewin to the ground with her.

They wound up with their legs knotted together, both laughing.

"I guess I wasn't ready after all," Quen said.

Aldewin brushed a stray hair from her eyes. "Me either." His gaze was intent and serious. "Your commitment to your family, your pod—to your people. It's admirable. And you're lovely, Quen. Do you know that?"

Quen's breath caught in her throat. She'd longed to hear such words, but had nearly given up hope that she ever would. Suddenly speechless, she merely shook her head.

He rubbed a calloused thumb across her cheek, cradling her head in his large palm. "There's something about you, Quen Tomo Santu. Something that makes me question everything I knew. I wish..." Aldewin looked away as if searching for something on the dark horizon.

Don't go to that far-off place where you spend all your time. She chucked a finger under his bearded chin and gently pulled his face back to look at her. "What, Aldewin? What do you wish for?"

He shook his head and sighed. "I wish I was not sworn to another."

His words were like Juka's coldest wind sucking away her warmth. Aldewin sighed and pushed himself up.

Her bewilderment quickly gave way to anger. She bolted up, hands on hips. "Sworn to another? Then what right do you have to toy with me this way?"

"No right." His previously twinkling eyes were cast downward, and the brightness faded. "I wronged you, Quen, and I apologize. No amount of drink can excuse my behavior. I promise it shall not happen again."

He began walking back to camp. Still holding Aldewin's staff, Quen knelt low and swooped the stick. Off-guard, the blow took his feet from beneath him.

Aldewin fell, and Quen, on fire with rage, used her preternatural speed for the first time since the day she nearly died in a haboob. She closed the gap between them before Aldewin had registered what happened. Quen loomed over him, the staff tip poised over his heart.

The ridges on her neck were hot and pulsated. Her fingertips tingled, and the bones in her hands ached. She panted hard, her arms trembling. She wanted to ground the stick into his heart—to punish him for humiliating her.

Perhaps sensing this, Aldewin put his hands up, palms facing her, showing he had no wish to fight. "You have every right to be angry. If you do this, no one will be there to protect..."

It might have provoked her further if he had shown the slightest fear. But Aldewin was as calm as Still Water. His eyes were warm and friendly, not pleading and pathetic. She took the staff from his chest, and Aldewin rose and brushed off his backside.

"What did you mean, 'protect'? You think I need protecting?"

He smiled at her but ignored the question. He held out a hand. "Can I have my stick back?" Gone was the hint of double meaning in his voice.

Quen twirled it. The staff felt good in her hands. More natural than a blade. "On one condition."

His eyebrow rose in surprise. "Maybe."

"If you ever toy with my emotions—or any woman's—again, I'll shove this stick so far up your arse, it'll come out your nose."

Instead of looking afraid of her threat, he smirked but nodded. "I can agree to that."

She held out the staff but didn't let it go. "And another thing."

"I'm listening."

"You will train me to use this. No love games. I want to know what you know about this weapon's Orrokan power."

Aldewin laughed nervously. "What makes you think I know about the Orrokan arts?"

"I don't know, but I've been watching you, Aldewin di Partha. You are more than Jagaru. To defeat the damned beast, I must know more about the Orrokan arts."

Aldewin's face relaxed. "I agree to your second term as well. Anything else you'd like to add? Want me to wipe your arse every time Lumine goes crescent?"

Quen smiled and released her grip on the staff. "I can wipe my own arse, but I'll hold you to your vows." She headed toward the camp, the fire nearly out.

Behind her, Aldewin said, "I have no doubt you will."

CHAPTER 8

S alivating for salacious details about what had happened the night before, Shel badgered Quen as they left Juinar. Nursing both a bruised bottom and ego, Quen's mood was sour. Her hangover was an unwelcome companion in the saddle.

"Come on, you gotta tell me what happened. You look like you lost every pit and dar you'll ever have in a game of Duple di Marc."

Quen ignored her, and Shel, thankfully, got the hint and didn't push further. Quen was glad of it. She was too tired to keep a civil tongue, and she didn't wish to pick a fight with her best, and perhaps only, friend.

After a few hours of riding ever north, Quen's mood had evened out a bit. Shel was chewing kabu stalk to stay awake. When she offered some, Quen took a piece and proffered a weak smile.

"I'm sorry I acted like a drey's behind back there," Quen said. She sucked on the bark, its tangy flavor refreshing.

Shell spoke with the bark held between her teeth. "I'm used to it." She gave Quen a sideways smile.

They rode in a more peaceable quiet for the rest of the ride to the Tilaj Gate. *I love that Shel knows when not to pick at someone's scab.*

Druvna had been true to his word, and in less than a day's ride, the Tilaj Gate loomed on the horizon. The picture Quen had of the famed gate didn't do it justice. *Why has no one told me it's a massive, white-plastered wall and not really a gate?* The Tilaj Gate undulated along the contours of the land like a giant white snake.

At least that's what she first noticed on the approach from the south. There was an actual gate, and from afar, it looked small. But as they got closer, the gate's elevation above the road from the south made it loom large. A massive wood structure covered in thick black lacquer, it was an imposing symbol of Kovan Dynasty power. Timbers making up the posts on either side were as big around as Quen. The dark wood was inlaid with copper cast in intricate patterns mimicking plants unlike anything growing in the Sulmére. Flickering in the sun, the polished copper inlay appeared like swirling molten lava.

A guard hut was perched above the wall on the right side, and a small guardhouse below. Outside the guardhouse stood a short, round woman dressed in black robes edged in silver, the hallmark of a Kovatha mage.

Druvna approached, and his mount, Dauer, snorted. Druvna took off his dinged helmet and tipped his balding head. "'Minster Imbica." His tone was more deferential than Quen would have expected, given how much their entire pod of Jagaru complained about all things having to do with the Dynasty.

"Good day, Druvna," Kovatha Imbica said. Her hair was mousy brown, streaked with grey and braided down her back. Her face was as round as her middle and red from the midday heat. "Do you bring a detainee for me to transport to the capital for dynasty justice?" She spoke with perfect diction, not the sloppy dialect of many in the southern provinces.

Druvna shot Mishny a glare then said, "No criminals for you to fuss with today, 'Minster."

Kovatha Imbica sighed. "Well, if you have no detainees for me, why are you here wasting my time?"

The area around the gate was quiet. Serene even. *She doesn't look busy to me.*

"We're tracking quarry more important than a common thief. The thing was last seen headed this way." Druvna dismounted. "You squibs stay here. Mishny—"

He didn't have to say more. Mishny had already left Boy's back and was at his side.

Imbica gave Mishny an appraising look. "Mishny's with you now?" By the Kovatha's expression, it appeared as though she disapproved of Mishny.

Druvna waved a hand in the air as though he could speed past the obvious discomfort the two women felt in each other's presence. "Yeah, yeah. Old news and a story for another time."

"All right, Druvna, you have my attention. It must be something big to get this close to the capital. Which reminds me, you are due for another honorarium, aren't you? The generous kind that seals my lips and keeps you out of prison?"

Mishny took a step toward Imbica, but Druvna held out an arm and pushed her back. He coughed lightly and jingled the coin purse at his belt. "I'll make the proper payment, as agreed, but first I need to know if the beast has been this far north and what you know of it."

Imbica smirked at Mishny as if daring the woman to try her. When Mishny remained in check, Imbica returned her attention to Druvna. "What are you on about?" Her wide silver belt had slid below her paunchy belly, and she tugged it up and smoothed her tunic.

"Been dragon attacks."

At first, Imbica said nothing. She looked sternly at Druvna then Mishny. When neither said anything further, she broke into loud, cackling laughter. "The Brothers have finally boiled your brains, Druvna." She wiped a laugh tear from her eye. Her laughter cut off as quickly as it had begun, and her voice was stern. "Now, I'll collect an honorarium for each in your party to forget I saw you here, then be on your way."

Aldewin dismounted and was quickly at Druvna's side. With Imbica only a smidge smaller than Druvna, Aldewin towered over them both. Imbica had to crane her neck to look at him.

"The old Jagaru here is in earnest. Two villages. Juinar, and before that, Solia." He pointed back at Quen and Rhoji. "Two of them saw the beast set fire to their village of Solia."

Imbica snapped her finger. "Down then, witnesses. I'll hear your sunbaked story, but I've not got all day." The

Kovatha continued badgering them to make haste. "Down now. Quickly, quickly."

Rhoji and Quen exchanged a look, and Rhoji dismounted from Gambol. He smoothed his riding tunic and unwrapped his keffla as he ambled toward the Kovatha.

Imbica had to look up at him, too. "Where did all these long poles come from?" She muttered to herself, "Didn't know there was anyone taller than Druvna south of the wall." Imbica retrieved a tiny pencil from the back of her braid and a small leather-bound book from her belt. With hand poised over the opened book, she was ready to take notes. "You, tall one with the blue feather. Tell me of this so-called dragon."

Rhoji began to speak, but Kovatha Imbica interrupted. "No, no, no. Your name first."

As he spoke, she wrote. "Rhoji Tomo Santu di Sulmére."

Before Rhoji could begin his story, a loud, mournful keening filled the air.

"What in Hiyadi's realm is that?" Quen asked.

Shel had her hands over her ears, but she could apparently hear Quen. "It's yindrils. Awful, heh? Wait 'til you *see* them. They look even worse than they sound."

Imbica looked impatient. "Dune blossoms." She rolled her eyes. "Get on with it. I need to set out for the capital soon. The yindrils are impatient for a journey." She pointed to Quen. "You a part of this story?"

Quen nodded.

"Well, get down here and let me take your statement as well."

Quen was happy to stretch her legs. Nabu gave an appreciative grunt, as he always did when rid of Quen.

Kovatha Imbica didn't look up, writing in her notebook. "Name."

Quen cleared her throat. She'd never been a witness before. "Quen Tomo Santu." Though it was not strictly necessary to add more because she was a woman, she added, "di Sulmére."

The Kovatha looked at her then, truly taking her in for the first time. Imbica had to look up at Quen too. "Another leggy one." She bent to write Quen's name in the book but stopped, her hand still on the page. She squinted up at Quen. "Your eyes…"

No one had mentioned Quen's eyes for a while. Rhoji, Eira, and Shel were, of course, all accustomed to Quen's oddity.

Kovatha Imbica crooked her finger at Quen. "Come closer. Show me those eyes."

Sweat pooled in Quen's armpits. This Kovatha's demeanor reminded her how she felt as a child when in trouble. She stooped to give the mage a closer look.

Imbica stared first at the glacial-blue eye, then the amber-yellow one. She repeated this another time, looking first at one, then the other as Aldewin had done when they first met. Finally, she said, "Druvna, you were holding out on me."

Druvna looked at Mishny, who shrugged, then at Aldewin, who shook his head.

"What's that, 'Minster?"

Imbica returned to Druvna. "You said you didn't have any detainees. Looks like you had one after all."

Druvna responded with a blank stare.

"Come now. Edict 42?"

Aldewin put in, "We truly do not know what you're referring to."

Imbica pointed at Quen. "She's a Doj'Anira." When all of them shrugged, Imbica explained, "Twice blessed. Two different eyes. One of Enara, one of Vatra." She stared intently at Quen as she spoke.

Quen's stomach roiled. *Twice blessed. That's what Aldewin had said, too. But he acts like he has no idea what she's talking about. What's going on?* While the others may have been puzzling over Imbica's terminology, Quen focused on the word she knew: detainee.

The voice from deep inside her fairly screamed, "Run!" It may have been prudent, but she'd never trusted the Nixan before. Quen didn't heed the inner warning this time, either.

Druvna donned his helmet. "I do no'a know about Edict 42, but I know this one is a member of my pod, 'Minster. I'll no'a turn her to the Dynasty just on your word."

Apparently sensing trouble in the air, two Dynasty guards came from the small building beside the outer wall of the gate. Both wore the Kovan Dynasty standard emblazoned on their crimson leather plate armor: a blazing golden sun. Their hands were on the hilts of the curved swords at their waists.

One said, "Any trouble there, Kovatha Imbica?"

A yindril's mournful keening sounded.

Druvna's hand was on the hilt of his blade, and Mishny pulled daggers from her belt, one for each hand. Aldewin's staff was in his hands as well, and Shel and Eira dismounted, weapons in hand, and came forward, creating a circle around Quen.

"Nothing I can't handle." Imbica wound her hands one around the other as though she held an invisible ball. "Do not test me, old Jagaru."

"*I'm* not old," Mishny snarled. She rushed the Kovatha, slashing her daggers, apparently intending to slice the Kovatha open from side to side.

Before Mishny was close enough to land a blade on the mage, Kovatha Imbica flicked her wrist and hurled a small ball of swirling fire at Mishny. It grazed Mishny's left wrist, causing her to yowl in pain and drop one of her daggers.

Imbica flicked her other hand and sent another fireball at Mishny, this time hitting her in the thigh. Mishny slapped her leg, trying to put out the flames. Her riding tunic was singed, but the fire extinguished quickly.

"I suggest you stand down and allow me to take this detainee into custody before you all end up in a Qülla cell with a lost key." There was a bead of sweat on Imbica's upper lip, and stray hairs had broken free of her braid, but her hands still circled as though gathering power. The air between her hands glowed, and sparks flew from the invisible ball of energy the Kovatha mage held.

Mishny's lip was curled in a snarl, but she didn't attack Imbica again. Druvna exchanged looks with Aldewin, but neither moved to prevent Imbica from taking Quen.

Rhoji stepped forward, lightly shoving Quen behind him. "She is my sister, and I am her First Kin. I demand to know the charges against her. What crime could she have possibly committed to warrant arrest and detention?" He stood tall, his chin thrust out, his demeanor and bearing as regal as one could be after riding with the Jagaru.

"You're an articulate young man, so I assume you can read?"

Rhoji nodded.

"Then what excuse have you for not knowing the Dynasty's edicts?" Before Rhoji could answer, Imbica continued. "In the Second Era of the great Kovan Dynasty, the fifth year of the reign of Xa'Vatra, the Exalted issued Edict 42. I quote, 'Any person bearing the mark of a Doj'Anira—blessed by both Lumine and Hiyadi—are hereby detainees of the Kovan Dynasty and shall be commandeered and delivered to the proper authority for processing forthwith.'"

Rhoji shook his head. "I don't understand. Quen committed no crime, and she's no sack of flour or skein of skins to be bartered." He didn't move aside.

The poignancy of Rhoji's words made Quen's throat tight. Pahpi had said nearly the same thing to Nevara.

"We did no'a know of this Edict." Druvna rifled in his pouch and pulled out a large silver coin. It was a kovar and worth an entire year's worth of skins. "It would no'a harm a thing if you look the other way, just this once."

Quen had known Druvna for less than a month. That he would part with a small fortune of silver to protect her moved Quen to tears.

Imbica tsked and shook her head. "You test me to the limits of patience today, Druvna. If I did not know better, I would think you want me to hand you over to your old friend Cinwa, head Reeve of Qülla prison."

Druvna blanched. His hand shaking, he quietly dropped the kovar back into his bag.

Kovatha Imbica opened a large pouch at her belt and retrieved wrist shackles with a chain between them. She moved toward Quen, but Rhoji's tall body blocked her. She stared up at him evenly. "Step aside, young Jagaru, or I'll send you to Druvna's old friend Cinwa." She glanced over at Druvna. "Did Druvna ever tell you how he got that scar that split his face in two?"

Quen felt as though her knees would buckle. She couldn't let harm befall Rhoji on her behalf. Whatever this Edict 42 was about, surely the Dynasty had no use for her. *This must be a mistake. I will go with this Kovatha and get it sorted in the capital.*

She pushed in front of Rhoji and submitted her wrists for cuffing. "Pahpi would want us to follow the law."

Rhoji's voice was panicked. "No, Quen, you can't." He looked at Druvna then Aldewin. "Please, you can't let the Kovatha take her. Quen's done nothing wrong."

Imbica muttered, "I do not have the time for this." On her tiptoes, she touched her pointer finger to the middle of Rhoji's forehead. "Be calm, young man. The Exalted is wise and does only what is best for all."

Rhoji's forehead crease softened. The tears twinkling at the corners of his eyes dried. He looked nearly serene where seconds before he appeared on the verge of ripping Imbica's limbs off. He backed up a few paces, allowing Kovatha Imbica to approach Quen.

A scorpion-shaped mechanism locked the iron manacles. Six 'legs' interlocked the two sides of the wrist restraints, while the 'pincers' came together with a loud click, locking the mechanism. *I never expected to wear prisoner's shackles.*

Shel sniffled, and Eira put an arm around his sister, his cheeks wet with tears.

Quen wiped her face on the shoulder of her dusty tunic. "Do not fret for me, friends. The Kovatha is right. The Exalted and her advisors are wise. I mean, they must be, right? To manage all Indrasi. I will speak to her. She'll see—this is a grand mistake."

Kovatha Imbica pulled the chain attached to the shackles. "The Exalted does not make mistakes. Come, Doj'Anira. My yindrils await."

Aldewin still held his staff and looked ready to use it. As Imbica steered Quen by him, she said, "Do not try me, mageling."

Without heeding the Kovatha's warning, Aldewin swung his staff toward Imbica's head.

Somehow sensing what was coming from behind, Imbica raised her free hand, and Aldewin's staff snapped. The break took him by surprise and threw off his momentum. He stumbled and landed in the rocky soil, holding two ruined pieces of splintered wood.

Though still miffed at Aldewin for toying with her emotions, she was heartsick he'd lost his 'stick.' He spent more time oiling and cleaning it every night at camp than talking with the pod. It was clear the well-worn staff meant a lot to him. *But he cared enough to try to stop her.* The way her new Jagaru family had attempted to come to her aid made the parting more bitter. *I don't want them to meet harm, but I hope they don't give up on trying to find me.*

Kovatha Imbica tugged the lead chain, pulling Quen toward the gate. The tower guard shouted to someone on the other side of the wall, "Open for Kovatha."

The colossal gate creaked, and the doors swung inward. They opened just enough to let them pass.

Druvna, now astride Dauer, clicked his tongue, and Dauer sauntered toward the gate. Mishny and Aldewin mounted too and followed.

Imbica turned and held up her hand. "Turn them back. We've no need for more Jagaru north of Tilaj."

Before Druvna made it through the gate, four guards pushed the massive doors closed. Rhoji stood between Eira and Shel, their arms around each other. "I'll find you," he called.

The massive black doors slammed shut, and Quen could no longer see her brother or Jagaru family. Even with the gates closed, Rhoji screamed, "I will find you!"

Not if I become someone—or something—you no longer recognize. The chains rattled as she wiped a tear from her cheek. Guards secured the gate with a massive block of timber, closing Quen off from her friends, family, and the only life she'd ever known.

PART II

KOVAN CAME
(Forever May He Reign)

Dragos o'er our heads, they soar.
Joy and dance, we have no more.
  Fire storm and Devil's breath.
Behold a pillar o' ash—
   Our sons and fathers!
   Mother's arms, no more.

Rock towers echo our cries.
Plea to the heavens, hear us.
  Pray ye end Terror's reign.
Our Father, oh Hiyadi,
   We lift praise to you,
   End the dragos scourge.

Brave warrior's heart is born.
With blade swift and true, take aim.
  Dragos head still and dead.
Our Father's son, Kovan, came!
   His eyes shone gold.
   Of the ash no more!

Great Kovan came,
Our Father now reigns!

Great Kovan came,
Our Father forever reigns!

  Great Kovan Came (Forever May He Reign),
Traditional Hymn, 1st Era, Kovan Dynasty

CHAPTER 9

Heartless Imbica tugged at Quen's lead again, forcing her away from the gate even as Rhoji's pained cry echoed. Rhoji and Quen had fought each other like starving rats all their lives, but they'd also been allies against the world's ills. Rhoji was her nemesis, but also her blood kin. Now she was being pulled from him, maybe forever.

"Rho-ji!" she screamed. Her eyeballs were hot, her chest in a vise.

There was no response from the other side of the massive gate. Imbica yanked at Quen's bindings.

Her throat tight and dry, Quen gave another parched cry. "Rho-ji!" Her knees buckled and nearly toppled the Kovatha.

The mage tugged again on the chains, but more intensely this time. "He cannot hear you through the thick wall. Come, Doj'Anira, you are debasing yourself."

The squat woman was tougher than she looked. As she jerked the chain, the shackles dug painfully into Quen's wrists, forcing her up. Quen followed Imbica, but was sure it was all a big mistake. Before the gate closed, Rhoji had said, "I'll find you." His promise to come for her was the only thing preventing stupefying panic.

Imbica led Quen to a small square building plastered bright white. Its red clay-tiled roof swooped up and out at the ends before meeting a high point in the middle. Seen from the front, the building looked like it wore a mustache over its walls.

The building was squat, and the wooden door rounded at the top and low. Quen had to duck to enter. Once inside, she kept her head bowed to prevent hitting it on the ceiling. Dimly lit with small oil lamps, the tiny clerk's office smelled of pipe smoke and body odor.

A small man with a shock of short orangey-red hair sat at a wooden desk with a slanted top. Like the Tilaj Gate, the desk's smooth, worn wood showed use by several generations. The clerk's light-blue tunic pulled tight against his thick middle. He was writing with an ink pen in a giant ledger book. Upon seeing them enter, he looked up and frowned. "Now what's this, Imbica?" He sounded annoyed by the interruption of his work.

"I need two yindrils and a carriage."

The clerk raised his eyebrows. "You do, do ya? And what in Hiyadi's name for?"

Imbica thrust her chin out. "Edict 42 business, Rhomley, and not your matter to mind."

His blue-grey eyes grew dark. He glared at Imbica as though she'd asked for the skin from his own back. He marked his place in the ledger with a cloth-covered weight and pulled a second ledger from the shelf above. "You'll get one yindril and a cart. No carriage."

Imbica stamped her foot. "Not satisfactory. Edict 42, Rhomley. I require—"

"This Edict 42 may be your business." He flourished his pen at Quen. "But keeping count of Dynasty property is my business, Kovatha, and not *yours* to mind. I don't forget losses, and…." He flipped backward in the second ledger book. "Ah, yes—two turns ago, you cost the Dynasty a yindril *and* a carriage."

Imbica's voice got pitchy. "But that wasn't—"

Rhomley held up his hand to silence her. "Rules are rules, eh, Kovatha? Or do you think they don't apply to you?" He gave her the kind of imperious stare only a bureaucrat armed with regulations can pull off.

When she didn't argue further, he wrote in the book then on a slip of paper. He applied a seal and handed the scroll to Imbica. "One yindril and one cart. Good day."

They said no more to each other. Imbica snatched the scroll and led Quen out the back door of the clerk's cramped hut.

Behind the clerk's office was a small compound of buildings, all in the same style as the clerk's hut. Imbica led Quen to stables, in front of which were lined up a row of impressive carriages. All shone with black lacquer, symbols of Hiyadi painted in gold on the doors with more gold and red accents on the wheels and trims. At the end of the row of imperial-looking carriages sat a small, simple wood wagon cart. It wasn't any more impressive than the typical traveling merchant or herder's carts passing through Solia.

There was no one around save for herself and Imbica. Quen's eyes darted wildly, considering potential avenues for escape. Though the Kovatha had shown she was physically strong, Quen had Nixan strength. *I can overpower her. I'll make a run for the gate. No one can outrun me.* She didn't have a plan for what to do once at the gates and could think no further than the immediate desire to run. *Rhoji and the Jagaru can't have made it far yet. I'll catch up to them. This may be my only chance.*

Quen dashed away from Imbica without restraining her speed. She tried to prize open the restraints on her wrists as she ran, but the lock held fast.

From behind, Imbica called out, "*Loa Vatra. Loa Vay'Nada. Sunginare di Vatra, sunginare di Vatra, sunginare di Vatra.*"

Under the shackles, Quen's wrists burned. Fire seared in her veins, like her blood had become molten. Sweat beaded on her forehead, and her breaths were shallow. The scorching sensation traveled up her arms and to her neck.

Quen didn't stop running, though her extreme speed was gone. She scratched at her wrists, trying to rid herself of the bindings. The heat overtaking her, Quen dropped to her knees, panting and breathless. It was as though she was being burned from the inside out.

Quen's voice was a parched croak. "Please. I beg of you. Stop."

Imbica approached, her hands circling, sparks flying between them. Her lips moved as she quietly chanted. Imbica stood over Quen with an expression of dispassionate interest. Quen's hands and arms turned a violent red color.

Finally, Imbica said, "Nil Vatra. Nil Vay'Nada. Sunginare di sunginare." As Quen lay in the dirt, writhing in pain, Imbica snatched Quen's amber pendant.

"This is the price for your foolish attempt to disobey Dynasty law." Imbica studied the amber necklace, shrugged her shoulders, and tied it around her own neck. "With this payment, I shall forget your escape attempt, so you don't end up in Cinwa's dungeon like Druvna. Since this is your only valuable item, you might consider that before trying to run again."

The searing pain stopped as suddenly as it had begun. Quen's throat was tight, her face wet with sweat and tears. The relief was sweeter than any feeling Quen had known. She wiped her face and noticed the veins in her hands were visible, making them look bruised purply blue.

"The bruising will be gone in a few days. Now get up." Imbica's tone was flat, containing neither anger nor compassion.

Quen's arms trembled as she pushed up. She had to stop midway to catch a breath. Though the sensation of veins filled with boiling blood had ceased, she throbbed from head to toe with achy, lingering discomfort. She wished for Dini's fever tea followed by rest in her own bed. The bed in Solia. *The one I no longer have.*

Quen had met few people she didn't like and none she loathed. But she despised Imbica. The desire for revenge simmered in her gut, taking residence with the smoldering fires of vengeance against the dragon and its rider.

Once Quen was upright, Imbica said, "You will obey me, yes?"

Quen nodded, though it made her skull swim with dizziness. *I have no other choice if I want to survive this day.*

Imbica tugged a thin leather cord from inside her tunic and retrieved a whistle carved of bleached bone. It was narrow and about a finger long. She put it to her lips and blew, but it didn't make a sound audible to Quen.

Within a few moments, a yindril bellowed. Its deep call rumbled her chest. The voice was mournful, as if whatever made it had suffered a substantial loss. Another yindril returned the cry, this time from farther away.

Footsteps scraped across the sunbaked clay road as though of a giant man who had lost a foot in battle. The thing slowly moved towards Quen and Imbica with a thump-step-scrape, over and over.

A thick mist of moist sea air and blowing sand obscured her vision. Quen could see only twenty paces in any direction.

A creature half again as tall as Quen emerged from the soupy fog, its wide grey horns jutting from a narrow, grey-skinned head. Skin resembling scaly bark covered its spindly arms and legs. The creature's eyes were tiny slits. Copious, sinewy threads covered a hole in the creature's throat. The hole breathed, growing larger then smaller. The overall appearance was of a walking man-plant. Quen backed away from the encroaching creature, but the lead chain pulled taut and halted her.

Imbica noticed Quen's unease. "You have never seen a yindril before?"

Quen shook her head, her mouth open but unable to form speech.

"No need to fear them. They are simple-minded, docile creatures."

"I've never heard of them," Quen said. Her voice was an awed whisper. "Not even in trader's tales."

"They are new to Indrasi, brought from the swamps of Tinox by the Dynasty. They have special... properties."

The yindril had no claws or sharp teeth. It made no threatening moves, yet Quen broke into a cold sweat. The hole in what should have been a neck sucked in and out unnervingly, the baleen-like strands quivering. And its mournful cry, coupled with its slow, foot-dragging gait, struck terror in her. She had difficulty understanding why the Dynasty would purposefully import such terrifying creatures. "What is special about them, other than how strange they look and sound?"

"They are simpletons, as I said, and incapable of mastering magical understanding themselves. But they enhance a mage's ability to receive the gifts of Menaris from gods and spirits. Useful for Kovatha mages, no?"

Receive gifts of Menaris? "I don't understand."

Imbica sighed with impatience. "Menaris, the gift of magic. It originates in the Void, you know."

No, I didn't know that. She'd been taught that the Void was the home of Vay'Nada—the Shadow. It was the place poor Niyadi went as he left the comfort of his brother, Hiyadi, and his unrequited love, Lumine. "You said it was a gift from gods and spirits. So what does the Void have to do with it?"

"Gods and spirits are intermediaries. They wash raw magical energy of the Void clean of its taint and gift Menaris to those patient enough to learn the complexities of Menaris."

"The Void is magic?" Quen shook her head. "What the heck *is* the Void?"

Imbica let out an impatient breath. "The is that isn't." Seeing that Quen still didn't comprehend, Imbica threw up her hands. "The unseen realm of the spirits and gods. Look, I can't explain it any better than that. It's something you understand, or you don't. And if you don't understand, suffice to say you probably don't have Menaris gifts."

I don't know about Menaris, but does a shadow-spawn heart of a Nixan soul count? "So if you pull magical energy from the void, why do you need yindrils to cast spells?"

Imbica harrumphed. "*I* don't need yindrils to cast. But some Kovathas never made it past the novice stage, known as Rising at the Pillars, and most have only a year of Kensai training at best. The yindrils are an important new tool for Kovathas to enforce the Dynasty's edicts across Indrasi."

Imbica makes the yindrils sound important. Odd that I've never seen one before. But then again, she'd rarely seen Kovathas in Solia.

The yindril held two leads, a horse on each. Covered in short black hair and well-muscled, the horses were stockier than kopeks. Though of standard size for a horse, they looked miniature next to the yindril.

The yindril had gotten the horses within ten paces of the cart, near enough for the beasts of burden to take up Quen's scent. Their reaction toward her was like that of kopeks. They skittered, keened, and showed the whites of their eyes.

Their reaction flustered the yindril. It halted and emitted a deep, low, mournful yowl from its gaping maw.

Imbica sighed. "For the love of Hiyadi's light, what has gotten into the lot of you?" She splayed her hands again, preparing for another spell.

Having recently experienced Imbica's immolation spell, Quen flinched away. But Imbica didn't intend her spell for Quen. The Kovatha swirled her arms, rolling her hands as if she held a ball. This time she thrust her hands toward the yindril and horses.

"*Usiru ôhmla cureā.*" Imbica invoked the spell in the same dead language she'd used before. Quen made out only the word 'fear.' Imbica repeated it several times. At first, her voice was calm and confident, as though she had spoken the spell many times and expected it to have the desired effect.

But by the fifth or sixth statement of the incantation, having had no effect on the animals, her words became higher-pitched and more clipped. The horses reared and whinnied shrilly. The yindril flailed its great long arms like trees blowing in a mighty wind as it tried to get control of the spooked horses.

"What in the Three is wrong with them?" She hurled her hand at the horses while chanting, "*Usiru recine.*"

"I am what is wrong with them," Quen said. Her voice weak from the burning spell Imbica had cast on her, Quen's words got lost in the commotion.

But Imbica's new spell calmed the horses. While their eyes were still wild and their nostrils flared, they stood still as stones.

The yindril stopped moaning. It held the leads of the now-bespelled animals, its tendril-covered maw slowly expanding then shrinking like a fish's mouth out of water.

Imbica pulled a neatly folded cloth from her belt and wiped sweat from her brow. The early evening was chilly, but the spell work apparently stoked Vatra within her. "What did you say?"

Quen cleared her throat. "It's me. Animals fear me." The horses had reacted to her as kopeks did. *But the yindril is more flustered by the nervous horses than by being near me.* The yindril was more plant than animal, though, and plants had never been afraid of her.

"All of my life, I've been cursed in this way. Kopeks barely tolerate me." *Though Nabu tolerated me well enough.* Thinking of Nabu, a gift from her eldest brother and his wife, made Quen recall Lio, Zarate, and wee Lumina. *Lio holds Lumina so gently in his burly arms.* She coughed and pushed aside memories of family, for now anyway. "How have you dealt with this before? With other Doj'Anira you've taken to the capital, I mean."

Imbica brushed the arms of her tunic as though they were dusty or soiled from her spell work. "I have not yet had the honor of delivering pursuant to Edict 42. You are the first, and by Hiyadi, I will get you there."

Imbica yanked on the chain, pulling Quen to the wagon. "Up and in you go." She heaved herself into the front seat, richly upholstered with deep-purple fabric embroidered with symbols of Hiyadi in golden thread.

"And don't think about jumping out once we ride. Not only can I set fire to your arse from a hundred paces, but I locked those shackles with a spell." She thumped the side of her head with a finger. "Only I have the key."

It's like she can read my mind. Quen leaped into the back of the cart and sat on the plain wooden bench. She continued pondering the possibility of escape, keeping her eyes and ears open for an opportunity.

The yindril sat on the upholstered seat next to Imbica, its great mass making the wagon creak and groan. It had hitched the still spell-drowsy horses to the wagon. It let out a screechy cry at Imbica, as if to complain about the situation with the horses.

"Worry not, woody friend. It will be slow going for a while, but the spell will soon wear off. Now proceed—to the Niri Bridge."

They rode in relative peace for close to an hour. The horses did indeed liven up with each mile they traveled. Soon Hiyadi kissed the horizon, setting the sky ablaze in crimson and orange. They climbed ever higher in elevation, the cactus and desert scrub giving way to dense greenery and small trees.

Bored, Quen peppered the Kovatha with questions. "Do all Kovathas know how to cast spells?"

Imbica snorted. "Spells." She folded her arms across her chest and looked indignant.

"Then what do you call the magic you wield?"

"The art of Vaya di Menaris we learn at the Pillar is unlike your village Bruxia's healing arts. It goes beyond what common people call magic. It is understanding."

If magic is understanding, that explains why I can't conjure fire in a wood stove. Though Pahpi had taught her much about calming her mind and focusing, he'd imparted no knowledge of Vaya di Menaris. Quen didn't understand what magic truly was, where it originated, or how to wield it. Her attempts to tap into the power of the magical Corners were amateur flailing and always failed. "Understanding?"

Imbica sighed loudly. "Of the Corners. Vatra, Enara, Qüira, and Doka. Fire, water, earth, and wood. And of course Juka of the æther and air, presiding over and among them all."

"Oh, you mean like the naming? I saw a woman once call Vatra to her aid. It was terribly frightening." She recalled Nevara conjuring a column of fire in Pahpi's trading post.

Imbica scoffed. "You think you can call spirits or gods to your side so you can perform tricks?" She laughed with incredulity. "Vatra does not simply come when called like a dog. Even Juka's winds, easily understood, come only because Juka enjoys making mischief in the world of men. Many teachers begin with lessons of calling the wind, thinking Juka easily manipulated." She chuckled. "Juka's pleasures are fickle. If it pleases her to answer prayers, she'll send soft breath to cool or tickle us. Or she might send a powerful gale to bandy us about and whip the sands into a haboob. Juka's japes can be cruel and are little understood by most."

Quen tried to follow the mage's explanation but didn't really grasp what Imbica was going on about. *But I agree with her about Juka. That spirit answered my prayer with a cruel jape that nearly killed me.*

Apparently recognizing Quen's lack of comprehension, Imbica said, "When a mage casts a spell, she is dancing with spirits." Her eyes were alight with excitement, her voice animated. "In a dance, one must pay attention—listen, watch—feel your partner. The best dancer responds to her partner's moves. Otherwise, you trample toes, and the dance is an ugly mess. A mage's power is a gift from the gods of the cosmos and the spirits of Menauld."

"That explains a lot."

"How so?"

"Every time I pray, the gods are silent or answer with a punishment. I don't think they like me much."

Imbica harrumphed. "It's not a matter of them liking us or not. It's a matter of respect and experience. Training at a Pillar, one learns how to show proper respect to the gods and spirits. And one learns restraint, lest one pull so much power from the Void—the realm of gods and spirits—they burn or freeze themselves to death."

"Did you know anyone that happened to?"

Imbica brushed hair from her temple and smoothed her tunic. "Yes, of course. Study in the Pillar long enough, and you'll..." Imbica sighed. "Enough about Vaya di Menaris. I doubt it matters for you—where you're going." Imbica glanced at Quen's bound wrists.

The Kovatha's pointed stare made Quen achingly aware of the metal wrapped about her arms. The shackles' chain looped through an iron hook affixed to the inside of the carriage at Imbica's side. *I'll wait for her to fall asleep. She must sleep sometime. And then I'll wrap this chain around her neck and....* But Imbica had said the lock on the shackles was magical. *If Imbica dies, maybe then I can unlock the chains.*

Quen weighed the pros and cons of attacking Imbica, but soon chased herself in a circle over it. She asked Imbica, "Where are you taking me?"

"To the place designated by the Dynasty for all Doj'Anira."

"And what place is that?"

Imbica ignored her question.

When Quen attempted to speak again, the woman held up her hand and said, "Shh. Listen."

There was only the sound of the wagon's wheels rolling along the clay road and the gentle creaking of the wooden carriage. Imbica's head was slightly tilted, her eyes closed. The wagon stopped.

"There," she said. "Do you hear that?"

Quen heard nothing, but before she could answer, the horses shrieked. Her chest rumbled with the yindril's low, mournful keening.

A now-familiar sound rose above the yindril's dirge. A primordial sound.

The horses nickered. Somewhere close, fire crackled.

"Lumine's teats, what now?"

A dark shadow flew over the wagon.

Quen sprang to her feet, ready to leap from the wagon and run. But Imbica held her by the lead.

The older woman searched the skies. When she glimpsed the fire-spitting beast, her mouth twisted into a shocked expression.

Imbica pulled the chain attached to the shackles and roughly yanked Quen from the wagon. The shadow swooped lower and headed toward them.

Imbica jerked Quen along as she put distance between themselves and the wagon. The yindril stood at the helm of the carriage, its long arms flailing, its grotesque mouth-hole sucking in and out.

"Get down from there," Imbica called. But the yindril acted as though it didn't hear her.

Dragon fire rained on the wagon, lighting the horses on fire. Trying to free themselves of their harnesses, the horses pranced and kicked. The wagon pitched as it rolled at the whim of the horses drawing it. Not knowing what to do, the yindril remained on the wagon bench, wailing its deep lament.

A tremendous roar followed a low grumble as fire erupted behind them. Imbica pulled Quen down a small embankment, and they ran through a ditch filled with weedy, knee-high grasses.

Quen didn't need to gaze upward to know what bedeviled them. The dragon's sulfurous odor assaulted her nostrils as fire rained from the sky and scorched the ground. The surrounding hills echoed with the creature's thunderous screech.

Imbica looked back over her shoulder and stared, her mouth agape. "For the love of the Three, it cannot be."

Quen didn't want to look. The beast already haunted her dreams. She chanced a look backward, anyway.

This is the dragon of my nightmares. Its iridescent purple scales reflected the light of the fires it had started. Its eyes shone vibrant yellow, except one appeared partially closed. *Is it possible I injured it with my dagger after all?* She had convinced herself the whole thing had been a dream.

Its wings spread wide, and the creature glided effortlessly. The dragon gracefully turned, its long body undulating like a sand snake. It had legs like those of a giant lizard and claws like a winged bird of prey. Its jaw opened wide, rows of sharp teeth glistening. The dragon's low rumble added to the yindril's as fires burned in the beast's gullet, ready to rain down on them.

Imbica's voice was an astonished whisper. "It cannot be—a dragon?"

"But it is." Quen added, "And it's after me."

CHAPTER 10

Nevara had prophesied Quen would bring destruction wherever she went. *Is this the terror the woman foretold?*

"You spook animals, and a dragon is after you?" Imbica frowned while circling her arms. "You may prove to be more trouble than you are worth."

She doesn't realize how true that is. Quen's neck ridge burned and ached. *Is my shadow soul a Rajani like Nevara and gladdened by the sound of the dragon?*

Imbica hurriedly looped the end of Quen's chain around her belt. She thrust her hands at the circling dragon, flicking her wrists with such force they snapped. "*Loa Hiyadi. Loa Vay'Nada.*"

As best Quen could piece together, Imbica had called upon the god of fire, Hiyadi, and Vay'Nada, the Shadow. *Drawing on the Shadow is dark magic. Pahpi and Dini would disapprove.*

Imbica stood firm on stout legs and tiny feet, her round face concentrating fully on the dragon. "*Sunginare di Naj.*" She repeated this phrase quickly and repeatedly.

Quen recognized the word 'Naj.' It was the frozen form of Enara and something virtually unknown in the perpetual summer lands of the Sulmére. But the word 'sunginare' was familiar. *Imbica used that word when she cast the horrid spell on me.* It had made Quen feel as though fire filled her veins.

Blood. Sunginare must be blood. Blood of Ice. A cold spell indeed.

Imbica's attempt to freeze the dragon's fiery spirit didn't work. The dragon didn't falter.

Quen crouched behind Imbica, trying to stay out of the beast's vision as if Imbica could shield her. Quen had no weapon to fight the dragon or its Rajani handler.

While her preternatural speed might give her a chance to outrun the beast, she was bound to Imbica. *I'll never escape pulling dead weight behind me.* Quen considered calling on the gods. Her past attempt resulted in disaster, but prayer was the only thing she had.

Quen imitated Imbica as best she could. She wound her arms, but sensed no magical energy flowing to her. She repeated the words Imbica had said. *Sunginare di Naj.*

Nothing changed.

The dragon circled and bore down on them again.

All she could do was run. Quen scampered up the hill. The chain briefly caught, but she tapped her deepest reserves and dragged Imbica. She stumbled out of the ditch and set off toward a copse of squat, spiky trees. Imbica fell and yanked painfully on Quen's wrists, forcing her to slow down.

Imbica let out a string of curses. "Stop, imbecile. The beast can outpace you. Our only chance is another volley."

Quen panted and watched helplessly as the yindril, still at the wagon, caught fire. The wagon was soon a remnant, and the yindril keened no more.

Imbica recovered and thrust her hands up again, this time speaking different words. *"Incanticle d'Hiyadi simir."* A spear of blazing white-hot flame materialized in Imbica's hands. It was as though Hiyadi had placed a weapon forged from his own fires into Imbica's grasp. She hurled the spear at the dragon.

The dragon reared back and screeched. Imbica's magical weapon opened a gash in the dragon's upper front leg, but the wound didn't deter the beast. Its eyes opened wider, glistening orangey-yellow, and it bore down again.

The dragon swooped lower. As before when Quen had seen the dragon, someone clung to the dragon's black mane. A cowl and mask obscured the rider's face.

Quen pointed to the dark figure behind the dragon's thick neck. "Look, a rider."

Imbica ignored Quen and repeated her last incantation. She conjured another white-hot spear and hurled the magical weapon at the black-clad rider.

A woman cried out in agony. The dark figure slid from the dragon's back but hung onto its silky mane with one hand. The rider scrambled onto the dragon's back, and it turned.

With the dragon momentarily distracted, Quen set off again, running as quickly as she could. Imbica's dead weight hindered her. "I could run more quickly if it weren't for these shackles."

164

Imbica panted behind her. "I will not cut you loose. The law requires that I deliver you to the Dynasty, and I *will* do my duty."

Quen sighed, continued running, and avoided glancing behind. At first, it was quiet, save for their hard breathing and footfalls. Quen hoped Imbica's last attack had injured the beast and its rider enough that they'd given up. Her hope was brief. Behind them, crackling fire set the spiky trees aflame.

"Stop running." Imbica panted hard. "We must face this beast."

I can't face it. Not yet. She had no sword, staff, bow, or even a small blade. Her hands were bound, and her attempts to call the Corners proved futile.

But Imbica stood her ground. Having little food or sleep for days, Quen's remaining reserves were exhausted. She couldn't pull the woman against her will.

"I know I said Vaya di Menaris does not concern you, but I fear we won't survive this attack without your help."

Quen didn't see how she could be of help to Imbica. The woman wielded magic far beyond what Quen had known existed. *But I'll try anything to survive this beast again.* "What do you need me to do?"

"This is a fire dragon, so I must draw on Enara to weaken it. I want you to summon Enara's power—"

Quen protested. "But I have no—"

Imbica jerked the chain harshly. "Do as I say, or so help me, I will throw you to the beast for its dinner."

Imbica's wild-eyed look of desperation left no doubt the woman would live up to her threat. Quen nodded.

"Menaris touches everyone's soul, even if they do not know it. Now calm yourself. Search inward for what gives you strength."

"I don't know what gives me strength." *Lie. You know, but avoid it.* Quen focused on the faint whisper of her Nixan soul.

Perhaps sensing that Quen had touched upon the source of her inner strength, Imbica said, "Yes, that's it. Draw it to the fore. Put your hands like this." Imbica demonstrated. "That is it. Now, gather your inner power and push it to me."

Quen ignored the sweat dripping from her temples and closed her eyes. Her chest pounded with a double beat. *Tharump-tharump.*

"Do you have it?" Imbica's voice sounded nearly panicked.

Quen kept her eyes closed, sure she'd lose concentration if she saw the danger headed for them. She nodded.

Imbica screamed, "Push, Doj'Anira! Drive your power to me."

Quen was certain Imbica wouldn't ask this of her if she knew a shadow soul, not Menaris, provided Quen's inner strength. The dragon was coming for them. Her Nixan soul was their only hope.

Quen's spine tingled, and the hairs on her neck and arms stood on end. She was cold, yet sweating. Raw power surged through her. Quen felt like she could sunder a boulder or rend Menauld beneath them. She'd never had this feeling before, and she wanted to keep all the energy she'd gathered.

But her arms shook, and as quickly as the feeling had come upon her, she feared she could hold it no longer.

Using her hands as a funnel, Quen mustered all her intention and pushed the gathered power into her captor.

Quen's legs wobbled and threatened to buckle. She was like a cup drained of drink. But Imbica looked ten years younger, her eyes radiant and refreshed.

Imbica swirled her arms again and hurled the crackling energy she'd gathered toward the dragon, now less than twenty paces away. She shouted at the flying beast. *"Incanticle di Lumine simir."* Instead of launching a white-flamed spear at the dragon, she hit the rider square across the chest with an unseen but effective weapon.

The woman screamed and fell sideways. She didn't snag herself in the dragon's mane, and yelled, "Vahgrin!" as she fell.

Fortunately for the dragon's passenger, the beast was close to the ground. The rider landed with a thud, but the impact didn't kill her. "Vahgrin—*ashta di Rajani,*" she said.

Curling its body and swooping, the dragon scooped the rider into its mouth. That the dragon carried its rider gently in jaws that could easily have snapped her in two amazed Quen.

Vahgrin's voice thundered. His sounds were a language, albeit a strange one made of long vowel sounds and tongue clicks. The sky in front of him wavered like heat rising from the dunes at midday. A swirling vortex of clouds formed in the previously clear sky. Vahgrin, the dark-clad rider still held gingerly in his great maw, flew into the gaping void. Though no storm threatened, the air smelled of lightning. As Vahgrin disappeared, the sky sounded as though it had been cleaved.

As suddenly as the sky had changed, it returned to its normal appearance. Vahgrin, the murderous dragon, and his Rajani were gone.

Quen should have been relieved she'd survived the attack. Instead, one word echoed in her mind, causing her chest to tighten. *Rajani.*

Rajani. That is how Nevara referred to herself in Santu's Stand. Is that Nevara riding Vahgrin? The rider was tiny atop the magnificent beast's back. With full dark approaching and the cowl, the passenger was in shadow, her features not discernable.

Vahgrin. Merely thinking the name brought a shudder. Nausea washed over her. Quen swallowed hard and instinctively drew herself into Still Waters.

Imbica stared at the sky where Vahgrin had been. She huffed, her hands on her hips. Dark circles edged her red-rimmed eyes, and her face was crimson and sweaty.

The chain hung loosely from Imbica's belt. *Exertion has drained her. Now is the time to attempt an escape. I could wrap the chain around her neck.*

Quen imagined picking up the chain. It was nearly in her hand. She envisioned pulling the chain across Imbica's throat, extinguishing the light in the woman's eyes. *I can find a smith to cut these shackles.*

Yet Pahpi's words echoed in her mind. *'Blood on the hands forever scars the heart.'*

Imbica didn't turn to face her. "You will fail."

Quen's hesitation cost her the opportunity to escape. "Succeed at what?" Her voice came out squeaky.

"You wanted to use the chain to end me." Her words were matter-of-fact.

"No." Quen tittered. "Why would you say that?" She really wanted to ask what sorcery allowed the woman to read her mind? *And can I also learn that magic?*

Imbica turned. Her eyes were tired, her color pale. "Because it is what I would do." She peered up, studying Quen's bicolored eyes. "You harnessed considerable power for an uninitiated. No simple Sulmére dune flower." Imbica squinted at Quen. "What are you?"

What kind of question is that? Especially coming from the woman who'd quoted law and taken her prisoner. In a far-away city she'd never visited, someone Quen had never met had decided Quen was subject to their whim. By extension, the Kovatha holding her chain, empowered by the Dynasty, held Quen's life in her hands. *Shouldn't she be the one answering my questions?*

"I'm Quen Tomo Santu di Sulmére. I'm a person, same as you."

"No." The Kovatha snorted. "We are not the same, you and I." She looked over her shoulder toward the sky. "Rajani. You heard the rider say this, yes?"

Quen nodded.

Imbica narrowed her eyes again at Quen as though squinting at her would allow the Kovatha to see something beyond ordinary sight. "Perhaps *you* are Rajani."

Ever since meeting Nevara, Quen had considered the possibility that she was Rajani, like the shapeshifting bird-woman. Hearing it from another's lips gave the idea space to grow.

"I don't think so. I mean, I should know it if I were, wouldn't I?" She had the urge to rub the ridge on her neck. *In truth, I don't know what I am. I could be a Rajani.* The idea made her queasy.

Imbica's eyes softened a bit. "Perhaps." She smoothed her tunic and pushed a few stray hairs from her face. "Or perhaps not. Like dragons, everyone thought Rajani had died off, too."

Quen desperately wanted to know everything she could about Rajani—about the undesirable thing she feared she was becoming. She tried to sound nonchalant and hide her urgent need for answers. "What do you know of Rajani?"

Imbica shrugged. "Precious little. Legends claim Rajani are a form of Nixan, like slints, but intelligent. Able to move effortlessly between beast and human form. Some texts claim that before dragons existed, humans used Rajani as spies." Imbica pulled the now-wrinkled cloth from her belt and wiped her sweat. She looked in the approximate direction they'd last seen Vahgrin before he disappeared into a rip in the sky.

"If Rajani are spies, why is one riding on a dragon?"

Imbica neatly folded her cloth, put it back on her belt, and smoothed her hair. "Other legends say that during the Dragos Teplo era, humans pressed Rajani into service as Dragomancers." As if expecting Quen's next question, she said, "Able to control dragons."

Dragomancers. Things were beginning to make sense. The woman on the dragon's back was giving Vahgrin commands. "But—"

Before Quen could ask another question, Imbica put her hand up. "This is all I know. It likely amounts to only collected gossip, tall tales, and speculation passed among the young impressionable students at the Pillar where I studied." Imbica eyed Quen warily. "But for all I know, if they exist, you could be Rajani."

170

Quen considered Imbica's words. *If I'm a Rajani, will I become a raven like Corvus?* Imbica's speculation contained a valuable nugget of information. Rajani were Dragomancers, able to command the most powerful creatures in the land. *What if I allow myself to become Rajani? Could I then control Vahgrin?* She wasn't sure how things worked. Each new piece of information grew threefold questions.

Her most pressing question she gave voice to. "If I were Rajani, why would the dragon be trying to kill me?"

Imbica's brow scrunched, and she rubbed her chin in thought. She shook her head. "These are mysteries beyond my ken. My masters are wiser than I. They'll know something of this mark upon you—something beyond the understanding of Dynasty subjects or even Kovathas." She tugged on the chain. "Come. We delay no longer. I will deliver you as my mandate requires."

Quen followed as they returned to the awful sight of scorched soil and ghastly charred yindril and horses. The wagon had been overturned. Extreme heat melted the metal parts, and the lacquered wood gave off a strange aroma nearly as nauseating as the odor of scorched flesh and hair.

The cart's remains smoldered, smoke eddying into the darkening sky. Imbica searched the rubble and pulled her pack from under the bench. Soot blackened Imbica's fine leather bag, but it hadn't burned through.

Imbica slung the pack across her body and wiped her sooty hands on her previously spotless black linen tunic. She resumed their northward journey. The chain pulled taut, and Quen followed.

They walked silently for at least a mile, each ensconced in private thought. It was full dark now, and Lumine was only a sliver in the sky. Quen saw only a few paces ahead. The chilly air was soggy. *I wish I had warmer clothes.*

Quen forced one foot in front of the other, trying to soothe her unmet needs with thoughts of her time with the Jagaru. Of Druvna's nightly stories and how pipe smoke escaped the hole in his lip and curled into the twilight air. Gossiping with Shel as they sucked kabu stalk and oiled their kopeks. Rhoji and Eira talking, Rhoji's head thrown back in laughter at Eira's jokes, happier than she'd ever seen him. Quen even longed for Mishny's haughty glare. She craved time with the family they'd cobbled together. People she cared about, and who cared for her. Yet the question nagged. *Would they stand with me if they knew?*

And then there was Aldewin. Though no one was around, her cheeks colored as she recalled the night of drunken songs and Aldewin lying atop her, telling her she was lovely. *He would run from me if he knew the truth. Nixan die alone. I can't dwell on something I'll never have.*

She turned her thoughts to wee Lumina, but that was even worse. Her chest tightened as she recalled saying goodbye to Lio, Zarate, and Lumina. She didn't allow herself to think about Pahpi. *No matter where my thoughts turn, I have no peace.*

They'd gone about six miles on foot when Imbica announced they'd bed down for a few hours. Their "bed" was the ditch at the side of the Trinity Road.

"We are nearly to the Niri Bridge." Imbica yawned. "There we will find a wagon headed to Qülla."

Quen admired the woman's self-assured nature. Since she'd hitched herself to Quen, a dragon had attacked, and she had lost two horses, a wagon, and a yindril. She now had to cart her cargo behind her, yet she confidently assumed they would find a ride to Qülla. *It must be nice to be Kovatha.* The black tunic and silver belt signaled what she was for all to see. Imbica was probably right. If there were travelers on the road going north, it was unlikely they'd refuse a request from a Kovatha.

As tired as she was, Quen slept fitfully. Each time her lids closed, she relived this second encounter with Vahgrin. If not for Imbica's battle-mage skills, Vahgrin would have made Quen into a cinder. Yet there was a connection with Rajani, one she could no longer deny. *What does it all mean?*

Imbica yanked the chain, ending Quen's fitful sleep. Hiyadi was already four fingers above the horizon, overpowering his little brother, Niyadi. Quen rubbed the sleep from her eyes and stretched. Her shoulders ached, and her neck was stiff from cramming herself into a ball to fit the narrow gulley.

"Come, Doj'Anira. We will find a wagon, then you may rest."

Hiyadi burned away the morning mists, revealing details of the landscape. Ice domes shone pinkish-white in the morning light atop high mountains to the west, while the lower slopes were craggy and barren grey stone. To the east, the land ended as it met the sea.

Finally, the Niri Bridge was visible ahead. It soared into the sky in a large upside-down 'V' of polished pale grey stone, expertly set so hardly a seam showed. The road turned from hard-packed clay to side-by-side wood planks. Wood planks met the stone entrance and covered the bridge for the entire length. Though the Tilaj Gate had been impressive, the Niri Bridge surpassed its grandeur. *I didn't know people built such things.* As soon as they stepped onto the bridge, a yindril keened a rumbling lament.

Quen had never particularly yearned to see Qülla, the capital, but her excitement stirred. She was nearing the end of this journey. *I don't know what lies ahead, but it must be better than being shackled to Imbica and enduring her magical torture.*

The bridge creaked beneath their feet. Unlike wood buildings in the Sulmére, the Niri Bridge's wood appeared more supple and not desiccated.

The bridge spanned the vast chasm of the churning Suab River, flowing from the mighty TasūZaj range to the western sea. Beginning as a small meandering brook, it gathered water as it traveled across the eastern portion of Indrasi. By the time it entered the capital's province of Suab'Hora, its waters were a churning torrent raging through the chasm it created.

Imbica drew a curvy twist in the air with her finger. "The river snakes along the Suab'Hora Province's southern border, marking it off keenly. The Suab carves a chasm passable here on the Niri Bridge. It is the only way in or out of Suab'Hora's southeastern border. Allows the Dynasty tight control of goods and people traveling through Suab'Hora."

Imbica rested on a large stone bench on the Suab'Hora side of the bridge. Catwalks built above for guards and archers were empty. Four guardhouses created corners. A lone guard occupied one guardhouse. Policing the southern border of the capital province fell to this one bored-looking guard. *It seems odd that they wouldn't have more guards here.*

The man yawned when Imbica inquired about catching a ride north on a wagon. "Been two days since even a three-wheeled fruit cart happened along."

Imbica rapped her fingers on the wood ledge she leaned on. "That is unusual, is it not?"

The guard nodded. "Yes, 'Minster. But trade is slower now that…"

Imbica stopped tapping. "Now that what?"

The guard shifted uneasily on his wooden stool.

Imbica sighed. "Oh, for the love of the Three, spit it out, man. My hands are full. I am in no position to arrest you."

He studied a spot on the small ledge he'd been leaning on, his fingers tracing an invisible circle. "Since the new levies on the southern provinces—on food and skins—"

"The Exalted has equalized the burden on all citizens. For many years, our southern friends enjoyed the benefit of unduly favorable treatment by the Dynasty, thanks to the generosity of Exalted Xa'Vatra's grandfather, Zal Kovan."

The guard rubbed the back of his neck. "I do no'a know 'bout that, 'Minster. I only know what I seein', and since them levies, fewer carts comin' up through the gate."

Imbica's brows knitted at the news.

He gave a nervous chuckle. "Of course, there's bound to be someone comin' eventually. Why, I bet there'll be a wagon this morning. Just wait and see."

There was nothing to do but wait. Imbica returned to the stone bench, her fingers nervously tapping her thigh.

Nearly an hour passed before Imbica pulled the last of the food from her charred pack. They ate nuts made smoky by the fire. *Surprisingly good.* The hard cheese was more challenging to choke down with an ashy flavor, but Quen forced herself to eat her entire portion. Quen's stomach rumbled loudly even after licking the last crumbs from her fingers.

Quen's hunger was intense. *I fear this constant hunger is more than just the meager rations Imbica provides.* She'd never cared much for eating meat, but since the day of the fire in Solia, she'd craved animal flesh like never before.

As they finished their meal, wagon wheels rattled onto the wooden bridge. A small, dark-haired man sporting a wide-brimmed reed hat drove an open-air cart pulled by a lone horse. The horse was stockier than the ones that had drawn Imbica's wagon. This horse had a long, shaggy mane and tufts of white hair at its ankles.

The guard groaned as he rose, bothered to be made busy. The man pulling the wagon retrieved a slip of paper from the breast pocket of his loose linen shirt.

While the guard inspected the man's proof of taxes paid at the Tilaj Gate on the goods he hauled north, Imbica pulled Quen toward the man. "Come along, Doj'Anira. Our ride is here."

As the cart driver returned the receipt to his pocket, Imbica approached him. "Are you headed to the capital?"

The man didn't glance in their direction. He gave a terse "Yes'n."

"Then you shall take us there."

He chuckled and said, "I do no'a know 'bout that." He finally looked over, and upon realizing he'd been talking to a Kovatha, his eyes grew wide, and he shifted nervously. "Oh, 'Minster, I did no'a know you was—I mean, of course, for the Dynasty." He got out of his seat and hastened to move bundles in his small wagon to make room, dusting the cart's bed as best he could with his straw hat.

"'Minster, you could ride on the bench up front with me." He looked down at the chain. "I do no'a think it will stretch that far. I suppose if you do no'a want to drop the chain for fear your prisoner will run away."

Imbica looked searchingly at Quen, but only briefly. "I will ride with the Doj'Anira."

The man smiled and offered his hand to help her into the wagon. "As you wish, 'Minster."

Imbica was sprier than Quen guessed, based on her size and being in her middle years. She didn't need the man's help, but accepted it graciously. The cart driver didn't offer Quen help, not that she needed it.

As he hoisted himself back into the driver's seat, he said, "Name's Besha." He smiled back at them, looking like he expected a pleasant greeting in return.

He didn't get it. Imbica kept her face stoic, her demeanor imperious.

"What are you taking to the capital?" Quen asked. Imbica shot her an angry look, but the way Quen saw it, Imbica hadn't quoted edicts about a Doj'Anira not having the right to speak.

"Got unworked thukna and drey wool in the sacks," he said. "They say folks in the capital be wanting to dye it themselves. Not liking the country dyes no more, they say." He spat. "Fah." He gave a furtive look back, eying his Kovatha passenger. "Anyhows, if they be wanting raw wool, ole Besha'll cart it. I'm only hoping it's worth the extra taxes."

Quen curled into a pile of sacks and inhaled the familiar odor of drey's wool. *Besha's cart smells like home.* She avoided thinking about the past. With each passing mile, life in Solia became a hazy dream.

They climbed steadily uphill. The vegetation transformed from the odd, spiky squat trees, tufted grasses, and low bushes to taller trees with broad leaves and vibrant green short grasses.

Quen ignored Imbica's glares and peppered Besha with questions. She was anxious for news of Solia. "What town are you coming from?"

"This load is comin' from Linzaô."

"Oh."

"That disappoints you?"

Quen sighed. "No. I had hoped you were from the Sulmére."

"I picked this load up from another fella, so I've no'a been to Sulmére lately."

Imbica chimed in, suddenly interested. "What village in the Sulmére, Doj'Anira?"

"I'm from Solia. *Was* from Solia."

Besha gasped. "Solia? Now that I heard about. Terrible fire down there. People claiming it were a dragon." He chuckled and slapped his knee as if he'd told a great joke. "Can you believe it? Some people got more 'magination than sense."

Quen considered setting him straight about the dragon. *I could regale him with a horrific tale of charred bodies and scorched sand.* But she decided not to. For a time, he'd be happier believing dragon stories were false. People were anxious about Niyadi's return to Vay'Nada, the night's shadow encroaching more each day. And frightened people were prone to spin calamity into superstitions to prove their fears.

As Hiyadi descended to the horizon, they came to a small town called Embrir. It wasn't much more than an inn with an attached tavern, a smithy, a tiny common goods store, and a smattering of houses. The grey stone used to build the Niri Bridge's facade was used to build the buildings. Still, nothing in Embrir was extraordinary like the Niri.

Besha pulled the wagon to the back side of the Exalted Inn. It was an impressive name for an insignificant place. A mild wind would have turned the rear stables into kindling. Interior light leaked out through the disintegrated mortar between the stacked stones of the main building.

The interior of the Exalted Inn was similar to the outside. The dusty floors bothered Quen. In the Sulmére, people kept their floors clean despite the constant battle with sand and dust—or perhaps because of it. Twice-daily sweepings were the norm. *No respectable establishment would allow dust to gather.*

A woman with arms the size of small tree trunks wiped a table. Her chubby face was red, and her neck flushed as though she'd overexerted herself.

Besha flushed and gave her an appreciative smile. "Finira, it's been long with no see'un you." He took off his reed hat and nervously twisted the brim in his fingers.

Finira's breeches stopped at the knees like Besha's. Her copious bosom nearly popped out of her front-laced linen shirt, and her ample buttocks made the fabric of her pants strain at the back. Quen hoped the entire ensemble didn't rip apart, leaving the woman exposed for all to see.

Finira smiled a broad, gap-toothed smile and pushed a clump of sweat-wet orange hair from her cheek. "Besha, I'll be a yindril's skinny arse." Only after she'd spoken did Finira notice the black tunic and silver belt on the woman coming up behind Besha. "Oh, pardon, 'Minster. Did no'a see you there." Her face reddened another shade.

Imbica sighed and smoothed her tunic. "We need a room for the night. And a hot meal."

The chain connecting Quen to Imbica rattled as they went farther into the inn. Finira stared down at it and gave Quen a pitying look.

Quen's face reddened. Being a prisoner hadn't embarrassed her because she knew she'd done nothing wrong. But Finira's look of pity made Quen's stomach lurch. She'd leave without supper or sleep if she didn't have to receive that look again.

They ate a bland meal of greasy, fried jishni tubers, day-old flatbread, and roasted meat. The meat was so tough, Quen worried she'd still be digesting it when her next birthday came around. Finira served sweet wine, the meal's only highlight. To Quen's surprise, Imbica allowed her a cup.

Besha lifted his wine cup and nodded a toast to Quen. "You treat your prisoner well there, 'Minster."

Imbica struggled with the tough meat, sweat on her upper lip as she attempted to cut it with a knife and fork. "She is no ordinary prisoner. In fact, I suppose one could say she is not truly a prisoner."

Besha pointed at Quen's shackles with a hunk of bread. "It's a-lookin' like she is one."

Imbica chewed Finira's tough meat and finally swallowed loudly. "This detainee is Doj'Anira, and I am delivering her to the capital pursuant to Edict 42."

Besha drank wine and wiped his mouth with his hand. "Did no'a know 'bout that law." He stared at Quen as if trying to make sense of it all.

Imbica sipped her wine. "The Dynasty needs to redouble its efforts to inform the citizenry beyond Qülla of its laws."

Besha nodded in deference. "As you say, 'Minster. You know best."

Imbica and Quen shared a tiny room with two narrow beds raised off the floor by a primitive handmade wood platform. Lumpy straw filled the mattress covered in rough spun linen. But it was Quen's best sleep since she left her bed for the last time in Solia.

The new morning brought a fine grey mist and a cooler temperature. Besha said the fog would burn off by midmorning.

Besha's stocky horse pulled the cart and riders on a gradual ascent, and the mountains to the west disappeared behind them. The clay road gave way to a path of deep-brown soil cut through a forest of trees so green, Quen questioned if she was, in fact, awake. As they ascended, the trees grew taller, and the canopy widened, blocking Hiyadi's warm rays. Quen wriggled deeper into the sacks of raw wool. The damp air made the cart's cargo smell of wet animal.

Mile after mile of pristine woodland answered how the peoples of the northern lands could build such a massive bridge or gate of wood. Since the time of legends, the Sulmére hadn't seen so much wood.

Midmorning of the third day, the trees thinned, and the air warmed considerably. Shackles still bound Quen to Imbica. Her future remained uncertain, but she threw her head back and basked in Hiyadi's light. She said a silent prayer of gratitude to Hiyadi for his healing rays.

"Qülla be ahead now, 'Minster." Besha whistled through his teeth. "Ah, now ain't she a beaut'."

Quen climbed atop the wool sacks for her first view of the capital. The entire city rested upon a steep hill rising from the bedrock. It looked like a giant had plucked a handful of rock and dirt and plunked it down atop the mountain. A single-lane road cut through the stone, winding up the steep cliff to the city above.

Atop the cliffs were brick and stone buildings, many with smooth columns at the corners topped with conical caps of copper. Some cones were orangey-gold, but most had weathered into a pale-green patina. Like the Tilaj Gate, intricate carvings cut into the stone mimicked vines and plants or ornate geometric patterns. Domes capped most buildings, some inlaid with elaborate tile mosaics, others plastered white or gilded with gold or copper. The overall effect was of a colorful city reflecting Hiyadi's light for several leagues.

The spires, domes, carvings, and color of Qülla paled compared to the palace. At the northernmost edge of the massive limestone bluff, a bit of land covered in mossy-green plants rose like a remnant of what used to be. A sliver of land curled down in an impossible structure, still somehow attached to the limestone cliff below but also curving from above, creating a great ladle of emerald land. Waterfalls poured from the spoon of land on either side.

A spoon of land cradled a palace of splendor. Quen rubbed her eyes to make sure she was awake. Artisans had carved the palace from the limestone cliffs into a delicate lacy structure. Cones of gold punctuated the walls. The castle sprawled down into the spoon. At the apex, an enormous gold dome covered a ring of glowing, jewel-like stained-glass windows.

As they got closer, something flew from the palace and disappeared below. Quen's muscles tightened, and her stomach roiled. "Was that a dragon?" she whispered.

Imbica laughed. "Hiyadi's light, no. It was a gib-rig."

As she was poised to ask another question, another object flew near the palace. It looked like a smaller version of the gold domes atop the buildings but made of rigid cloth. A small wooden boat hung from it.

Quen pointed to the flying thing. "What is it exactly?"

"Hmm, how to explain to someone from the Sulmére?" Imbica rubbed her chin. "It is like Besha's cart, except it flies instead of being pulled by a horse or kopek."

"It hasn't got wings. How does it fly?"

"It is a clever invention. Beneath the palace lies a bubbling tar pit. Prelate Vidar of Vatra Pillar, a talented alchemist, discovered the air around the tar pit is special. He captures the magical air with a contraption he built and puts it into the gib-rig. Then the whole vessel floats."

Unlike some people, Quen didn't yearn to fly. *I like my feet firmly planted and preferably in Sulmére sand.* She never considered the possibility of people flying. "Can everyone in Qülla travel by gib-rig?"

Imbica shook her head. "Oh no, the air the alchemist uses is sacred since it only exists beneath the palace. Only Kovan Dynasty or honored guests travel by gib-rig, and only to travel to the Palace di Solis. Once they deplete the magical air, the gib-rig is merely cloth and wood. Until Prelate Vidar refills it with magical air, that is."

They began their steep ascent up the crushed stone path to the capital. The horses didn't grumble, but the cart creaked and groaned.

Quen hated that she was coming to the capital in chains. But she couldn't help staring with her mouth open in awe of the majesty of Qülla, Indrasi's capital city.

"It is magnificent, is it not?" Imbica asked.

Quen nodded.

"Just wait 'til you see what's inside them city walls," Besha said.

CHAPTER II

Awed by the soaring city, Quen arrived at Qülla's gate with a cricked neck from staring upward. Twin towers flanked the pale-gold limestone city gates. A guard in maroon leather armor staffed each tower. The Kovan Dynasty sigil, a fiery dragon against a sun, covered their chests. A guard from the right turret called down, "Kovatha. Open the gate!" By some hidden mechanism, the massive limestone gates swung open.

The peacefulness of the countryside evaporated in Qülla's din. Carts' wheels squeaked. Dogs barked, and children cried. The noise became a sinuous thrum.

As they entered the city's major boulevard, tan brick pavement replaced the crushed rock path. Expertly laid, the pavers created a smooth road. The esplanade tapered to side streets, shooting off in every direction. Some were narrow alleys for foot traffic. Others, wide enough for wagons, radiated from the primary route. Towering over the roads were buildings carved of stone, some three or four levels high.

At the ground level of both alleyways and boulevards were shops and inns. Hawkers stood in front of many of them, calling out to passers-by about their wares.

"It's a fine day for a cup o' wine," a buxom woman shouted. She teetered as she waved customers in. *Looks like she sampled some of her own wares.*

The aroma of roasting meat filled the air, and Quen's stomach rumbled. A man held up an odd meat stick. Upon closer inspection, the "stick" was the neck of a bird, complete with head and beak.

Quen pointed. "What is that?"

Imbica's upper lip turned up in disgust. "Horrid."

"What bird has a neck that long?"

"A swan," Imbica said.

Over the man's head hung a painting of a black-beaked bird. A young boy handed the man a coin and received the swan's neck, holding it by the beak as the salesman had. He licked the greasy meat from his lips as he ambled away, happily munching.

Besha's cart rolled by shops dedicated to things such as traveling satchels made of smooth, exquisite leathers and a tiny store selling nothing but parchments and pen and ink.

How do these shops thrive? Paper was a rare extravagance in the Sulmére. *What professions allow these people to afford such luxuries?*

A young girl with long black hair woven into elaborate braids stood outside another shop. Her cheeks were unnaturally wan, her lips made red with paint. Her dress was pale-gold silk overlaid in a gauzy fabric so sheer it was hardly there. The U-cut neckline barely covered her tiny bosoms.

She stood next to an older girl, perhaps Quen's age. This young woman, dressed in a gauzy red dress, held the petite girl's hand and twirled her on her toes. The two giggled, and the older girl called, "Dressmakers for the Kovan Dynasty. Wear what the princesses wear."

Quen had never thought about Kovan princesses because she hadn't known there were Kovan princesses. It mattered little to a child in the Sulmére what girls hundreds of leagues away wore.

In Qülla for a short time, Quen already had the measure of its people. *They spend good coin for a nearly meatless bird's neck and wear clothes so impractical they might as well go naked.* Qülla was beautiful beyond imagination, yet Quen couldn't ignore the lingering odor of the place, foul with excrement and dank water.

A few more wheel turns down the road, a man took off his black wool hat, rolled it down his arm using only his arm muscles, then put a purple hat atop his head with his other hand. "Caps, hats, and headwear, as worn by Princess Feray."

The hat seller gave a low bow to the Kovatha as they passed. When he noticed the shackles on Quen's wrist, he frowned and looked away.

Quen had been riding high atop stacked sacks, but she slumped down into the nest she'd made among the wool the first day they had begun their journey. Her face was fiery with embarrassment. Sometimes Sulmére people avoided her, but they never made her feel small like she felt now.

"Ignore their rudeness, Doj'Anira. Most Qüllanians are small people, sheltering in the Kovan Dynasty's shadow." Imbica remained stoic, her eyes gazing ahead and over the heads of everyone they passed.

"We Sulmére people may be poor, and we don't live in fancy houses or wear expensive clothes. But we aren't rude to strangers."

"Maybe. Or perhaps you never noticed it. People talk about others rather than make a name for themselves. 'Tis easier for most people."

"They respect you, though."

The Kovatha adjusted her silver belt. "They respect the emblems of my station. They know nothing of me other than to fear me." She looked down into Quen's eyes. "Do not mistake me. They should fear Kovatha."

True. She'd never been a nervous person, but Quen had cautious respect for the power Imbica had shown.

"One day, the Exalted will reveal the true significance of being Doj'Anira. Then people will understand you are no ordinary prisoner."

"Whatever that means," said Quen.

Imbica's brows furrowed. "Yes, whatever that means."

The Kovatha appeared bothered that she didn't know the full implication of Quen's status as Doj'Anira. It chafed Quen as well. *Hopefully, I'll have answers soon.*

Ahead, the buildings thinned and gave way to another wide esplanade. Besha steered to the eastern side of the boulevard and down a narrow alley barely wide enough for his wagon. The dank odor grew more insistent and mixed with the smell of rotten fish. Quen pulled her keffla up over her nose. Infused with years of huson pine oil residue, it shielded her from the rancid smell.

Gilded storefronts and people hawking wares gave way to dingy, compact, utilitarian buildings lacking ornate decoration. *It doesn't seem like a place for Kovatha.* But Imbica didn't protest.

They came to a one-level building constructed of orangey-red bricks that looked like they'd melt in a hard rain. The wide doors were open, and Besha drove the wagon through.

A stout man with silver hair called down from a platform. Smoke curled up from a long, thin-necked pipe he had clamped between his teeth. "Besha, by Lumine's teats, I figured you got swallowed by the sands." He hobbled on legs so bowed they looked like they would snap. The man's pipe smoking and bowed legs reminded her of Druvna, and her eyes got hot with unspent tears. *I wish I could cry alone in peace.*

Besha chuckled. "It was slow goin' with only ole Jini here." He patted the horse's rump, sending up a puff of dust.

The man approached them. "What happened to Jon?"

Besha climbed out of the wagon and offered a hand to Imbica. "I had to sell Jon to meet the levy last fall." He glanced at the Kovatha, then lowered his head as he helped her down.

When the man saw the Kovatha, a nervous laugh replaced his jovial smile. "Ah, Besha, you brought a 'Minster with you." The man took off his wool cap and bowed as deeply as his bowed legs would allow.

Imbica ignored the man and waited for Quen to disembark before she walked farther lest she jerk Quen harshly. The man glanced at Quen's shackled wrists then diverted his gaze. Neither man offered Quen a hand.

Besha removed his hat and gave his thinning grey hair a good tousle. "The 'Minster required a ride from Niri Bridge, see? 'Minster, this here is Castor, manager o' this warehouse and a fine trader. Does his part for the Dynasty, he does."

Castor tittered. "Fah, Besha, you're too kind to this ole man." His face colored.

None of this seemed to touch Imbica's ears, or if it did, she cared not a whit about their chatter. She brushed road dust from her tunic, adjusted her wide silver belt, and finger-brushed her hair to smooth it. Finally, she said, "The Dynasty thanks you for your service, Besha di Tikli."

Besha gripped the rim of his hat and stood expectantly, perhaps waiting for a tip. But Imbica exited the warehouse without looking back, pulling Quen along.

Besha and Castor were silent behind them. They knew better than to complain within range of a Kovatha. Quen waved goodbye with her bound hands. Besha rubbed the brim of his hat, his expression gloomy. He gave her a single nod in reply. Besha was polite to her, even though she was in chains. *If I ran for it now, would he help me escape?* She knew the answer was no. Besha had been deferential to Imbica, clearly fearful of her power. *Would anyone here risk themselves to help a person unjustly held against their will?* Quen glanced down at the restraints. *That's just it, though. How could anyone know I'm innocent?*

The streets in the lower city gave way to canals. An incessant roar filled the air.

"What's that sound?" Quen towered over the Kovatha as they waited at the water's edge, but for what, Quen didn't know.

"What?" Imbica looked up at her. "Oh, the water? The roar of the waterfalls pouring from Mount Néru, where the Palace di Solis rests."

Ah, the waterfalls I saw from outside the gates end up here.

A small boat sidled to them as they waited at the dock. The boat was the same shape and size as the flying gib-rig Quen had seen floating from Mount Néru.

The boat was driven by a thin young woman with long black hair pulled into a sleek tail. She wore a wide-brimmed straw hat, like Besha's. She gave the Kovatha a hand into the boat. Unlike others Quen had encountered, the woman helped Quen board, unfazed by the shackles on her wrists.

"Where I be boating you, 'Minster?"

Quen's heart fluttered with anticipation. *Soon I'll meet the Exalted. Please, Hiyadi, shine your light on me so I can get this nasty 'Doj'Anira' business behind me and reunite with Rhoji and my pod.*

"To the Menagerie," Kovatha Imbica said.

Imbica and Quen settled onto the narrow wooden benches. As they were wide enough for only one passenger, they sat facing each other.

The water-carriage driver whistled through her teeth as she shoved off from the dock with a long pole. "To the Menagerie, heh? Not being impert'nint, 'Minster, but only Kovan family allowed in the Menagerie, you know?"

Her eyes wide and dark with anger, Imbica spat, "Are you blind, woman? I am Kovatha, and transporting an important prisoner on Dynasty business. Just take us there. With haste."

The driver shrugged but didn't look nervous or frightened by the Kovatha's chastisement. She did, however, give Quen a pitying look before she set to work turning the boat around. "As you say, 'Minster. I'll have you there lickety-split." Her strokes were long and fluid, barely rippling the water.

Imbica's anger dissipated. Soon her brow was smooth, and her eyes relaxed. "Home at last." Her voice was a whisper. Though it was hardly a display of excitement, it was the closest thing to emotion the woman had shown since their encounter with Vahgrin.

Quen had hoped they would go directly to the Palace di Solis. *How disappointing.* It meant a delay in securing her freedom.

"There are no mistakes. Only opportunities," Pahpi said. Quen tried to emblazon the labyrinth of canals and alleys on her memory. *I can disappear in this city.* Quen peered at the shackles on her wrists, something she'd avoided, as if seeing them would make it more real. *These restraints are only a brief setback.* She tried to convince herself it was true.

The brief recollection of Pahpi brought hot tears to her eyes, and her throat got tight with the effort to hold back emotion. She hadn't permitted herself to grieve him yet. Not truly. *I'll grieve another day.* Pahpi's killer was still at large. The slightest recollection of Vahgrin made her jaw tense and her back stiffen.

If I can't talk my way to freedom at the Palace, I'll escape this fetid city some other way. And as soon as I'm free, I'll find my Jagaru pod and continue our hunt for Vahgrin. Fires of vengeance still smoldered in her core. *I will avenge you, Pahpi.*

• • •

The water-carriage driver steered the boat onto a side canal of green water. They floated past buildings of salmon-colored stone, many with intricately carved balconies. Most buildings were three levels high, with long balconies framed by gauzy curtains blowing in the breeze. The curtains were silky jewel tones of emerald, azure blue, deep gold, purple, or turquoise. *I wonder if the colors mean anything the way tent colors in the Sulmére represent different herdclans?*

Lush gardens covered most rooftops with carpets of grasses, blossoms, bushes, and trees. Vines cascaded from roofs, creating vibrant living curtains of red, magenta, and golden yellow.

On the balconies, people lounged and watched the boats. They fanned themselves with flickering gilded fans. Others laughed and drank from delicate white cups with thin handles, unlike the thick clay handleless mugs used in the Sulmére. Languid music lilted from an upper balcony.

The overall energy of this area of Qülla was of wealthy vibrance. *Does no one work? How in Hiyadi's name do they afford this luxurious life when idle at midday?*

The canals were busy with water taxis darting past each other. The drivers called out "Hi" and "Ho" as they passed, sometimes coming so close they slapped hands in convivial greeting.

Their driver appeared well-known as she got many hand slaps and cheerful greetings as she wound her way through the bustling city. The bustling canals gave way to ground covered in a carpet of grass. *It looks soft and inviting.* An impossible building stood alone at the terminus of the canal system, gleaming and resplendent.

Clear glass held together by brass spines made the walls look invisible. The building wasn't rectangular, and there were three sides visible. Inside, lush greenery grew to the two-story-high ceiling, rounding to a point.

Exotic flowers, trees, and bushes surrounded the building's perimeter. Even outside the Menagerie, a cacophony of bird calls and songs rang.

The boat operator sidled up to a small pier. "Welcome to the Menagerie, 'Minster."

Imbica accepted the driver's help from the boat but said nothing in response. The driver maintained her cordial smile and gave Quen a hand up. *It's refreshing to be treated like a person rather than livestock.* The chain rattled as Quen sprang from the boat.

Once on land, the boat driver held Quen's hand and examined her face, staring into her dual-colored eyes. "You are *Doj'Anira.*" The woman dipped her head, pulled Quen closer, and whispered, "You have friends in Qülla." She released Quen, returned to her boat, and shoved off.

Quen decided against calling to the woman and asking what she meant. *I can't reveal this prospect for escape to Imbica.* The chain connecting her to the Kovatha pulled taut.

"You have friends in Qülla." Quen's heart pounded. *Did my Jagaru pod find a way into Qülla?* The mere hint of allies in the city made her heart race with newfound hope.

Imbica led Quen up a wide walkway paved with the same tan bricks that had welcomed them inside the gates of Qülla. They were the only ones in the Menagerie gardens.

Despite the circumstances, Quen wanted to learn what was inside the see-through building. But Imbica turned and led her down a lesser path. On either side were tall trees, the branches touching each other over the sidewalk, light streaming through the canopy in thin bands.

The path took a bend and climbed a knoll. The trees were shorter here, the leaves sparse and feathery. Clusters of purple flowers hung from the smaller trees and filled the air with a delicious odor. Ahead was another building, grander than all she'd seen before.

Iron beams rose skyward, beginning as a circle but near the top, jutting again to form a peaked arch. Each iron door was larger than the last until it reached three stories tall. At the back, another ironwork structure formed a spider's web pattern. The construction gave the effect of walking through a grand iron hallway to a spider's web.

They entered a courtyard, with a rocky spire for a back 'wall.' *It must be part of Mount Néru itself.* The roof of interlaced veins of ironwork allowed ample light and air through its open weave pattern. A waterfall trickled down the spire's face, filling a small pond. Water flowing over rocks and boulders created a soothing, babbling sound.

The courtyard was abuzz with the sound of insects and the song of birds. A giant snow tiger lounged atop a flat rock overlooking the pond. The cat was as large as the black wolf Nevara had ridden into Solia. The tiger's fluffy snow-white beard was braided and bejeweled with golden rings and red tassels. A golden clip adorned the base of each of the big cat's ears.

The gorgeous snow tiger sniffed the air, and its gaze rested on Quen. Like Quen's right eye, the tiger's eyes were the color of a clear blue sky.

The magnificent cat made no move toward them, content to receive the affections of the woman stroking its back. Quen recognized the woman. *She's Pelagia, Mistress of the Menagerie. Fano told me stories about her and the Menagerie.* His description of Pelagia was flawless.

A cape flowed from her bare shoulders to the ground. The cape made it look as though she wore butterfly wings of bright yellow, orange, and red rimmed in black. Light spilled through the iron latticework, and the woman's wrap shimmered. Quen stared at the cape, and upon the woman turning toward them, she realized why it glittered. The butterfly effect was, in fact, made from real butterfly wings. Somehow, Pelagia had placed hundreds, maybe thousands, of butterflies, creating the illusion of enormous, flowing butterfly wings.

Pelagia's skin was so pale it looked like she'd never seen the Brothers' light. Beneath the elaborate cape was a collar of bleached bone. Attached to this collar, held by perhaps a single strong filament, a thin wisp of silky cloth skimmed her long, slim body. More wings adorned her pale-grey eyes, creating the effect of butterflies kissing her eyelids.

Her accent was northern, like Aldewin's. "Imbica."

The woman moved toward them, gliding as if on unseen rollers. *It's like she's made of smoke rather than flesh and bone.*

Pelagia approached Imbica and gave a curtsy, dipping low but still at eye level with the Kovatha. She was as tall as Quen, perhaps even taller. She never took her eyes from Imbica's. Her lips curled into a small, courteous smile. "To what do I owe the pleasure of a Kovatha visit?" Her voice was low and smooth.

Imbica yanked on the chain, forcing Quen to stand beside her. "Under Edict 42 in year five of the reign of Xa'Vatra, Exalted Ruler of the Kovan Dynasty, Hiyadi's Third Epoch, I deliver this day a Doj'Anira."

Excited anticipation rendered Quen breathless. She'd never met a woman taller than her, nor one with such pale skin, hair, and eyes. Pelagia was like an incarnation of Lumine, fallen from the heavens as a butterfly. Pelagia's otherworldly beauty and grace disarmed her.

Imbica yanked on the chain and hissed, "Kneel."

Quen was about to obey, but Pelagia waved her up. "I am not the Exalted, Imbica. No kneeling is required here."

Pelagia locked eyes with Quen. She peered first into Quen's right eye, the clear blue one, then the left amber-colored one. "A Doj'Anira from the Vindaô?" Her voice was a whisper.

"No, from the Sulmére."

Pelagia circled them as if inspecting the package Imbica had delivered. "Where did you find her?"

"Recovered at the Tilaj Gates. She'd been traveling with Druvna's little band of rogue Jagaru."

What did Imbica mean by 'rogue' Jagaru?

Pelagia stood less than a pace in front of Imbica. "And you, loyal servant of the Dynasty, took the Doj'Anira off Druvna's hands." She wore a bemused smile.

"Of course, as Edict 42 mandates. And I have delivered it forthwith to the Mistress of the Menagerie, as the law requires."

Pelagia was silent but gave Imbica a cordial smile. She clicked her tongue, and the magnificent tiger rose from its

197

perch atop the rocks, leaped over the stream in one easy jump, and sidled up to Pelagia.

The tiger's head was half again as large as a person's head. He was tall enough to stare Imbica in the eye. Pelagia stroked the cat's head.

"Were you under the impression you may abuse and neglect a Doj'Anira?" Pelagia asked.

"I never." Imbica attempted to sound aghast at the accusation. *She's a terrible actor.*

Pelagia smirked then once again regarded Quen. Her movements were slow and deliberate, and she ran a long, thin finger along Quen's jawline. Her touch was gentle. Pelagia grasped Quen's hands, thrust her palms up, and examined them. Quen's chains rattled, and Pelagia's smile disappeared.

Spidery blue veins threaded Quen's palms. They radiated from an intense blue at the center to a purple-red at the fingertips. Imbica had said the evidence of her immolation spell was temporary, but in the days since, the bruises had bloomed an even nastier shade of purple.

"You immolated her." Pelagia's calm grey-blue eyes grew dark with anger.

"She attempted to escape."

"You could have subdued her."

"How else could I counter her power?" Imbica asked. "I had to prevent her escape."

The giant snow tiger curled his upper lip, showing a mouth full of pointy teeth fit for tearing and shredding flesh. His chest rumbled with a low growl.

"Be still, Nivi." Pelagia patted Nivi's massive head, soothing him. "You see. Such primitive methods are unnecessary, even when calming a ferocious beast." She glared at Imbica, her pale eyes now dark with anger. "Now remove the shackles and chains."

Imbica didn't invoke the spell to open the scorpion lock. "I do not recommend it. Not until you have shown you can control this Doj'Anira."

Pelagia's laugh was deep and throaty. "I need show you nothing. You have delivered the Doj'Anira as required. Your service is complete. Remove the shackles. Take your chains and go." All feigned amiability toward Imbica was gone from her voice and demeanor.

Nivi growled again and bared his teeth. Pelagia's glare could have withered a day-blooming desert marigold.

The Kovatha wound her hands and thrust them toward the lock while whispering an incantation in the ancient tongue. "I came far, you know. Lost a wagon, a yindril, and two horses on this errand."

The scorpion lock's legs clicked forward and up, releasing their grip on Quen's wrists. The shackles fell, revealing pale skin in contrast to the dirt covering the rest of her. Quen rubbed her wrists. *I feel freer already. Unlike Imbica, Pelagia seems kind. Maybe she'll help me plead my case to the Exalted.*

Imbica retrieved the clunky cuffs. Pelagia held two shiny gold kovars between her fingers. *Where did those coins come from?* Pelagia had no purse, pouch, or hidden pockets in such a thin shift.

Imbica snorted. "You think you need to pay me, like a common trader, and I will be happy for your gold?"

Pelagia smiled wide. "You are a money collector, no?"

Imbica still didn't grab the coins.

Quen knew little about how money worked beyond the Sulmére, but she knew a copper kovar was worth many skins. A silver one could buy a half-dozen thukna or a small herd of drey. She couldn't imagine how many thukna a gold kovar was worth. She'd never seen one gold kovar before. Before her eyes were two. *A fortune in the Sulmére.*

"You want to leave empty-handed? And after all your troubles," Pelagia said. She slid the coins together, and they clinked.

Imbica held out her hand. Pelagia dropped the coins into Imbica's open palm, avoiding touching her skin.

"You will tell the Exalted, won't you? I am the one who delivered this Doj'Anira?" Imbica's voice had lost its stoic indifference. She now sounded like a begging child.

Pelagia again focused her attention on Quen, and gave her a bemused smile.

"Mistress—you will tell the Exalted?"

Pelagia waved her off. "Yes, yes. You did your duty. If I were you, I would go back to southern sands. Who knows, Imbica, you may be lucky enough to find another Doj'Anira wandering the dunes. A few more gold kovars, and you can buy yourself out of the slums."

Pelagia turned and flourished her remarkable cape. As she did, a few butterflies moved, breaking the pattern. Quen gasped. *I thought they'd used dead butterflies to construct the cape, but these are alive. How does she control them to make them behave in such an odd way?*

If Pelagia's living cape awed Imbica, she didn't show it. "Mark my word. You must watch yourself and take care with this one."

Pelagia continued strolling away, and Nivi padded after her.

"She may be Rajani," Imbica called.

Pelagia stopped. She called over her shoulder, "Are you coming, Doj'Anira?"

Quen turned her gaze to Imbica, the woman who had taken her from her First Kin, friends, and future. *I wish Pelagia would allow Nivi to sink his teeth into Imbica. It would serve her right.*

Imbica, her voice higher and more shrill, implored Pelagia. "There are strange things afoot in Indrasi. What are these 'Doj'Anira'? Is it related to the dragon?"

Pelagia continued walking, as though oblivious to Imbica's strident queries. She showed no interest in what Imbica said. *Not even Imbica's mention of a dragon.*

Quen turned her back on Imbica. She followed Pelagia through the courtyard garden toward the impressive black-lacquered door set within an intricate brass web. Quen hoped she'd never see the puffy-faced Imbica again.

Pelagia slid through the doorway into a metalwork spider's web. Desperate for answers, Quen entered Pelagia's web.

CHAPTER 12

Temerity in check, Quen hurried after Pelagia. A grand iron door banged shut, the sound echoing off the glass walls and stone floor. Pelagia led Quen through a hall of iron ribs and glass, the only sounds the subtle swish of her silken gown and the occasional flap of butterfly wings.

"I am sure you have many questions." Pelagia didn't stop to allow for conversation.

"I have so many questions, my head feels like dust in a sandstorm."

Pelagia chuckled softly as she opened the last door in the long hall. "You must be exhausted from your journey." She took Quen's hand in her long, thin one. "And I fear you were badly mistreated." She gazed at Quen's purple palm and shook her head. Pelagia favored her with a friendly smile. "There will be plenty of time for questions. And under the Edict, I must arrange an audience for you with the Exalted."

Quen's hearts double-thumped.

"But first, you need rest. And a bath."

They entered a room larger than all the living space Quen's family had occupied in Solia. Light shone through a vibrantly colored glass ceiling, casting a warm glow on plastered walls painted violet. A raised platform occupied the center of the room. On it, a sumptuous bed splayed with silk covers and pillows of teal, aubergine, and emerald-green pillows beckoned for sleep. Potted plants, both tall and small, undulated from the wall edges, making the bed look as though plopped into a forest. A copper tub, large enough for Quen to lie In, invited her for a bath.

Pelagia pushed a silent black button on a panel beside the door and pulled a fire starter kit from a wood table. She struck a spark and lit lamps on either side of the door and one on the table.

By the time Pelagia lit the lamps, two small women had appeared. Both wore long silky pants billowing about their legs. The pants rested low on their hips while their small chests were covered with little more than strings, their stomachs bare. The women wore their dark hair down, not braided as most people in the Sulmére.

Both women, like Quen, had two different-colored eyes, though each had one brown and one green instead of blue and yellow-amber. *They are Doj'Anira. Were they brought to the Menagerie under Edict 42 like me? Is this what I am to become?* It was strange for the Exalted to create a law to conscript people to be house servants. Plenty of desperate people across the continent readily sold themselves into indentured servitude in the capital. For a set time, they exchanged their freedom for a roof over their head and food in their belly. *Not a life I would choose.*

The twins bowed slightly to Pelagia as they entered, then stood side by side.

"Luz and Caz, welcome our new Doj'Anira."

The two women bowed to Quen. They wore a mask of neutrality, evincing no curiosity about Quen. Unsure whether Qülla custom called for a bow, curtsy, or something else entirely, Quen opted to nod and smile. The twins responded with stoic, emotionless masks.

Pelagia returned her gaze to Quen. Her welcoming smile stoked Quen's hope that being Doj'Anira was an honor, not a curse. *Maybe the Exalted didn't intend for Imbica to mistreat me.*

"The Doj'Anira has had a long journey." Pelagia gently took Quen's hand in hers, staring down at the purple and blue bruises. She frowned. "And has been ill-treated. Bathe her, and massage away the soreness from her journey." Pelagia squeezed her hand, her eyes glistening. "And feed her well."

At the mere mention of food, Quen's stomach rumbled loudly. *I hope Pelagia didn't hear that.*

Pelagia let go of Quen's hand and turned to leave.

"Wait. I'm not too tired to talk. What is this place? Why was I brought here? What does being Doj'Anira mean?" She glanced at Caz and Luz, still standing like statues, their faces expressionless. "And when will I get to meet with the Exalted and get this whole thing sorted?"

"Oh, my dune flower," Pelagia said. "You say you are not tired, yet your face looks careworn. It is my job to see to your needs, and I cannot deliver you to the Palace in your state. Besides, one does not simply pop in for a visit with the Exalted. I must follow protocols. While I work on that, allow Caz and Luz to massage the knots from your back and the cares from your mind. Sleep. Eat. Recuperate." At the door now, she looked back before crossing the threshold. "Food and rest are nearly as good as O'Dishi chants to cure whatever ails you."

Dini had said something similar. *Pelagia knows of Sulmére healing arts?* Amidst the glamour and wealth of Pelagia's palace, she longed for tea out of Dini's handmade earthenware cup and a bit of Rhoji's simple stew eaten with family. *Unless your drink can transport me back to the life I had before Nevara darkened my door, then I doubt you can cure what ails me.*

Pelagia glided out the door, her butterfly cape outstretched behind her. She left Quen with more questions than before.

The women wasted no time drawing Quen's bath. In the parched Sulmére, bathing was a weekly basin of water and cloth, with wipe downs of huson oil between. Quen rarely had the opportunity to immerse fully in water.

"Thank you. I can bathe myself."

Rather than taking the cue to leave, they helped her undress. Before Quen could protest, they'd peeled off her filthy, frayed riding tunic, scorched riding apron, outer pants, and leg wrappings. The two even stripped off her treasured inner silk tank and long underpants, luxuries Pahpi had bartered many skins for as a gift to Quen. She stood naked and instinctively covered her breasts and tender parts with her hands in an attempt at modesty.

Caz took Quen by the hand and led her to the bath. The brass and bead necklaces Caz wore jingled as she walked. Luz poured scented oil from a small ewer into the steaming water.

Each took a hand and helped Quen step onto the platform then down into the scented water. Quen lay back, splashing some of the water out. She giggled, and the two women smiled amiably but said nothing.

The water was the perfect temperature. The steam carried an intoxicating spicy floral scent. Quen rested her head on the curved tub back and nearly cried with joy. The water buoyed her, and Quen relaxed fully into Enara's loving waters.

She closed her eyes and nearly drifted to sleep. Caz lifted an arm and washed Quen from armpit to fingertips and cleaned underneath her nails with a small metal tool.

While Caz bathed Quen, Luz washed her hair. She gathered a separate basin and let the water drain down from Quen's head, the warm water whisking away weeks of sand, sweat, and grime. After running through three fresh changes of rinse water, Luz turned her attention to massaging Quen's neck and shoulders, pressing the tension out of her.

Quen drifted in and out of sleep. She would float into a dream only to wake as they moved to another body part to wash or massage. They spoke neither to Quen nor to each other. There was only the gentle slosh of water and the fragrant odor of flowers.

By the time the bath ended, Quen felt like she had been given nys't. Her limbs were fluid, her mind free of questions or cares.

Caz and Luz steered her to the bed when the bath was done. Quen didn't argue.

Quen was used to sleeping on the ground with only a pallet of reeds for comfort. The fluffy bed was like resting on a cloud. Quen was asleep before Luz and Caz had turned out the lamps.

• • •

Quen slept the rest of the day, the night, and into the following day. She might not have woken then, except her stomach protested its aching hunger.

Not knowing where to go or what to do, she pressed the small black button on the wall she'd seen Pelagia use. Within a few minutes, Caz and Luz appeared. As before, neither of them spoke.

"I'm hungry," Quen said. Unsure if they understood, she rubbed her stomach and pantomimed eating.

They nodded in unison, and Luz waved her to follow. Someone had dressed Quen in a creamy-white tunic tied about her waist, with bell sleeves dropping from the wrists in long tails. Her legs were naked beneath the tunic. *It's odd to have bare legs. I like it.* Caz retrieved a pair of white silk slippers that matched the gown. The slippers were whisper-light on her feet.

She followed Caz and Luz out into the sun-filled hall, back to the vestibule with three doors, and this time they took the middle door leading to another courtyard. It was as though she had stepped outside, but beneath her feet was a floor of polished stone, overhead a ceiling of glass and brass. Bird song filled the sultry air.

Quen followed the women on a winding path of time-worn stone that opened onto a large patio of polished orange-red marble. In the center was an ornately carved wood table surrounded by at least a dozen chairs. At the far end of the table, Pelagia perused a scroll while Nivi sat by her side.

The scroll was attached both top and bottom to a brass mechanism that held it flat for reading. Pelagia wound a lever on the side to reveal more of the manuscript. As Quen entered, Pelagia looked up from the scroll, and her eyes brightened at the sight of Quen.

Pelagia's butterfly dress was gone. Instead, she wore a sleeveless gown of feathers in rainbow colors. The neckline was a low V, outlined in vibrant red feathers. Under her bust, the feathers morphed from red to orange, blending to yellow at the hip, then green, blue, and deep indigo at the floor. Stylized wings at her shoulders gave the impression Pelagia had spread her wings and was about to fly.

A small feather headdress adorned her pale silver hair. The feathers flowed from her head to mid-back.

She looks horribly uncomfortable. Does she ever wear anything except extravagant gowns?

"Ah, our dune flower arises at last." She smiled warmly at Quen. "You must be famished. From the look of you, neither Druvna nor Imbica took care to feed you adequately."

It was true she'd been famished for weeks, but she blamed neither Druvna nor Imbica for it. The Nixan soul's needs stoked her hunger. She kept that information, though, to herself. For now, all she wanted was to put whatever smelled so tasty into her belly.

Caz pulled out a chair for Quen. Luz was busy readying a plate for her while Caz poured a pale-pink liquid into a deep-blue goblet.

Luz used a small knife and long fork with two tines to slice meat from a roasted fowl and piled fluffy bread onto her plate. She placed it in front of Quen while Caz brought her a bowl of tiny ripe red berries, a plate of creamy cheese, and a porridge with spices, sugar, and milk.

Quen tried, at first, to be polite and take small bites. But one taste of the fresh bread with creamy cheese and the ravenous hunger took over. She shoved food into her gullet like a wild animal hoarding its kill, her head down over her plate. Occasionally she sipped from the cup to wash it down. The beverage was a tangy citrus drink flavored with a hint of spice and honey. Each time she emptied the cup, Caz filled it.

She ate until she was just past gorged. *I'll probably soon regret eating so much rich food.* After weeks of eating little more than dried meat, hard cheese, and nuts, her system wasn't used to food in such quantity. Quen belched loudly, and her stomach rumbled like pipes filling with water after a long dry spell.

Pelagia looked up from the scroll she'd been reading. "You must go slowly, Quen. Like the rest of you, your stomach needs time to heal."

Quen wiped her mouth and belched again, this time trying to cover it with her hand. It occurred to her that Pelagia had used her real name. "How do you know my name?"

Pelagia smiled. "I know much about you, Quen Tomo Santu di Sulmére. But what I do not understand is how you came to be in the company of Druvna's rogue Jagaru pod?"

A bird as orange as a Sulmére sunset after a sandstorm landed on the table near Quen's hand. The bird sported a mohawk of black feathers. *Did Pelagia use feathers from a bird like this to make her dress?* The bird gazed at Quen as if expecting food, but her plate was empty.

"Imbica said the same thing. What do you mean by 'rogue' Jagaru?"

"You didn't know?"

When Quen shrugged and shook her head, Pelagia laughed. "Now I see how old Druvna got a pod together. He did not tell his young recruits that the Exalted exiled him from the Jagaru. Druvna's Jagaru pod is— unsanctioned, shall we say?"

Pahpi would sooner be stripped of his skin in the Phisma tar pits than know not one but two of his children were illicit Jagaru. The rich food coupled with the shock of Druvna's deception made Quen's gut a roiling cauldron. She sipped the nectar to avoid vomiting, or worse, showing Pelagia how surprised she was at the news. "What did he do to earn such a punishment?" *I'm afraid to hear the answer.*

"The worst sin one can commit in the Exalted Xa'Vatra's eyes."

Quen took a deep breath and swallowed hard. "And what might that be?"

"He disobeyed." Pelagia coolly regarded her as if waiting for her reaction.

Quen had expected her to say that Druvna had murdered an innocent. "They sent him to prison for disobedience?" Her voice was incredulous.

Pelagia nodded and stroked Nivi's head. "Instead of delivering a prisoner to Kovatha for judgment, he summarily executed the accused. Can you imagine?"

I'm imagining it right now. She recalled how angry Druvna had been at Mishny when she slit the throat of the people traffickers they'd encountered in Juinar. She held her tongue, though, not wanting to say something that would land Druvna back in a Qülla cell—or worse. *I'm sore at him for deceiving Rhoji and me, but I don't want Druvna to go to prison again.*

"You did not answer my question. I would love to learn how Druvna's band of ne'er-do-wells ended up at the Tilaj Gate. It is risky for an exile to travel so far north."

Answering Pelagia's questions required a long story and would reveal more than Quen wanted to share. "It is a long tale."

Pelagia rolled the manuscript she'd been reading back into the brass reading device. She reclined in her chair and steepled her fingers beneath her chin. "I have time for a story." She wore a bemused expression.

Quen sipped the honeyed nectar, trying to compose herself. *I wish Rhoji were here. He always knows what should—and should not—be said.*

Rhoji. Quen wiped her wet cheek with the silk sleeve of her gown.

Pelagia's expression softened. "Ah, I see. It is a tale of woe. Too many have such tales." She held up her cup, and Luz refilled it. "Do not speak of it if you wish to forget."

To forget? *I don't want to forget. My life in the Sulmére is already like a hazy dream. I must tell the story, if only so my life in Solia doesn't fade into oblivion. Pahpi cannot be forgotten.*

She'd intended to describe only the bare minimum about a burned village and her time with Imbica. Instead, she spoke of Nevara and the black wolf, the dragon and its mysterious rider, and the Jagaru riding north. She ended the story with her last moments with Imbica. The tale took so long to tell she ate another plate, speaking at times with her mouth full. Pelagia listened patiently and intently, interrupting only a few times to ask a question or get clarification.

Quen finished by saying, "I don't think the gods like me much."

Pelagia laughed. "The gods dislike us all, Quen. Why do you think they made us human?" She rubbed Nivi's head, and he blinked slowly, appearing content with her affections. Pelagia made a chirping sound, and within a few moments, two blue-black birds landed on her outstretched arm.

The birds made the same chirping sound back to her. Pelagia gave each a gentle ruffle beneath the chin, and they danced on her arm and vied for her attention.

"If the gods loved us, they would have given us lives as birds," she said. Pelagia lifted her arm and shooed the birds off. They flew to the top of one of the tallest trees in the indoor courtyard. "To fly." Her eyes looked wistful.

She turned her attention back to Quen. There was a gleam in her eye. "Dragons fly."

At the mere mention of dragons, Vahgrin's immense maw filled with razor teeth came to mind, followed closely by visions of her burning village—and Pahpi. Quen squeezed her eyes shut and swallowed hard. *Pelagia wouldn't be enamored with dragons if one had incinerated her palace or killed someone she loved.* "Dragons also kill."

Pelagia offered the prayer for the dead. She touched the fingertips of her right hand to her chest, then mouth, and finally her thumb to her forehead. "May the Sister welcome your loved ones in her embrace."

Quen touched her thumb to her forehead between her eyes and gave the rote reply. "And be welcomed by the light of the Brothers."

Pelagia held a reverent look as the prayer required, but only for a few seconds. She edged her seat closer, excitement gleaming in her eyes. "Tell me. What did you do when you first saw the magnificent flying beast?"

"I nearly dirtied myself."

Pelagia laughed. "The mighty Quen Santu, afraid of a dragon."

Of course I was afraid. She imagined Fano, his chest as broad as a thukna arse, likely quaked upon seeing Vahgrin. "I'm hardly mighty. Any attempt I make to call on the Corners goes horribly wrong. And animals are afraid of me, which usually leads to disaster."

Pelagia looked astonished. "Afraid of you? Nivi does not fear you." She gestured to the air above them. "The birds in my sanctuary have come right up to you."

I should be happy about this change in circumstances, but something about it feels wrong. It added to the growing sensation that her previous life was the dream, not this new one.

"Maybe the ones here are—well, they're tame, aren't they? Anyway, I'm not mighty." *Why would she say that?*

"Maybe not now." Pelagia stared intently at her. "But you will be."

"What do you—"

Before Quen could finish her sentence, a man burst into the patio area. "Oh, dear Mistress, you have been hiding from me." Short, thick black hair cut to the shoulders topped his cleanly shaven face. *I haven't seen a single beard in Qülla.*

213

Pelagia rose to greet this newcomer, the feathers of her dress rustling as she moved. Gold liner rimmed the man's dark-brown eyes, and turquoise shadow covered his eyelids. A chain hung from the silver cuff at his ear and connected to a large hoop through his nostril. The chain lightly tinkled as he feigned a kiss on Pelagia's cheek. His purple-tinted lips never touched her face. Pelagia did the same, barely grazing his clean-shaven face as they held hands lightly.

"Anu, you have been away too long." She gestured to a seat.

He swung the long tails of his turquoise-colored silk coat behind him, his purple silk pants swishing as he sat. After settling in his seat, he grabbed a few grapes from a bowl on the table and took notice of Quen for the first time. "My dear Mistress, what have you been up to?" His eyes were wide with wonder, and a smile lit up his face.

Quen wasn't sure if she should stand or remain seated and quiet. She did nothing, sure if she was wrong, Pelagia would correct her.

"Anu'Bida di Māja Wix—meet Quen Tomo Santu di Sulmére. The first Doj'Anira from the Sulmére to make her way to the Menagerie."

Quen was about to correct Pelagia. She didn't 'make her way.' *More like kidnapped, tortured, and unceremoniously sold to the Menagerie for a small fortune.*

"Doj'Anira from the Sulmére," he whispered. "By Lumine's teats, and one eye is blue."

Pelagia drank from her cup. "Blue as a mountain pool." She popped a grape into her mouth.

Anu grabbed a goblet from a serving tray, and before he'd even set it down, Luz was at his side, ready to fill his cup with the honeyed fruit juice they were drinking. He put a hand over his goblet.

"None of that piss for me. Come, Pelagia, it must be time for wine. If not here, then somewhere." He faked a pout.

Pelagia nodded at Luz, and the silent woman sped through the trees, presumably to find wine for the new arrival.

"Who brought her?" Anu asked.

Pelagia leaned her elbows on the table, her chin on her hands. "Imbica. Can you believe it?"

The man chortled. "I would not have thought the little climber had it in her."

"Do not credit her with courage. The nasty cornerless fool immolated her."

Anu gasped. "She did not."

Quen spread her hands open. The blue network of veins was still visible under her skin, but it had already faded a bit since she arrived.

Luz returned and filled Anu's glass with dark-red wine. Pelagia snapped her fingers, and Luz brought her a fresh cup and filled it as well.

"One wonders how she even got a post as a Kovatha, what with being born in a granary." Pelagia took a long drink of the wine. "She gets far more respect in the world than she deserves."

Quen wanted to take issue with the idea that Imbica didn't deserve to be a Kovatha. *Apparently, neither has suffered Imbica's magical torture or witnessed her besting a dragon and its Rajani.*

"I suppose she wanted you to run to the Exalted, squealing about what a loyal servant to the Dynasty she is," Anu'Bida said.

They chuckled.

"You know her far too well."

"An easy book to read," Anu said.

Quen drained her cup. Luz was ready to pour wine into it, but Quen put her hand over her cup as she'd seen Anu do. Should the chance for escape present itself, it was best to be sober.

Pelagia apparently couldn't abide an empty goblet. "Fetch her more nectar." She turned her full attention back to Anu. "Enough about that little root dweller. Tell me about your travels. Did you bring me anything wonderfully ugly from Tinox?"

Anu looked over the rim of his cup at her as he drank. "I am afraid I came empty-handed, at least for you."

It was Pelagia's turn to puff her lips in a mock pout. She let out a loud sigh. "Ah well, at least tell me gossip of our friends to the north."

Anu had been full of mirth, but his smile disappeared, and his eyes grew dark. He chanced a furtive look at Quen and sighed. "That is a conversation best left for another time." He forced a light laugh. "Besides, what news could compare to this?" He gestured toward Quen with his cup. "Did Imbica know what she had in her hands when she delivered the Doj'Anira to you?"

Pelagia stared at Quen pensively. "I am not sure. Of course, Prelate Vidar must examine the Doj'Anira."

Anu wiped his mouth with a silk napkin. "Of course."

"Imbica raved about Rajani and dragons as she left, but I do not think she had a clue." Pelagia took a long draw from her cup. "Thank Hiyadi's light. You can always count on a bureaucrat to do the job but not look past the plain lines of an Edict."

Anu laughed. "Hear, hear!"

They clinked their goblets, red wine splashing onto the wood table. Caz rushed to wipe it.

"What more is there to know of it?" Quen asked.

They stopped laughing. Both stared at her as though they'd forgotten she could speak. Nivi, who had been napping a few paces behind Pelagia, rose. He looked at Quen as if he awaited an answer as much as she did.

Pelagia coughed lightly. "The Exalted has expressly forbidden anyone to discuss the purpose of Edict 42 except among members of the Conclave. Alas, we are not members—"

"Yet." Anu's eyes twinkled.

Quen had had it with people trying to deny her information about an unjust law that singled out people for capture based solely on eye color. "By Lumine's tits and Hiyadi's ass, I am a person, not a jizz-spewing drey. If you can't tell me what this is about, then... well...."

She ran out of curse words. *I'm glad Pahpi didn't hear me.*

They were momentarily silent, then both Anu and Pelagia laughed heartily. Anu wiped tears of laughter from his eyes.

"Jizz-spewing drey." He drank deeply of his cup and laughed. "I must remember that one. Straight from the Sulmére, that is. The people of the dunes have a quaint culture, don't they?"

Pelagia rose, her feather dress rustling. "I would enjoy nothing more than to speak with you for hours—days— about all that is behind Edict 42, Quen. Alas, I am only a simple zookeeper, not a Conclave member. I am not privy to the Dynasty's mysteries."

She knows more about Edict 42 than she'll say.

Seeing Quen's face fall with defeat, Pelagia added, "Have good cheer, dune flower. The Exalted has called me to present you to her court this evening." She raised her cup to Quen. "The Exalted has planned a fête in your honor. Perhaps tonight, we will learn more of what is behind this edict."

Pelagia drained her cup, and Luz immediately refilled it. "Come to my study, Anu. It grows hot here with the afternoon suns. We have much to discuss."

She turned to leave, Nivi at her heels. Anu followed.

Quen shouted after them, "What am I to do?"

Pelagia turned and held up her cup. "Eat and drink your fill. Then visit the Menagerie. Caz and Luz will show you the way and later prepare you for your audience with the Exalted."

Pelagia clicked her tongue, and Nivi rose and stood at her side. He gave Quen a mournful look, then the three disappeared behind the thick foliage along the path.

Quen should have been full still from gorging herself. Yet her stomach rumbled with a hunger that was feeling insatiable.

She reached for more of the roasted fowl, but Luz motioned her to sit as soon as she did. Caz grabbed the platter and swooped to her side to fill her plate.

"I can serve myself."

She hadn't meant it as a slight, but Luz's stoic demeanor gave way to a droopy frown. Caz cast her eyes downward as though she, too, had been offended.

"I'm sorry. I meant no offense."

Neither woman said anything.

They clearly understand me. "Are you forbidden from speaking to me?" Quen had always had companions to chat with. If not her father and brothers, there was always Dini. During the rains, Shel, Eira, and countless people from herd clans, or Fano and other traveling tradespeople, merchants, and entertainers. *The silence of these two is maddening.*

Luz opened her mouth wide, showing Quen the inside. There was only a little stub of flesh where a tongue should have been.

Quen gasped. She looked at Caz. "And you too?"

Caz opened her mouth and showed the nub where her tongue used to be.

Bile filled Quen's throat. Either someone had mutilated the twins before they served Pelagia, or the woman who had treated Quen like royalty wasn't what she seemed. *What if this happens to all Doj'Anira?*

"Did Pelagia do this to you two?"

They didn't respond. Their stoic expressions returned.

Quen pondered how she could ask it another way. Finally, she said, "When you arrived here, were you able to speak?"

They nodded in unison.

Unbridled anxiety about her future quashed her hunger, and she pushed the plate away.

Were they maimed as punishment, or are all servants clipped like that? The warmth of the glass-domed garden, previously soothing, now suffocated. She'd dodged the bonds of shackles only to be imprisoned in a glass cage. *There's only one way to ensure I don't become a speechless thrall. I must escape Qülla.*

CHAPTER 13

Handicapped and with no means of escape, Quen was still adamant she wouldn't succumb to fate as a maimed servant. She recalled what the water-taxi driver said. *"You have friends in the capital." What does that mean?* Qülla's canals and water alleys were her best bet of finding these so-called 'friends.' *I'll find a way out of this glass prison and seek the water-taxi driver.*

Quen asked, "Can you show me to the Menagerie?"

Luz nodded and gestured for Quen to follow. *I don't want to harm them, but....* As they rounded a narrow and secluded path, Quen was about to make her move, but a deep voice boomed from behind.

"Hold up, you two. They sent me to guard the Doj'Anira." The voice came from a massive man, his arms as big around as one of Quen's thighs. He caught up and said, "Name's Hem. I'm with House Neyda, Ser Anu'Bida's personal guard, but he said I'm to watch over you today."

Guard me from harm, or ensure I don't flee? Quen closed her eyes and sighed. *I could have easily bested these small, unarmed women.* Hem wore a pair of khopesh in scabbards hooked to his waist belt, where he also stowed a belt knife. Without weapons, Quen couldn't best Hem in combat. She forced a wan smile. "Welcome to the party. We're headed to the Menagerie then."

Hem's golden-brown eyes widened, and his full lips curled in a smile. "There's perks to my job, yes. Only the Kovan family gets to even peek into the Menagerie. You must be real special, Doj'Anira, to get to go inside when you're not a Kovan."

Quen didn't feel special. *More like cursed.* But she remained silent and followed Caz and Luz through the sun-filled glass enclosed halls, Hem close on her heels.

They walked through a labyrinth of glass-enclosed halls and inner stone corridors. They finally arrived at a massive iron gate from which came bird calls and animal sounds. Caz opened the gate and gestured for Quen to enter. She made a sign with her hands that indicated she and Luz would stay, but Quen could go inside.

Quen entered the gates and assumed Hem would go with her, but he remained with the women.

"You came to make sure I won't escape, didn't you? So why aren't you coming with me?"

Hem smiled and chuckled. "'Cause there's no way out of the Menagerie 'xept through me." He crossed his arms over his bare, burly chest. "And if you try something in there, most likely you end up eaten, so be on your best behavior." Seeing Quen's frown, his eyes softened a bit. "Look at it this way, Doj'Anira. You get a rare peek at something most people'll never see. Enjoy it."

He had a point. *What was it Pahpi said about unpleasant tasks? 'Bask in Hiyadi's light when you can, for Vay'Nada's shadow hovers on the horizon.' Rhoji hates that saying.* Throat tight with welling emotion, Quen sighed and walked the stone path, passing glass enclosures containing exotic birds and unfamiliar beasts. Quen meandered through a maze of glass cages. Though separated from Quen by glass walls, the animals paced, panted, squawked, and chittered. The gentle birdcall swelled to a cacophony of nervous screeching. *My curse remains.* Her stomach churned from rich food mixed with growing unease with the place. *There is something unnatural at work here.*

The Menagerie ended at a massive enclosure built around a natural rock outcropping. Wildly overgrown vines and foliage filled the entire pen. Water trickling from the rocks created a peaceful background sound for the dark, cave-like cage.

The iron railing here was taller, at least an arm's reach over Quen's head. The rails were set more closely together, creating a pronounced prison-bar effect.

Quen searched high and low but saw nothing move within. *This pen must be empty.*

She was about to walk away but stopped when Nivi roared. He leaped out of the shadows, his white fur glistening in the sunlight. Though she knew he couldn't escape the enclosure, she jumped back. Nivi cleared the moat in one smooth stride, clearly undeterred by efforts to prevent him from approaching the bars. Up close, he was even larger than she'd thought he was.

Nivi stood as close to the rails as possible and stared at Quen. He roared again and paced back and forth by the bars, panting and making small chirps.

She didn't know what his calls meant. Seeing such a magnificent creature confined as he was, Quen's heart filled with sorrow. "Do you want to be free of this place?"

Nivi roared again.

"I wish I could free you, Nivi. But right now, I can't even free myself." She took a step closer to gauge his reaction.

Nivi sat on his haunches, still panting.

"Are you hot?" She held out her hand for him to smell her. Her fingers shook as she got closer.

Nivi sniffed at her and intently stared. He didn't bare his teeth.

She moved in a relaxed and deliberate way. *"Never stare a wild predator in the eye," Pahpi said.* Quen cast her gaze downwards. As her hand approached his nose, Nivi showed no sign he would nip her.

She touched his wet nose and, seeing he wasn't uncomfortable, Quen gently stroked his furry cheek and neck. Nivi blinked languidly, apparently content with her attention. Quen mimicked the slow blinking, hoping to show she was no threat.

Quen's hearts fluttered. She'd always wanted to pet an animal the way she saw people caress dogs, cats, and even drey and thukna. His fur was clean and fluffy. The bells hanging from his braided beard lightly jingled as she stroked him.

The anomaly on her neck tingled like a limb waking after falling asleep. She rubbed it and willed herself into a calmer state.

Quen knelt, slowly reached through the bars, and wrapped her arms around Nivi's neck. The big cat rubbed his head against hers through the bars, a deep rumble coming from his enormous chest.

Quen lay in the grass and petted Nivi. "You belong in a cage no more than I, Nivi." His braided beard jingled. "We are meant to roam." He purred, and when she stopped stroking, he nuzzled her hand for more affection.

She remained by his side, content in his company despite the sweltering heat of the late-afternoon suns. Nivi's wild heart was not afraid of the Nixan shadow soul Quen carried. "You're the first animal friend I've ever had, Nivi." Quen was happier than she'd been in weeks, at least so long as she kept herself from contemplating the fate that would befall her if she was unsuccessful at convincing the Exalted that Quen wasn't whatever she sought.

Suddenly, Nivi yelped and kneeled, his head on his front paws, his eyes downcast.

"He did not hurt you, did he?" Pelagia called.

Quen rose and wiped dirt and grass from her behind. She shook her head.

Pelagia wore pants fashioned from the skin of a ringed snake. Its red, gold, and black stripes now wound around Pelagia's thighs. On top, she wore a sleeveless shirt of light-tan-and-grey lizard skin. She wore no headdress, and her wrists and fingers were unadorned. It was odd to see her so plain compared to her usual elaborate dress.

Pelagia's pink skin glistened with sweat. She had a pair of smooth, finely tanned grey leather gloves in her hand, and she waved them at Quen. She sounded out of breath. "It is time for you to get ready to go to the Palace di Soli." Pelagia ran her hand along Nivi's nose. He stared up at Pelagia without lifting his head, his look contemptuous.

Quen couldn't explain how she knew it, but she was certain Nivi despised Pelagia. *He obeys against his will. I don't understand how Pelagia does it, but she controls him. And her control causes him pain.*

As this realization bloomed, Vatra's heat rose in her belly. *If only I could command Vatra.* She imagined hurling a ball of flame at Pelagia as she'd seen Imbica do. But acrid sweat was the only thing coming from her hands.

"Have you enjoyed your time in the Menagerie?"

Rhoji would play it cool and suck up to Pelagia. But Quen wasn't good at hiding her feelings. "Cages aren't really my thing." Her neck ridge buzzed like a beehive.

Pelagia's expression remained cool, unbothered by Quen's lack of enthusiasm for the animal prison the Dynasty was so proud of. "Most beasts here came to us ill, injured, or orphaned." She stared intently at Quen. "We fix broken things here."

"I'm not broken," Quen said.

Pelagia smiled. "Aren't you?" She cocked her head to the side and narrowed her eyes at Quen. "I wonder."

"And what of Nivi? He wasn't ill or broken. They forced him to leave his family. Same as me." Quen didn't want to cry, but thinking about the injustice of it all brought hot tears. Her hands were tight fists at her sides.

To Quen's surprise, tears swelled in Pelagia's eyes as well. "You are correct, Doj'Anira. Nivi is a rare beast and brought here from Tinox under the Exalted's order, as were you. It is not my law, Quen. I am but a spoke in the great wheel. My full purpose is unknown even to me."

225

Pelagia's sentiment seemed sincere, but Quen wasn't convinced she could trust the woman. The vision of Caz and Luz's nubs where tongues used to be made her wary. Besides, Nivi's venom toward the woman was unmistakable. Quen trusted the tiger more than she trusted a person who adorned herself with the bones and skins of others.

"Now is not the time for this conversation. Hem will escort you back to your chambers."

Quen was glad to be free of Pelagia's company for a while. The way she wavered between honeyed sweetness and unripe bitterness made Quen nervous.

"Do not dally. Caz and Luz await you." She called back over her shoulder, "And I will stop by your chamber before we leave to ensure the twins have properly prepared you."

Quen called after her, "How can women without tongues or the ability to speak properly prepare me for an audience with the Exalted?"

Pelagia stopped, and it looked as though she'd turn and answer. Instead, she resumed walking and acted as though she hadn't heard the question.

Quen knelt once more and held Nivi's face in her hands. "You belong in a cage no more than I, Nivi." His braided beard jingled sweetly as she petted him. "I promise you this. If I find a way out of this mess, I will come for you." She hoped she could keep this promise.

•   •   •

Hem escorted her through the palace's maze of corridors and guarded the door to her room. Once inside,

Luz was filling the bath with warm water while Caz poured in the scented oil. *I just bathed yesterday.* She'd never bathed two days in a row. "I suppose she told you to spiff me up, like a prized drey going to market." Her voice held a bitter edge.

Luz gestured to the bath and gave her a wan smile. The two women scrubbed Quen like a dirty tuber freshly plucked from the ground. They worked a lovely spice-scented oil into her hair and rolled it onto large bone rollers.

When they'd finished scraping away any lingering bit of Sulmére sand, they gently lifted her from the bath and wrapped her in a luxuriant robe of fluffy, baby-soft wool. Luz showed her to a seat, Quen's eyes drowsy from the warm bath.

While her hair dried, Caz worked on her face. People in the Sulmére didn't wear face paint. Caz used what looked like charcoal to draw lines above Quen's lashes. Caz took a small shallow footed bowl from her apron. She wet her pinky finger with a dab of water and rubbed it along the lip of the shallow bowl. Her finger turned dark red, and Caz wiped the color onto Quen's lips.

Once her face had been painted, Luz indicated she should get up, and Caz removed the cozy robe. Quen stood naked, her nipples hardened from the chilly air. Since the two women had attended to her every need, from serving her breakfast to cleaning her chamber pot, she was less inhibited than she'd been the day before, and she didn't cover herself.

Luz produced a dress of turquoise and aubergine silk. A tiny braid of silk secured the dress at the shoulders. The fitted turquoise bodice wrapped from the sides with a gauzy drape of purple silk flowing into a loose skirt, bits of turquoise silk showing through from underneath. Caz motioned for Quen to raise her arms so she could slide the dress on over her head. She did so, but Luz being at least a head shorter than her, there was no way she could reach over Quen's head.

"Give it to me. I can dress myself."

Luz hesitated and glanced behind to see if anyone was watching.

Quen held her hands out. "I've been dressing myself since I was a child."

The woman finally relinquished the dress. Quen shimmied into it and accidentally put her arm through one loop of silk that wound around from back to front, meeting at the waist. *Okay, so I did need help.* She'd never worn such a complicated garment. Quen righted the wrong and finally got the dress on correctly.

It fit like the silk undergarments her father had gifted her. Snug against her body, yet not constricting. She twirled around, enjoying the feel of the whisper-thin silk on her bare legs.

Caz motioned for her to look in the mirror. Quen gasped, barely recognizing the young woman in the glass.

Black kohl drew attention to the two distinctly different colors of her eyes. The dress fit like someone had made it from a mold of her body. Like fashions she'd seen in Qülla, the neckline was cut low enough to show nearly her entire tiny breasts, stopping above her nipples. Fabric draping from the sides made her waist appear even smaller, and the long, loose folds to her ankle made her look even taller.

If Pahpi saw me dressed like this, he'd probably throw a poncho over me. She smiled at the thought. Quen enjoyed seeing herself this way and hated that she liked it.

Luz presented her with a pair of silk slippers dyed to match the lavender of the dress's skirt and escorted her back to the chair. The two women unwound her hair from the bone rollers and brushed it through only once, her hair now nearly dry and slightly fuller as it flowed down her shoulders and back.

The door swung open, and Pelagia burst in, clattering as she walked. "Ah, good work." She waved her hand to dismiss the two.

Caz and Luz bowed their heads, lowered their eyes, and made their way from Quen's chambers. As they left, loneliness overcame her. *Even silent companions are preferable to the chattering noise of my thoughts.*

Quen was about to rise, but Pelagia said, "Stay put for a moment. I have something for you."

At first, Quen thought Pelagia's dress was creamy white embroidered silk. When Pelagia got closer, Quen realized the dress was made of teeth and bone, not fabric. The collar was an animal's vertebral column. The rest of the gown was constructed of tightly fitted row upon row of polished shark's teeth. As Pelagia moved, light shone off the polished teeth, making the ensemble glimmer. Tiny animal skulls covered her shoulders, giving the appearance of pauldrons.

Topping the ensemble, Pelagia wore the most elaborate headdress Quen had yet seen. Tiny pink, creamy white, and gold shells flowed from a small animal skull, forming a crown across her forehead. From the crown of skull and shells flowed a train of feathers. At the top of her head, the feathers were fluffy and snow white. As the train progressed down her back, the feathers became creamy white, golden brown and finally mutated through neutral colors. At the small of her back, the train ended in black feathers. Pelagia was both a walking vision of loveliness and a harbinger of death.

Pelagia carried a small brown velvet box. Her eyes twinkled as she opened it, revealing two lustrous gold ear cuffs. Pelagia removed a cuff and swept Quen's hair aside.

The draft on her neck made Quen's skin goose-pimpled. Pelagia's thin fingers were like ice as she wrapped the gold cuff around Quen's upper ear. She put the other gold band on the opposite ear.

Pelagia stood back a few paces and smiled. "You look lovely, dune blossom."

The cuffs pinched, and Quen tugged at her ear. "I'm not used to wearing jewelry." Her ears were hot under the bands. "Is this a fashion in Qülla, gold cuffs like these?"

"As a Doj'Anira, the bands befit your station." Pelagia brushed stray hair from Quen's eye. "Ah, now you are ready to meet the Exalted. I know what Xa'Vatra wants."

Quen met her gaze. "And you give it to her?"

Pelagia moved closer, the teeth of her dress rattling as she moved. Their faces nearly touched now. It was unsettling to have Pelagia within her intimate space.

"It is wise to give the Exalted exactly what she demands." Pelagia ran the back of her hand down Quen's bare arm. She moved her face closer, her lips at Quen's ear, the cold shark's teeth up against the skin of Quen's nearly naked chest. She whispered into Quen's ear. "Terrible things happen to people who do not know their place in this Dynasty."

Molten tightness seized Quen's core, but not in the same way it had when Aldewin touched her. Pelagia's caress brought fear, not excited anticipation. *I can never feel affection for a woman who presides over a palace of unwilling captives, their lives subject to her whim.*

Pelagia remained close, looking intently first at one of Quen's eyes, then the other. "If you were not Doj'Anira, I should like to have you for my own." Her voice was low and husky. Pelagia momentarily hovered near Quen, then pulled herself away with a sigh.

"Have me for your own?" Quen spat the words. "I'm a person, not a dreyskin to be traded at market."

Pelagia laughed. "Sulmére child. Such innocence." She grazed Quen's chin with a long, thin finger.

Quen jerked her face away.

Pelagia's eyes darkened, and her voice was a low whisper. "You have much to learn about life outside the sands."

"Maybe I don't want to learn." *Qüllanians are bound by silly customs and subject to the Exalted's whims. I'd never trade Jagaru freedom for silken luxury or an overstuffed bed.*

"Xa'Vatra, the Sixth Exalted of the Kovan Era, has choice. You do not. In fact, no one else has free will. We live only to serve her."

"You're in a sadder state than I am," Quen said.

Pelagia raised her eyebrows. "How so, dune blossom?"

"The Dynasty forced me into bondage. You chose it."

Pelagia laughed again, throwing her head back, her voice echoing off the tiles. "You still live by the illusion of options. So be it. Soon enough, you will learn what little choice anyone truly has."

This woman has been too long in Qülla. If Pelagia visited the Sulmére, she'd see how people could dwell in the sands their whole lives without once thinking about the capital or the Exalted. For all people in the Sulmére knew, the capital was ruled by a giant rat making decisions by spinning a wheel of fortune. The petty squabbles and territorial battles of the Exalted and the Mājas mattered little to the people of the Sulmére. *But there's no point arguing it with her.*

"Come, Quen. It is time for you to meet Xa'Vatra, your true master."

Doubt crept in like a shadowed beggar. *If even Pelagia considers herself a subject of this so-called Exalted, how can I expect this person to nullify her own edict?*

Quen fingered the back of her neck. Nausea swelled in her gullet, and chills ran along her spine. A fresh idea grew like a seedling planted in her mind. *I have a destiny.*

Gods, what destiny did you plan for me? Will my actions be in the name of peaceful Lumine or warring Hiyadi? She had no more answers about Rajani, dragons, or the Dragos Sol'iberi now than when she'd left Solia. *I still don't understand what being Doj'Anira really means, or what the Exalted wants with me.*

Quen gingerly pressed her fingers to the bony anomaly at the back of her neck. Visions of Vahgrin came to mind. Vatra fire ignited in her core. *I must flee this city.* She didn't know what the gods had planned for her. Frankly, it didn't matter. Quen had plans of her own. *Vahgrin, and any Rajani who compel him, will pay for their crimes.*

CHAPTER 14

Exalted Xa'Vatra had summoned Quen to the Palace di Soli, the height of opulence and grandeur in all Indrasi. Quen wanted to hope she was bound for honor, but the lingering malodorous stench of Qülla set her on edge. Thoughts of the mutilation endured by Caz and Luz—and poor Nivi's capture—made her insides roil. If she had any chance of escaping Qülla, she needed her audience with Xa'Vatra to go well. But Quen feared the Palace di Soli was, like Pelagia's Palace, a webweaver's trap, and she was the insect likely to get snared.

At the doorway where she'd entered the Palace with Imbica, Anu'Bida stood with Hem. Anu clapped his hands to his mouth, his eyebrows raised in astonishment. "Oh, Pelagia. The Exalted will be more than pleased." His eyes rode up and down Quen's body.

"Let us hope so." Pelagia faced Quen. "Anu and Hem will escort you to the palace. I will meet you there." The shark-tooth dress rattled as she walked swiftly away.

"This way." Anu held the door open for Quen.

Hem followed and stayed only a pace behind. Anu led them to a narrow sidewalk rounding to the back of the palace. It ended at a stone-paved landing beside a sheer cliff face.

They were at the edge of the city—the part that looked like a piece had been broken off. Above them loomed Mt. Néru. Quen couldn't see the Palace di Soli cradled in the land like a bit of stew resting in a spoon. She glanced over the edge, careful not to get too close for fear she'd slip on a bit of loose rock and tumble over the side.

Below was a chasm so deep the bottom was a dark void. *Reminds me of descriptions of Vay'Nada—the realm of the Shadow.* The waterfall's rushing water drowned all other sounds. The water appeared to drop off into nothingness as it toppled from Mt. Néru into the valley.

A large bronze gong stood between them and the chasm. Anu retrieved the hanging mallet and struck the gong. Its clatter echoed across the deep canyon.

Anu and Hem stood patiently, staring straight ahead as though the sight of a mountain suspended over them was so mundane as to be of no interest. Quen got a sore neck from straining to glimpse the palace. The structure was fascinating, but Quen was even more curious about the sort of people that lived in such a remarkable place.

"Be careful at the edge, Doj'Anira. If you fall, you will be dead before landing. The valley fills with poisonous vapor," Anu said.

A mountain in suspense. A palace precariously resting over a valley of poisonous gas. *Peculiar mechanics of nature—or machinations of the gods—have brought this to be.* She stepped away from the edge.

An updraft rustled the skirt of her dress. With the slight breeze came an awful odor of rotten eggs, the same smell that lingered inside the entire walled city.

"You there, back away from the edge," a man said. His voice was low and muffled, as though spoken through a rolled scroll.

The breeze picked up and brought with it an even fouler odor. Up from the chasm wafted a giant canvas balloon. Attached below was a flying boat of the sort used to traverse the canals.

Inside the boat was a round man wearing a leather sack about his head with a mask protruding forward into what looked like a long bird's beak. The man wore goggles of thick glass, and a long-sleeved grey suede shirt over long pants of the same material tucked into tightly laced black leather boots. Over the entire ensemble, he wore a long black leather coat. Not a speck of skin was exposed.

The gib-rig operator was a vision scarier than even a child's nightmare. *Why would Xa'Vatra allow someone so disfigured to drive a gib-rig to the palace?*

As the gib-rig floated to the edge, the squat man threw a lasso and landed it around the pole holding the gong on the first try. He pulled the rope and brought his flying boat to the chasm's edge.

With his face entirely covered, it was impossible to view the man's reaction to seeing Quen, Anu, and Hem. His breathing was loud and labored behind the mask. "Careful gettin' into the gib-rig." He offered Quen a hand.

Reluctantly, she accepted his aid, though she worried she was touching a diseased person. His glove was dry, the fingers stiff the way leather gets after years of use. The butterflies in her stomach eased when she got both feet inside the boat. She tried not to think about hanging in the air over a poisonous pit.

Anu entered the flying boat with the driver's help while Hem hoisted himself in. Quen's stomach flip-flopped as the small vessel swayed with Hem's considerable weight.

The driver undid the rope from inside the boat, and they floated up effortlessly and quickly, air whooshing by them. Quen felt as though her belly had dropped to her toes. She laughed a nervous, involuntary giggle.

Anu laughed as well, his nose ring jingling. "So, Pelagia's dune blossom can smile."

Quen didn't like how Anu ogled her chest. "I smile when there is something to smile about."

Anu'Bida took a tiny round bronze box with a colorful lid out of a pocket hidden inside his tunic. He pinched a snowy-white powder between two fingers and stuck the substance between his cheek and gum. "I would offer you some, but I suspect Pelagia would be cross with me if I delivered you to the Exalted in a swooning state of ecstasy." His pupils grew large. Anu stood, and the gib-rig wobbled. "Exhilarating, is it not?"

Quen remained silent, trying not to show fear as the gib-rig swayed with Anu's every move.

He threw his arms out to the side. "Ah, to fly." He had his eyes closed but opened them suddenly and looked gravely at Quen. "Enjoy this part."

"What? Watching you try to tip us over?"

He giggled as if he couldn't stop. "No, shite blossom, the flying. It is the best part of visiting the Palace di Solis." He flopped down and waved his hand in the air. "The rest will be all kiss this arse over here and talk behind your hand about that one over there. Bend and curtsey and try your best not to kiss the wrong arse or talk about the wrong person. And above all, never contradict the Exalted or anyone on the Conclave. Don't allow your face to express disagreement, no matter what shite spills from their mouths." Anu's expression had grown dark, his last words holding a distinct edge of bitterness.

"This must all be *so* exhausting for you."

Anu laughed maniacally. "Sarcasm?" He held his ribs as though the laughing pained him. "I didn't know that flotsam from the Sea of Dunes had the capacity for it."

Quen held herself erect, her chin out. "We people of the Sulmére have the capacity for many things."

Anu's lips turned up in a churlish smile. "Oh, I bet you do."

It wasn't how she'd meant her words to be taken. Quen sighed and decided it wasn't worth arguing with him. *Whatever he pinched from that tiny box has made him like a second-sitting drunk.*

Quen made the mistake of looking over the side of the gib-rig. The grounds of Pelagia's Palace, the Menagerie, and the landing pad zoomed away. Her head swam. She gripped the sides of the gib-rig.

"Have no fear, Doj'Anira. Lyas has not lost one. Yet."

Lyas snorted, the sound muffled by his mask. He ripped the goggles from his head, pulled the face mask down, and spat over the side. Though puffy and red from the horrid mask, Lyas's face was normal enough.

"Of course, there is always a first." Anu's dilated eyes twinkled with mischief.

Lyas whistled a mournful tune as he worked the ropes that steered the boat as it ascended. *Pahpi used to whistle as he worked, but his songs were always cheery tunes. Lyas sounds like he's headed to a Nilva pyre.*

The chilly air made Quen's flesh bumpy and her nipples taut beneath the gauzy fabric. She wished for her tunic, riding apron, and more than anything, her keffla. It wasn't so much from modesty. Pahpi always said bodies are gifts from Doj'Madi—the Great Mother—and not something to be ashamed of. But showing one's mouth to strangers was something a person in the Sulmére rarely did. It made her feel vulnerable and naked.

Hem kept his arms crossed over his broad chest, his face pinched into a scowl. He stared at Quen as if daring her to try for an escape.

Quen ignored Hem's persistent glare. She tried to forget she was flying in an impossible machine perched over a poison-filled chasm.

Lyas steered the gib-rig away from the black chasm and up over the lip of the sheer rock face. Ahead lay a verdant hill, tender green grass and moss-covered rocks.

Up and up, higher still, past a smaller cliff opening to a deep valley below. And within the verdant bowl was a glowing castle carved from the mountainside itself.

The palace was constructed of sunset-colored marble and stone. Golden pyramids capped soaring spires of red-gold. Intricate carvings, repeating the motifs Quen had seen in Qülla, covered the windows. Vines and birds, flowers, and bees. Soli were abundant, especially Hiyadi. In some depictions, he cradled Lumine like a lover. *Hiyadi might long for her, but everyone knows Lumine's heart yearns for Niyadi.* At least that was how people in the Sulmére told the story of Menauld's most well-known love triangle.

A grand portico, supported by giant marble columns, shone in Hiyadi's setting light. A massive staircase led to the entrance. On the ground below the stairs was a large stone landing around which stood several gib-rig operators by their rigs. All wore the same protective gear Lyas wore, and they'd removed their headwear as he had. A few smoked pipes. One lay across the seats of his gib-rig, taking a nap.

Lyas worked the ropes to open the hole in the top of the giant balloon. As he did, they descended, touching down in the middle of the stone landing pad. "Welcome to the Palace di Soli."

Above them, atop a stone staircase that seemed to go forever, the grand palace glowed like a burning ember in the setting sun's light.

"It's magnificent," Quen whispered.

Lyas gave Anu a hand, but he still wobbled as he disembarked. Anu slurred his words. "What, this old thing?" He waved his hand up at the castle. "It is just a hunk of rock." He drew near to Quen as she descended from the gib-rig. He whispered in her ear. "It's what's inside that will blow the Sulmére sand from your arse."

All eyes of the idle gib-rig operators were on them. A few mouths were agape as they took in Quen. She wasn't sure if it was because of her unusual height or eyes. Or perhaps the too-revealing slip of a dress Pelagia made her wear. Her cheeks colored.

No older than Quen, one young man took off his hat and bowed low to her.

Anu clapped his hands. "Here now, get yourself up."

The young man hastily stood, his face red.

"You best never let a member of the Kovan Dynasty see you do that to anyone who is not Kovan."

The man mumbled, "But the eyes—"

Anu pulled the man by the wrist and shoved him in front of Quen. "Do you see golden eyes here?"

The man shook his head. "'Pology. 'Pology."

Anu roughly dropped the man's wrist and shooed him away. The other gib-rig operators, at first unable to take their eyes off Quen, averted their gaze. They minded their own business in an overtly measured way.

Anu turned his attention to Lyas. "Where are the palanquins?"

Lyas chewed whatever wad of something was in his mouth and spat to the side. "No rides up the steps tonight."

Out of the flying boat, not a lick of air moved. A thin film of sweat had formed on Anu's upper lip. *Will his nasty sweat melt that beautiful purple from his lips?*

Anu raised his voice. "For the love of Niyadi's skinny ass, why are there no palanquins? You will fetch me one this instant. The Exalted awaits my delivery of this Doj'Anira."

A few other gib-rig operators bowed to Quen, and Anu looked as though his head would explode with anger. "Stop doing that. You do not bow to anyone but a Kovan. Why can you not understand?" He dabbed his brow with a silk handkerchief. "And why is no one fetching a palanquin?"

The young man who'd initially bowed said, "We heard the 'Xulted says no rides."

Anu snorted and stowed his handkerchief in his tunic's sleeve pocket. "I think you are all lazy and do not want to do your job. The Exalted will hear about this."

A young woman operator spat out tobacco juice. "Listen here, Ser, it ain't like that. My da said he heard the 'Xulted ordered no rides so visitors be thinking 'bout the glory of Hiyadi as they climbing the steps of Infinite Light. That's what the steps be called now."

The stone steps before them had been polished to a high sheen. The light of the two suns shone brightly off the stairs, making them glow as the palace did in the early evening light.

Anu clenched his jaw. He mumbled something under his breath that sounded to Quen like he said, "More shite here than on a baby's behind."

"What say you, Ser?" Lyas asked.

Anu'Bida harrumphed.

"You best get to climbing if you want to be at the Palace afore Hiyadi bids us all 'night." Lyas's face lit up, his dark eyes twinkling, and his ample cheeks dimpling.

Hem said, "I can carry you, Ser, if you need to rest your legs. You be small as a woman, and ole Hem can get you up."

Anu's glare at Hem could have withered even the sturdiest desert vine. His face was so red it was nearly purple. "I am no invalid. You will walk behind." He pulled a small vial from his pocket, filled his long pinky nail with pale-blue powder, and sniffed it up his nose. Anu wiped a bit from the tip of his nose and licked it from his fingers. "Come, Doj'Anira. Apparently, we are destined to climb this together."

241

The stairs were more than ample enough for two people to walk side by side. They were shallow and easy to climb, but copious. Clad in silk slippers that barely qualified as shoes, Quen slipped on the first stair of slick stone and nearly went down.

Anu'Bida rolled his eyes.

"Should I carry the Doj'Anira?" Hem asked.

Anu's voice was pitchy. "For the love of Lumine's tits, you are not carrying anyone, you cumbersome oaf. What has gotten into you tonight?"

Hem looked genuinely taken aback by his master's chastisement. "I only thought—"

"I do not pay you to use the jelly inside your thick skull, Hem." Anu held out his arm to Quen. "Give me your hand. They'll throw me into a dark cell if you crack open your head on the way to the Palace."

Anu's hand was clammy, but she was glad for his help to steady her. They climbed with Hem trailing a few steps behind.

The stone at the bottom of the stairway of Infinite Light had been pearly-pink. As they climbed higher, the color changed to light orange, then darker, and higher above them still were stones of deep red.

Anu stopped to rest, and Quen looked behind them. The stairway had narrowed as they rose. The narrowing gave the stairs the appearance of being higher than they were. There were many stairs, to be sure. She had already counted over one hundred. But the effect from below was of a stairway to the heavens.

"Contemplate Hiyadi," Anu grumbled. He dabbed at his sweat again as he panted. He looked up at her. "Do people of the Sulmére not sweat?"

Quen shrugged. Her legs were slightly tired, but the climb was more exhilarating than tiring. Smooth, even steps were a blessing compared to climbing sandy dunes. *If not for these silly slippers, I'd be in the palace by now.*

Anu stowed his handkerchief. "Ah, to be young."

As they walked, Quen did contemplate, though not Hiyadi as the Exalted intended. Instead, she imagined a roleplay of what she would say to the woman who held Quen's freedom in her hands. She tried out demanding release, but knew it wouldn't work. She was in no position to order anything. Quen could beg, but that was no more likely to achieve freedom than commanding. As they neared the top, she concluded that her only hope was to argue it was all a mistake. She would have to prove she was not whatever the Exalted Xa'Vatra hunted. *What is she searching for?*

The stairs narrowed, and finally, there was room for only one. Anu gestured for her to go ahead of him.

Quen stepped onto a grand walkway paved with smooth grey stones. The mundane stone contrasted starkly with the luxurious marble of the stairway.

As if expecting her question, Anu said, "The stones in this plaza are from the beginnings of the Kovan age. Each ruler has left them here to remind of how their ancestors struggled to bring order to Indrasi and unite the provinces under one liege."

Given the affluence she had seen so far, it was difficult for Quen to imagine the Kovan family toiling at anything. They appeared to have plenty of servants struggling on their behalf.

A grand staircase of creamy white marble curved up on each side. She followed Anu up the left side of the stairs. Red silk curtains covered the walls and billowed in the breeze. As they climbed even more stairs, faint sounds of lively, toe-tapping music grew louder. High, melodious flutes fluttered over dulcimer stringed instruments all in time with deep, mellow drums. If Quen had been there under different circumstances, she would have liked to twirl, feeling the dress's silk against her bare legs. The music made her daydream, if only for a moment, of swaying to the sultry music with Aldewin.

She shook her head and took a deep breath. *Aldewin's not here. I'm alone in this beautiful but terrible place.*

At the top of the stairs, an expansive landing was empty save for guards posted at a wide-open doorway to a massive room. A glass dome topped the hall's soaring ceiling, giving the appearance of the room being open to the sky. Twilight's pink light bathed Xa'Vatra's court in a rosy glow.

Rectangular tables were arranged in a semicircle, divided by a wide aisle. People dressed in fashions like Quen had seen in Qülla filled the seats. There were no long tunics, kefflas, riding aprons, or long pants of rough-spun or linen. A few well-endowed women left little but their nipples covered, and both women and men sported bare midsections and shoulders and showed ample leg. Gold bracelets jingled, and rings glinted in the candlelight of the tables.

Anu'Bida held his head high as he escorted Quen up the middle aisle, leaving Hem in the hall with the guards. As they moved forward, a hush came over the crowd. Quen felt their eyes on her. Their whispers were like the buzz of a cornered desert rattler.

Anu whispered, "Pay the onlookers no mind, Doj'Anira. They may whisper and even gawk. They will pretend they are better than you in public, but most would give anything to be you."

Quen couldn't imagine why anyone would want to be her—a prisoner who might end up a tongueless thrall. "And the rest? The ones who don't wish to be in my shoes?"

Anu gave her a sideways smile. "The rest fear you."

The concept that anyone would fear her, a woman in bondage, was stranger still. "Why would anyone fear me?" Anu didn't know her, but anyone who did would likely find the idea laughable. *At least anyone who's seen me try to mount a kopek.*

They were near the end of the walkway. Anu ignored her question.

Before them was a raised platform of red marble. In the middle was a small table with a large wooden seat carved with Hiyadi and inlaid with solid gold. The chair was empty, at least for now.

Disappointment filled Quen. She'd hoped she could speak with Xa'Vatra right away, but the Exalted wasn't even at her own feast. *I wanted to get this over with.* The need to rejoin the hunt for Vahgrin was a persistent nagging itch, ever present in her deepest thoughts. Pondering the hunt for Vahgrin made her Nixan heart flutter, and her neck ridge tingled.

Quen reached for Still Waters. *Bide your time, Quen. Patience is your only ally in this.*

To each side of the raised dais was a long table with vacant chairs. Pelagia had spoken of the Conclave, presumably Xa'Vatra's inner circle. *I bet the empty seats are for the Conclave.*

At the end of the middle aisle was a man dressed in a silk tunic and pants, much like what Anu wore, though the silk wasn't as finely spun. He wore a pale-pink sash across his body, pinned at his waist. His hair was pulled into a high bun.

Anu stopped and held out his arm, motioning for Quen to halt. The man whispered something into Anu's ear, and Anu whispered back. The man's eyebrows rose, but only for a moment before he composed his face into a stoic mask.

"Please welcome Anu'Bida di Māja Wix, guest of Mistress Pelagia."

People banged their water cups on the table and said, "Welcome, son of Hiyadi," and cheered.

"At the Mistress's request, the Exalted grants accommodation for Ser Anu'Bida di Māja Wix to accompany honored guest Quen Tomo Santu di Sulmére, pursuant to Edict 42, a Doj'Anira."

The assembled gasped, followed by hushed whispers and pointing. No one cheered or bid Quen welcome. It would have bothered her if she cared what these strange people thought.

The man in the pink sash gestured for Anu and Quen to sit at a table on the left. Their table was closest to the aisle and directly in front of the dais. Quen had the best seat in the house to see Xa'Vatra.

They'd barely sat before a young serving woman wearing only flowing silk pants and long hair to cover the tips of her breasts came bearing a cold pitcher of wine. Anu turned Quen's wine glass over.

"Apologies, Doj'Anira, but by strict order of the Mistress, you are to have no wine this evening."

The young woman was about to walk away, but Anu objected loudly. "Is my cup upside down?" He held his wine glass up for her to see. "Pour liberally, voiceless hen, or I shall inform your master of your error."

The woman hastily poured his cup full, her eyes downturned. She waited for him to take a drink, then she topped off his goblet before she glided away to fill more glasses.

"Do all servants have their tongues cut out?"

Anu drank deeply from the wine goblet. He dabbed the corners of his mouth with the orange silk napkin. "Only the women."

"How awful." Her heart picked up speed as she worried she would be next to lose her tongue. "Why not the men?"

Anu used a small silver spoon to scoop kikoi nuts into his hand, and he popped them into his mouth. He didn't bother to swallow before speaking. "Oh, the men lose something else." He looked down at his lap and pointed to it. "If you get what I mean." Seeing the aghast look on Quen's face, he chortled. "What, they don't take the fortitude of male servants in the Sulmére?"

Quen wasn't sure which was worse, losing speech or of the ability to—well, to leave one's mark on the world. "We don't have servants in the Sulmére."

Anu faked a shudder. "Why, you practically live second era Dune Blossom."

After her time in the capital, Quen couldn't argue against what he said. It was as though Solia and Qülla were of two different times and places. "Why a woman's tongue and a man's, er—"

"Surely you have seen kopeks lose their stones. Does it not make them more docile? Men are no different. Besides, they say Xa'Vatra takes from each condemned that which they cherish most. Women love to talk and men to, eh—Well, I do not think I need to tell you."

"Not all women like to talk." Quen wasn't sure she believed what she said, though. Being around girls and women from the herdclans, and Dini and other women in Solia, she couldn't recall meeting a woman who didn't enjoy chatter.

Anu popped more nuts into his mouth and shot her a disbelieving look. He took a sip of wine, moved closer, and whispered, "Of course, there are other uses for a woman's tongue, so perhaps both men and women lose something equivalent, eh?" His eyes were lazy from the alcohol, and his smile too vulgar for Quen's liking.

They announced more guests, and the crowd welcomed them with cheers, some more enthusiastically than others. When the seats were nearly full, the man in the pink sash announced a name Quen knew.

"Please welcome Kovatha Imbica di Tikli, guest of the Exalted Xa'Vatra."

The welcome was reserved. Quen noticed Imbica's back stiffen, her chin thrust out in prideful defiance.

Anu lightly tapped his cup once and quietly clapped a few times. "Skeeving little climber," he hissed under his breath. "I am surprised the Exalted bothers to honor Imbica in public for bringing you to the capital."

As much as Quen detested Imbica, she didn't agree with Anu's assessment of her. Perhaps the woman was a social climber, as he and Pelagia said. But Imbica had battled Vahgrin and lived to tell the tale. Quen doubted either Anu or Pelagia would survive such an encounter. *With a dragon circling Indrasi's skies, they might consider adjusting their priorities.*

A low gong interrupted the buzzing babble of nearly a hundred people speaking at once. The room went silent save for the gong's echo.

Quen had been mindlessly eating olives. She wiped her fingers and sat up straighter, looking around to see what the hush was about.

At the back of the room, a brilliant ball of light appeared. It bounced first off one wall, then swirled to the other, dancing around the assembled guests.

People laughed and pointed. A few clapped like giddy children.

As the light moved forward up the aisle, two men followed behind. The first man, bent with age, had milky eyes and walked with an ornately carved black cane with a copper knob. Quen had never seen such a long beard. Silken black embroidery edged his deep-crimson robes, and a broad gold silk cummerbund was wrapped around his waist. On his head was a round box-style hat of the same crimson and black, embroidered with a golden Hiyadi. Painted in red between his eyes was the mark of Vatra Pillar. It was merely a sun, the symbol of Hiyadi, painted so it appeared as a third eye. Niyadi and Lumine were missing from the mark.

This is what Rhoji told me about changes the Dynasty has made. Kentaros used to display their devotion to Vaya di Solis by wearing the Trinity symbol.

"Who's the old man?" Quen asked.

"Prelate Vidar of Val'Vatra Pillar. He's a legacy member of the Conclave." Anu sniffed. "But probably not for long."

At first, Quen thought Prelate Vidar made the light. But the Prelate held his cane in one hand, and the other remained at his side. Behind him walked a much younger man, about Rhoji's age, Quen guessed. With golden hair to his shoulders, he, too, wore a round box-style hat of crimson, though it was not as richly embroidered as Vidar's. He wore a short wrap-style tunic in crimson linen over black linen pants to his knees.

As Qülla's fashion dictated, the man had a clean-shaven face. With an outstretched hand, he controlled the ball of magical light.

When the two men approached the dais, Quen gasped.

"What is it?" Anu asked, his mouth full of olives.

Quen's breaths were shallow, her heart like a stampeding thukna herd. *How can this be?*

Anu's eyes grew wide with alarm. "Speak to me, Doj'Anira. Please, by Hiyadi's light, tell me you have not been poisoned."

Still unable to speak, she shook her head. She took a sip of water. "I'm—fine."

Everyone now standing, they bowed. Though still playing, the musicians genuflected.

Prelate Vidar bowed.

And Aldewin bowed.

CHAPTER 15

Wild cheers, shouts, and cup pounding filled the grand hall of the Palace di Soli. Like rowdy herders during Solia's summer festival, Xa'Vatra's guests cheered, their voices echoing off the stone walls and glass dome. Raucous exuberance replaced elegant restraint.

Quen's two hearts thumped wildly with renewed hope. *Aldewin is here, and if he's here, maybe Rhoji is, too. I'll escape the bonds of being Doj'Anira tonight.*

Still standing, Anu'Bida pulled her arm. "Bow to the Exalted, dune blossom."

She wanted to call to Aldewin, but she couldn't acknowledge him. He was Jagaru, not a member of Xa'Vatra's court. *He must be here by subterfuge.*

Aldewin directed the mage light to the throne. The musicians played a fanfare, and a circle of young women wearing only cocourie shell belts danced gracefully before the throne.

Bowed low, Aldewin caught Quen's eye. After giving her a nod, he focused on the throne above.

Aldewin saw me. He came to help me.

The water-taxi driver—what had she said? "You have friends in the capital."

It took a colossal effort not to go to him. *Still Waters, Quen.* She had no idea how Aldewin had gotten past the Niri Bridge and infiltrated Xa'Vatra's court. He looked like he belonged in the palace, though, and the observation renewed her belief that Aldewin was more than what he claimed. But she'd take those questions up with him once they were beyond Qülla's walls.

Anu again yanked on her. "Bow!" he hissed.

Quen stood tall. They'd wrongly imprisoned her. *They're the criminals, not me. I won't bow to injustice.*

She glanced to her right and realized the eyes she felt were Imbica's. Though Imbica bowed like the others, her dark eyes bored into Quen. The mere gaze brought memories of the searing pain of being cooked from the inside out.

Pride be damned, Quen. Bow before Imbica burns you again. Quen grudgingly bowed.

From behind the throne, a woman approached the raised platform. She held Quen's life in her hands. Quen had planned to reason with her—woman to woman.

As soon as Quen glimpsed Xa'Vatra, doubts arose about her plan to talk her way out of confinement. Many considered the Exalted the representative of the god Hiyadi on Menauld. The vision of Xa'Vatra rising from the shadows made Quen believe it could be true.

A gold headdress spread from the crown of Xa'Vatra's head like sun rays. Her flawless, dewy brown skin highlighted golden eyes so bright they glowed. With eyelids and lips painted gold, Xa'Vatra's face shimmered like twilight on rippling water. Quen gasped at Xa'Vatra's beauty, the personification of Hiyadi's heavenly light.

The tight-fitting bodice of the Exalted's sleeveless dress clung to her bosom. It looked as though the artisans who'd carved the palace's lacy stonework had cut similar patterns from thin sheets of gold to create the dress's fabric. Xa'Vatra's bronzed skin showed through the cutouts.

As she stood on the raised dais before her throne, the room stilled. Xa'Vatra surveyed the assembled, her face calm as she scanned the room. The Exalted nodded to the man in the pink sash.

His voice rang out louder and more robust than before. "Behold Her Eminence, born Néru Kovan, daughter of Sunya, raised to Exalted in the auspicious year 1444 of Hiyadi's Third Epoch, crowned Xa'Vatra, ruler of Indrasi and Exalted over all. Exalted Xa'Vatra welcomes her guests to Palace di Soli in this tenth month of the year 1449."

With a loving voice like a mother to her children, Xa'Vatra finally said, "Rise, beloveds."

The Exalted gracefully lowered herself to her throne, and the guests returned to their seats. They murmured hushed whispers until someone pounded a glass. That was enough to urge the assembled to renew their cheers, whistles, and pounding in admiration for their leader. Xa'Vatra nodded and basked in the ongoing adulation.

After many minutes of cheering and adoration, Xa'Vatra raised a single slim hand, and everyone quieted. The pink-sashed man announced Xa'Vatra's Conclave: Xa'Vatra's sisters, Nyx and Morana; her brothers,

Djeuthui and Hauké; her husband, Asar; and last, Prelate Vidar. They didn't announce Aldewin, and he was nowhere to be seen. *I hope he remains nearby.*

Also joining the Conclave at the upper table were Xa'Vatra's five children. *She doesn't look old enough to have one child, let alone five.*

Once the family was seated, Xa'Vatra rang a tiny gong with a small mallet. More topless servers, both female and male, sashayed into the hall from behind the tiger's eye columns encircling the room. They carried trays of lightly fried orange slices, creamy cheese, and thin slices of bread.

Servants took the first platter to Xa'Vatra's table. A woman stepped from behind the Exalted, inspected the food, and tasted a bit of each item. After a few moments, she nodded, then returned to the shadows. Waitstaff placed some of each type of food on the Exalted's plate.

Servers circulated around the room, dishing similar food to each guest. No one ate until Xa'Vatra had taken her first bite, then everyone happily dug in.

Quen was unsure about cooked oranges, but she devoured a plum-like fruit in two bites and downed the lightly buttered bread as if it were air.

"Be slow with eating," Anu'Bida said.

Quen finished the bite of bread in her mouth. "Why? Are my manners too Sulmére for you?"

Anu put down his fork. "No, because there are five courses in this feast to match the five Corners. This is but the first. If you stuff yourself now, you will be sad when you cannot taste the delicacies offered at the end."

"Five corners? But there are only four." She stuffed bread into her mouth, not heeding Anu'Bida's warning. Her perpetually hollow stomach growled for more.

"I keep forgetting you are from the south." He took a long draw of wine. "Enara, Vatra, Doka, Qüira, and the Exalted is the fifth." He used his fingers to create a rough pyramid shape. "She is the pinnacle."

"But…"

He shot her a shushing look. "Look around you, dune blossom," he hissed. "Is anyone questioning the pronouncement that there are now five corners rather than four?"

Quen swallowed a wad of bread. "But—"

Anu'Bida's withering look cut her off. His voice was a hoarse whisper. "Sycophants do not question because they curry favor. By Niyadi's skinny arse, some of them will even come to believe what they're told because they choose not to think for themselves."

Quen glanced around the room. "These people change their beliefs solely because she says to?"

Anu sipped his wine and dabbed his painted lips. "Others know the truth but choose to go along because they fear losing the few crumbs the Exalted allows them." His eyes fixed on the dais, and he tipped his wine cup toward Asar, Xa'Vatra's husband. "Still others go along with the fictions because they bide their time, waiting for an opportunity. If you hold your tongue, you live to see another day. Tomorrow often brings an opening when one did not exist the day before."

Quen quietly considered what he'd said. "And in which of these three groups do you belong?"

He drained his cup. Anu'Bida snapped his fingers at a wine bearer and ignored Quen's question. "Take care what you say of the Corners in this palace."

No person, not even an Exalted, could make themselves a guardian spirit or god ruling over a realm of elemental energy. As far as Quen knew, the elements were already spoken for. But it sounded like Anu'Bida talked from experience, so she took his advice and let the topic go.

Anu adjusted his hoop nose ring, the chain connecting it to his ear lightly clinking. His voice lost its ominous and reprimanding tone. "The point is, there are five courses of food tonight as there are five Corners." He leaned closer and whispered, "At least there are five in Qülla." He winked at her.

As soon as the food servers vacated the room, the musicians rejoined, bringing a half-dozen women dancers. The dancers' lithe bodies undulated, bare save for the wide gold belts worn low on their hips and rows of bells on their ankles. Their hair was tightly braided and adorned with colorful beads. As they whipped their heads and danced around the room, their hair beads and ankle bells created their own music.

The crowd clapped and laughed as the dancers whirled about the room. As the musicians finished the song, the nearly naked dancers twirled in a frenzy, their long, braided hair whipping as they spun.

During the entire dance, Xa'Vatra ignored the show and her food. She talked to her sisters, seated to her right, as though there were no other people in the hall. Seated to her left and below, her husband Asar stared at the dancers and drank heavily.

When the music stopped, the dancers stood in a circle, back-to-back, their arms swept up. Quen clapped, but no one else did. There was only silence.

Interrupted from her conversation, Xa'Vatra barely took notice of the dancers, but gave a polite clap using her left hand on the back of her right. That was all the raucous crowd needed to pound their cups and cheer.

As soon as the dancers exited, waiters came with another course of food. They followed the same ritual as before, giving it first to Xa'Vatra's taster, then once approved, serving the hall.

This course was a savory fish dish of whole salmon stuffed with saffron-spiced rice with a delicate creamy sauce on the side. As soon as Quen smelled the fish, her stomach growled. She'd eaten the equivalent of what she'd ordinarily eat for two meals for the first course. Yet, the enticing aroma of spiced fish renewed her hunger.

Anu picked at his fish, taking small bites. He dabbed his mustache with his napkin. "Where are you putting this food, Doj'Anira?"

Quen shrugged. "Perhaps I am growing still." She finished the fish as a half-dozen jugglers and acrobats entertained the hall.

The third course consisted of roasted fowl with spiced apples. It surprised Quen that the Exalted allowed mundane fowl at such a decadent banquet. *In the Sulmére, it isn't a feast until we've eaten a whole roasted drey.*

She asked Anu about it, and he told her the Exalted liked to eat things that fly. It made her think about how Pelagia kept talking about flying and the gib-rigs.

"Is the entire city of Qülla obsessed with flying?"

Anu pointed to the dais with his cup. "Not so much enamored with flying itself as with the things that fly."

I doubt Xa'Vatra would be so smitten if she was staring down Vahgrin's gaping maw.

257

After everyone enjoyed the fowl course, the pink-sashed man announced the next entertainment. Quen expected mummers like they had at feasts in Solia. Instead, a portly, middle-aged man carrying a large wine bottle entered. Two younger men followed the wine merchant. One of the young men had black hair falling to nearly his mid-back. And in his ear, a single blue feather earring.

Quen shot to her feet. Her throat tight with emotion, she called, "Rhoji." Her voice came out in a hoarse whisper, but joy soared within.

"Sit, Doj'Anira," Anu hissed. "It is rude beyond measure to stand before Xa'Vatra has stood."

She allowed Anu to pull her to her seat. It was probably a good thing her voice had come out thin and not carried. *First Aldewin, now Rhoji. They didn't forsake me. Does this mean our entire Jagaru pod is here?* She hoped Anu didn't notice how flushed from excitement she was. She cautiously wiped sweaty palms on her silk dress, not caring it would create unsightly puckers in the fabric.

Rhoji was with a Bardivian wine merchant. He didn't look in her direction as he went about his business. As the merchant spoke with Xa'Vatra and Asar, Rhoji worked the Kovan women's side of the dais with his flashy smile, polite conversation, and filling their cups.

Quen couldn't guess how they got Rhoji into the palace with the wine merchant. It took great restraint not to run to him. *He risked himself to help me.* Even if they ultimately failed, it gladdened her heart that her brother had come for her.

Rhoji was in his element. Morana favored him with a smile and made sure their hands touched as he poured her more wine. Rhoji gave Morana a sultry look beneath long, thick lashes. Born to live a courtly life, Rhoji played his part well. *Is he playing the game well? Or is he here to woo the court, not help me escape?*

Once at the end of the table, Rhoji gave Quen an inconspicuous nod. She trembled with relief. *He's my First Kin. Of course he's here to help me.* His acknowledgment gave her relief and gladdened her heart.

The fourth course of cheeses, fruits, nut spreads, and thin baked bread arrived. A tight knot of anticipation seized Quen's gut. *What have Rhoji and Aldewin planned?* She picked at the food placed before her, the excitement of what was to come overshadowing her hunger.

Copious wine drinking fortified Anu's appetite. He ate more with each course.

The hall buzzed with politely whispered conversation, but soon a hush fell as a chorus of birdsong swelled. Small yellow finches circled tables then flew toward the ceiling. Larger birds with long red tails and crowns of black feathers followed. Flying in a similar pattern, they joined the finches in an intricately choreographed flight.

Xa'Vatra ended her conversations, her eyes gleaming with delight as she watched the birds circle over her head.

Two more birds flew in from the right. Their feathers were pure black, their eyes golden, and gold bands adorned their necks. Their wings were nearly five feet across when outstretched, and they whistled to each other as they swooped low by the tables in front, one almost grazing Quen's head. They circled near the Exalted before soaring to the palace's glass ceiling.

Xa'Vatra clapped her hands, not politely as she had before, but with the zeal of a fan cheering a favorite team of thukna roping at a Sulmére feast.

After the birds came more flying creatures, but this time small ones. A swarm of purple and gold butterflies swirled in a column of shimmering color in front of Xa'Vatra's table. Hundreds of delicate wings fluttered, creating a light breeze.

The butterflies spread and flew up, revealing Pelagia.

The crowd gasped, and Xa'Vatra clapped loudly, her face afire with delight. Pelagia bowed deeply, the shark's tooth dress rattling as she moved.

"Rise, Mistress of the Menagerie."

Pelagia did as told, then turned to the crowd and blew a kiss to each side of the room. She turned back to Xa'Vatra and made a low chirping sound.

Nivi roared and bounded to Pelagia's side. The bells in his mane jingled as he ran. As he approached Pelagia, she motioned him up with her hand, and he did as commanded, standing on his hind legs. He towered above Pelagia and roared again. He made a full circle before dropping to all fours.

Nivi roared again before sitting beside Pelagia like a dutiful dog. Xa'Vatra continued to clap, her smile as wide as a child's.

"Bravo," she said. "You have outdone yourself, Mistress. And you brought Nivi, a court favorite." The assembled cheered loudly and whistled appreciation for Nivi. "But I hear you brought me something exceptional."

Pelagia bowed her head. "I humbly accept your praise, Exalted, but I can hardly take the compliment for myself alone." She lifted her hands to the sky to indicate the birds and butterflies overhead, bringing on another round of applause. She then pointed to Nivi, and the crowd cheered loudly again for him.

Xa'Vatra raised her hand, and all fell instantly silent. "Keep me in suspense no longer. Where is my new Doj'Anira?"

Quen bristled at her use of 'my' regarding her. Before the night was over, she intended to make sure everyone knew she was no one's property.

Pelagia turned, her eyes immediately finding Quen. "Come forward, Doj'Anira."

Quen sat stone still. Sweat dripping down her back made the silk dress cling to her.

Anu'Bida nudged her with his elbow and whispered, "Go to her."

Quen rose on shaky legs. She used the table to steady herself, then came forward. Her ribs ached with a band of anxiety. *This is my chance.* She stood tall, collecting herself as she walked.

The room was so silent she could have heard a hair drop from her head. She made her way slowly, Xa'Vatra's golden eyes on her the whole time, appraising her.

Once Quen was at Pelagia's side, Pelagia said, "I present the first Doj'Anira found in the Sulmére Province. And the first with one blue eye the color of pure Enara waters." She bowed low, and the crowd gasped.

Pelagia pulled on Quen's hand, trying to get her to bow. When Quen didn't take the hint, Pelagia whispered, "Bow to the Exalted, Quen."

But Quen refused to bow.

Xa'Vatra sat forward in her chair, her eyes glowering at Quen. "Do you refuse your master's command?"

No longer whispering, Pelagia said, "Bow to the Exalted, Doj'Anira."

Quen didn't move.

Xa'Vatra rose, and the pink-sashed man strode toward Quen. "You will bow to the Exalted."

"I am a free person of the Sulmére, and in the Sea of Sands, we bow to no one."

The crowd gasped for a second time, then a murmur of disbelief followed by hisses of disdain.

Quen's heart pounded, but she felt better than she had in weeks. She was a woman of the dunes, lost in a sea of excess and strange customs. Her beloved Pahpi was dead, her home destroyed. A dragon hunted her, and a ruler condemned her. *My only crime is being unlike others.* She had little left except her life. *I'll lose that too before bowing to someone claiming ownership of me.*

She hadn't stopped to think that she might have ruined the escape plan Aldewin and Rhoji had made. But it was too late to backtrack. She stood firm and unbent.

Xa'Vatra's eyes were wide and dark with anger. Her voice was low and seething. "Mistress, you have my permission to discipline the Doj'Anira."

Pain twinged Quen's ears as if a wasp had stung her. Quen tugged at her right ear, but the sensation leaped from ear to chest. *It's like someone slammed Fano's forge hammer into my bosom.*

Pelagia's voice was a low growl. "Lower yourself before the Exalted, or soon this pain will be a fond memory of better days."

Quen gasped for air, sure her chest was empty of life-giving breath. Instead of receding, the pain grew steadily worse as it traveled from chest to navel. Pelagia had filled

Quen's body with Juka's sky-fire, and the agony permeated her lower gut.

It wasn't the same as the immolation visited on her by Imbica. It was worse.

I'll do anything to stop this agony.

She would do anything to make it stop. Quen bowed low, not because she'd been told to, but because the excruciating pain doubled her over.

Xa'Vatra clapped with apparent delight, and the crowd did the same. "Bravo, Mistress. Bravo," the Exalted said. After forcing both to bow for a moment, she said, "Rise, Mistress. Rise, Doj'Anira."

Pelagia rose first and ended her torturous spell. Quen slowly rose up, still unsteady from the torture. Because Pelagia had displayed no command of the corners, Quen had assumed the woman had no magical skill. *But how else can she command animals and fill my veins with sky-fire?*

Quen touched the gold band on her ear. It was warm. She'd been so swept up in the evening's energy she hadn't put it together. The gold bands adorning Quen's ears were the same as the ones on Nivi's neck and the necks of the birds flying overhead. The mechanism of the bands was still unknown, but they had to be involved in Pelagia's control of the animals. *And now me.*

Trying to dislodge the gold cuff, she tugged at her ear again, but it didn't budge. Somehow, the gold had bonded to her.

"I understand we have one of my Kovathas to thank for this acquisition. Kovatha Imbica. Come forward."

Imbica quickly but soundlessly strode to the front and tried to stand beside Pelagia, but Nivi snarled and showed his teeth. Xa'Vatra and her sisters laughed, as did her children. Imbica was forced to stand a bit to the right of Pelagia and gave Nivi a wide berth.

"Kovatha Imbica, please tell the Conclave how you found this Doj'Anira. And do not skip a single detail." Xa'Vatra leaned forward, her chin resting on her hands, her face rapt with attention.

Imbica told the tale accurately, from first encountering Druvna's Jagaru, to the wagon journey north over the Niri Bridge and the bumpy ride in Besha's cart. She even told about the run-in with Vahgrin. This part of the story drew gasps but also jeers and laughs from the assembled court. The Conclave tittered at that part as well, though Xa'Vatra didn't. Her face was a veritable mask throughout the telling, her gold eyes unflinching as she listened.

Imbica left the immolation out of her story. *Will Xa'Vatra ask me to verify Imbica's story? If so, I intend to set the record straight.*

"Druvna appears in this tale, huh? I thought I'd sent him to my dungeons to rot. Has our jailer Cinwa become lax?" She sipped wine and gave the air a wave of her hand. "I will deal with old Druvna another day." She pointed to the scribe hovering behind her. "Note that."

The scribe hurriedly dragged her quill across a parchment while Xa'Vatra returned her attention to Imbica. "Kovatha Imbica, you had quite a journey. Such bravery with the dragon." Her voice dripped with sarcasm.

Imbica bowed her head. "I did my duty to the Dynasty."

"Oh, and modest too." There was mock enthusiasm in her voice. "Do tell me, Kovatha, did you deliver this Doj'Anira unharmed to the Mistress of the Menagerie?"

Imbica shifted. "Yes, Exalted." She bowed again.

Xa'Vatra sat forward again, her golden eyes wide and piercing. "You did not use immolation on this property of the Dynasty on at least one occasion."

Another collective gasp from the assembled.

Imbica stuttered. "I tried to... But the Doj'Anira attempted to—"

Xa'Vatra shot to her feet, towering over them. "Did the Edict say you were permitted to damage *my* property?"

"No, Exalted One." Imbica bowed low.

"No. I should say it did not. As Kovatha, you know the penalty for intentional damage to Dynasty property."

Imbica threw herself to her knees, her hands clasped in front of her. Tears welled in her eyes. "Please, Exalted One. I beg of you. I am Kovatha, a faithful servant to the Dynasty. There is no one more devoted to your service than I."

Xa'Vatra let out a throaty laugh. "You already proved yourself unfaithful, Imbica. Why would I keep around such a disloyal, Cornerless fool?"

Because she might be the only mage in Indrasi who can defeat Vahgrin.

The Exalted plopped into her chair and steepled her fingers beneath her chin. "What say you, Conclave? Shall I spare this befouled Kovatha? Or send her to the blade?"

Nyx spoke first, her pronouncement a single word. "Blade."

Morana seconded the notion, and the brothers Djeuthui and Hauké followed suit. Only Xa'Vatra's husband, Asar, disagreed. After he said, "Spare," the siblings hissed their disagreement.

"Oh, spare is not the word though for my recommended reprimand," he said.

He had his wife's attention now. "Speak then, husband."

He narrowed his eyes at Imbica then turned his attention to Pelagia. "I hear the Mistress of the Menagerie could use more servants. And given the Mistress's loyal service to the Dynasty, does she not deserve this boon?"

Xa'Vatra's eyes gleamed with excitement. Her voice was a soft purr. "Why, husband, you are full of worthy ideas of late."

He nodded and raised his cup to her. "I am inspired by your astute leadership." His smile was as phony as his words.

She favored him with a languid look and drank from the cup he offered. Her siblings looked dejected.

"And what say you, Prelate Vidar? Shall I send this disgraced Kovatha to the blade, as most of the Conclave favors, or gift her to the Mistress to do with as she sees fit?"

Vidar's look was grim. Disinterested in the whole affair, he showed no joy in his vote. "The Kovatha was loyal to the Dynasty until the Doj'Anira's escape attempt prompted a serious lapse in judgment. Still, the Kovatha has otherwise been a faithful Dynasty servant."

Nyx chimed in, "It does not matter if her life was in danger. She committed a crime against the Dynasty, Prelate. An offense against Xa'Vatra, our Exalted. If the Exalted excuses every Cornerless fool—"

Vidar waved his hand in the air. "Yes, yes. I know all that. I was merely pointing out that given her past service, and since she is the one who brought this prized possession into Dynasty control—and protecting it from a dragon, no less—"

People spoke behind unfurled hand fans and tittered and outright laughed at Vidar's mention of a dragon. *People think Imbica made that part up.* But neither Vidar nor the Exalted showed mirth at the mention of a dragon. *What does Xa'Vatra know about Vahgrin?*

Unshaken by the derision from the crowd, Vidar continued. "It's fitting that Kovatha Imbica should continue to oblige the Dynasty by being a servant to the Dynasty's Menagerie."

"Vidar, you spill words as though you expect speaking will add years to your life." Xa'Vatra sat back again and was quiet, perhaps thinking about what to do. She stared intently at Imbica, who still knelt, but pivoted her attention to Quen.

"And you." She pointed to Quen with a thin finger. "What say you, Doj'Anira?"

The crowd murmured whispers.

Morana said, "This is most unusual, Exalted. To ask the opinion of a chained one."

Xa'Vatra snapped at Morana, her words clipped. "Do you question me, Morana?"

"No, Exalted One, of course not. It is just—"

Xa'Vatra slammed her tiny fist down on the table. "I am Exalted, not you. Mind your place, or there will be an empty seat on the Conclave."

Morana bowed her head. She retreated to the back of her chair, making herself small in the shadow cast by Xa'Vatra's looming figure.

Xa'Vatra regained her composure, her voice now as calm as Still Waters. "Doj'Anira, former Kovatha Imbica harmed you with an unsanctioned immolation. You are a victim here, though not as great a victim as the Dynasty, to be sure. Still, I would hear what you have to say on the matter. The blade for this *former* Kovatha, or service to the Mistress?"

Quen had much to say on the matter. First, she wanted to set the Exalted straight. *I'm the victim of Imbica's torture, not the Dynasty.* If the Exalted disagreed, she would like to see Xa'Vatra suffer a few moments of Imbica's immolation. She also disagreed with killing Imbica for violating the Exalted's command. Sulmére laws and traditions discouraged death as a punishment for anything, even murder, because of the firm belief that taking another's life forever scars the heart.

But Quen didn't speak out. Pelagia's torture was fresh in her mind. She tugged at her still-burning ear.

Though she knew sending Imbica to Pelagia's meant she would likely lose her tongue, Imbica would still live. *Is life without the ability to speak better than a blade through the heart?* Quen wasn't sure. Her palms were clammy, and sweat beaded her forehead.

"Choose one, Doj'Anira," Pelagia said.

"Servitude," Quen blurted out.

Pelagia smiled widely.

Xa'Vatra's eyes glistened with excitement. "Intriguing choice." She looked down at her husband. "It appears you have another convert to your cause."

Asar bowed his head to her. "What say you, my love?"

"Imbica di Tikli, born in a granary, you have clawed and climbed your way to a place of respect, but what a scheming, belchiforous ratling you are. The Conclave has

268

never cared for you, to be sure." She looked at her sisters, and they laughed along with her. "My husband is a poet of sorts, and his justice grows e'er more poetic with each passing year. I am ready to pass judgment."

Xa'Vatra stood, and the scribe raised her quill, poised to take down the Exalted's pronouncement.

The pink-sashed man said, "Rise, Kovatha Imbica di Tikli."

Imbica rose, her face wet with tears and sweat, her head still bowed.

"For damaging Dynasty property without authority, I sentence you to serve the Mistress of the Menagerie. The term… for your natural life."

Murmurs rose, and people spoke quietly behind their hands. Being forced into bondage as a punishment wasn't unusual, but it was for a set number of years, not for life. *I thought slavery was illegal.*

If Imbica was shocked by the harshness of the sentence, she didn't show it. Imbica bowed low again and muttered, "Merciful Exalted."

"Those may be the last words you ever speak." Xa'Vatra banged her little gong, and guards came forth from both sides of the room. "She is Kovatha no more. Strip her of signatories."

One guard seized the silver silk scarf from around her neck. As spectators pounded their cups, two other guards ripped her embroidered tunic into pieces. Imbica's top was now bare except for the amber pendant—Quen's pendant—tied around her neck. But the guards were only interested in stripping Imbica of things denoting her office as Kovatha. They left the pendant alone.

The banging of cups grew louder, and people clapped as well. Two other guards tugged at her black linen pants until they too were rags, and she was naked before the Conclave and all onlookers. Wild cheers echoed in the cavernous chamber.

To her credit, Imbica didn't weep or attempt to cover herself. She stood stoically, the fat rolls around her middle bare for all to see. She accepted her sentence with the grace befitting a woman who was once a powerful Kovatha.

Xa'Vatra raised a single hand, and the crowd grew quiet. "Prepare her for delivery to the Menagerie."

The guards escorted Imbica from the room. Somber quiet replaced the once-joyful chatter.

Xa'Vatra broke the silence. "Prelate Vidar, I hope wine has not dulled your senses this evening. The Dynasty requires your services."

Prelate Vidar had snuggled back into himself and appeared to be asleep. He roused and said, "I stand ready for service to the Dynasty, as I have since the time of your grand-sire."

Xa'Vatra waved her hand in the air. "Yes, yes. We all know how ancient you are. As if age automatically entitles you to respect."

"I humbly apologize for any offense, Exalted. What do you need of me tonight?"

She indicated Quen, who still stood, as did Pelagia, in front of the raised platform. "I need you to inspect this Doj'Anira."

A grave look came over Vidar. "Here, Exalted? Now?"

Xa'Vatra rolled her eyes and sighed. "Yes, here and now. I have waited long for this moment, Vidar. I will wait no more."

What does any of this mean? How could the woman have been waiting for anything having to do with me when we just met? The word 'inspection' made her break into a cold sweat.

Aldewin bounded to the dais from behind and assisted Prelate Vidar to step down from the platform.

"Today, Vidar." Xa'Vatra's voice contained the edge of a blade in it.

Pelagia moved aside to give them room, and Quen stood alone.

Vidar smelled of smoke, body odor, and stale breath. Quen was already on the verge of nausea from the evening events and the rich food. She swallowed hard and tried not to throw up fish all over the man.

"This is a mistake. I am only a simple woman from the—" Sky-fire jolted Quen, and she gasped for air.

Prelate Vidar's voice was soft and kindly. "Please do not fight this, Doj'Anira. I do not want to see you harmed. I will not hurt you, nor will my assistant."

Aldewin gazed at her, his pale blue-grey eyes rimmed in red. He forced a wan smile, but it didn't reach his eyes. Quen appreciated his attempt to allay her fear. He looked younger without his grizzly beard. Quen liked what she saw.

"I assure you, this examination is purely medicinal. You are from the Sulmére, no? Think of my assistant here as a Bruxia. My hands are shaky, and my eyes nearly blind, so he will be my sense of sight and touch."

Aldewin moved closer and whispered, "I'm sorry if my hands are cold. And for touching you, but I must."

Please touch me. Tell me again you think I'm lovely.

Aldewin first lifted her arm. He moved his hand up her arm, lingering, feeling every inch.

Does he linger because he enjoys the intimacy as much as I do? Quen's skin prickled. His fingers were warm, not cold as he'd warned. Heat rose from him, making her insides stir.

Aldewin investigated her other arm and her face. Close enough his breath warmed her cheek. He smelled of orange blossom soap, tobacco, and sweat. She closed her eyes and swayed. Aldewin held her face in his hands, his thumbs rubbing along her cheekbones, then up through her hair.

She wished the moment would last forever. And that it wasn't being shared with Xa'Vatra's entire court.

He whispered apologies to her again. "Please forgive my invasion, but I must touch along your sides and spine. May I?"

"Do I have the option to say no?"

His eyes were full of sadness, and he shook his head.

"Go ahead then." She cast her gaze downward and slumped her shoulders, giving the impression she was resigned to something unwanted. *Please touch me.*

Aldewin felt along her ribs. Her gown was so thin it was as if he touched her naked flesh. When his warm hands moved across her belly, she shuddered.

"Do you feel anything?" Vidar asked.

Is he talking to me? She wanted to answer, "Yes!" To admit that her legs had become molten, and that the desire to seek Aldewin's lips had overcome her. *I'm like a string*

272

pulled nearly to breaking. She'd never experienced such sweet yet agonizing tautness.

But Aldewin answered. "Nothing yet, Prelate Vidar."

"The upper spine is the last hope," Vidar said.

Hope for what? Her neck tingled as though anticipating his touch.

Behind her now, Aldewin placed his hands on either side of her spine, just above her buttocks. Nervousness made the edges of her vision swirl. She sucked in a breath. It wasn't merely because her nether region was tight, and her nipples hardened. Embarrassed by what felt like a display of passion in front of a room of people, Quen's face grew hot.

As he got closer to her neck, panic gripped her. *Rajani. Nixan.* Her heart thumped furiously, her ears and neck hot and flushed. *What if he feels my deformity?*

When he got to her neck, he paused. He pulled her hair to the side. The cool air made her skin goose-pimply. He got closer still, his breath hot against her neck.

Quen feared she'd topple from weak knees. He rested his calloused fingers on either side of her neck and circled his thumbs over her spine, pressing lightly. When he got to where he should have felt her spinal deformity, he stopped. Aldewin let out a long exhale.

He removed his fingers and put her hair back over her neck. Aldewin's warmth now gone, Quen felt like she'd been thrust into Vay'Nada's frozen void.

"Well?" Prelate Vidar said.

Aldewin was behind her, so Quen couldn't see what he did, but Prelate Vidar closed his eyes and looked as though he had been told something awful. He nodded once, his look grave.

Aldewin stepped to Quen's left side. He was silent and stared straight ahead.

He had to feel my deviant spine. How could he not notice it? Yet he neither mentioned it to Prelate Vidar nor looked askance at her. If he felt it and said nothing, it must not be noteworthy to the Exalted. *Why else would he keep it from Xa'Vatra and even Vidar? Is Xa'Vatra searching for Nixan? No, not Nixan. She searches for Rajani. But why?*

Xa'Vatra's eyes were wide, her body forward in her seat with anticipation. "What say you, Prelate? Is this the Doj'Anira we have searched for?"

His voice was low, his eyes downcast. "I am afraid not, Exalted."

Xa'Vatra shot to her feet. "Are you certain? This one is from the Sulmére. It has the blue eye." Wine slurred her speech. Her voice was loud and filled with venom.

"Perhaps I should inspect her," Pelagia said. She turned to the Prelate. "You can't rely on an apprentice. Tell me what you seek, and my capable hands will find it."

Prelate Vidar slammed his cane onto the marble floor, sending an echo throughout the great hall. He looked in the general direction of Pelagia, but being nearly blind, he looked past her as he spoke. "I have had a seat on the Conclave since before you were born," he hissed. "You dare question my authority? Do not forget yourself, Mistress."

The cavernous room was silent.

"Be that as it may, Vidar, the Mistress has a point. You must confirm your apprentice's assessment," Xa'Vatra said.

Prelate Vidar looked up at Quen with milky eyes. The condition was common among elders in the Sulmére. She doubted he saw more than a shadow when looking at her.

"Guide my fingers," Vidar said to Aldewin.

Aldewin took the Prelate's hand and guided it toward Quen's neck. He placed the old man's fingers at the base of her skull.

Vidar's fingers were ice cold. It sent a chill through Quen, but unlike what she experienced when Aldewin touched her. Aldewin guided the old man's fingers up and down the upper region of Quen's neck.

The Prelate shook his head and removed his hand from her neck. Aldewin had not put the Prelate's fingers over the protruding bone in her neck.

Quen shot Aldewin a sideways look. His face was calm. Serene even. *What game does he play?*

"And?" Xa'Vatra asked.

"It is as my assistant said. This one may be Doj'Anira, but she is not the one you seek."

Quen didn't know if this was good news or bad.

Xa'Vatra sat heavily in her chair. "Your fortune, Mistress, is the Dynasty's loss. You gained two servants this night."

Quen had feared this outcome. She moved her tongue around her mouth. By tomorrow, she might have only a nub of butchered flesh where her tongue once was.

She peered sideways at Aldewin again, hoping he would say something to urge Xa'Vatra to not exile Quen to Pelagia's service. *If you're here to rescue me, now is an excellent time to unfold your plan.* But Aldewin avoided looking in her direction and said nothing.

Pelagia bowed deeply. "My humblest gratitude, Exalted." She rose. "I will ensure this one serves the Dynasty well in the Menagerie."

Xa'Vatra's chin rested on her hand. She looked bored beyond measure now, and she waved Pelagia off. "Away with her then." A servant filled her wine cup, and Xa'Vatra drank deeply then slammed it down on her table, crimson liquid shooting out and staining the white linen cloth. Her voice echoed off the tiger's eye columns and marble walls. "I command an entire country, yet no one is competent to find me the one Doj'Anira I seek."

One servant replaced the soiled linen while another refilled her cup. Xa'Vatra waved them off and drank deeply again. "Where is Imbica?"

"You sent her away to be a servant," Morana said.

Xa'Vatra glared down at her husband. "I should not have listened to you," she hissed. "Vile Imbica delivered a pile of detritus. I should order her flayed until skinless."

Her sisters nodded, their heads bobbing.

Xa'Vatra rose and swayed. Her radiant gold headdress had gone askew. "I will flay to death the next person who brings me trash Doj'Anira." She pointed at the scribe. "Make that an Edict."

"My love, if you make that a law, no one will bother bringing Doj'Anira to you. They will be too afraid. Only a few of the Conclave know what you search for exactly."

Xa'Vatra swayed as she leaned so close to him their noses nearly touched. "Do not question the Exalted, husband, or you will be the next one flayed."

Asar closed his eyes and looked away.

Quen knew no more of what happened in the great feast hall. Pelagia dug her thin fingers into Quen's arm

276

and pulled her roughly away. She exited to the left, Nivi at her heels.

As they passed Aldewin, he stopped them. "I am sorry it didn't work out for you, Mistress."

She glared back at him. "Apparently, a lowly assistant may know the secrets of the Conclave, but the Mistress of the Menagerie, entrusted with the care of the Dynasty's Doj'Anira, is not."

As Pelagia spoke, Aldewin moved closer to Quen and whispered into her ear, "Keep faith. You have friends in the capital."

It happened quickly. With Quen's body between them, Pelagia appeared not to notice.

Pelagia roughly jerked Quen forward. As they exited the room, Quen looked back, searching for Rhoji. He was busy pouring wine for the Conclave, but his eyes were on her. He gave her a slight nod then returned his full attention to his duties.

Though Pelagia led Quen toward a life of servitude, hope swelled in her breast. *Rhoji and Aldewin have a plan to help me escape. They must. And hopefully the rest of the pod are in Qülla too.* Aldewin now knew she was something other than human—had to know—yet he'd not betrayed Quen to the Exalted. *I don't know why he'd risk himself for someone he knows is Nixan, but I'm grateful for his aid. I'll worry about what's really going on with him once we're free of this city.*

Thanks to Aldewin's deception, she was no longer bound by Edict 42. *And with Jagaru help, I might even escape the Menagerie before the butcher's blade takes my tongue.*

CHAPTER 16

Imagining Rhoji and Aldewin had planned to liberate Quen from the Palace di Soli, she was disappointed they allowed Pelagia to take her. Excited anticipation of a reunion morphed into panic. She was free of the Edict 42 business, but now Pelagia held Quen by an invisible leash, and Hem was close on her heels. *Running isn't an option.* To escape Qülla, she first had to break free of Pelagia's restraints.

Pelagia gripped the sides of the gib-rig, her knuckles white, her eyes wide and wild. Pahpi once told Quen that a person without control over Vatra fires within was more dangerous than a mother thukna guarding a newborn calf. *Pelagia looks like she's ready to erupt with Vatra.* Quen's innards were a mass of tangled knots.

Quen tugged at the embedded ear cuffs, making her earlobes burn. Blood covered her fingertips. She sucked them, trying to hide the blood from Pelagia.

"Go ahead, yank as much as you want." Pelagia's voice was a low hiss. She narrowed her eyes and pressed her face closer. "Only I know how to control—or remove—them."

The spiny ridge on Quen's neck—where Aldewin's fingers had lingered—pulsated. The Nixan soul was pushing itself to the fore. *I'm tempted to let it. If I'm Rajani, like Nevara, maybe my inner beast can rid me of Pelagia.*

But Quen wasn't sure she was Rajani. For all she knew, the second beat pulsing within was a spawn of Vay'Nada, like a slint or darmanitong. Worse still, she worried that if she allowed the Nixan to come forth, she wouldn't know how to become Quen again. She pushed away the urge to let the shadow soul within consume her. She focused on stillness, as Pahpi had taught her. *Lumine light my way,* she prayed.

It was challenging to quiet her mind with so many questions swirling. Aldewin had felt her spiny ridge, yet he lied about it to the Conclave, as did Prelate Vidar. *What game are they playing?*

Nevara's prophecy haunted her. *"Wherever you go, tragedy will follow. You will lay waste to entire villages, kingdoms even."* Nevara's cryptic prophecy was the key to answering many of her questions. Yet Quen was still missing critical pieces of the puzzle.

Upon their arrival at Pelagia's Palace, Caz waited for them inside the northeastern entrance. She offered a hand to Quen to help her in the dim light.

"You need to attend to her no longer." Pelagia's voice was taut with bitter anger. "She is Doj'Anira no more." Pelagia spoke as though it was Quen's fault she wasn't whatever the Exalted hoped she would be.

Caz drew her hand back. Luz stood a few paces inside the door with a lamp.

"Luz and Hem, come with me. We will take this new servant to the lower holding cells. Caz, wake Timming. Tell him to bring his butcher's blade."

Quen shuddered at the mention of the butcher's blade. Her palms were wet, and her mind raced as she tried to figure a way out of her predicament.

"You have friends in the capital," Aldewin had said. *Rhoji, where are you?*

Luz led the way, and Pelagia followed with Nivi at her heels. Quen didn't follow. *I won't voluntarily enter a life of mutilation and servitude.*

Hem shoved her in the back, and Pelagia rounded on her. Pelagia's pale-grey eyes were wide and shot through with red. "Must I force your obedience? You had but the slightest taste of my prod. Do you hunger for more?"

The gold cuffs warmed, and a jolt of sky-fire pulsed through Quen. It recalled the torture Pelagia inflicted on her at the Palace.

The swirling spasms of pain reminded her of the mage the Exalted had given to Pelagia earlier that night. *Imbica. If they brought Imbica here, maybe....* Imbica was the last person Quen wished to help, but if Aldewin and Rhoji didn't assist her soon, working with Imbica might be her only hope.

Now on her knees, her breathing labored, Quen croaked, "I will obey." The words were rancid in her mouth.

Hem yanked her up by the hair.

Reluctantly, Quen followed Pelagia. At Quen's heels, Nivi panted loudly. The big cat likely wanted to take a bite out of Pelagia. But the same magical device that forced Quen's obeisance also subjected Nivi to Pelagia's control.

Pelagia led them through the servant's quarters, an infirmary, and a kitchen. Unseen from the doorway, at the back of the room, a narrow staircase wound downward.

As they descended, the air grew chilly and moist and smelled of mold, wet fur, urine, and rot. At the bottom, they entered a large dungeon. Haphazardly placed lanterns did little to chase away the dark. Iron-barred stone cells lined the jail's walls, while a smith's fire and bellows glowed red in the middle, casting an eerie glow.

Pelagia snatched Luz's lantern. "Did you know that the Menagerie used to be a palace for the Kovan Dynasty?"

Quen shook her head, wary of voicing her thoughts on the subject. *I don't care about the history of a power-hungry family.*

"The castle's original dungeon is all that remains." She swung the lantern, illuminating empty prison cells as she stepped into the dungeon. "These cells held the Dynasty's political enemies. Important people, even if ultimately deemed traitors." She swung the lantern back toward Quen. "And now you will spend the night among the ghosts of greatness."

Perhaps Pelagia meant to impress her. *What do I care about Qülla's political squabbles?*

"Why am I here, Pelagia? You know I did nothing wrong. My only crime was being born with strange eyes."

The large stone in Pelagia's ring took a chunk of Quen's skin as she smashed Quen's jaw. Blood gushed from her chin, ruining the thin slip of a dress.

The shock was greater than the pain. *What have I done to anger her to violence against me? Nothing makes sense anymore.*

"Why—?" Quen tried to ask.

Pelagia walloped her again, landing a solid punch to her side. "You disobeyed me—dishonored me—in front of the Exalted and the entire Conclave."

Quen turned to run back up the stairs, but Hem blocked her path with his wide body. He shoved her roughly toward Pelagia. Two guards, previously hidden in the shadows, stepped forward, flanking Pelagia.

The Mistress swung at her again, but Quen blocked it with her forearm this time. "This punishment is unjust, and you know it." She kept her arms up, ready to defend herself from another attack. Quen was losing hope she'd see beyond the dungeon again, but she wasn't about to kneel and simper like a cornered pup.

Pelagia threw her head back and let out a low, throaty laugh. "There you go again, talking of justice. Your crime? You stole the Exalted's moment of glory. People have died for less. Consider yourself fortunate to live still." Pelagia's pupils were dark and dilated with rage. Sweat beaded on her brow as a jolt pierced Quen's chest. "Of course, you are no longer an honored Doj'Anira."

A metallic taste filled Quen's mouth. The agony made Quen's legs buckle, and she sank to her knees.

Pelagia's nostrils flared. "Servants die all the time."

Tendrils of fiery pain radiated from Quen's core to her toes and fingertips. Quen tried to scream, but her voice was thin and hoarse. She writhed on the floor and moaned. Sweat and blood soaked her now-muddy dress.

Pelagia loomed over Quen, her headpiece askew. Pelagia flung it off, the delicate bones shattering on the floor. Kneeling, she cupped Quen's chin, stuck two fingers in her mouth, and found her tongue. "It is a waste to take away your ability to pleasure me."

The fiery tendrils of sky-fire energy eased. Quen panted as she tried to fill her burning lungs with air.

Pelagia trailed the same fingers down Quen's neck and across her breast. "The Exalted said I could do with you as I pleased."

Quen coughed. "I would—" She sucked in a breath. "Rather lose my tongue than be forced to lie with you."

Pelagia kicked Quen in the ribs. Quen curled into the smallest ball she could make of herself.

Nivi roared and leaped between Quen and Pelagia. He was about to swipe at Pelagia with his mighty claws, but she activated the gold cuffs on his ears. Nivi yowled and pressed his nose to the dusty floor in forced obeisance.

"The damned cat has taken a liking to you."

Nivi cried out again and slapped a paw at his ear until it was bloody.

"You ruined my faithful kitty." Pelagia kicked Quen again before pulling her by the hair, dragging her across the hard-packed dirt floor of the dungeon. "Sulmére trash."

Quen screamed in agony, her scalp pulling like it would soon peel from her skull. *Will Hem or the guards help me? Surely they won't let her do this to me.* But none tried to intervene. They stoically watched as if they, too, feared what Pelagia might do to them. Luz watched as well, her eyes rimmed in red from crying.

Pelagia twisted Quen's hair in one hand. She pulled a set of keys from a peg on the wall. The cell was utterly dark inside.

"Luz!" she called. "Bring the lantern."

There was no answer, but soon Luz arrived at their side, and a warm glow illuminated the dank cell.

Pelagia dragged Quen into the cell and delivered a kick to her back. "When next we meet, you will be a speechless mewling quim, competing with the other servants for my favor."

"Never," Quen croaked.

Pelagia spat on her then delivered a kick to her head. Quen tried to deflect the blow, but Pelagia landed a solid shot, and blood trickled onto Quen's upper lip.

Pelagia's breath was ragged from her exertion. Luz whimpered.

Quen called out, "Help me!"

"Cry all you want. Scream and gnash, but no one will come for you because you are nothing. You are nothing because the Exalted commanded it so."

"You're wrong." *Rhoji cares. Aldewin cares.* Even if they didn't find her in time to save her from a prisoner's fate, they'd risked their lives coming to the capital to help her.

Pelagia was about to deliver another kick, but a commotion at the dungeon entrance stopped her. Men grunted as steel clashed against steel. And a man with a pronounced lisp was swearing.

"Suda, but he's wide as a thukna's arse," Druvna said.

"Duck!" Mishny hollered. There was a loud thwack and an 'oof.'

Quen's heart skipped a beat. *The pod is here.*

"What in the name of Hiyadi—?" Pelagia stepped out of the cell. At first, annoyance knitted her brows, but Pelagia turned to Quen and laughed. "How sweet, dune blossom. Druvna the Dishonored has brought his little band of rogues to attempt a rescue." She turned her gaze on Quen, her lips pulled back in a sneer. "Too bad they'll all die here tonight. Better yet—" She returned to the cell and grabbed Quen's hair again, dragging her to the ring of red-hot coals in the room's center.

Pelagia twisted Quen's hair in one hand while she gripped a poker with the other. Furiously stoking the fire, she yelled, "Stand down, Druvna, or your young Jagaru gets a poker in her pretty blue eye."

The fighting ceased.

Quen's vision was sideways and bleary from sweat and strands of hair plastered across her face. She couldn't tell if Aldewin, Rhoji, Eira, and Shel were with Mishny and Druvna.

"Bring them to me," Pelagia said.

Pelagia's damned chunky ring dug into Quen's scalp. Quen kicked and twisted, which only made Pelagia twist her hair more tightly.

Hem and the two guards held Druvna, Mishny, and Aldewin at sword-point. Caz and Luz stood behind and held each other, tears streaming down their cheeks. A slash of crimson crisscrossed Hem's broad chest, and his left eye was smeared in blood from a cut in his brow, but his wounds didn't hamper him. The two guards and Druvna's Jagaru were unscathed.

But where is Rhoji? And what of Eira and Shel? That something terrible had happened to her brother and friends brought hot tears, and her neck ridge pulsed.

"I was going to save this work for Timming, but I will wait for him no more," Pelagia said. She dragged Quen to a vise-like device with metal clamps.

"He weren't comin' anyway," Druvna said. He threw what looked like a raw, bloody piece of meat to the ground at Pelagia's feet.

"Killed my butcher? That'll cost you." Her hand squeezed Quen's throat, holding her down as she used the other hand to screw a clamp to hold Quen's head in place.

Quen clutched at Pelagia's hand, trying to pry it from her throat. Pelagia's wild eyes met Quen's, and her grip remained firm. Pelagia's graceful, pale beauty had vanished. Her red face dripped sweat. Her mouth twisted into a grimace, her neck veins bulging. Quen's throat was afire, her breaths ragged.

The sounds of clashing steel filled the air. A man yowled, and Mishny growled. No, it wasn't Mishny. Nivi roared, and a man screeched, then there was the sound of blood gushing from a neck wound.

Pelagia turned toward the commotion, her hand still squeezing Quen's neck. "You may be a court favorite, but I'll tolerate your disobedience no longer." Her voice was strained and thin.

Nivi yowled, a cry so full of pain it was unbearable. A staff made a loud thwack. *Aldewin must have found a replacement stick.* Druvna grunted, and Mishny taunted Hem. "Come at me, puffed-up cock-waddle."

Quen blinked, trying to see Nivi. He lay on the ground, his legs twitching, his tongue lolling out of the side of his mouth.

She's killing him. Quen's breaths were shallow and rapid. Nivi was more of a kindred spirit to Quen than anyone she'd ever met. *He's rare and beautiful and has the right to live as much as anyone.* Knowing he would soon die if she did nothing, Quen stopped trying to suppress the Nixan. *Damn me to Vay'Nada's frigid eternity, if you must, Lumine. But I must protect Nivi.*

Quen released any lingering Still Waters remaining within her. Instead of her usual prayers to the Sister, she called on Hiyadi. He was the god of war. *Bless me, Brother, and fill me with Vatra. Burnish and hone me into a weapon of your design.* Quen didn't still her turbulent thoughts. Instead, she allowed fear, sadness, and anger to fill her like steam from a boiling kettle. She had lost plenty, and the repressed emotional toll fueled her. For the first time, Quen invited the Nixan's power to surface.

White heat seared her neck ridge, and chills rang the length of her spine. Hot tears poured. Threads of pain wrapped around her sides. A scream formed deep in her belly, rose, and she released a primordial yell. Her eyes were hot, her vision bleary. It felt like something had pushed through the skin along her spine.

Agony gave way to the thrill of an unfamiliar power coursing through her. Hiyadi's strength filled her. Quen wrested Pelagia's fingers from her throat, the woman's finger bones snapping like twigs breaking.

Pelagia's expression changed from sadistic joy to utter shock. She held one hand in the other. "You broke my fingers." Her voice was an awed whisper as she staggered back from Quen. "What in the name of the Three?"

Pressing upward with all her strength, Quen broke free of the clamps Pelagia hadn't finished pressing into her scalp. She swiped at Pelagia with her fingers outstretched, using her nails like claws. Bloody scratches bloomed on Pelagia's chest, but it was only a flesh wound.

Aldewin broke free of his battle with Hem and swung his body toward Pelagia, his staff twirling. It looked like he'd land a solid shot across Pelagia's back, but she thrust up an arm, and the staff flew from his hands. Her broken hand did nothing to hinder her magical abilities.

Aldewin was only momentarily off-kilter. He pulled the broadsword from his back and fended off a blow from Hem at his backside.

Mishny stood on a guardsman's chest, thrust her curved blade into his gut, and ripped upward. The smell of urine and offal filled the air. Mishny wiped blood spatter from her face as she rushed toward Hem, while Aldewin defended himself from Hem's blade. Mishny fileted the large man's back, distracting him enough that Aldewin found a landing for his broadsword. Aldewin lunged forward, piercing Hem's well-muscled torso and plunging his sword into the man's gut. Aldewin twisted the blade as he pulled it from the dying man's belly.

The Jagaru fought against Hem and the guards, but Nivi still writhed. He'd been furiously panting, but now his breaths were shallow.

Storm energy crackled in the air. A shock of sky-fire exploded in Quen, searing her from crown to toes. Before she could cry out, her chest tightened. Pelagia's attack sucked life-sustaining air from her lungs.

While she still had breath left, Quen called out, "Gold ear cuffs, Aldewin. She controls—us." She hoped he had the magical knowledge to determine how to remove the gold control devices from both Quen and Nivi.

Quen writhed on the cold stone floor like an eel with a severed head. Drool spilled from the corner of her mouth, her head jerked, and her legs twitched. Pelagia's magical control device siphoned off whatever power Quen's inner beast had lent her.

Aldewin chanted in a strange language, yet different from the one Imbica had used. *"A-zhi ni-wa hō-na kai."* He repeated the phrase several times.

Quen hoped the words were a spell to remove the cuffs from her ears and thus interrupt Pelagia's power over her. But the cuffs remained dug into her flesh, hot and sending searing sky-fire through her.

Pelagia laughed. "Old Tinoxian magic. Smart, mageling, but not smart enough."

Aldewin thrust his greatsword toward her, but Pelagia sprang backward like an acrobat in a traveling show, flipping herself out of harm's way.

While Aldewin's blade didn't land a blow, his attempts momentarily distracted Pelagia. She lost enough concentration that the fiery tendrils of torture coursing through Quen eased a bit.

Aldewin was near enough that Quen could touch him. Quen moved slowly, not wanting to attract Pelagia's attention. Aldewin always had a dagger strapped to each of his boots. Quen hoped they were still there. Her hands shook as she lifted Aldewin's pants leg and pulled the blade from its scabbard.

The steel was reassuring in her hand. *Forgive me, Pahpi, for the scar I'm about to sear into my heart.* The soul scar was necessary to free Nivi from Pelagia's control.

Pahpi's advice to her while hunting came to her now. *"Aim for your quarry's heart, Quen, and never take your eyes from it."*

Armed solely with a dagger, Quen was no match for Pelagia. Quen spoke internally to her Nixan soul. *You've been trying to poke out of the shell for months and push me aside. Well, come then. Show me your power.*

A wave of heat and something else. Something raw rolled from toes to head in a spiral. She pulled energy directly from the soil beneath and the air around and filled herself with it. The ground trembled, and the air crackled.

Spindles of fiery pain threaded from the base of her spine. Her skin was tight, as if it was someone else's she'd borrowed.

Pelagia blinked, and it was like a crash of falling stone. Nivi's breath was like a tiny fly's wings fluttering at her face. Movement around her slowed as if all were caught in amber.

It was as it had been when she'd first faced Vahgrin. As though time itself paused for her.

I don't know how long this power will last. She advanced on Pelagia swiftly, never taking her eyes from the Mistress of the Menagerie's chest. Pelagia's heartbeat was like the thundering roar of a herd's hooves, rattling Quen's teeth and thrumming within her. She could nearly see Pelagia's heart beneath her skin, barely more than a thin membrane of water covering brittle bone. *So easy to crush.*

Quen leaped and plunged the dagger into Pelagia's chest. Her aim was true, her arm strong. She pushed with all her strength, forcing the blade up to the hilt. Quen let go of the dagger handle.

Pelagia, still moving as though in air made of honey, fell to the ground. Her eyes were wide, her mouth open in astonishment. Blood gurgled out of her open mouth like a fish stranded on land. She flung her arm toward Quen and uttered her last words, "Doj'Anira...." Gasping for breath, the haughty Mistress of the Menagerie died in the dungeon where she'd meted out pain and punishment at her whim.

Quen had assumed she'd feel remorse, but she felt only satisfaction. *That horrible woman will never torture a beast or person again.* Quen turned her attention to Nivi, wasting no more thought on Pelagia.

Kneeling at Nivi's side, her hands on his chest, Quen felt for the beat of his giant tiger heart. She nestled her face against his downy white fur, listening for breath. Her mind was a rope pulled in a single direction, focusing only on whether she'd succeeded in time to save him.

His chest was still, his lungs quiet. Quen pushed on his massive chest with all her strength. Again. And again. She didn't understand what called her to do it. To pound on the dead was surely taboo, but she couldn't stop herself.

"Live!" Salty sweat and tears mixed with blood and streamed down her face. She compressed Nivi's ribs, pushing through layers of fur, blood, and bone.

"I need you, Nivi." She pushed again as sounds returned to her like a sudden burst of thunder.

Beneath her hands, a great heave. Nivi panted, his massive tongue lolling as he sucked in precious air.

"I told you I wouldn't leave without you," she whispered into his blood-caked ear. Quen stroked his chest, hoping he wouldn't be in pain from her efforts to revive him.

Nivi chirped, his eyes bleary but finding hers. Quen stroked his fur. "You are free now." Tears rolled down her cheeks. "We are both free of her." She tugged at her ear, expecting the cuff to release. It didn't.

Yet there were no more shocks. No crackling pulses of sky-fire.

Pelagia lay still, her eyes lifeless lenses to an empty vessel.

CHAPTER 17

Nivi lived, and Pelagia lay dead. Quen released a quivering sigh. She was free of Pelagia's grasp, but they had still to escape Qülla.

There was a hand on her shoulder. "Will he make it?" Aldewin asked.

Quen tried to speak, but her throat was tight. She swallowed and said, "He is strong."

Nivi and Quen both pushed up. As she stood, the eyes of her Jagaru pod and the two silent women were on her, their mouths slightly open, their faces full of questions.

Mishny held her blade in a defensive position, ready to attack. "What in Vay'Nada's bloody shadow are you?"

Quen sighed and held her hands out to her side, palms up. "I am Quen Tomo Santu di Sulmére. The same as I was when I joined you in Solia."

"No, you bloody aren't." Mishny moved from a defensive to an offensive stance.

Druvna put himself between Quen and Mishny. "She's Jagaru. 'Member the creed, woman. Jagaru protect our own."

Mishny looked stricken, her voice full of rage. "You're taking her side?"

"We do no'a have time for your attitude. You can rip my arse later."

"You're hiding something from me, Druvna, and I don't like it." Mishny puffed her chest and leaned toward him.

Her bravado didn't cow Druvna. "Like it or no, I lead this pod, and I say leave off. Let's get our arses to the meetup with the others."

Quen was relieved to hear Druvna mention others. *Rhoji and my friends are alive.*

Nivi growled at Mishny, and she stomped her foot, snarled, and flicked her blade. "I'm not afraid of you, either. I've skinned critters bigger'n you."

"No one's skinnin' nobody," Druvna said. "Now, the lot of you, make haste."

Mishny grudgingly sheathed her dagger. "Mark my words, Druvna. This one'll be the death of you." She still looked ready to gut Quen if given half a chance.

I need to watch my back now with Mishny.

Someone called from a cell across the dungeon, "Doj'Anira."

All stopped save for Mishny.

"Doj'Anira, please."

Imbica.

I have good reason to leave Imbica in this cell. With Pelagia gone, no one—save for Vahgrin—was more deserving of rough justice than Imbica.

Aldewin yanked her hand. "Come. I promised our mutual friend I would get Caz and Luz out of this place. We don't have time to help her."

I should leave the boar's bowel here to rot. But dammit, I've seen what she can do. If we have an encounter with Vahgrin, she's our only hope of survival. "We might need her."

Mishny groused. "You cannot be serious. She's the one who brought you to this place."

"You don't yet know the half of it." Quen glanced at her hands. The purple veining was nearly gone, but she'd never forget Imbica's torture. "Someone find the keys."

A strange blue light emanated from Imbica's cell. Twisting, glowing bands encircled Imbica.

Luz jangled keys and unlocked the cell, Aldewin at her heels.

"What is that light?" Quen asked.

"Mage shackles." Imbica sat in a cross-legged position. Her shoulders were slumped, her arms loose at her sides. She was free of bruises, cuts, or other apparent injuries, yet she looked defeated.

Druvna poked his head in by Aldewin's side. "By Lumine's light. What magic is this?"

Aldewin tilted his head and squinted at the blue lights as if studying them. "Tinoxian magic, straight from Māja di Menaris in Partha."

"Can you undo it?" Quen asked.

Aldewin circled Imbica, his arms outstretched. "I'm uncertain."

"If Pelagia set the spell, why is it still active? She's dead. Shouldn't all her spells, I don't know—dissolve?" Quen asked.

Quen had asked Aldewin, but Imbica answered. "Remember what I told you, Doj'Anira. Magic is understanding. An agreement made with spirits or gods. Some promises survive death."

Aldewin raised his eyebrows. "An elegant way to state it. You sound like an Ascended Master from a Pillar."

Imbica stared at him dispassionately. "You know Vaya di Menaris?"

Aldewin shrugged. "Some. Healing mostly. I recognize the threads, but I've never seen this weave."

"Take a stab at it," Imbica said. It was a command, not a request.

Quen held out her arm and blocked Aldewin. She spoke to Imbica. "I despise you."

Imbica's tone was even, without a hint of sarcasm. "I do not blame you."

"We have every reason to leave you behind."

"I would if I were you."

Quen folded her arms. "I know. But I am not you. There are four of us. Soon three more. If you try any mage tricks on us, you will die."

Imbica nodded once.

"If Vahgrin attacks and you fail to protect us, we will end you."

She nodded again.

"You work for me now, not the Kovan Dynasty. If you do anything against my interests, you'll die."

"Freedom always comes at a price," Imbica said.

Mishny said, "This one is like the beetles that devour thukna dung. Leave her to rot."

"I had not said I would pay the price for my freedom." Imbica's voice was calm. She eyed Quen, squinting as if

296

attempting to see something far beyond her. After a few seconds, she nodded. "I vow to abide by your terms."

Aldewin circled Imbica, his arms outstretched as if feeling the swirling magical binding. Finally, he stopped. "Aha. I see it now. Novel weave, but not as clever as she thought." He chuckled. "I'm surprised this held you."

Imbica blushed. "Bindings are not my forte."

But magical combat and torture are. Reason to have you on our side.

Aldewin's eyes closed again, and he muttered something low and inaudible. Within seconds, the glowing rings sputtered and then flashed out of existence.

Imbica rose and brushed herself off. Though she'd been naked when taken from the Palace di Soli, they'd clothed her in a pale-green rough-spun wrap-style tunic and wide-legged pants. Her face was dirty, and her hair was out of its braid and frizzy. She smoothed her hair and plucked bits of straw from it.

She slightly bowed her head to Aldewin and briefly touched her thumb to her forehead. "Je'en li, Kentaro."

Aldewin bowed his head, touched his thumb to his forehead, and said, "Di'nira. But please, call me Aldewin. I am no Kentaro."

Imbica narrowed her eyes at him, but she didn't argue. "As you say. Lead, and I shall follow."

"Finally," Mishny said.

Mishny strained to pry the rusty sewer grate open but succeeded. "Go first, Aldewin, and make light for us."

Druvna followed Aldewin, Caz and Luz on his heels. Quen motioned for Imbica to go next. *She hasn't earned my trust yet. I'm not about to show her my back.*

"That oversized cat is *not* coming with us." Mishny crossed her arms and looked ready to put a dagger through anyone who opposed her.

"He's a powerful fighter," Quen said.

As if he understood her, Nivi roared, showing a mouth full of pointy teeth made for ripping throats open.

"He killed a guard, remember?"

Mishny rolled her eyes. "By Lumine's bloody fuckin' teats! If that fur bag so much as sheds a hair in my direction, so help me—" She continued cursing and threatening, but her words faded as she slid down the ladder to the dark Qülla sewers.

Nivi squeezed through the hole and leaped into the dirty water, splashing Quen.

"Come, my friend. I want you to meet my brother."

•　　•　　•

The night waned as Hiyadi's first light filtered through the sewer grates overhead. They rushed to the city's western edge, moving silently save for Nivi's splashing.

Before long, they arrived at a tall circular grate leading to the river far below Qülla's walls. Mishny yanked on it, but the rusty hinges held. Nivi roared at it.

"Barking at it won't help," Druvna said.

"It was more of a roar than a bark," Quen said.

Mishny glared at Quen. "I expected resistance. Where are the guards?"

"Why would they put guards in a sewer?" Druvna harrumphed. "Especially when the gate has us inside the walls still." He gave the gate a good shake, but it didn't budge.

Imbica waddled forward, closed her eyes, and hovered her hands over the hinges. "Not to worry. Give me some room."

Everyone backed up. Imbica wound her arms and mumbled an incantation. Quen caught the word 'Vatra' but couldn't decipher Imbica's spell.

The space between Imbica's hands glowed. Sweat beaded her upper lip, and her face was bright red as she concentrated. Small but nearly white fireballs appeared near Imbica's hands. She hurled them at the gate hinges, where they hovered briefly. Nivi growled at the flame. His mane puffed, his tail twitching. The rest watched in quiet awe. At last, there was a loud snap, and the grate splashed as it fell.

"Impressive," Aldewin said.

Imbica wiped her brow. Druvna trudged through the gate and waddled toward the light at the tunnel's end. Aldewin ushered Caz and Luz into the passageway, and Imbica followed.

"After you, Doj'Anira," Mishny said.

Quen rounded on her. "Don't call me that."

"Or what? You'll tell Druvna on me?" Her lip curled into a mocking sneer.

Quen's core sizzled with Vatra fire. For the long weeks of riding north, Mishny had ridden her ass. It was annoying, but expected for a new Jagaru recruit. But now, Mishny was openly hostile—as if goading Quen to allow the fires of Hiyadi to consume her.

Pahpi's voice, often a whisper in her mind, said, *"Still Waters, Quen."* She breathed deeply, calling on Lumine's peace, but they weren't yet out of the city. *We'll have a reckoning, Mishny and I. But now isn't the time.* She ran after the others, Nivi at her heels.

Mishny laughed. "Run to Druvna, *Doj'Anira.*"

With each step, the air sweetened, the sour stench receding. Quen exited the tunnel at a rocky cliff above a river. The sticky air smelled of sweet grasses, earth, and fresh water. Voices below made her heart soar with hopeful anticipation. *Rhoji.*

She hurried down the rocky slope to her waiting friends and family. From afar, they looked none the worse for wear.

Nearly to the bottom of the hill, Caz and Luz began sprinting toward a familiar-looking woman. Tears streamed down the woman's face as she embraced Caz and Luz.

"Your sisters, Biveta, as promised," Aldewin said.

Biveta was the water-taxi driver who had whispered, *"You have friends in Qülla."* She had an arm around each of her sisters. "The blessings of the Three to you, Aldewin. You kept your promise."

He gave her a slight bow. "As did you." He turned to Quen and Imbica, joining the others gathered at the embankment by the river. "Biveta helped me get the Jagaru into Qülla through the tunnels beneath the city."

"Sounds like the Dynasty needs to tighten their security," Imbica said.

"But that's not your problem anymore. Is it, *former* Kovatha?" Mishny said.

Imbica ran her hands down her tunic to smooth it. "Yes, well, old habits die hard."

Aldewin turned his attention back to the reunited sisters. "What will you do now?"

"We'll return to Ginarli and continue serving Vaya di Qüira as we have our whole lives," Biveta said.

Caz and Luz each made the crescent sign on their forehead with their thumb. Biveta pulled her long hair aside, revealing a Qüira tattoo on her neck—a triangle with three dots beneath, the symbol for the earth element. Caz and Luz each had the same mark.

Rhoji was at Quen's side now, his arm around her. He gave her a light squeeze. "Ginarli is at the farthest tip of Suab'hora. How did you end up in Qülla?"

"About a year ago, two Kovatha came to Ginarli, searching for Doj'Anira," Biveta said.

"A remote area for Kovatha to range," Imbica said.

Biveta nodded and squeezed her sisters tightly.

Quen's innards churned. "Did they say why they were looking for Doj'Anira?"

Biveta shook her head. "Took one look at the twins' eyes and had cuffs on 'em before we could argue." Her voice cracked. "Hauled them from their family—home and work—like they were criminals."

"Sounds familiar." Shel glared at Imbica.

Quen rubbed her wrists. She'd been in chains only days before. "It makes no sense. It's not like there's a registry of people with bicolored eyes."

"Agreed, Doj—I mean, Quen. It was happenstance that I came upon you," Imbica said.

"I don't know what such eyes have to do with anything." Biveta wiped her face on her shoulder. "People throughout the upper Suab'Hora knew about my sisters. It may have been Altair, the Archon of Val'Qüira, who first used the term Doj'Anira. He always referred to Caz and Luz as Doj'Anira, but he meant it as an honor. He said their brown eyes were the colors of earth and their green eyes a harbinger of spring." She smiled at them. "Both Vaya di Qüira and Vaya di Doka in one person. And they were twins. Doubly blessed." She hugged her sisters again.

Doubly blessed. That's what Aldewin said to me when we first met. Quen eyed him and still wasn't used to his clean-shaven face and short, smoothly combed hair. He looked younger than when they first met. *And innocent looking.* Yet her gut churned at the idea that his use of the term "twice blessed" hadn't been a coincidence.

Biveta continued. "When they took my sisters, I thought they were being taken to a place of high honor in the Exalted's court."

"I had assumed that as well—for Quen, I mean," Imbica said.

Then why did you treat me like a criminal? It was a question she intended to put to Imbica at some point. Quen, too, had at first hoped Doj'Anira was a term of honor. But whatever the Dynasty truly wanted with so-called Doj'Anira, eventually, they'd figure out she was Nixan. Then being Doj'Anira, whatever it truly meant, wouldn't have saved her from the dire fate awaiting all Nixan.

Biveta took her sister's hands in hers. "I followed them to the capital and got work in the canals. When I found out what had befallen them, I stayed. I never gave up hope that I'd get them back." She wiped a lone tear from Luz's cheek. "And now, I take them home."

"The Dynasty might search for you there," Rhoji said. "With us, you will have safety in numbers."

"Or make our group even more noticeable as we travel," Imbica said.

Aldewin had untied his dappled horse from a nearby copse of trees. "He's not much to look at, but he'll get you there." He helped Caz and Luz onto the horse's back while Biveta retrieved her horse.

"May the Sister shield you in her arms," Quen said.

Biveta kissed two fingers and then held them to the sky. "Until the Three bring us together again, the blessings of Hiyadi upon you." She clucked her tongue, kicked her horse lightly, and galloped across the stream, Caz and Luz following behind. None of them looked back.

The Jagaru and Imbica watched for a few minutes in uncomfortable silence. Quen was glad Aldewin had helped Caz and Luz and that she had played a small part in reuniting the twins with their family. But she had many questions and was eager to have it out with him.

Druvna wasn't about to give them time for a reunion or questioning. "Mount up, mush-brained squibs, or you might as well put your own arse in a Qülla prison cell."

He has a good point. We're barely outside Qülla's walls. Answers could wait, but warm clothing could not. "Hold up. I can't go anywhere dressed like this." She still wore a dress of wet, torn, bloody silk. "And did no one realize we're now an animal short?"

Mishny, atop her kopek, Boy, smirked at her. "You can ride with Aldewin. Or maybe your new friend, Imbica."

"Actually, we're short two mounts," Aldewin said. "We weren't counting on having Imbica along."

"Then ride the hair bag, Doj'Anira, seeing how you insisted on bringing him along." Mishny clicked her tongue and followed Druvna.

Rhoji handed her a pair of pants he'd dug out of his pack. "They're at least long enough."

Shel offered her a dusty pale-yellow tunic. "It'll be tight, but better than that smelly silk rag."

As Quen disrobed, Rhoji scowled at Aldewin. "Look away."

Quen sighed. "Niyadi's ass, Rhoji. The guy practically felt me up in front of the entire Conclave."

Rhoji arched an eyebrow.

Aldewin smiled but turned his back.

The shirt was tight across her shoulders. Quen stretched, and a seam ripped. She had to hold the pants up to keep them from falling off her slim hips. "You can turn around now."

As soon as Aldewin saw her unable to let loose of her waistband, he took off his secondary belt. It had a short, thin sword and a dagger sheathed on it. He handed the whole thing to Quen. "They're not the best weapons, but all I could find in Qülla. Weapons are in short supply here, for some reason."

"Probably because Xa'Vatra fears someone will stab her in the back," Shel said.

"A reasonable fear," Imbica said.

Quen wrapped the belt around twice. The steel on her hips was reassuring. They scrounged well-worn boots, a size too small, but better than the useless silk slippers she'd worn in Qülla. *If only I had a keffla.*

As if reading her mind, Eira handed her a tatty muslin keffla. "It's as ugly as Mishny's attitude, but will protect you from the Brothers—and the stink coming off you from the sewers." He screwed up his face and pinched his nostrils shut.

Nivi lay on the grass, busily washing off the blood, guts, and grime from the sewers. His paws were nearly white again.

"If he lets you ride, Imbica and I can share Nabu, if you don't mind," Aldewin said.

Quen nuzzled Nivi's mane. "You're just an overgrown kitten, aren't you?"

Nivi purred.

Aldewin stroked Nivi's back. "He's truly magnificent."

"You're both from Tinox. Do you have any tips on convincing this sweet boy to let me climb aboard?"

Aldewin was so close she felt the heat rising from his skin. Remembering his muscular hands so delicately touching her at the Palace made heat spread from her loins to her navel. *Would he push me away again if I pressed my lips to his?*

Aldewin's eyes were dark, his pupils large. "I suppose you should begin by speaking to him sweetly."

"Do you think he likes sweet talk?"

"He seems to enjoy your voice." He glanced at her, his pale blue-grey eyes peeking at her beneath long lashes. "And your touch."

His hand brushed against hers, and he stepped back. "I'm sorry."

Quen sighed. "Don't be."

"I didn't violate the rules you gave me?"

She had intended to press Aldewin to answers about referring to her as twice blessed and his subterfuge in the Palace di Solis. But being close to him, Quen only wanted to feel him pressed against her, his lips on hers. To forget she was Nixan and now a fugitive. And to ignore that Aldewin knew what she was, but said nothing.

"There is much to discuss, but it will have to wait, won't it?"

He nodded. "Do you need help—to get on his back, I mean?"

She wanted his hands on her waist, lifting her, if only to feel his touch again. But she shook her head. "Only stay near—just in case."

She leaned her head on Nivi's mane, his snowy fur as soft as a kitten's. She whispered into his ear, "May I ride upon your back, friend? If I cannot ride you, I may have to saddle up with a man." The idea of mounting Aldewin made her blush.

Nivi chirped, and she took that as assent. Quen gripped his mane but with care not to pull out hair as she launched onto his back.

To her surprise, Nivi didn't buck or rear. He pushed up and roared.

Aldewin jumped back. The kopeks pranced and nickered.

"You look like you belong there." Aldewin smiled up at her.

"I feel like I belong here." She gave Nivi a pat. "I hope the kopeks get used to my new mount."

"Sorry, Aldewin. Quen is now spoken for," Shel said.

"Shel!" Quen blushed dark crimson.

Aldewin laughed with the rest as he helped Imbica onto Nabu's back.

Rhoji smiled at Quen and gave her a nod. "We must make haste to catch up to Druvna."

"Please tell me he does not intend to head south on the Kovan Road," Imbica said. "It will be crawling with Kovatha."

"We follow the stream west to where it joins the Mitosh River." Aldewin clicked his tongue.

"Then where are we going?" Imbica asked.

Rhoji pointed to the misty mountains in the distance. "To the northern foothills of the TasūZaj range."

"That range is wild and unforgiving. What business could you possibly have there?" Imbica asked.

"The business of staying out of Qülla's dungeons," Rhoji said.

CHAPTER 18

Turbulent waters roiled below Druvna's Jagaru pod as they hugged the precipice overlooking the Mitosh River. Qülla at their backs, the churning river created a deafening roar as they sped toward the wild terrain of the TasūZaj mountains. Druvna pressed the pod hard and brooked no complaint from human or beast when they didn't stop for food or rest.

After a few hours, Imbica called from the back of the column. "Druvna, you must allow the animals to rest. And permit us a bit of sustenance."

"You was the one that warned of Kovathas, wasn't you? You wanna be a feast for scavengers, woman? Or live another day?" Druvna's glare was sharp enough to peel hide from flesh.

None suggested rest after that.

Shel steered alongside Imbica and handed her a rod of kabu stalk. "It'll take the edge from your hunger."

Imbica hesitated. After looking around and noticing all of them sucked the stalks, she took Shel's offering. Imbica's smile looked forced, and she uttered a stiff "Thank you."

This is the first time I've seen her thank someone.

By late afternoon, the rocky slopes were behind, and a vast valley lay ahead. The hazy purple peaks of the enormous TasūZaj range loomed on the horizon.

The closer they got to the craggy peaks, the more relief set in. *We somehow escaped Qülla.* But the respite from worry was brief. Ahead loomed a wall of black basalt and grey granite. Quen whispered to Shel, "Do you know where we're going?"

Shel pointed to the forbidding grey peaks. "We gotta get over the Mitosh River and up into those mountains."

"Imbica told me you can only cross the river at the Niri Bridge."

Shel spat kabu juice. "That's what the Dynasty wants people to think. That way they can tax 'em and control what comes in and out. But people find ways to get around the Dynasty's rules." She winked.

Quen gazed at the path ahead. Now the gorge was visible to the south. Their trail appeared to end at a vertical wall of granite. "I don't have spider legs." *At least not yet.* "I see no way beyond that wall of rock."

Shel laughed. "If I told you what we've gotta do, you'd turn that tiger around and run in the other direction."

"Not an option." While she was still trying to imagine what Shel was talking about, the air crackled.

Shel yowled. Her backside was afire.

From behind, Aldewin and Imbica called in unison, "Kovathas!"

Shel leaped from her kopek and rolled on the ground, dousing the flames. Her leather riding girdle and jerkin were smoking, but it appeared the mage-fire hadn't severely injured her.

Imbica turned backward in the saddle, her leg looped under Aldewin's. Her lips moved as she wound her arms, readying to cast a spell. "By the Three, there are more Vay'Nada spawn than just the giant purple one. And my former friend, Indris." Imbica tsked. "*She* needs a yindril." The contempt was evident in her tone.

Mishny, Druvna, Eira, and Rhoji pulled up and halted, their kopeks dancing nervously. Shel scrambled back to her kopek, apparently unfazed by being on fire moments before.

The ridges on Quen's neck tingled. Her vision narrowed as if she were looking through a dark tunnel. *Don't pass out.* Bile rose in her throat as the now-familiar Nixan voice spoke to her. *Turn*, it said. Quen hesitated, and a chilly breeze prickled the skin on her arms. "*Jijig,*" the inner voice said. Quen recognized the word as a name. *How do I know that?*

A fireball intended for Mishny zinged past Quen's head. It missed its mark and hurtled instead onto a large black boulder.

Face them, the inner Nixan voice commanded.

From above, someone called out, "Rain fire on them!"

Mage fire sizzled past. Quen's bowels quivered, fearing what was behind, but she glanced back anyway.

Three dragons rapidly approached, flying in a tight V formation. Each carried a Kovatha mage on its back, and the largest, lead dragon also had a yindril passenger. The three approaching dragons were smaller than Vahgrin.

The lead dragon's pale-green scales shone like fresh pea shoots in spring. To its left, a vibrant chartreuse dragon flew, and on its right, a dragon the color of yellow-orange spring desert poppies. *These dragons aren't cute like a pet cat, but they're not as fearsome looking as Vahgrin.*

The lead dragon in the formation screeched in pain, its eyes wide and frightened. The Kovatha riding it, the one Imbica called Indris, screamed. "Fly straight, you stupid beast!" The mage held a rod she slapped against the dragon's backside. Sky-fire erupted from the prod jolting the creature. The dragon uttered a soul-rending howl. The yindril riding behind Indris opened and closed its baleen-filled maw and wailed a lament.

The two other Kovathas had similar prods. All three mages smacked at the scaly flesh of their flying mounts, urging the three dragons to fly faster.

I'd like to put an arrow through the Kovatha who harms Jijig. The sentiment arose from the Nixan soul. Somehow, the Rajani soul within her knew these dragons. "*Doka,*" the inner voice said.

Nivi sprinted to catch up with the rest of the pod. *'Doka'? My Nixan soul is trying to tell me something—but what?* Quen pondered Doka, the Pillar associated with wood, plants, spring, birth, and renewal. Considered the opposite of Vatra Pillar, the Corner of war and masters of the Orrokan arts, Doka was known as a Pillar of healing and peace. *These are healing dragons, like Doka Pillar?* Her neck ridge burned, and her second heart fluttered.

"Damn us all to Vay'Nada's cold ass. There's more of those shadow-spawn," Druvna said.

The Dynasty has gotten its hands on dragons. But how? Even with the extra Menaris power the Kovathas pulled from the yindril, they were unable to control the dragons the way Rajani controlled Vahgrin. Still, the Dynasty's dominion over three dragons deeply troubled Quen.

No wonder the Dynasty is desperate to force a Rajani into service. Is that why Aldewin lied to Xa'Vatra? Intuition told her he was trying to protect her. *But how could he know I carry a Rajani soul inside?*

More questions to be reckoned with. *Later. After we've dealt with these Kovatha.*

Imbica met Indris's sizzling fireballs with water, creating puffs of steam. Aldewin kept Nabu running at full speed, though the frightened beast needed little encouragement to run from the dragon-riding Kovathas hurling mage-fire at them.

At the southern horizon, the mighty Mitosh cut a deep gash through the land and cut off escape in that direction. The Mitosh River's steep banks threatened on their left while the three Kovathas behind forced them into a gauntlet. Straight ahead, into a wall of ice and basalt, was the only way forward.

Mishny brought her kopek alongside Druvna and yelled out, "Jagaru-jab!" Raised off the saddle and gripping with only her thighs, Mishny leaped from her kopek, aiming to land behind Druvna. It was a daring move, and she nearly made it, but missed. Druvna grabbed her, and Mishny's legs dragged the dirt for a few seconds.

"Push off, damn you," Druvna hollered. "I can no'a hold you for long."

Mishny hollered as Druvna hoisted, and Mishny flung herself onto the saddle. Now riding backward, she pulled her bow and nocked an arrow.

While Mishny was busy getting onto Druvna's kopek, Shel slowed and rode alongside her brother. Quen had often seen the two perform the Jagaru-jab at Tide di Solis festival, but Quen was still worried for her friend. If Eira missed, a galloping kopek could trample him.

Eira knelt with both feet on the saddle while Shel kept her eyes on him, doing her best to match the speed of his mount. Eira yelled, "Hika!" and leaped onto Shel's kopek. His foot slipped, and he nearly fell, but Eira grabbed the saddle and pulled himself up, Shel lending a hand.

Mishny let two arrows fly, but she was better at stabbing than shooting. One arrow flew left of anything. The other bounced off Jijig's thick, scale-covered skin.

Within seconds, Eira had a bow in hand and an arrow nocked. Quen had seen him split another's arrow while riding at full speed. *Juka's luck be with Eira.*

Eira took a deep breath and aimed. He loosed, and his arrow struck Indris's leg. The woman grunted, but Eira's hit did nothing to slow the dragons' advance.

The closer they got to the mountains, the clearer Quen's vision of what lay ahead. A vertical rock-face walled off escape to the north. The mountains were only approachable if one got across the river chasm.

Rhoji must have seen what Quen did. He said, "We ride kopeks, Druvna, not mountain goats."

"Trust me, young Jagaru, and follow," Druvna called.

Aldewin rode beside Quen. "There's a tunnel through the mountain. We just must cross the chasm."

His words weren't reassuring. From a mile away, it didn't look like there was a way across the canyon.

Fire sizzled, and Nivi yowled. The mage-fire singed the fur on his rump, creating an oozing red wound.

Enraged, Quen wished she could hurl a cartful of Hiyadi's fire at the Kovatha who'd injured Nivi. The Nixan power she pulled from within, though, was unpredictable. If she allowed herself to unleash it, she could harm Nivi rather than injure his attacker.

Aldewin pulled a small pouch from his waist. "Use this." He tossed the bag to Quen.

She opened the pouch, and the odor of rot assaulted her. Quen's nose scrunched up at the smell of the tarry brown substance.

"Trust me," Aldewin called. "It will help him."

Quen pinched some goo between her fingers and rubbed it onto Nivi's angry wound. He growled but didn't throw her and kept pace despite his injury.

"You are a brave warrior, Nivi."

"Is he okay?" Rhoji called.

"He'll live, but the Kovatha that did this to him won't." She pulled a throwing knife from the scabbard on her left hip. *Lumine be with my blade*, she prayed. Quen doused her anger with Still Waters as Pahpi had taught her. Keeping her eyes on the mage, Quen trusted Nivi to watch the path ahead while she aimed for Indris, the lead Kovatha. Aiming for the woman's heart, she flung the steel blade with all her might. The blade's tip struck below the chest, missing the Kovatha's heart.

As the knife struck, the Kovatha's eyes grew wide, the blade sticking out of her side. The Kovatha dropped the prod she'd been using to control Jijig. As she grabbed the hilt of Quen's blade and pulled, her face turned ashen. No longer gripping the dragon's neck, the Kovatha wobbled. She tried to right herself but couldn't get a grip. Her black robes spread like bat wings as she plummeted from Jijig's back. She landed in the powdery soil behind them, sending up a cloud of grey dust. The yindril ceased yowling but remained on Jijig's back.

Shel and Rhoji both whooped. "One down, two to go," Rhoji said.

"You've got one more shot. We need to cross that canyon."

Mishny had sent at least a half-dozen arrows, but all failed to hit a target. She nocked another arrow and pulled back the bowstring. Mishny's arms shook as she waited for the right moment. The arrow zinged and hit the Kovatha on the chartreuse dragon in the shoulder. It didn't kill him, but he screamed as though the arrow had pierced his heart.

Druvna held up a fist, the signal to stop. They were at a dead end. Solid ground gave way to a forty-foot span across a deep chasm. Below, the raging Mitosh roiled in a deep chasm.

"The mounts will no'a step onto the bridge, so you need to leave 'em behind. Hurry now, Rhoji, Eira, and Shel. Step up and go. Quickly. We'll hold 'em off for you."

The 'bridge' that Druvna spoke of was a rickety-looking contraption of wood ladders lashed together and spanning the chasm. The wood was sun-bleached and looked like it would splinter if breathed upon.

Shel looked in no hurry to be the first across. "They'll pick us off if we don't take out the mages before we cross." She nocked an arrow.

Eira hesitated at the edge and tested the ladder with one foot, keeping the other safely on solid ground. Placing a foot on the ladder made the whole apparatus sway and creak. He gingerly placed his other foot and held his arms to his sides for balance. *Just don't look down, Eira.*

Imbica, now off Aldewin's dappled horse and with both feet on the ground, wound her arms. "Hiyadi scimir." When she'd used the same spell during Vahgrin's attack on their way to Qülla, Imbica had produced a long, shining sword that looked like sky-fire. This time, the weapon she pulled from the void was a small, shimmering blade that looked like it would blink out of existence before she could hurl it.

She must be tired. The woman had conjured countless water shields to counter the barrage of fire attacks from the Kovathas. *We wouldn't have made it without her.*

Wet hair matted the squat woman's puffy red face. Imbica launched the small blade, and it struck the last remaining unscathed Kovatha in the side. The conjured blade dissolved nearly immediately. Though it didn't kill the mage, it seared a deep burn into the woman's side.

The distraction gave Shel ample time to line up a shot. She let go of the tension, and her arrow hit the same mage in the forehead, squarely between the eyes.

Rhoji was now on the ladder, about a body's length behind Eira. They inched along, stepping carefully in unison, so they didn't bounce the other.

Two dragons were now without Kovatha riders. They hovered and altered their formation, so the only dragon with a rider was in front. The remaining Kovatha pulled a poultice from his waist pouch and held it against his shoulder. *Maybe it's the same medicinal Aldewin gave me for Nivi's burn.* The Kovatha spoke to the dragons, but the din of the churning Mitosh River ate his words.

Eira whooped happily as he set foot on the other side of the canyon. He held out a hand to help Rhoji tackle the last few feet of the treacherous, swaying ladder. Once Rhoji was across, they happily embraced, and Quen sighed with relief.

Eira called out to his sister. "Come, Shel."

Rhoji added, "It's not that bad."

Shel said, "Is that why you now have a brown stain in your pants?" Shel held out a hand behind her to Imbica. "Move across with me, Imbica. We'll step together, as Rhoji and Eira did."

The two women eased across the ladder.

The remaining Kovatha was having trouble bending the dragons to his will. Jijig, no longer subject to a prod, flew erratically, the yindril gripping Jijig's long neck with overly long arms and hands. Using varying chirps and clicks, Jijig called to the other two dragons. The last Kovatha slapped hard against the hide of the dragon he was on, sending jolts of sky-fire into it.

Quen had vowed to bring Vahgrin to justice, but she couldn't find it in her heart to despise these three dragons. *The Dynasty has done them an injustice, like Nivi and me.*

Dump your rider, Jijig. Lead the others and fly away. To where, Quen didn't know. *There must be a place where dragons can be free of the Dynasty and that dragon cult.*

From deep within, Quen's second heart thrummed wildly. The unwelcome voice within said, *"Bídea wheha, Jijig."* The Nixan repeated this inside Quen's mind, making her head pound and ache. Finally, Quen blurted out loud, "Bídea wheha, Jijig!"

The chartreuse dragon cocked its head as if listening. Quen's neck ridges burned, and her Nixan counterpart forced the foreign words from her mouth again. "Bídea wheha, Jijig!" This time, Quen's voice came out deeper and more sonorous.

Jijig called again to the other dragons and, with the yindril still riding, turned north. The dragon with a Kovatha passenger swooped straight up, then lunged downward. She whipped her tail against her rider's thighs and unseated him. The Kovatha tried to cling to the dragon, but its scaly skin was slippery, and he couldn't find purchase. Flying low to the ground, he tumbled. The mage pushed off the ground, covered in grey dust, winded but alive.

By the time the Kovatha stood, Jijig had led the other dragons away. She called in a low, mournful voice, not unlike yindrils keening, and the yindril's cry joined Jijig's, but soon their voices were heard no more. The dragons flew higher and higher until they were dots in the sky. Quen didn't know what she'd said or where the dragons and yindril went.

Aldewin was now across the divide, as were the rest of the pod save for Druvna, Quen, and Nivi. Druvna practically danced across the ladder. "You've gotta leave the hair bag behind, Quen."

The remaining Kovatha with the injured shoulder ambled toward them. "I'll take good care of him." He sneered. "He'll be back in a cage where he belongs. As will you." The mage hurled a tight ball of fire at Quen.

Quen's reflexes, only part human, were swift. She bent backward, and the mage's fire attack scorched the air over Quen's bent body.

The mage's face was red like Imbica's from exertion. He wound his arms, but they were shaking.

He's tuckered out as well. Quen suspected the last volley he'd thrown had been the strongest he had left. *But I'm not waiting on the edge of this precipice to find out.*

"I promised my friend he'd never see the inside of a cage again. If you want to take him, it will be over my dead body." Quen pulled the thin blade from the scabbard on her right hip and leaped. She had spring in her legs she hadn't known before, and she bounded unnaturally high and far. Quen slashed downward with the blade, slicing the front of the man's tunic clean in two. His torso gushed crimson, and his hand instinctively felt at his chest to assess the damage. While he was still gaping at what she'd done, Quen sliced from right to left, opening his belly. The Kovatha mage, his mouth agape, fell into his own entrails with a sickening squish.

"By the grace of the Three, I'm glad you're on my side." Druvna motioned for her to hurry across the ladder. "Be quick now." He grabbed for the hammer hanging at his belt. "After you get across, I'll break it down, so no chance of any Dynasty guards following on foot."

Quen wasn't keen on putting her life in the hands of such weak-looking wood and was even less enamored with leaving Nivi behind. She pressed her mouth to the cat's ear. "You can make it, my friend. With the heart of Niyadi, the grace of Lumine, and Juka's breath at your back, we can do this."

Nivi knelt, and Quen hitched her leg astride. She tugged lightly on his mane, steering him from the edge.

"Suda, Quen! What in Vay'Nada are you doing?" Rhoji screamed. "It's too far. Even for Nivi."

The Jagaru pod and Imbica stood on the other side of the gorge, eyes wide and clearly worried for her. All except Mishny, who stood with arms crossed, glaring.

Quen gripped Nivi's ribs tightly with her thighs and leaned forward, her face next to his ear. "Don't listen to them, Nivi. I know you can do this." The encouragement was more for her sake than his.

"Hika!" Quen shouted. She kicked lightly, and Nivi ran at full speed. His muscles rippled beneath her. Icy, damp wind whipped out of the river gorge.

The exhilaration of danger made her head swim, and her heart thrummed its unusual double thump. The ground melted away, the path lost in a black void.

Nivi roared as he stretched his mighty front legs and pushed off with his back. He leaped into the icy air.

Time stretched ahead while below, her friends shouted encouragement. Nivi's roar still rippled through the air. *We're going to make it.*

Nivi's front paws grabbed at the edge of the canyon wall. His long claws dug into the frozen dirt, his eyes showing whites. Quen wound her arms tightly around him as his back end swung downward. Her knees hit the rock wall as they slammed into the cliff face.

Druvna's hammering echoed in the deep canyon. Shel screamed, and voices shouted out to her.

Nivi's muscles shook with the effort of holding them.

"Hold on, and trust me. I won't let you go." She hollered into his ear to be heard over the roar of the raging water below. Quen found a handhold on the rock above, dug her fingers into frozen dirt, and pulled herself up. She reached the top of the rock wall and crawled on her belly as she edged onto a patch of frozen ground.

Without taking time to regain strength, she leaned over the side. While Quen reached for Nivi, someone grabbed her legs.

Aldewin fell to the ground at her side and grabbed Nivi's paw. "Pull us, Rhoji."

Rhoji yanked Quen backward as she and Aldewin pulled Nivi with all their might. Together, they hoisted the giant snow tiger out of the canyon.

On solid ground again, Nivi shook his mane, icy droplets spraying them. He roared approval.

Rhoji hugged Quen. "Come before Mishny gets so angry she stabs one of us."

I wouldn't put it past her. She seems to enjoy stabbing people.

Mishny stood atop a rock wall nearly eight feet tall and gestured for them to follow. Hoisting herself and Nivi out of the canyon had made Quen's arms feel like they would come out of their sockets. She hoped she'd make it up because there was nothing behind to run back to.

Imbica, Shel, and Eira were already running through the dark tunnel into the mountain. Aldewin entered the tunnel and created a ball of mage light, illuminating their path. Rhoji followed behind him, and Nivi chirped as he entered the tunnel.

Quen stood at the base of the rock face, waiting for Druvna. She yelled, "Come on, Druvna!" *The old man might not make it up the wall without my help.*

Druvna drew back his hammer and gave the sturdy wood a firm whack. "One more strike and—" The wood finally split, severing it from the canyon's edge. The ladder fell into the chasm and crashed on the boulders below.

Druvna pushed up and looked pleased with himself. He wiped the sweat from his brow, his split lip curled in a smile. "That'll do it." As he stowed his hammer, the air crackled with the hiss of fire.

The mage Indris, who'd fallen like a huge black bat, limped toward them. Her face was so pale she looked ghostly. Her black robes clung to her side where the blade had struck her, but apparently, it wasn't deep enough to be fatal. Indris's hair was disheveled, and pale-grey dust covered her once-pristine black robes. The lone and injured Kovatha conjured a sky-fire blade and flung it at Druvna's back.

Quen called out, "Druvna!" But the magical blade conjured from the void hit Druvna while Quen's words still echoed off the granite walls around them.

His look of joy gone, Druvna cried out in agony. Quen rushed to him. Druvna lay face-down, his back an angry bleeding ulcer, his fingers still gripping his hammer.

Engulfed in rage, Quen didn't consider the additional scar on her heart. *I'll get justice for Druvna, even if I still haven't gotten justice for Pahpi.* She grabbed Druvna's hammer and flung it with all her strength. By the grace of the Three, the hammer struck the mage's chest, knocking the wind out of her. As the mallet fell into the icy canyon, the mage's chest opened like a cracked egg, the insides spilling out. She fell into the deeps below, crashing onto the jutting rocks at the bottom of the canyon.

"Good riddance, you blighted shadow-spawn bitch." The curse felt good. Quen knelt and pulled Druvna over and toward her. His breaths were ragged, his eyes glassy. She searched her belt pouch for the poultice Aldewin had given her. "Stay with me, Druvna." Her hands shook as she opened the bag, hot tears welling.

Mishny scrambled down the rock wall and rushed toward them. "Get away from him. Don't you touch him." Mishny's voice reeked of contempt. She pushed Quen away and gave her a look that could boil leather. Quen kicked at the rocks and backed away to give Mishny room.

"Them Kovathas got no honor among 'em, do they?" Druvna said. His voice was hoarse, his split lip making his shallow breaths whistle.

"Not a shred of honor," Mishny said. Tears rolled down her dusty cheeks as she held him to her. "You'll have to teach the lot of 'em a lesson, you will. 'Bout honor." Her lower lip quivered.

"The pod is yours now. Watch over 'em, woman. They're young." He coughed. "They need you guidin' 'em more than they know."

Mishny rocked him. "The pod's still yours, you crusty old bastard. Don't leave me. You promised you'd always have my back." Black kohl liner streaked her face.

Druvna raised a shaky arm and pointed at Quen. "Get that one to Val'Enara." His glassy eyes looked as though he was trying to bring her face into focus. His hand plopped to the ground. "She's…"

Druvna's eyes were vacant, his body as still as stone. His head flopped to the side. Druvna was no more.

Mishny shook him. "Wake, you bastard!" Her guttural scream echoed in the canyon. "You promised we'd be a team to the end."

Hiyadi now kissed the horizon, his light fading fast from the world. The temperature was dipping quickly.

Cold and grief-stricken, Quen shivered. She lightly tugged at Mishny. "Come. We must meet up with the others."

Mishny flinched. "Leave me! You as good as killed 'im."

The words stung. "I know you're hurting, but he died trying to protect us. We do his memory no service if we remain here and perish from the cold."

Mishny turned on Quen, her eyes red with tears and rage. "He died protecting *you*—a freak. A damned slint wearing a human skin is what you are. And it's your fault he's dead." She rocked him harder, her voice cracking with emotion. "And don't dare tell me how to honor him. *You* don't speak of him again. Ever."

Without another word, Mishny cut Druvna's coin purse from his belt and pulled his good khopesh blade from the scabbard. She took his dented Jagaru helmet and put it on her head. There was no Nilva. No prayers to Lumine or the Brothers. Mishny unceremoniously rolled Druvna to the edge and into the chasm. The roiling water was so loud that it masked the sound of Druvna's body crashing on the below rocks.

Mishny wiped her face and ran to scramble up the rock wall. She didn't look back and didn't offer to help Quen.

Staring down into the deep gorge, Quen tried to see where Druvna had landed. She wished Mishny had allowed her to say a quick Nilva for the man before abruptly pushing him into the chasm's shadow. Druvna followed Vaya di Vatra—the Way of Fire—in life. She hoped he'd find his way to the arms of Hiyadi in death. *Please, Brothers, open your arms for Druvna. I pray Hiyadi shines his light upon you, Druvna, now and forever.* She wiped her runny nose with her sleeve.

Grief made everything ache. Her arms were like two soggy tubers gone to mush. Quen clambered up the wall and dug her fingers into the ice on the ledge above, but they were already tired from helping hoist Nivi. Heartache sapped her strength to pull. She hung like a carcass, her legs scrambling in vain to push up. She howled in frustration.

Strong hands gripped her wrists. "Mourn him later," Rhoji said.

Hearing his voice renewed her resolve. With Rhoji's help, Quen pulled herself to the rocky ledge. Imbica had come back with Rhoji. *I figured she'd leave us behind the first chance she got.*

"Quickly, Quen," Imbica said. "We must catch up with the others."

Imbica mumbled an incantation, and a mage light hovered in the air ahead, casting a bright blue-white light onto the chiseled stone walls. Quen followed Imbica, and Rhoji took up the rear as they entered the mountain pass. Quen and Rhoji had to duck and walk single file and hunched over.

"How far is it?" Quen asked.

"I don't know," Rhoji answered. "I had gotten only partway when Imbica called me back to help you."

They walked into a dark abyss of unknowns, hearts heavy with another loss. Nivi's roar echoed ahead in the stone corridor. It was the signpost Quen moved toward as she ran through the dark, but to what, she didn't know.

CHAPTER 19

Extricated from Qülla but cut off from all routes save the one, Quen followed Imbica into a murky tunnel caked with ice. The cave's black basalt walls devoured Imbica's blue-white mage light. *It's like being trapped in a stone tomb.*

At last, a cool breeze chased away the dank, musty air, and the darkness dissipated. Ahead were familiar voices. Shel and Eira gathered wood in a green alpine meadow of silky grass and wildflowers. Nivi lay washing in a cozy grove of white-barked trees, their shimmery leaves dancing in the late-afternoon breeze. Protected from harsh winds, the grove was cool, but not frigid.

Across the clearing, Mishny hollered while Aldewin frowned and shook his head, his arms crossed. *I wonder what they're arguing about?*

Eira and Shel hurried to meet them. Nivi stopped washing long enough to nuzzle Quen's shoulder.

"We were concerned for you," Eira said. He gestured toward Aldewin and Mishny. "Your arrival might stop their bickering. Aldewin wanted to return to get you, but Mishny ordered us to stay."

Heat bloomed on Rhoji's neck. "You were going to leave us?"

Eira looked wounded. "No." He stretched out a hand to Rhoji but pulled it back. "I—*we*—wouldn't leave you."

Shel put in, "We knew that with Imbica, you'd be fine." Shel said to Imbica, "You're one powerful mage."

Imbica, possibly unused to praise, nervously pushed stray hair from her face. "I am happy to be of service."

Rhoji undid the leather thong tying his hair, and the late-day breeze caught his long, dark locks. "You two have ridden with Mishny longer than us. What's going on here?"

Eira hunched his shoulders.

Shel said, "She and Druvna were close in their own way. She mourns him."

"Mishny blames me for Druvna's death." Quen sighed. "She's right. If Druvna hadn't come to Qülla—"

"And you think blaming yourself, or accepting the lash of Mishny's tongue, will bring him back?" Imbica said.

"Well, no, but—"

"Druvna lived by his own terms." Imbica's eyes were watery, and she swallowed hard. "He died doing what he believed. That's more than most can say. He had an honorable death. One fitting a noble Jagaru."

The statement was true but surprising, coming from Imbica.

From behind, Mishny clapped slowly. "Gracious speech, Kovatha. Too bad you didn't live by that sentiment when it could have helped him avoid torture in

Qülla's dungeon. Or have you forgotten you're the one that put him there?"

Imbica smoothed her tunic. "I have not forgotten. I cannot undo it now."

Rhoji sighed. "You two can cast blame on the long walk ahead. For now, let us camp, rest, and rejoice that we still live. Druvna would want that, right?"

Shel raised her water skin in the air. "Hear, hear. We'll drink a Sayari ale toast to Druvna." She wiped a tear. "And pass the heja."

Mishny glared but held her tongue.

Quen didn't care about ale, heja, or even food. *All I want is answers only Aldewin can give.* But he'd disappeared into the thick woods. "Where did Aldewin go?"

Mishny growled her answer. "To hunt. Animals, not children, so you might go hungry."

It was a barb about Quen being a slint. Quen was moving on Mishny, intending to land a blow the woman wouldn't soon forget. But Rhoji and Shel held her back.

"Come. We'll hunt, too," Shel said. She whispered into Quen's ear, "And look for Aldewin."

Mishny crossed her arms and smirked, baiting Quen to act like the monster Mishny accused her of being. *Still Waters. I will not prove her right.* Quen left Mishny to glower and followed Shel into the forest.

Hiyadi set, and they finished hunting by Niyadi's pale light. Shel and Quen hadn't found Aldewin while hunting, but he showed up to help them dress the game. After the hard riding and the battle to escape Suab'Hora Province, the charred flesh of rabbit and squirrel was a feast. Mishny pointedly avoided Quen but gathered around the fire with the rest to share the pipe and drink.

Camp was uncharacteristically hushed. *Are they exhausted like me, or avoiding talk of Druvna?* No one had an appetite for baiting Mishny's ire. Eira played slow, sweet melodies on his double pipe flute. Shel's eyes were closed, and Imbica lightly snored.

Quen's body ached from the day's labor. Still, her mind raced with unanswered questions—and anxiety about the increasing encroachment of her Nixan soul. But the pod's plans were foremost on her mind. Since they were now wanted criminals, the pod needed to stay out of Qülla and the entire Suab'Hora Province for the foreseeable future. Though Indrasi was vast, knowing the Dynasty had a small army of Kovatha mages and possibly more dragons made it feel smaller to Quen than before.

She hesitated to bring up Druvna for fear of Mishny's wrath, but his last words concerned her. *I must know what he meant.* She prodded the fire with a long stick, sending up sparks. "Before he died, Druvna said to make sure I got to Val'Enara. What did he mean by that?"

Mishny spat sayari ale at the fire, sending the flames higher. "Ask those two." She pointed at Aldewin and Rhoji. "But I lead the pod now. I decide what we do and where we go. We're not getting swallowed by the Chasm of Nil so you can bury yourself in scrolls and escape the world. I'll never know why Druvna made a deal to escort you there. I told him you'd be more trouble than you're worth, and by Niyadi's ass, I was right." Her eyes were wide and dark, and her voice edged in a bitter tone.

"Deal with who?" Quen asked.

Previously reclining, Rhoji bolted upright, his jaw tensed, and he interrupted. "You were there when we made the plan, Mishny. You agreed—"

"*I* didn't agree to shite. Druvna agreed. As leader of the pod, it was his right. But he's dead now because of that one, and I'll not follow him to Vay'Nada's shores. Not today, and not on account of you, Doj'Anira." Spittle shone on her lower lip.

Fury rose in Quen's gullet. She rose, her whole body trembling. "Was anyone going to ask me what I want?"

Learning what she could of Vaya di Menaris and the Orrokan arts would give her the edge she needed to hunt Vahgrin. After all, she'd used Pahpi's lessons in Still Waters to keep the Nixan soul within her locked away. Each day, the changeling became more insistent. *And I now understand the meaning of its words when it speaks to me.* That thought disturbed her the most. *A deeper training in Vaya di Menaris might be the only way to eradicate my shadow soul.*

Val'Enara might be best for me now. But dammit, that's beside the point. Her companions hadn't bothered to ask what she wanted. Her father had told Nevara Quen wasn't a sack of flour to be traded. *But people have treated me like an object. First the Dynasty and now my brother and companions. And what of our hunt for Vahgrin?*

"Phsh," Mishny said. She laughed ironically. "You're complaining about us pulling your arse from a Qülla dungeon? 'Cause I'm happy to personally deliver you back to the Dynasty and collect a fat reward, I'd wager."

"I wasn't talking about that. Not one of you shite-eaters bothered to consider what *I* wanted." She glared first at Rhoji, then Aldewin. Both flinched from her gaze.

Mishny bolted to her feet and pointed a thin finger at Quen. "I don't give a fuck what you want. I don't trust you. Haven't since I first laid eyes on you."

"Why? I did nothing to—"

330

"I don't need to explain myself." Mishny looked around at the others. "And I don't owe any of you lot shite." She pointed to Druvna's dented helmet, still perched cockeyed on her head. "Druvna made me leader, and I decide who's in and out. I decide where this pod goes and what work we take on. And I say we're headed to Vindaô Province—like we planned. We'll find mercenary work and lie low for a while." She stared across the fire at Quen. "Except you, *Doj'Anira*."

Quen's body still shook, and she fought back the tears of anger and hurt. *I feared the pod would reject me if they learned I'm Nixan. It didn't matter. Mishny doesn't even know I'm Rajani, but she booted me anyway.* "I thought we—this pod—was a family. Are you going to let Mishny kick me out? Why not vote? Like we did in Juinar when we decided Earnôt's fate."

"Quen, don't…." Tears shone in the corners of Shel's eyes like bright jewels in the firelight.

Quen's throat was so tight she could barely speak. "My friends…" Her voice was thin, her words barely audible. "I thought we were—family."

Tears choked Eira's voice. "You are like a sister to us, Quen. But… I have to protect the others that I love too." He put his hand in Shel's, and his shoulder touched Rhoji's.

Quen's eyes bored into Rhoji's. Her voice quavered yet held an edge. "And you—my First Kin." She laughed a bitter laugh. "So you will cast me out, too. Finally able to be rid of me like you always wanted." She harrumphed. "I'm surprised it took you this long."

Rhoji pulled at her hand. "We must speak. In private."

Quen crossed her arms and remained planted. "Go ahead. Speak. We have no secrets from the pod." *A lie. We both have secrets, don't we, Rhoji?*

Rhoji pinched the bridge of his nose as Pahpi did when frustrated. The memory was like a dagger through her heart.

"This may be our last chance to talk. I have things to tell you. Things I know you want to hear."

Her need for answers was larger than her pride. Quen rolled her eyes but said, "Fine. Let us speak." She followed Rhoji to the clearing's far side. The night air made her shiver. Quen was ready to lash out at him, but as soon as they stopped, Rhoji scooped her into a hug.

Rhoji whispered, "I thought I'd lost you forever."

Rhoji's uncharacteristic tenderness caught her by surprise, and she hugged him tightly. Her voice was tremulous. "Why are you siding with Mishny? Why send me to Val'Enara when you know it's not what I want? Are you so eager to be rid of me?"

Rhoji held her face between his large hands. "Remember when you were a wee thing? Pahpi told you 'Still Waters' so much, people thought it was your name."

The tension in her shoulders eased, and Quen couldn't help but laugh. Because she didn't respond when people called her 'Still Waters,' the other kids thought she was a dimwit. "Still Waters. That was Pahpi's answer to everything." *Oh, Pahpi. Did you always know what I was? Did you really believe I could keep the Nixan from consuming me by repeating that mantra my whole life?* She let out a tremulous sigh. "He wanted me to study at Val'Enara. Did he—do you think he knew..." She couldn't bring herself to name the Nixan aloud.

Rhoji was pensive, his thoughts momentarily far off. "Honestly, I don't know what Pahpi knew. About many things." He returned his gaze to Quen. "Looking back— the excessive time he spent training you. Repeating that fucking mantra...." His jaw twitched. "I thought he loved you best. But maybe..."

"Maybe he was afraid of me or what I'd become?" Fresh tears welled, and her stomach was a hollow pit.

Rhoji's eyes softened. "His true feelings—about you, me, or any of this—died with him. But of this, I am certain. He loved you, Quen."

"But could he love me if I became... could he truly love a...?" She couldn't say the word out loud.

Rhoji didn't finish her sentence, perhaps also not wanting to give voice to the ugly truth. "What we saw— at the Menagerie. Are you truly—"

A shapeshifting Rajani sorceress dragon rider destined to take part in the destruction of the human world? He's not ready for the whole truth of what I suspect my future holds. "I'm uncertain what I truly am. Or what I'll become if I don't control this—thing inside me." *A partial truth, anyway. Should I mention the scroll Nevara showed Pahpi?* Proof their mother had colluded with the Dragos Sol'iberi to plant a Vay'Nada spawn soul in Quen. *That truth would cut a wound so deep in Rhoji's soul, it would crush him into emotional dust. Besides, he likely wouldn't believe me. People stick with the comfort of lies they've believed rather than truths they don't prefer.*

Quen sighed. "Perhaps it is best for me to go to Val'Enara. Maybe I should trust that Pahpi knew more than he revealed about me." She recalled his argument in Solia with Nevara.

Rhoji nodded. "This was my thinking as well."

"Well, I wish you'd spoken to me about it before acting like a lordly First Kin arsehole."

"I'm sorry I didn't discuss it with you. We've been busy trying to get you out of Qülla—and staying alive." He looked deeply into her bicolored eyes. "I don't understand this Doj'Anira business. Do you?"

She shook her head.

"You know Pahpi wanted you to study at Val'Enara. But did you know he and Lio fought about it?"

She shook her head. *I've never known Pahpi to be angry with Liodhan.*

Rhoji ran his hands through his long hair, unbraided and gritty with road dust. "Ah, Quen. I'm your First Kin now, and I'm supposed to guide you. To know what's best for you. But I'm lost in all this. Dragons. The Dynasty hunting you. Why?" He shrugged. "Before, you mentioned Pahpi knew things we didn't. Maybe Pahpi was right to insist you study at Val'Enara."

She wiped her nose on her sleeve and sniffled. "You, Rhoji Tomo Santu di Sulmére, are saying Pahpi was right?" She felt his forehead. "Are you okay?"

He chuckled. "I think so."

When they were growing up, the nightly meal often lasted for hours. Rhoji and Pahpi debated things like Kovan policy, the meanings of various sutras of the Vaya di Solis, or the best way to make a hide supple. Quen rarely entered the fray, content to listen and weigh both sides. Sometimes she agreed with Rhoji but kept her thoughts to herself, not wanting to cause Pahpi more consternation. "It's unlike you to agree with anything Pahpi wanted or said."

Rhoji picked at a tree's bark and flicked a piece off. "Maybe what we've been through—since the fires in Solia. My eyes have opened."

"Pahpi would have liked to hear you say that." Quen's throat was tight.

"I know you want to stay with the pod. You enjoy the ranging life."

"It suits me." *I'd gladly exchange a comfortable life for the intrigue of the unknown.* She glanced back at the pod, and her eyes landed on Aldewin. *And maybe more than wanderlust or justice binds me to the pod.*

"You can range again. Spreading the gospel of the Vaya di Solis around the Sulmére." He smirked.

Quen lightly punched his shoulder. "Don't make fun of me."

"I'm not." The breeze caught his blue feather earring and twirled it against his cheek. He laughed. "Okay, I kind of am. But the point is, we both need somewhere safe to land while we figure it out."

"Where do you intend to land? You never seemed like Jagaru to me."

Rhoji nodded. "I'll admit it was not Mishny's idea to head to Vindaô Province." His eyes caught sight of Eira. "The wine merchant you saw me with at the capital—Ser Chervais. He offered me a position at his estate in Bardivia. Said there's plenty of mercenary work. Tensions are growing between Bardivia and the Dynasty, so the wealthier merchants are bulking up their personal and house guards. The pod should easily find work."

There was still a question tickling her brain. Mishny had implied that Rhoji and Aldewin conspired in the plan to send Quen to Val'Enara rather than staying with the Jagaru.

"You were involved in the Val'Enara plan. But what of Aldewin? How did he figure into this?" That Aldewin would deign to make plans for her irritated her, yet it gladdened her that he cared enough to consider her. Quen vacillated between wanting to bed the man or break him.

"If you hate the monk's life, blame him. It was Aldewin's idea. He and Druvna approached me as your First Kin. I agreed it was a good idea even before what happened at the Menagerie."

"Why would you consider Val'Enara the right path before the Menagerie? You saw how much I've enjoyed ranging with the Jagaru. How I finally belonged somewhere." Hot tears sprang to her eyes again.

Rhoji's eyes watered too. "You've never fooled me. I've known you were different my whole life."

Her heart thumped wildly, and a band of anxiety tightened her chest. "What do you mean?"

Rhoji smiled warmly at her. "You could always jump higher and run faster than anyone. Like freakishly swift." He tucked a tendril of hair behind her ear. "How Pahpi spent so much time training you in Vaya d'Enara stillness, but hardly noticed I existed." His lips pulled tighter.

"I'm sorry." *I truly am. I never asked for Pahpi's constant attention.*

Rhoji shook his head, closed his eyes, and swallowed. "It's not something for you to regret. I know this now, though as children, I often resented you. Hated you even."

She'd often felt like he hated her, but hearing it spoken aloud still stung. She'd never understood what she'd done to make him so angry at her. At least now she knew.

"But you were also—my only friend." Fat tears welled in his eyes.

Quen threw her arms around him, her face buried in his shoulder. "I'm scared, Rhoji."

"I know, sol'dishi." He smoothed her dusty hair, and his hand swept over the bony ridge at the base of her skull. He pulled his hand away. "I am scared too."

He didn't have to say it. Quen, and the Nixan she'd become, frightened Rhoji. *Slints do not remember their family.* At least that was what stories said of them. *And if I'm Rajani? People don't trust women who consort with Vay'Nada spawn, like dragons.*

Rhoji forced a wan smile. "I know you hold Lumine's light in your heart. Perhaps Val'Enara, filled with the wisdom of ages past—you will find answers. And lots of bruises from training, according to Aldewin. Good luck with that." He playfully poked her ribs.

Quen smiled back at him. "Yeah, that's better than putting up with Mishny's sour ass."

He laughed. "She will be unbearable." Rhoji put an arm around her shoulder. "Remember, I love you, little sister, and always will."

"No matter what—I become?"

Rhoji held her shoulders. "You are Quen Tomo Santu di Sulmére, daughter of Santu Inzo Dakon di Sulmére. Never forget that." He hugged her. When they separated, he wiped away a tear.

Quen's throat was tight, so she nodded rather than trying to speak. If someone had told her a few months ago that parting from Rhoji would choke her up, she'd have accused them of having curdled drey's milk for brains. After all they'd been through together. And now to know Rhoji had known she was Nixan and loved her, anyway. It made her want to stay with him, yet reinforced why they must separate. *If he stays with me, I only bring the possibility of danger upon him.*

"Come." Rhoji rubbed his arms. "Let us join the others before we freeze."

When they rejoined the group, Mishny was asleep—or at least acting like it—her back to them. Eira, Shel, and Aldewin lounged and still passed the pipe. At the edge of their camp, Nivi was fast asleep, his long legs taking up the space of four men.

Imbica sat cross-legged, her palms resting on her knees, her eyes unblinking and focused on the fire. *Is she in a trance?* Imbica startled Quen when she said, "Welcome back."

Quen sat across from Imbica and accepted the pipe when Shel handed it to her. The bitter smoke burned in her chest yet soothed her mind. She turned her attention to Imbica. "You are my sworn shield. Tomorrow, I will ride with Aldewin and Nivi to Val'Enara. You will join us."

Imbica raised her gaze from the fire. "I will not travel with you to the Chasm of Nil."

The three lounging sat up.

"It took you less than a full day to break your oath," Eira said.

Aldewin blew out heja smoke. "She can't come with us because she's unwelcome at Val'Enara." He offered the pipe to Imbica. "Am I right?"

Imbica waved the heja away. "Val'Enara accepted me as a Rising at age ten. By twelve, the Archon promoted me to Ascended."

Aldewin whistled. "Kensai level by twelve. You were a Menaris prodigy."

338

Imbica nodded, though not with an air of arrogance. "The Three bestow blessings without preference for lineage or wealth. Something the Dynasty has yet to appreciate."

"I second that," Rhoji said.

"Did you get kicked out?" Shel asked.

Eira kicked her foot. "Don't be rude."

Shel kicked him back. "It's an honest question."

Imbica showed no offense at the inquiry. "Before being named Ascended Master, I left of my own accord."

"But you showed such promise. By now, you'd probably be a Zenith." Quen doubted she'd make it past Rising, given she had no aptitude for manipulating the elements of Menaris. Val'Enara might admit her to study the Orrokan art of war and the Vaya di Solis—together known as "The Way." But unless she mastered Menaris, Val'Enara would never promote her above the rank of Rising. *I can't imagine throwing away an opportunity like Imbica had.*

Imbica stretched her arm toward the fire, twirled her fingers, and raised sparkling embers, making them dance. "At Val'Enara, Ascended Masters and Zeniths spend their days charting the heavens, consulting scrolls, teaching younglings, and arguing amongst themselves. If they make it past Kensai, they grow old without seeing the world beyond the Moon Gate."

Shel stoked the fire. "We began traveling with our da while still in training pants. Hard to imagine not ranging across Indrasi."

Eira, leaning back on his forearms, took the pipe. "Our da taught us to read scrolls and tabulate, but he said Menauld was our best teacher."

Imbica yawned behind her hand. "Indeed. What good does command of the Corners do a mage if she's locked in a stone tower, unable to use the gifts the Three gave her to help people?"

Aldewin nodded, his jaw tight. "A fair point, and one I have asked myself since leaving the Pillar."

Imbica flicked her wrist, and the sparkling embers fell back to the fire. "It's enough to make one wonder if the Pillars are high places of learning or—"

"Prisons," Aldewin said.

Imbica sighed and shrugged her shoulders. "I transferred to Val'Vatra to study the Way of Fire and become a Kovatha. The Dynasty has faults, but it sees the value of Menaris." She gave a wry laugh. "I thought I would help people." She smoothed stray gray hairs away from her face. "Look at me now."

"You helped me," Quen said. "If not for you, I'd be dead." *If Imbica knew what I truly was, would she have saved me from Vahgrin's fire?*

"You could return if you wanted, right?" Shel asked. "If they didn't kick you out, you could go back, since you're not a Kovatha anymore." She blew a smoke ring.

"Perhaps I would be welcome. Archon Kine may see me as valuable now I've worked for the Dynasty."

"I imagine that's true," Aldewin said. "If you come with us, you may find a home again at Val'Enara."

Imbica shook her head. "I no longer want to live in a Pillar. And Aldewin, do not forget the Chasm of Nil. I doubt the Guardian will permit me passage." Her face was dour. "Not now. After what I've done—*had* to do— for the Kovan Dynasty."

"Why not?" Quen had more than a passing curiosity about the subject since she had to cross the chasm to walk the Steps of a Thousand Waters and enter Val'Enara.

Imbica stared at her. "I will allow Aldewin to explain it to you as he has crossed the Chasm of Nil more recently than I. You will have time to talk on your journey to the Chasm."

Aldewin and Nivi were capable company for a journey to the Moon Gate. *I took a risk rescuing her. She saved our arses from the Kovathas. But is she getting out of our agreement too easily?* "So, what will you do if I release you from your bond?"

Imbica's eyes grew wide. "I said nothing about release from my promise. I remain your sworn shield. The vow extends to your First Kin. If this arrangement meets your approval, I will be Rhoji's shield until we meet again."

All turned their attention to Rhoji. The memory of Vahgrin's shadow over the land made Quen shudder. With Imbica watching the skies over Rhoji, Quen was more at ease about their parting.

Quen nodded her affirmation, and Imbica gave her a single nod back.

Quen took them in, creating a memory of her strange Jagaru pod. *Nearly all the family I have. Even Mishny. She probably wants me dead, but I care about her, even if she doesn't care for me.* Though Shel and Eira's decision to side with Mishny stung, Quen understood their reluctance to remain in her company after what they'd witnessed in Qülla. *They must protect each other—from me.* Hot tears welled. "Shield them, Imbica. Protect them all."

From dragons, and from whatever I become.

CHAPTER 20

Rainy mist woke Quen from a fitful slumber. She was glad to end the game of trying to sleep. Every time she dozed off, she dreamed of Druvna's vacant eyes. Finally, Hiyadi rose and painted the horizon pale salmon. She tried to pack quietly, but Aldewin had the ears of a hunting dog.

Before the day was done, she'd get answers from Aldewin. But they had many hours ahead for talk. They packed in silence, Aldewin yawning as much as Quen.

Before long, Mishny roused her pod. "Indolence begets the lash of sorrows, and don't think I won't lash you." She was quoting renowned Vaya di Vatra master Vas O'Nai. When the scripture-backed threat of the lash didn't rouse them, she kicked their feet. "Get your arses up, you lazy squib."

Rhoji, Shell, and Eira grumbled as they rose. Imbica didn't curse Mishny, but yawned behind her hand.

With little to pack, Aldewin and Quen were ready before the others finished taking their morning relief. Aldewin clasped forearms with Rhoji. "May you know the Sister's embrace, my friend."

"And the Brothers light your way." Rhoji pulled Aldewin to him and whispered something in his ear.

Quen didn't know what they said, but Aldewin nodded. She imagined her older brother was admonishing Aldewin to watch over her. *Or maybe threatening violence if he becomes too familiar.*

There were teary goodbyes with Eira and Shel. "We will see each other again." Quen hoped it was true. As she embraced Shel, she whispered, "Watch over Rhoji for me."

Imbica gave the friends time to say their goodbyes, then came to Quen. "Hold out your hand."

Quen hesitated. Though her hand no longer showed the purple bruises of Imbica's torture, its memory lingered. Imbica pulled the amber pendant from under her tunic and untied the cord. Quen had forgotten Imbica had taken it.

"I believe this is yours." Imbica put the necklace in Quen's open palm.

In the first grey light of morning, the amber was a nondescript brown blob hanging from a fire-singed cord. Unremarkable in every way, it had no value to anyone but Quen and Rhoji.

"Allow me." Rhoji took the necklace and tied the cord around Quen's neck. The pendant fell to her collarbone.

Quen closed her eyes and took a deep breath of sweet alpine air. At first cold even through her tunic, the amber soon warmed, its weight comforting against her chest.

"You will learn much about Menaris and its secrets at Val'Enara," Imbica said. "But the most potent magic I ever learned was at the knee of my village Bruxia. You know the most important lesson she taught me?"

Quen's heart quickened. She was eager to learn about Vaya di Menaris. She nodded vigorously.

"Love," Imbica said.

Love? "Um, okay."

The crow's feet at the corners of Imbica's eyes crinkled. She gently tucked the pendant into Quen's tunic and patted it. "It's a lesson I have ignored for many years." Her eyes glistened, but she exhaled, and the tears never fell. "A time may come when this amulet will mean the difference between life and death. Use its magic wisely."

Like always, when Imbica tried to impart magical wisdom, Quen didn't understand what the woman meant.

"Until we meet again," Imbica said. She gave Quen a quick bow and left to help Mishny clean the camp.

Rhoji swept her into a hug. "Be well, sister." He kissed her forehead. His eyes were wet and rimmed in red.

"Watch over Shel and Eira," Quen whispered. "I promise to keep Pahpi's lessons in my heart."

Rhoji smiled and gave her a nod, then went to the others, leaving Quen alone with Aldewin and Nivi. "May you always know the Sister's loving embrace," she called to him.

Instead of the usual rote response, Rhoji called, "I know I will."

•　　•　　•

With only one mount animal to ride, Quen and Aldewin had no option but to journey to Val'Enara with Aldewin pressed against Quen's backside. She had planned to confront Aldewin about how he'd lied to her— or withheld information, anyway—from the start. But her mind was a swirling eddy. Aldewin was so close. His warm breath tickled the back of her neck, his firm thighs pressed against hers. Nivi's spine undulated beneath them, the sway forward and back causing Aldewin's loins to press her backside in a seductive rhythm.

Instead of interrogating him, she imagined his warm lips on hers as his firm hands caressed her. She'd never daydreamed about being with someone this way, even the awkward traveling merchant's son with whom she'd spent a few fumbling hours last summer. Her thoughts of Aldewin made her loins painfully tight and her breasts taut, her nipples aroused by the slightest rustle of her tunic.

When Aldewin spoke, it startled her out of her daydream. "You must have many questions for me." His voice was soft and deep.

Can a Val'Enara initiate consort with someone of higher rank? She was glad Aldewin couldn't see the blush bloom from her neck to her hairline. Quen cleared her throat. *Remember, you're still irritated with him.* "Yes, Aldewin di Partha. What do you know about me?" She shook her head. "No, first, what do you know about Doj'Anira?" He'd begun speaking, but she cut him off. "Wait. Why did you lie to the Exalted about me?"

Aldewin sighed. "A good question. Answering requires a lengthy story."

She waved her hand in a sweeping motion. "We've got nothing else to do but tell stories."

"But I'm not permitted to tell parts of this one."

Quen groaned and gently pulled Nivi's mane. She leaped from the tiger's back with the speed and agility she usually held back for fear of startling people. *The time for games is over.* "Cut the shite, Aldewin. We're not going one step farther until you answer my questions."

He shook his head and groaned, his fingertips to his forehead. "Dammit, Quen, I took an oath."

"The Jagaru don't require oaths. At least Rhoji and I didn't take one."

He slid off Nivi's back. "Forget the damned Jagaru. This is about Val'Enara. I took oaths to the Pillar and to Archon Kine. I'm soul-bound to obey the Archon's commands."

"How does this pertain to me? Or my questions?" Hot tears of frustration sprang to her eyes. "For fuck's sake, Aldewin. People have treated me like a sack of jishni flour for weeks. Traded like a common drey." She shook with anger. "And I thought we'd become friends. But no. We were never friends, were we?"

The anger was gone from his face, replaced by melancholy. "I want to be your friend. My feelings about you—for you—are genuine. My soul is...."

"Is what?"

Anguish twisted his mouth, and hot watery tears rimmed his eyes red. "Torn apart. I am bound by an oath—by honor—but it's more... complicated. When you take vows at Val'Enara—you'll learn—it's more than pride or honor. You commit yourself—even your soul—to do the Pillar's work."

Quen stamped the ground. The earth shook, and Nivi growled. "I don't care about the Pillar! I need to know...." Her lip trembled, and her throat was tight. "What am I becoming?"

It was the only question that mattered.

Aldewin stepped closer, gauging her reaction. He took her hand and smiled, his face pale, his eyes nervous. "The truth? I don't know."

She rolled her eyes and tsked.

"You don't have to believe me, but in the name of Lumine and Doj'Madi, I swear to you, I don't know the answer to your question." He sighed. "I'm probably going to spend eternity in the frozen void of Vay'Nada for telling you this...."

Quen moved closer and caught his eye. His look was despairing, but she matched his pain with pleading. Her voice quavered. "Please."

Aldewin let go of her hand and held his arms splayed to the sides, palms up. "About a half-turn ago, Archon Kine summoned me. You need to understand she doesn't do that. The Archon is ancient and spends most of her time in meditation. It is rare for the Archon to summon a Rising."

"Okay. And?"

He put his hands in his pockets. "Kine called on me to perform a task I'm uniquely qualified for, at least among those at Val'Enara." He'd avoided her eyes, but he looked into them now. "Acting on information she gained from a spy, she asked me to go south to retrieve what she called a Doj'Anira."

Quen's stomach felt like it had dropped to her toes. "The Archon of Val'Enara *knew* about Doj'Anira."

Aldewin sucked in a breath, his eyes roving upwards then finding hers again. "Archon Kine not only knew about Doj'Anira, but that *you* are one. She also knew I'd find you in Solia. And that you're *the* Doj'Anira the Dynasty searched for."

The world swirled around her. Quen's breaths were shallow, her head swimming.

Aldewin put out a hand. "You should sit down."

She let him help her to a rock. Eventually, the spinning stopped enough that she could form words. "Pahpi's letter." *What had he told Archon Kine?* It was making sense why Pahpi had reassured Quen the Pillar would accept her when she had no Menaris ability.

Aldewin knelt beside her. "I don't know how she knew. It could have been the letter from your da. However she found out, the Archon tasked me with bringing you to Val'Enara."

"But why you? And why were you with the Jagaru? I mean, I would have come willingly."

"Even for someone like me, it is dangerous to travel alone through the Sulmére. Archon Kine knew of a certain Jagaru captain who'd had trouble in the capital. She paid him handsomely to accompany me, all in the guise of the Jagaru. That way, it would not alert the capital to her plans or your location."

"Druvna knew I was—well, different?"

"Archon Kine ensures people only know what is required to perform her directives. Druvna knew I was from Val'Enara, but little else."

"But did he know about me? Know what I am?"

"Only that you are an immensely important magical being. I don't think he knew you were Nixan."

There. Aldewin said it. The ugly-sounding word was out in the open. *There's no need to tiptoe around it anymore, at least not with him.*

"But *you* knew. Before you even met me, you knew."

He nodded.

The implications made her head hurt. The moments and details of their journey together eddied. He'd lied to her from the start. Along with Druvna, they acted out the charade of hunting the dragon. They were never pursuing Vahgrin. They'd always planned to end up at Val'Enara. Inevitably, they'd break her out of Qülla, but not because they had affection toward her. They merely retrieved valuable cargo to fulfill oaths and contracts. *I was merely a commodity to transport.*

Silent tears streamed down her face. Like a seed husk empty and desiccated by Juka's hot breath, Quen was bereft. She had thought she'd found friends—a family. Even a lover. The memory of Aldewin lying atop her, telling her she was lovely.

"That night, in Juinar."

He averted her gaze and studied the horizon.

Quen gently tugged his face, so he had to look at her. She wanted to see his eyes, to gauge whether his next words were truth or lies. "You played at affection with me for weeks. You said loving words. Were those words lies too?"

"What I told you—" His pale blue-grey eyes softened. "I spoke the truth." He swept the hair from her eye. "The truest thing I've ever said."

Heat radiated from him. His pupils dilated, and his eyes glistened. His full lips parted, and his jaw tensed. Quen detected how his odor changed simply from

349

remembering the night in Juinar. This ability to sense a change in one's odor, evidencing fear or passion, was a new ability courtesy of her Nixan soul. *I'm becoming more animal each day.* It was an unwelcome change.

But she had her answer. Aldewin's affections were genuine. She didn't want that to make her heart soar, but it did.

"You can feel affection for a creature such as myself?"

Aldewin bent closer. He took one of her hands, opened it so it was palm up, and traced the paths and lines of her skin. "We are all creatures with hidden compartments. Where I come from, secrets and lies are common, but the truth rare." He zigzagged across her palm with his finger. "I escaped that life and found purpose at Val'Enara." He stopped and gazed into her eyes. "Then I met you, and I've been unmoored ever since." He cast his gaze downward.

"Are you ashamed to have feelings for someone like me?"

He looked like she'd smacked him in the face with a pan. "Ashamed? Gods, no." He rubbed a hand through his newly cut hair. "Oaths have bound me since my childhood. And I've never gone back on my word. Never." Tears welled in his eyes. "And now, my heart has pulled me in a direction...." He stood and paced. "I find myself questioning."

"The Archon?"

He threw his hands in the air. "Everything!" He rubbed his neck and chuckled. "By the Three, I sound like a novice Rising in his first week at the Pillar."

"Pahpi always said only people lacking the power to mind their way spoke oaths."

Aldewin stopped pacing, and his eyes grew wide. "Suda, Quen, that's exactly what I've been thinking lately." He laughed. "Your da sounds like a wise old Kensai. I wish I'd known him."

His words brought her grief to the fore. It felt like years since she'd seen her father's sun-weathered face, heard his hearty laugh, or listened over evening meal as he tried to bend Rhoji to his way of thinking. Pahpi's light had been extinguished from her world. It created a hole in her soul as raw and festering as the day Vahgrin took him from her. Her tears were silent. Her grief was like the gaping, icy void of Vay'Nada. It crept like a bandit and pilfered the last vestiges of her joy.

"I'm sorry." Aldewin took her hand in his. They sat quietly until her tunic was wet with tears.

The long cry of grief was overdue. Cathartic beyond what she'd expected, the tears dried of their own accord. A few long, heaving breaths and thoughts of her loss diminished and morphed into anxiety about her future. Aldewin had hit her with new information and a decision about her path.

"You said earlier that Archon Kine knew I was Nixan. Tasked you with bringing me to Val'Enara?"

Aldewin nodded.

Quen's gut seized in a knot just thinking about the question. "Do you know what she plans for me?" She wasn't sure she wanted the answer.

He shook his head. "Getting you out of Qülla? Easy decision. Nothing good would come from you being under Xa'Vatra's thumb. But Archon Kine?" He rubbed the stubble on his chin. "She's never shown me anything but kindness. She intervened when Prelate Hrabke wanted to deny my entry. Kine permitted me to study at Val'Enara, even though I exhibited little aptitude for Vaya d'Enara."

That was puzzling to Quen. *I thought Val'Enara rarely accepted people without natural Menaris ability.* "Why would she do that?"

Aldewin shrugged. "She gave me a chance, and for that, I've always felt—"

"Indebted."

There was the hit-in-the-face-with-a-pan look again. "I was going to say grateful, but indebted applies."

Aldewin didn't know Kine's plans for Quen, so there was nothing more about Kine to discuss. She could ask him what his intuition told him, but from the look about him, she feared she'd just shoved a hammer into the wheel spoke of his mind.

"I'm sorry I can't provide all the answers to your questions. I'm a tiny beetle caught in the great web spun by the Archons and the Exalted. They're always spinning, Quen." He flopped down with a thud, and his mood soured. "Like a fat, juicy bug wrapped in spider silk, snared and waiting for them to suck the life force from me."

Quen laughed and playfully kicked at his leg. "A bit dramatic, hey, Aldewin? Were you a mummer in your former life in Tinox?"

He laughed as well. "No, but maybe I should have been." He picked up a pebble and tossed it. "What now?"

The towering mountain's cold shadow brought a chill. Nivi had lain down and was snoring lightly.

"You're asking me for a plan? I haven't been making my own plans for weeks now." She laughed. "Hell, for my whole life, if I'm being honest."

"Maybe it's time you began." Aldewin tossed a pebble at her. "What do you want to do?"

Quen couldn't recall the last time anyone had asked her that. Most days didn't offer many choices. Most of her days were rote routines. When the path came to a fork, others had decided for her. First Pahpi, then Druvna, Imbica, the Exalted, or even Aldewin and Rhoji. She stared at the clear blue sky, beautiful and rare after living in the dusty Sulmére with pale yellow and orange skies. She took deep breaths of clean mountain air and considered what *she* wanted, perhaps for the first time.

Primal desire outweighed reason. A lifetime of longing insinuated itself into the internal conversation, the Nixan soul fanning the flames of her passion.

Quen didn't know what tomorrow held. The tenuous grip she maintained on her own skin was weakening. Forces she still didn't fully understand wanted her for a reason she didn't entirely know. Vahgrin's fiery breath and his Rajani, Nevara, loomed like a shadow.

I understand little more about Aldewin now than I did weeks ago. Maybe he speaks honeyed lies, but I smell his desire. He can't fake the odor of longing. I don't know what will happen tomorrow. But Aldewin is here now. To Vay'Nada with the rest! For now, he's my answer to everything.

Quen sprang and gracefully pounced off her rock perch and straddled his outstretched legs, their chests only a few finger widths apart, their lips nearly touching. His heart had picked up speed, his pupils now so wide his

353

eyes were almost black. He should have been afraid of her. She was at least a little afraid of herself.

But he didn't back away or flinch at her forwardness. He smoldered, his lips parted. He pressed himself forward, open to her touch.

His lips were soft, warm, and yielding beneath hers. Nothing else touching, only the moist flesh of his kiss. Her neck ridge pulsing, the second heartbeat pounding. The heat rising from Aldewin was like the warm sands of her homeland.

Aldewin's hand tangled in her hair, pulling gently but insisting. This kiss was firmer, the need known. He gracefully cradled and tumbled her, his thighs on hers, the full weight of his body pressed into her.

Aldewin stared into her eyes, his desire no longer in question. His thumb traced her bottom lip, and he looked like he did weeks ago when he'd whispered sweet words then retreated.

Will he pull away from me again? She feared what the raging Nixan in her would do if he spurned her affections again. "Do you remember what you promised me that night in Juinar?"

A roguish smile curled his lips, and he kissed her again, darting his tongue into her mouth. His hand swept down her body and found her taut nipples. He rubbed lightly, kissing her so deeply she thought their faces would meld. His voice was low and hoarse. "I have every intention of keeping my promises to you."

As he bent again to kiss her, Quen flipped him off and onto his back. She straddled him again and started working on his tunic's laces. "I will hold you to that."

"I expect you will."

One hand on his manhood, the other playfully tangled in his hair. She leaned down, their faces nearly touching. "You understand, this isn't a game." She squeezed his manhood gently. "Once you tend my garden, you have no right to walk away from me. That's not how it's done in the Sulmére."

His eyes were soft as he gently pulled her head down to meet his lips. "With Lumine as my witness and Doj'Madi to bind me, I promise you, Quen Tomo Santu di Sulmére, you have my affection so long as you choose." He sealed his oath with a gentle kiss.

She pulled her tunic off over her head, her breasts taut and her nipples hard in the chill air. "I accept your oath." Quen pressed her naked breasts to his chest and kissed him deeply. *I only hope I have not doomed you for loving me.*

CHAPTER 21

Dancing embers rose from the fire as they lay intertwined, Aldewin's arm encircling her, Quen's head resting on his bare chest. Love games with the merchant boy and timid covert kisses in her youth hadn't prepared her for the unbounded pleasure Aldewin had shown her. What he'd done with his lips and tongue... She had to shake herself free of thinking about it, or she'd pin him with her thighs, and they would get no farther than the riverside meadow.

His fingers absentmindedly twirled her hair. "I could stay like this forever." He chuckled. "They'll find two skeletons covered with moss and wildflowers." His voice lilted, carrying joy that hadn't been there before. *Like he speaks with a song in his heart.*

Quen's laughter echoed off the basalt.

Aldewin's fingers stopped twirling. "Are you mocking me?"

She pushed up and rested her head on a bent arm. "Of course not. I was thinking the same thing." Her fingers traced a figure eight around his chest, his muscles tightening beneath her touch.

Grief for losing Pahpi and her home, her imprisonment, and the unending battle to keep control of her very skin had left her exhausted.

Aldewin's warm encircling arms brought peace and comfort Quen had never known. *Is it terrible to want to stay here forever?* As if in answer to her question, her neck ridge warmed and subtly pulsed, reminding her she was Nixan, not human. *Nixan don't get to live in the arms of love's embrace.* Aldewin's face was bleary through her unwept tears.

"What's this now, sol'dishi?" Aldewin wiped the water from her cheek.

Quen sighed. His use of the Sulmére term of endearment moved her. She kissed him. This time, their pent-up passions spent, the languid kiss nourished her soul in a way the ignited Vatra kisses had not.

"In case you hadn't noticed, I'm not like other girls." Quen placed his hand on her neck ridge.

Instead of recoiling, Aldewin bent her to him again and kissed her. "I see you, Quen Tomo Santu di Sulmére. And I'm falling in love with you."

"But you don't—*I* don't even know what beast form I'll take. For all we know, I could become a giant snake."

He kissed her again. "Then I will love a snake."

"Or an eight-legged hairy beast that spins one of those webs you're so fond of." The idea made her stomach churn.

Aldewin laughed and kissed her again. "I'm already caught in webs. They might as well be yours."

Though slightly reassuring, she doubted anyone could love what she would become if she allowed the Nixan inside to come forth. "Do you think—well, the Ascended Masters and Zeniths at Val'Enara—is their magic and wisdom…"

"Enough to pry the Nixan soul from you?" Aldewin shrugged. "I've seen strange and even indescribable things at Val'Enara." He rubbed his chin. "If anyone in Indrasi knows how to help you, I am certain it is Archon Kine."

"Then I must do this," Quen said.

Aldewin said, "Wait. Remember what I said when I promised honesty? I'm no seer, Quen. I can't pry into people's hearts and know their intentions. The Archon is a mystery. I cannot ensure that her goal aligns with yours."

"That may be true, but answer me this. Is she kind?"

He thought about it for a bit. "I have known only kindness from her." He considered his words. "Except…" His brows furrowed, the dreamy gaze in his eyes gone. His mind had taken him somewhere else. Someplace dark from the look about him.

"What troubles your heart, sol'dishi?"

He sought her eyes then a kiss. "If you're asking me what you should do, I cannot both love you and be master of your fate."

She laughed. "So you don't want to act like my First Kin. Is that Northerner wisdom?"

"No, it's Aldewin wisdom." The twinkle was back in his eye. "I've told you what I know. It is up to you. Do you still desire to become a Supplicant? If so, I'll tell you all I know about seeking the favor of the guardian spirit, Hooxaura, so she'll open the Path of a Thousand Waters."

"And if I decide I no longer want to submit myself to testing at the chasm?"

He leaned into her, pinning her with his thighs. "Then we head north and find passage to my homeland. We can disappear there." He kissed her deeply.

Quen undulated her hips, and he rose beneath her. The Nixan within disturbed her peace, insisting she head south to Volenex. She didn't know how much longer she'd own the skin she wore. Quen pressed into him, enjoying the feel of his weight. She had finally found someone to love and who loved her back. *It's all I ever wanted.* Quen didn't want the feeling to end.

If my shadow soul is urging me to embrace Vatra's fires, I should instead seek Lumine's blessings at Val'Enara. She playfully bit Aldewin's lip. "Tomorrow, I will submit as a Supplicant at the Chasm." She arched into him. "But tonight, I submit only to you."

• • •

They rose at Hiyadi's first light. The air was thick with frosty fog. Stiff from sleeping on the ground and her lungs burning from the cold air, Quen longed for hot Sulmére air and a bed.

Nivi had hunted overnight and was ready to ride. With great, wide paws and thick fur, Nivi had no trouble bearing their weight as he climbed ever upward in frigid, mountainous terrain.

They arrived at Nil mid-morning. Compared to the rift they'd crossed at the mighty Mitosh river, the word 'chasm' was not apt for this wide spot in a small river. *It's neither wide nor deep. Nivi can clear it, even with Aldewin and me on his back.*

She rubbed Nivi's furry sides as they inspected the small gorge. "We could leap across with Nivi's help. Why do we need to seek the favor of this river's guardian?"

"Look up." Aldewin pointed to the rocky cliff above them. "You could cross the river, but how would you reach the Path of a Thousand Waters?"

Her hands shielding her eyes from the morning glare, she squinted where Aldewin pointed. In ancient times, they'd carved steps into the dark grey mountainside. Three stories up, the first step loomed. *Even I can't jump that high.* "Is this the only way to reach Val'Enara?"

Aldewin nodded. "I should add that if you attempt a hop across the river without first seeking the favor of Hooxaura, she'll destroy you."

Quen's breakfast sat heavy in her gut. She'd hoped she and Nivi could jump the chasm as a backup plan if Hooxaura didn't favor her. "How do I get Hooxaura to let me pass?"

"Well, she doesn't permit passage so much as reveal the path. There aren't scrolls on this. Each Supplicant has a unique experience."

Quen rolled her eyes and groaned. "So, you're telling me there's no help for me here?"

"Let me finish. Kensai compared stories, and Hooxaura doesn't test your Menaris ability. Prelate Hrabke does that. Hooxaura senses a Supplicant's true heart and guards Val'Enara against anyone who'd sow chaos or discord at the Pillar."

If Aldewin was trying to allay her fears, he was failing. "Great. I should pack it in now." Quen leaped onto Nivi's back.

"What are you doing? You said you wanted to—"

She glared down at him. "I have *two* hearts, remember? And Vatra rules one of them. Talk about chaos and discord. Hooxaura will never let a Nixan enter Val'Enara."

His face softened. "I believe in you, Quen. And it's about time you began believing in yourself." He kissed her hand, his stubble tickling her skin. "You're here for guidance from Val'Enara's Masters. You want to learn to control your shadow soul. To protect your loved ones, not destroy or sow disharmony. I know this about you, and Hooxaura will sense this in you."

And so that I become powerful in manipulating Menaris to bring down Vahgrin. Quen pondered whether Hooxaura would consider this a positive or negative concerning the Val'Enara pillar.

"Come down. You'll see, it's easy. You need to kneel at the edge and call upon Hooxaura. Tell her you're a Supplicant and wish to walk the Path of a Thousand Waters."

Quen picked a bramble from Nivi's mane. "And you've done this before?"

Aldewin chuckled. "More than once. And look." He wiggled his fingers. "I've still got all my fingers and toes."

Within her, the Nixan soul neither "spoke" nor trilled its shadow heart. She didn't know if it slept or by what mechanism it could bring itself to the fore of her thoughts. But she knew a tranquility that had been beyond reach for months. *There will never be a better time.* She dismounted and walked to the edge.

The water below was more a babbling brook than a raging river. The edge was a sandy path, clearly traversed with some regularity. She knelt, her knees nearly over the edge. "What do I say?"

"I usually introduce myself, something like your name, and that you submit as Supplicant." He waved his hand in a rolling motion. "You know, as we talked about. Then ask Hooxaura to reveal the Path of a Thousand Waters."

She'd hoped for more of a script. Though only Aldewin and Nivi were with her, Quen felt a thousand eyes watching. Her neck ridge tingled.

Quen sighed. "Here goes." Eyes closed, she grasped for the calmness of Still Waters. The crisp air smelled of pine, soil, and wet leaves. "Hooxaura, I am Quen Tomo Santu di Sulmére." Her voice squeaked. She cleared her throat and breathed, intending to calm herself. But the frigid, damp air burned her lungs and made her feel she couldn't get enough of Juka's life-giving breath. Quen tried again. "I submit as Supplicant to you, Hooxaura, and I humbly request you permit passage to the Path of a Thousand Waters so I can...." The ground shook, and the air smelled like it does before sky-fire erupts.

Quen blinked open her eyes. The obscuring mists coalesced to a single point as if sucked in by an unseen force. Quen had expected Hooxaura to rise from turbulent, churning river water. The river, though, remained calm.

The air wavered as a single droplet of water hung, suspended. It spun slowly at first, then it gained speed as it gathered moisture and grew. The spinning flung icy droplets at Quen, and she shivered. What began as a single droplet of water increased to a frozen ball the size of a melon, then a white-blue orb as large as a child. Though it no longer gathered Enara to itself, the globe spun, its thin, icy outer layer revealing a glacial-blue watery interior. Hooxaura hovered in the space between Quen and the far side of the chasm. Cool morning fog returned, thicker than before. The orb glowed as if lit from within, and its light pulsed like a beacon through the mists.

Though it had no mouth, eyes, nose, or other features, the Guardian spoke, its sound reminiscent of windswept sands dancing on dunes. "Supplicant unknown."

Juka's breeze stirred in a circle around Quen. The temperature dropped, and she shivered violently, clutching herself to preserve warmth. The air pressed in on her, compressing her chest and pulling air from her, making breathing even more challenging.

As quickly as the unpleasant sensation began, it ceased. Warmth returned. The air was again still. Quen gasped for air.

"You claim to be a child of the sands." The spirit drew out its S's. The guardian flickered like a lamp turning on and off inside. "But that is not true, is it? Begin again, Supplicant. *Who* are you, and why do you call me forth?"

Quen swallowed hard. There was nothing fearful in the spirit's being. Gazing at it was soothing. But something about Hooxaura made her bowels turn to water. "I told you. I am Quen Tomo Santu of the Sulmére."

The spirit spun wildly, flinging shards of icicles at Quen. She raised her hands to shield her face. Fortunately, the icicles were tiny and wet, not frozen solid. She was understanding the danger of facing Hooxaura. Sweat matted her hair to her head and made her tunic cling to her back. She shivered so hard she feared she'd fall into the canyon.

"Benevolent Hooxaura provides a third chance to the novice Supplicant." The orb returned to its peaceful state, emanating a pulsing light, its interior waters swirling. "Who are you? Why do you seek the Path of a Thousand Waters?"

Quen wiped her wet face with a damp sleeve. She wasn't sure what Hooxaura wanted. She'd stated her name. *What else can I be?* As soon as she asked herself the question, the answer came. This creature knew Quen's truth, perhaps better than she knew it herself.

"I am Quen, but I am also Nixan."

The strange pulsing light within the orb happened again, but no more icy shards were flung her way.

"I seek the Path of a Thousand Waters because...." *Careful, Quen. What truth to reveal?* Quen closed her eyes again, and hot tears welled, but she didn't know why. She wanted to open Vahgrin's throat, spill his blood, and send him and his rider back to the shadow of Vay'Nada, where they belonged. It was a desire so intense she could taste it.

But Quen would give up that quest, and every desire she had, if she could ensure she'd never endanger her loved ones again. *Suppose I allow my shadow soul to Promena. Then what will happen to Rhoji, Aldewin, Nivi, my Jagaru pod, Liodhan, Zarate, and wee Lumina?* Hot tears stung her chilled cheeks.

"Pahpi taught me of Still Waters. He was Kensai and trained at Val'Enara Pillar." She wiped away a tear. "He believed Val'Enara's wisdom would help me tame the shadow soul I carry. And Still Waters has kept me...

human." Her voice trembled. "I want people I love to be free from harm. I won't be responsible for more death." Her chest heaved. "If you indeed discern a Supplicant's true heart, then you know I speak with sincerity. Val'Enara is my only hope."

The orb had spun within itself, calm, and without lighting up as she spoke. It hung in the air, still and silent.

Rocks gnashed together in a deafening groan. It sounded like Menauld split into two. Ice splintered and tinkled on the ground as the orb swelled, then shattered, sending icy spray in every direction. The mists cleared, revealing stairs of ice leading to the rocky steps above. The Path of a Thousand Waters was open to her.

Quen stood on wobbly legs, wiping her face with her sleeves. Aldewin clapped and cheered behind her, and Nivi roared.

Quen gawked at what seemed like a thousand steps. The icy steps creaked and moaned as if they were breaking apart.

"Hurry. The Path will remain open for you only a short time."

Quen slapped her thigh. "Come, Nivi." She was astride the snow tiger in seconds. His long limbs took the steps by twos, and soon they were on solid, beautiful stone stairs.

Her heart fluttered like a crow stuck in a net. She slid off Nivi, her legs still shaky. Quen peered over the edge to find Aldewin below. The icy stairs they'd climbed melted, the water falling back to the river below. Aldewin would have to forge his own path.

Quen's head swam, dizzy from looking over the precipice. She grabbed a clump of Nivi's mane to steady herself. *I don't think I can fly on a dragon like a Rajani.* She looked up and ahead, and the swooning feeling subsided. "Hurry, Aldewin. If I keep looking down, I fear I'll fall off these damnable steps."

He said something, but Juka's breath latched onto his voice and carried it away. Aldewin waved at her before kneeling at the edge as she had. From her vantage point, he looked serene, without the rigid tension she'd felt. His hands hung at his sides, palms up. With eyes closed, he spoke, but Quen couldn't understand what he said. *He's probably saying something like what I said.*

As she'd experienced, the ground rumbled, and first a void, then a coalescence of water and ice appeared. Though she couldn't hear Aldewin, Hooxaura's voice sounded as though the spirit whispered into Quen's ear as she spoke.

"Aldewin di Partha. The Archon's Assassin. Successful in his mission, but tainted."

Archon's Assassin? What in Vay'Nada is this water spirit talking about?

Aldewin shook his head furiously. Only a few words were audible. "No... faithful servant... must—"

The water spirit was a white-blue blur, spinning and spewing needle-like ice shards. "Your directive was to secure the Nixan for the Archon, not taint yourself by coupling with it."

Icicles as long and sharp as knives were flung in every direction. Aldewin rose and stepped back, his palms out, trying to shield himself. His hands were soon bloody.

"Aldewin!" Fear of tumbling off the stone ledge gave way to worry that the pissed-off ice spirit would shred her beloved. Vatra fires roiled, and her fingertips burned. "Leave off him, you icy bitch."

"Quen, no. Don't interfere. You'll—"

She lost his words in the high-pitched, piercing whine of the spinning ice. Hooxaura's voice was no longer serene but crackling like a bolt of sky-fire and rumbling Quen's chest. Hooxaura spoke to Aldewin. "You are Supplicant at Val'Enara no longer." Hooxaura's orb advanced on Aldewin, moving with the preternatural speed Quen knew well.

Quen had leaped inhumanly high and far when she served justice on Druvna's killer. But even she couldn't survive a jump from this height. The mountain's edge trapped her, unable to reach Aldewin. But he couldn't outpace the swift Hooxaura. "What can we do, Nivi?" Quen couldn't watch the icy monster tear Aldewin to shreds or get sucked into its whirling vortex. Her neck ridge burned white-hot, and she screamed in agony.

The inner voice—the shadow-spawn's—called to her. *Embrace Vay'Nada. Allow Vatra and call me forth.* Over and over, it spoke these words. Quen's head felt like it would split open, gnashing friction like Menauld beneath her when Hooxaura appeared. Her insides burned. Heat emanated from her and seared away the frozen morning mist. The snow melted in a perfect circle around her, its vapor rising as steam. Plants dripped with thawing frost.

The tips of her fingers felt like someone had shoved wood splinters under her nails. Over the sound of dripping water and the high-pitched whir of spinning Hooxaura, bones cracked, and Quen yowled in pain. Razor-sharp, talon-like claws erupted from the tips of her fingers, her fingernails popping off, plinking on the stone.

The skin on her hands became mottled and scaly, like a pale-blue version of the skin around a chicken's legs. Her fingers had become talons.

The Nixan was forcing its way into control. *It's clawing through my core like a thrasher shearing a field.* Blackness played at the edges of her vision. Quen's guttural scream echoed in the canyon below.

Aldewin dropped his hand shield down and glanced up. "Quen!"

Quen's bloodcurdling scream distracted Hooxaura. Though Hooxaura spun, the knife-like shards stopped.

The air ahead shimmered like she'd seen when Vahgrin and his rider vanished. Movement around her slowed as if a dewy web had snagged all of Menauld. The odor of sky-fire permeated the air, and every hair on her body stood on end. Within the shimmering air, a window of darkest night. *Like everything in the cosmos has vanished.* "Vay'Nada," she whispered.

The Nixan soul urged. *Jump. Jump. JUMP.*

Below, Hooxaura resumed her twirling advance. Gaining speed, Aldewin couldn't hope to outrun the water spirit.

JUMP. JUMP. JUMP.

Quen propelled herself into the terrible black maw.

CHAPTER 22

Robbed of bodily sensation. Quen's gamble on Vay'Nada's Void left her paralyzed. Gone was the odor of wet leaves and water and Nivi's fur. The Void smelled like a cold, dark night. Soon, even that odor faded, as did sound.

Vay'Nada stole her senses, but Quen could still think. *I wish Vay'Nada took my mind as well.* Vay'Nada opened the locked chest of dark thoughts hidden deep within. Out poured memories of past hurts, bitter and inky black like the boiling tars of the Phisma pits. Quen had told Imbica that Sulmére people never treated her with contempt, as she'd experienced in Qülla. *A half-truth.* While she was growing up, children taunted her, and parents from visiting herdclans pulled their tots away. Whispered about her behind kefflas. Memories of offenses fueled her desire for revenge. To wound others as they'd hurt her.

This is unquelled Vatra, the fuel of warriors and murderous people. She'd seen this darkness in Earnôt, the slave trader, and it clung to Vahgrin and Nevara like a wet cloak.

She leaped into the Void, intending to emerge at Aldewin's side. To protect him from the crazed guardian spirit. Her time in Vay'Nada's Void was like an eternity, and she feared it would be too late when she emerged. But when she surfaced back in Menauld, Aldewin still ran from Hooxaura. It had been mere seconds, though what she understood while in the Void was worth lifetimes. *Opening this pocket of Oblivion must be a Rajani trick.* She couldn't have explained how she'd accomplished it, but it left her feeling wrapped in a dark storm cloud. *If this is a hint of Rajani sorcery, I dislike its lingering effect.* But the Rajani magic had successfully propelled her in virtually no time from the stony shelf to the river's edge beneath her, face-to-face with Hooxaura.

The bizarre black chasm remained open, and she kept one foot in its maw. The Void sucked at her and threatened to pull her in. Though she had only a foot still in the Void, Quen felt its effects and it heightened her perception of Hooxaura.

Deep within Hooxaura's swirling blue water, a woman's face appeared. It was the face of a wee child, sweet, wide-eyed, and innocent. The waters swirled and showed an elderly crone like a skeleton covered in thin onionskin. *Is Hooxaura truly a spirit? Or a manipulation of Menaris?* If it was a magical manipulation, it was so masterful, only a Pillar Zenith could create it. *Archon Kine.*

As soon as she formed the thought, Hooxaura rounded on her. The water spirit spun off icy spears, but Quen was a boiling mass of Vatra. Hooxaura's frozen assault became steam, feeding the misty air and obscuring Quen's vision.

Quen's face was wet with melted ice, steam, and salty tears. "You are no better than Xa'Vatra." Her voice trembled. "You put Aldewin into more danger than he knew. Sent him to gather me like a skein of dreyskin to be bartered." Anger shook her. "I tell you what I told Xa'Vatra. I am Quen Tomo Santu, a free person of the Sulmére, and I obey no master."

Hooxaura spun furiously and sped toward her with unbelievable speed. Still holding a toe in the shadow realm, Quen considered jumping wholly back into the Void to escape the spirit's icy assault.

Now only a few paces away, Hooxaura slowed and hovered, her interior waters peaceful. The child's face emerged, a watery replica of its original. "I do not intend to be your master. Val'Enara seeks only to assist you in that which you hold as your deepest desire."

Hooxaura ambled closer still, and Quen eased another toe into the Void. Her foot was numb, and she fought off despair. From the ledge above her, Nivi's low growl kept her tethered to Menauld.

"I will not harm you." Hooxaura was so close, Quen saw that the pulsing light within the orb was an icy-blue heart beating and fueling the creature. "If I intended to kill you, Quen Tomo Santu, I would have ended you by now."

Still trembling with cold and fury, Quen stood her ground. "You truly have the power to separate the two souls within me?"

"We have not attempted a soul fissure. But we know a Nixan can learn to live peacefully with two hearts. After all, Archon Kine is Nixan." The watery visage morphed, melting into a grotesque head of a darmanitong. *The gruesome creature Fano told of.* Changeling sea monsters that lured men to their deaths.

Quen recoiled in disgust from the ugly beast, even though it was only a watery copy of an actual darmanitong. *If this sea monster is Archon Kine's Nixan soul, how did Kine survive? People exterminate Nixan even when their shadow soul is a sleek cat or harmless raven.*

Hooxaura's voice was again a soothing warble. "The answer to your question is Vaya d'Enara, Quen." Kine's visage returned, again with the innocence of a child. "The Way is the Path. Permit me to teach you—to train you. You, too, can learn to quiet the shadow soul calling within you."

Vay'Nada's darkness sucked at her leg, threatening to wrench her from Menauld and back into Oblivion. No longer spewing icy spindrils, Archon Kine exuded tranquility and kindness. She had two choices. The soul-wrenching darkness of Vay'Nada or the loving kindness exuded by Hooxaura, representative of Val'Enara. *I should choose Val'Enara, shouldn't I?*

Nivi was unimpressed with Kine, no matter how sweet her voice or innocent her visage. He raised his hackles, and his growl was low but insistent. *Is he merely wary of the spirit? Or does he sense something about Hooxaura that I don't?*

And then there was her lover. "What of Aldewin? His only crime was to love me." She wiped at her tears. "Val'Enara must not be committed to kindness if it finds fault with love."

"Aldewin Kensai took oaths and submitted himself to rule by a master. He knew the conditions of his vows and the penalty for disobedience. Val'Enara treats its adherents with fairness. The Pillar makes no exceptions."

"He followed his passions, and now he has to die?" Quen's voice was tremulous. "If this is how you treat your Kensai, no wonder the Pillars have difficulty filling their halls these days."

Quen glanced beyond the swirling orb in search of Aldewin. He knelt, eyes closed, lips moving as he murmured. *Perhaps we are all devout in the end.*

Standing with one foot in Oblivion, Quen faced an ancient Zenith, the ultimate master of Menaris. In comparison, Aldewin appeared fragile. Human. And like all humans, capable of causing death, but also of making beautiful love. She'd felt it. Millions of souls walked on Menauld's back, but only one knew her—loved her—as Aldewin did. *I can't allow Kine to take him from me.*

The Nixan urged. *"Hooxaura linzini Vay'Nada."*

Quen shouldn't have understood the internal whisperings in an ancient tongue, but she did. One leg anchored in the swirling eddy of Vay'Nada, Quen grabbed for Hooxaura. She ignored the knife-like icy shards Hooxaura flung at her. Quen seized the beating center of the spinning orb. Quen extended her new talons and ripped Hooxaura's frozen heart from its watery home. "To Vay'Nada with you!" she screamed.

Back into the formless abyss. Numb. Still. Alone and despondent.

In the paralyzing Void, without sensation, she couldn't be sure if she held Hooxaura's icy heart. She should have yearned to escape Vay'Nada's realm, but misery can be a comfort. Familiar agony becomes a friend. *Best to remain in Vay'Nada's abyss than seek an unknown path on Menauld.* Melancholy was Quen's new best friend. Wretchedness her new home.

Resigned, Quen found peace in the Void. But the nagging Nixan voice wasn't content. Like the insistent ping of hurled sand against a tent in a Sulmére sandstorm, it said, *"Jump."* And *"escape."* The Nixan persevered until it finally roused Quen from the Shadow's hold.

"Aldewin," it said.

Aldewin. I must go to him.

As before, Quen emerged from the Void onto the firm ground of Menauld. Bloodied and soaked through, Aldewin still knelt in prayer. He likely didn't expect a talon-clawed lover to emerge from Vay'Nada and rescue him from the icy assault. But Quen had learned that the gods rarely answer prayers in expected ways.

Her fingertips still aching and sticky with drying blood, Quen snatched Aldewin in her talons and pulled him into the Void. Now more familiar with the soul-sucking feeling of the Shadow's realm, Quen didn't linger. She emerged onto the stone steps of the Path of a Thousand Waters, dragging Aldewin through with haste. *Did Aldewin feel Vay'Nada's pull into the dark abyss?*

As soon as Quen dropped him onto the stone steps, Aldewin rounded on her. "Suda, Quen! What did you do?" He trembled, his voice sharp enough to cut fog.

Quen moved to wipe the blood from his face. "Are you all right, sol'dishi?"

Aldewin drew his staff and stepped away from her touch. "You destroyed the guardian of my Pillar."

She'd expected gratitude, not anger. Aldewin's reaction puzzled her. *Is he still suffering from Vay'Nada's dark pull on his heart?* "Hooxaura was about to kill you."

He's freezing and wounded. Quen moved closer, wanting to encircle him in her warmth and comfort him as he had comforted her.

He took another step back. His voice was tremulous, scratchy, and strained. "I took vows, Quen—offered my life in service to the Archon. To Val'Enara Pillar. My life was Hooxaura's to take."

"But you were running—not submitting."

Aldewin leaned on his staff. Tears welled. "I should not have. I was afraid and unworthy." He wiped his eyes with a shaky hand. "A thriving pillar is more valuable than one man's life."

Quen stepped closer, her hand outstretched into the space between them. Hot tears welled in her eyes, too. "Aldewin—sol'dishi—"

Aldewin shook his head.

"Please. I couldn't stand like a helpless newborn drey and watch that monster murder my beloved. You would have done the same for me, wouldn't you?"

His face softened. "I would, and that's how I know Hooxaura rightly pronounced me no longer fit to enter the Moon Gate. I vowed to put the needs of Val'Enara first. Instead, I put my desires ahead."

Before Quen responded, the air cracked with thunder, though the sky was clear. Ice groaned against ice. Juka's breath swirled, wet and cold.

A grey-blue cloud materialized a few steps above as enormous icy shards crashed onto the stone. In a blur of white-grey like a dirty snowball, a man appeared, standing on a column of ice.

Nearly as tall as Aldewin, with skin dark as night, the man had icy eyes that glared beneath bushy snow-white eyebrows. Pristine pale-blue robes flew behind him as he somersaulted from his icy tower and landed gracefully on the step above them.

His voice boomed like an earthquake and erupted like a volcano. "By the Sister's holy light, I will ice-burn you into Oblivion." The man wound his hands the way Imbica did. But ice-blue crystals hovered there instead of a warm golden glow.

Still shaky, Aldewin stepped in front of Quen. "Prelate Hrabke, please. She did not know the ramifications of her actions. She only meant to—"

Prelate Hrabke flicked a hand, sending an icy shard to Aldewin's feet. Hrabke's voice was an angry hiss. "Hold your tongue, Kensai. Or have you forsworn all allegiance to Val'Enara Pillar and now swear fealty to Vay'Nada?"

Aldewin shook his head. "Vay'Nada? How can you say that, Master?" His voice shook with rage. "I left the Pillar—my home. Risked my life." Bitter acid tinged his words. "I added scars to my heart—something I vowed I would never do again. All so I could fulfill the task the Archon set upon me." He wiped at the water, blood, sweat, and tears with the back of his soaked sleeve. "Now that I succeeded—brought this woman to Val'Enara as the Archon ordered—you claim I am at fault for the same action." He trembled and shook his head. "I do not understand, Master."

Hrabke's face softened, but only slightly. "Your true Master, Archon Kine, lay ill, Kensai. Kine and Hooxaura, their souls intertwined. And now that—" He raised an arm and pointed at Quen, his voice accusing. "The shadow-spawn creature you brought to our gate destroyed the loving heart of our guardian, and our Pillar will probably lose its Archon as well."

Aldewin fell to his knees, his voice a whisper. "No. My Master…"

"You are not the first Kensai a shadow-spawn has seduced. Though likely not a slint, this vile shadow-spawn pulled you in just the same—promised love and affection, no doubt. Beguiled you as only the Shadow can." Hrabke's voice rose again, and he thrust an icy shard toward Quen. It shattered on the stone steps at her feet. "Look, Kensai Aldewin. Gaze upon Vay'Nada's child. See her through eyes illumined by Lumine's light. This is what you broke your vows for. What you thrust Val'Enara itself into chaos for."

Aldewin raised watery, red-rimmed eyes to Quen. His eyes grew wide as he noticed her talon-tipped fingers, perhaps truly seeing them for the first time. His mouth twisted in agony as if pulled like a dreyskin being stretched taut for drying. "I didn't mean for this to happen." He stared at her with eyes like blue-grey stones in a pool of clear water. "Are you of the Shadow?"

Quen shook her head. "No." Her heart—the human heart—thumped like a spooked herd. "You know what we have is real. I am Quen. You know me." She took his hand and meant to place it on her chest. But she was unused to having claws, and she accidentally scratched his hand, drawing blood.

Aldewin flinched away.

"This is what you brought to the sacred door of Val'Enara, Kensai Aldewin." Prelate Hrabke flung another icy shard at Quen's feet. It sizzled and evaporated instantly from the heat emanating from her. "My next shard will slice it open so you can see the true nature of this Nixan seductress."

To her surprise, Aldewin rose and again stood between Hrabke and Quen. "My head swims with unanswered questions, my Prelate. But I know this to be true. The Archon tasked me with bringing this woman to Val'Enara. Why? It is not my place to know. The Pillar's Guardian opened the Path of a Thousand Waters for her."

Hrabke relaxed his stance slightly, folded his arms, and stroked his long white beard. "Is this true?"

Both Aldewin and Quen nodded.

"You can banish me or kill me if you must. I broke vows, and I deserve punishment. The Archon wanted Quen for a reason."

Prelate Hrabke stroked his chin and appeared to be considering Aldewin's plea. "Though the Archon is virtually all-seeing, who is to say if the Shadow's dark magic obscured her vision on this matter? Or perhaps she underestimated its strength. That no longer matters. As she cannot perform her duties, it falls to me to take up the mantle of Archon. And I cannot allow this shadow-spawn to darken the Pillar's halls." He took up a wide-legged stance and raised his arms. As he did, a wall of snowy ice rose around him and soon towered over them. "I will carry out Hooxaura's will and protect the Pillar from Vay'Nada's chaos."

The heat emanating from Quen melted the ice and snow in a perfect circle around her. Vatra fires roiled within, though Quen doubted her Nixan heat could protect them from the avalanche of ice and snow Hrabke intended to send upon them. Quen didn't understand how she'd created the door to Oblivion, and she wasn't sure what would happen to her if she kept pulling on Vay'Nada's dark power. Now she saw no alternative. *Aldewin may have given up, but I will not.* She snatched Aldewin in her talons. "Nivi, with me." She towed Aldewin into the now-familiar Void. She hoped Nivi would follow and not get separated from her in the unfamiliar Shadow's land.

They emerged by the river's edge, Aldewin alive but shaking in her arms, Nivi at her side. Both looked dazedly at their surroundings. Aldewin looked despondent, and even Nivi wore a melancholy expression. Quen hoped their sadness wasn't permanent.

Though Quen accessed the Void to bypass the ledge, Hrabke had his own method. He transformed the snow wall into an icy slide and slid down. "Sucking power from the Void. You are the Shadow's spawn, all right."

Quen pushed in front of Aldewin, feet planted squarely. "I am Nixan and no longer afraid to admit it. Kine is as well. Did you know that?"

Hrabke's expression changed from ire to wariness. "You speak with the Shadow's tongue, too." He wound his arms, readying for a volley, and hissed, "Lies."

"A darmanitong, in fact." Quen allowed the rage that had welled in her since the day Vahgrin attacked her village to spill out, no longer tamping it down with the Still Waters mantra. "Your Archon was a Nixan, and you never knew."

Hrabke's eyes were far off. The icy energy he'd gathered dissipated into frosty mist.

"You didn't know of her plans to bring another Nixan into Val'Enara's walls, did you?"

Hrabke's eyes narrowed, his mouth twisted into a sneer. "How can I trust the word of Vay'Nada's agent?"

Aldewin pushed Quen aside. "Trust me, then. Archon Kine called upon me three Lumine cycles ago. She ordered me to embed with a rogue Jagaru pod. She knew the Dynasty had recently exiled Druvna, the pod's leader, and forbidden him from Jagaru service. So Kine gave Druvna the job of escorting me to the Sulmére village of Solia. There, Archon Kine said, I'd find a woman who was Doj'Anira. This 'Twice Blessed' would have one blue eye and one yellow. Kine tasked me with escorting the Doj'Anira to Val'Enara. 'No matter the cost,' Kine said. I swear this is the truth by Lumine's grace, the light of the Brothers, and the life-giving bosom of Doj'Madi, Prelate Hrabke."

Hrabke crossed his arms and stood defiantly on his icy pillar, towering over them. "Assuming this is true, Kensai, did Archon Kine tell you this woman was Nixan?"

Aldewin shook his head. "The Archon withheld this, and her plans for Quen, from me. But during our journey, I figured it out."

Quen's two hearts thumped their asynchronous beat. "How long did you know?"

Aldewin sighed. "Does it matter?"

"It matters to me."

"And it matters to me as well. Answer her, Kensai."

Aldewin closed his eyes and took a breath, steeling himself. "I suspected it that night in Juinar. The way you moved. It was—unnatural."

Visions of that night flooded her mind. "Is that the true reason you spurned me? Not because of vows, but because—"

"No. It was my vows."

Prelate Hrabke wasn't about to give Aldewin any benefit of the doubt. "Though you later broke them."

Aldewin nodded. "Yes." He turned to Quen. "And when I broke my vows, I knew you carried a shadow soul within you. Doj'Madi and the Three help me, but I love you anyway."

It should have been a touching moment ending in a kiss, but the air crackled with sky-fire and carried the odor of a thunderstorm. Quen's hackles rose. A thunderous boom shook the mountain valley as if cleaving the air. Juka's breath sucked at Quen's back, and Menauld rumbled beneath them. Quen had experienced this enough times now to know Vahgrin would soon emerge from the Void, a Rajani dragomancer on his back.

Hot wind warmed her back, but it was not Juka's breath. The air smelled as it did in the heart of summer when Juka's winds came from the southeast, blowing the odor of the Phisma tar pits all the way to Solia.

The strange bird that had sat like a statue atop the stone outcropping finally moved. Quen followed its path with her eyes as it landed on Vahgrin's giant black-haired head.

The beast knelt, and Nevara, the woman she'd first met on that fateful day in Solia, slid off Vahgrin's back. She wore a finely hammered light steel helmet with a faceplate shaped like a bird's head. Though helmeted, Quen recognized Nevara.

Gone were Nevara's black Kentaro robes, a ruse she'd worn to assuage fear. She'd traded the monk's robes for a form-fitting black leather corset, segmented so she could ride a dragon and cast spells. Atop the leather was a dress of deep red, barely covering her breasts before flaring to a split skirt. A golden girdle adorned her hips, linked chains joined in the front by a dragon-head clasp. Her shoulders bore pauldrons emblazoned with golden dragon heads against a background of Hiyadi's rays of light.

Nevara approached, removed the helmet, and shook out her long, sleek black hair. She flicked a steel-vambrace-covered wrist, sending a tight fiery projectile at Hrabke's ice wall. That single zinging ball of Vatra energy sizzled and spread across Hrabke's snowy wall, disintegrating it in mere seconds. "This Doj'Anira is not yours to destroy, Hrabke. Her madi promised her to me before she was even born."

Vahgrin tilted his head to the skies, and from his throat came a sound that began low and rumbling, then crescendoed to a pained cry. As if egged on by the dragon's lament, Nivi roared and began pacing while he chirped and flared his nostrils in displeasure.

Nevara held out a hand at Vahgrin, her face stern. "Zhijnatu, Vahgrin." She flicked a wrist, and the giant dragon bowed his head. Beneath bushy black brows, Vahgrin's amber-yellow eyes glared at the Rajani sorceress.

She has power over him. It was like how Pelagia had controlled Nivi and Quen, though there were no ear cuffs or other adornments on Vahgrin. *How does she do it?* Nevara both repulsed Quen and stoked her curiosity. *I want to learn this power she has over Vahgrin. If I allow my Rajani soul its Promena, will I then learn how to control dragons?*

Yet again, there was another person claiming they 'owned' Quen. Though she wanted to understand Nevara's power, she hadn't come this far to submit like a pet to the Dragos Sol'iberi. "I belong to no one, Nevara. Not the Exalted, not Val'Enara. And not you. I am a free person of the Sulmére, and I will not submit myself to you or anyone else."

Quen wanted the Nixan to show itself, at least a little. The shadow spirit gave her strength. Drawing on its power likely meant she was siphoning dark energy from Vay'Nada, but at this moment, she would welcome it. But her neck ridge didn't tingle or grow hot. No phantom whispers plagued her mind, or painful joints as the Nixan strained to usurp her very skin. She was utterly alone, and that thought frightened her more than she would admit.

Nevara laughed, the cold, shrill sound echoing off the basalt rock. "This freedom you squawk about...." She shook her head. "Such freedom never existed. We are all bound by something, Quen Tomo Santu. Bound to another, or to a cause. To an Order. And some, like you, are created to be bound. *I* made you, child."

Nevara's odor assaulted Quen. It was a combination of tar, feathers, and a scent reminiscent of her family's meat cellar in Solia. Quen backed away. "Why can't everyone let me be? Allow Aldewin and me to live in peace?" Vatra's fires roiled in her belly, and a sheen of sweat covered her neck and arms. Heat rose in her throat, and anger brought hot tears.

The ground rumbled again, but it wasn't Vahgrin or his Rajani that shook the world. Quen's white-hot anger shook Menauld's foundation.

Hrabke's voice boomed over the rumble of Menauld's quaking. "You say you stake a claim to this Nixan, but no law of man, Menaris, or Vaya di Solis allows you to bind the soul of the unborn."

Quen carped. "Moments ago, you tried to bury me beneath an ice avalanche. Now you argue on my behalf?"

Quen's retreat from Nevara's stench pressed her against Aldewin. He was now backed up to the riverbank's precipice. His voice was soft but clear. "'The undercurrent of emotion must not breach the dam of the Pillar's principles.' A core tenet of Vaya d'Enara. Etched in stone just inside the Moon Gate."

The current of emotion kept in check? The more Quen learned of Val'Enara, the more convinced she became that she didn't fit there. Pahpi had trained her to suppress feelings. To tamp them down and shunt them away with the Still Waters mantra.

But Quen didn't want to dampen her emotions. She released the dam on her emotions, and her anger quaked the ground. *I want to own what's inside me, good and bad. To shout it to the Three. Even to Vay'Nada and back again so all can hear. What are laws, if not proclamations by rulers far removed from the people who toil to keep everyone alive?* Xa'Vatra, in her elegant palace, perched precariously over a poisonous pit. Archon Kine and her like, cloistered in a lofty tower, secluded and protected from the nasty business of everyday life. *What do these 'lawmakers' know of the real world?*

The more Quen seethed, the more Menauld trembled.

Aldewin put a hand on her arm. "Calm yourself, sol'dishi."

His use of the Sulmére term of endearment caught at her heartstrings and pulled until it stretched nearly to breaking. When she faced him, the look of utter sadness he wore almost broke her. *I'm not meant to study scrolls in a tower.* She'd expressed this doubt to Pahpi, but he'd ignored her. *You were right about many things, Pahpi, but not this.* Her doubt had been born of reason, and now she knew it wholly to be true. *And Aldewin now understands it too.*

Hrabke might have been an eminent scholar on the laws of men and Menaris, but he was overlooking one crucial fact. Quen wasn't human. *As far as I've seen, the 'laws' meant to protect people never apply to creatures like me. Or Nivi or yindrils.*

Quen was something other than human, and as the power within her grew unchecked and untrained, she became a danger. Instead of hunting the dragon to protect the ones she loved, she was becoming the thing most likely to put them in harm's way.

Nevara claimed she 'made' Quen. *Whatever that means.* Quen sighed. *Damn my human soul to Vay'Nada. I know what must be done.*

"These weeks riding with you..." Her voice broke, and she wiped at a tear. "I didn't believe I could know love like this." She kissed Aldewin, and to her surprise, he returned the affection. "Even if I sprout hairy legs or a raven's wings, I will never forget the love you gave me." She released him and backed away, putting cold distance between them. "I will love you all my days." Quen hugged Nivi and whispered into his furry ear, "Take care of Aldewin for me, my friend."

Tears welled in Aldewin's red-rimmed eyes. "You can't go with her. She'll use you, Quen. You'll be a slave to these Rajani for the rest of your life."

Hrabke shot a giant ice shard from above, missing Quen only because she heard it slice the air before a normal human would have registered a flying object. She sprang, feet over head, mere seconds before the ice crashed on the ground.

Nevara flicked a purple-white projectile of sky-fire at Hrabke. He leaped from his buttress of ice, escaping the jolt of Nevara's blow.

"Old man, if you hope to see your precious Night Sister again, stay out of Rajani business." With haste, she flung another sky-fire bolt. Hrabke, still recovering from his jump from the ice tower, didn't deflect. The flesh on his thigh sizzled, and his burnt hair and skin smelled foul. Hrabke yowled in pain and grabbed at his leg.

"Kensai Aldewin, you still want to be an acolyte of the Pillar. If so, prove your worth. Seize the Nixan. You must destroy her for the good of the Pillar—and the world."

Aldewin pulled the staff from behind his back, arms shaking. He looked into Quen's eyes and dropped his weapon. His arms at his sides, palms facing out, Aldewin was utterly defenseless. He closed his eyes, bowed his head, and shook it. "The Pillar asks too much of me."

Quen imagined herself and Aldewin mounting Nivi and galloping away. To the North, across the Straits of Minea, to Aldewin's homeland. *We could disappear there.*

Quen gazed at her hands, now covered in scaly blue-white skin. Black talons protruded from her fingers. *I no longer pass for human. No return to that life now. I don't know where it leads, but there remains only one path available to me.*

"Take Nivi, Aldewin. Run from this place. Across the pass to Vindaô Province. Find Rhoji and our Jagaru pod. Take refuge with our friends."

She didn't wait for arguments, pleas, or more icy shards. Quen thrust her chin up and her chest out. It was important to feel it was her decision—to not allow Nevara to believe she'd won. "Take me to Volenex."

PART III

DRAGOS TEPLO

Once, the Queen soared over Menauld's sea, forest, and sands. Then Kovan danced upon the wave's crest as it kissed Indrasi's bloody shore. With influence as frothy as the sea's foam, Kovan ushered in Nomo Teplo—Age of Man.

But be patient, fair sisters, for every tide turns. The Dragos Primeri will rise and we, the Rajani, will rejoice. Oh, how fervently we long to see the Queen's shadow upon the dunes! Raise your voices and sing praise for the coming of a new Dragos Teplo. Until that glorious day, we endure at Volenex and hold vigil over the venerable Queen's sacred sacrament.

> —from the *Sitta* of the Dragos Sol'iberi, held in the Dragos Archives at Volenex

CHAPTER 23

Aldewin leaned on his staff, head bowed, shoulders slumped. *He looks defeated.* Quen's human heart ached with bitter anguish for the turmoil she'd brought to him. *Oh, Aldewin. This is the only way I can protect you from the Dragos Sol'iberi and Vahgrin.* The lingering ache in her newly emerged claws reminded her how dangerous she'd become to him as well. *You must understand, my love.*

Quen hadn't imagined ascending into Vay'Nada's realm on the back of the dragon she'd vowed to destroy, yet it didn't feel as strange as it should have. *To my Rajani soul, this feels familiar.* Since the fateful day Nevara visited Solia, Quen had feared she'd end up in Nevara's clutches. She stared down at her taloned hands. *Volenex is where I belong now.* The only consolation was that she'd finally have answers to the questions that had plagued her.

Below, Hrabke launched upward on a cone of ice then took the stairs of the Path of a Thousand Waters by twos, agile for an elder with an injured leg.

Vahgrin's scales were smooth beneath her, and Nevara's heat seeped into Quen's backside. She hadn't allowed herself to feel the cold air of the mountain, but now, as warmth returned, she shivered.

"Soon, you will know cold no more." Nevara's voice was low and warm. "Deep within Menauld beats the heart of a fiery dragon. Did you know that?"

Quen didn't. In fact, it sounded wrong to her, but Nevara didn't wait for Quen to answer.

"We travel to the place where Menauld's Vatra core shows itself to Hiyadi. There you will find the answers you seek. Now grip tightly with your thighs. Volenex awaits." She spoke in the language the Rajanis used when talking to Vahgrin. *"Ashtanga Volenex, Vahgrin."*

The dragon lowered his head. Vahgrin's body rumbled with vibration beneath Quen's thighs. Quen's second heart thumped faintly, signaling that her Nixan soul, which had been uncustomarily quiet, remained.

The air shimmered ahead, and a doorway dark as a cave on a starless night opened. Quen steeled herself for the dread feeling she'd soon encounter.

As if expecting Quen's trepidation, Nevara said, "Fear not the knowing touch of the Shadow. Vay'Nada reveals truth. It is difficult for some to face. But you are strong, Doj'Anira, and your journey has prepared you well for the honesty of...."

The Void pilfered Nevara's last words and her warmth. As before when Quen entered Vay'Nada's realm, all sensation faded. Vay'Nada deprived her of everything but her most dreadful thoughts.

Within moments, another dark door appeared with an orangey-red sky on the other side. The late-summer skies of the Sulmére. *A familiar sky.* Vahgrin flapped his massive wings, and they cleared the dark portal, the air crackling with sky-fire.

Seeing familiar skies brought tears of joy. Quen hadn't realized how much she missed burnt-orange skies, Hiyadi a hazy yellow blob rather than a bright white denizen she had to shield her eyes to look upon.

Vahgrin tilted to the left and pointed his nose down. Quen's stomach flopped, and it felt as though her heart had risen to her throat. She let out an involuntary gasp.

Nevara's laugh was hearty and vibrated at Quen's back. "Have no fear, Doj'Anira. Vahgrin hasn't lost a Rajani yet."

Vahgrin yowled loudly. Whether it was a cry of pain or agreement, Quen couldn't tell. The phantom Nixan heart was silent and still. *Sure, now you're silent when you might actually have something useful to say.*

Juka's relentless summer breath hurled sand, making the air thick with dust. Wee Niyadi was a few hand widths past zenith, while Hiyadi hugged the horizon. It was late, though still five or six hours until the full dark of Niyadi's brief rest. The air smelled of dirt and the faintest odor of the tar pits to the northeast. Ahead lay Volenex.

Where desert meets sea, a mountain rose from an ancient crater. The craterous land hugged Indrasi's southernmost waters, where the Zhongdu Ocean met the Orju Sea. Odors of saltwater, kelp, and rotten fish mixed with the tarry aroma. The smell made Quen's nose twitch.

She donned her tatty borrowed keffla to ward off the stench.

Inside the large outer crater sat an inner crater, smaller and less worn. Seawater filled the ring between the two. The craggy outer crater was volcanic black, while the inner cone was rusted-iron red. From their high vantage point, the formation of the two extinct volcanos with a ring of ocean water looked like an eye. Volenex's double caldera was both bleak and beautiful.

She despised the excitement that welled in her. This most foreign place—a place she'd never been before—felt like... home.

As they got closer, a complex of buildings came into view. Carved from the inner cinder cone's black stone, towering spires like midnight glass glistened.

Vahgrin landed in a courtyard paved with square tiles cut from black basalt. In between grew vibrant green moss, delicate in contrast to the spiky towers rising around them. As Vahgrin flapped his mighty wings to gently land, the air he produced blew the gauzy, flowing garb of a circle of women ringing the courtyard.

Two of the women, covered head to toe in sheer white linen, came forward to assist them in disembarking. Quen had seen Nevara leap gracefully from the beast without needing help, but Nevara didn't deny their aid. The women carried wood steps and placed them on the ground by Vahgrin. They stood on the top step and offered delicate hands, their wrists jingling with gold bangles, their faces obscured by the thin gauzy fabric.

Nevara took their petite hands in hers, and they bowed as she descended. Once on the ground, she kissed their hands as they kept their heads low. "How blessed by the mighty Dragos heart you are this day, sisters, chosen to be the first to touch the Doj'Anira."

The two white-clad women raised their heads and looked up to Quen. Beneath the gauze, their lips and eyes were rouged red. They glanced furtively at Quen but quickly averted their gaze as if it was taboo to stare at her.

"They are Atyro, Doj'Anira. Nixan, like all here. Atyro are neophytes, pure and untouched by their first Promena. They eagerly await shedding the confines of the human skin they've worn, and all hope for the feathers of Rajani. Atyro serve the Order. Sisters, lend a hand to the Doj'Anira."

Quen took their hands in hers. They were the hands of young women, most likely not yet of age. They were hands that had known little of the rough work Quen had grown up doing in the harsh Sulmére.

Like Nevara, Quen didn't truly require help. Though Vahgrin's back stood a person and a half high, Quen's Nixan agility allowed her to leap from such a height. But, following Nevara's lead, Quen allowed the women to help her disembark.

The courtyard was quiet save for the gentle lapping of waves as the sea pounded the volcanic shore. The gathered Atyros, the neophyte Rajani, were silent as an eavesdropper listening for gossip.

"Come, Doj'Anira. I have the great honor of preparing you for a ceremony in your honor." Nevara walked toward the tallest spire.

It was late, and Quen was exhausted. She'd gotten a lifetime fill of pomp and ceremony at the capital. Now, she had energy only for answers. "Ceremony. Now?"

"The Rajani have planned for your return for many years. We will allow no one to interfere. Besides, we are creatures of the night."

An Atyro on either side pulled open a massive door of solid granite. Quen followed Nevara into a vestibule of polished grey marble, open to the sky above. Nevara's boot heels clicked on the floor while Quen's dreyskin boots made hardly a sound.

"How could I be returning to a place I've never been?"

Nevara ascended a stairway of stone steps, much like the ones Quen had climbed in the capital. Quen followed, taking the steps by twos so she could get ahead of Nevara. On the landing, Quen blocked the path. "I need answers, Nevara. How could you plan for me? What is a Doj'Anira, really? And why under Hiyadi's sky are so many people trying to claim me as their own when I'm a simple Sulmére woman? I will go no farther without answers."

Nevara smiled, her eyes twinkling. "You truly still believe yourself a simple woman?" She laughed, the cackle echoing off the stone. Nevara stepped onto the landing and took Quen's hand in hers, deftly avoiding the talons. "Come with me, and you will have the answers you seek."

Nevara strode down the wide hall and dragged Quen behind. They soon ascended yet another column of stairs leading to a small courtyard. In this outdoor circle stood another ring of women, this time wearing red robes and girdles of gold chain, much like the one Nevara wore, clasped at the front with a dragon's head. Hammered golden headdresses affixed to the backs of their heads echoed Vatra's fire and reverence for Hiyadi's power.

As Quen entered the courtyard, the women came forward. Nevara held Quen's arm outstretched, and the women touched her talon-tipped hand.

"Sisters, welcome our Doj'Anira."

They surrounded Quen, their hands covering her shoulders, back, arms, and hands. Their voices were hushed as they mumbled words in the ancient tongue Quen couldn't understand without aid from her Nixan. But her shadow soul remained hidden, even to her. *Is it still with me?* The thought simultaneously raised hope but also panic. *What if killing the Nixan kills me too?*

"These women are Drago'Sorceri, like me," Nevara said. "Many older even than me, we have faithfully studied the ancient ways. Kept the language of Dragos Menaris alive, you see. Waiting for the day we would welcome Ishna, the Winter Dragon, back from her sleep in Vay'Nada."

Though Quen understood the words Nevara spoke, the meaning eluded her. The Drago'Sorceri, these odd, red-robed women groping at her, made her head swim. Bile rose, and a band of anxiety tightened around her middle. *I am Quen, not Ishna.*

"Welcome home, Ishna, our venerated Dragos'Madi." The women whispered this phrase as they pawed at Quen with silver-nail-tipped fingers.

What are they babbling about? They're all addlebrained.

But Quen couldn't ignore the rod of searing pain that began at her middle and jolted her entire body like a bolt of sky-fire. *Ishna.*

She swayed, and her vision narrowed.

Deep inside, she'd always known. *I am Doj'Anira — twice blessed.* Not because of her bicolored eyes, but because she carried two souls. *And my shadow soul—the Nixan I've imprisoned... It belongs not to a Rajani changeling, but to... a dragon. My second soul is... Ishna. The Winter Dragon.*

Quen's temples throbbed, and her legs wobbled. "I'm going—"

The women bore Quen to a stone bench, where they laid her down. They continued whispered prayers or spells or whatever they were saying. To Quen, their mumbling was like fingers scraping sandstone. It didn't ease the feeling that she would either pass out or vomit.

With a hand to her head, she bolted upright. "Please, stop. I must... I want to speak to Nevara. Alone."

Nevara spoke in the odd Rajani language, full of tongue clicks and long-drawn-out vowels like Vahgrin's dragon-speak. The women went silent. They laid their hands on Quen one last time, bowed, and left her alone with Nevara.

Without the onslaught of the women's buzzing words ringing in her ears, the urge to slip into unconsciousness faded. She bent her head low, between her knees, and took deep gulps of air as she tried to gather her thoughts. Finally, she said, "Tell me everything. From the beginning. What did you show my Pahpi that day in Solia? How did you know my mother? And what of this beast I carry inside?"

"Instead of telling you, I will show you."

"Show me—what?" The idea that her mother was still alive took Quen's breath. She clasped the amber pendant at her neck. *Could it be?*

A dark shadow passed over Nevara's face. "I have nothing to show you of your human family. No human before has walked the corridors of Volenex. What I will show you is of Ishna. Come with me, and I will show you what remains of the first Winter Dragon."

•   •   •

Quen had often imagined conversations with the mother she'd never known—the woman who'd schemed to doom Quen to life as a Nixan. *Did she realize what she'd done? Or did she think she could override Nevara's will? I will never know. But maybe Nevara will finally answer the questions tormenting me like a bug in my bedroll.* She followed on Nevara's heels as they traveled a winding corridor, spiraling down into the belly of the extinct volcano.

They arrived finally at a deep cave. Two iron sconces bearing torches near the doorway provided dim light, but the central part of the room remained shadowed. Two white-robed Atyro sat on ancient wood benches just inside the stone opening. When they saw Nevara, they quickly rose and bowed low.

One of the Atyro spoke, her voice thin and low as if a babe slept, and she didn't want to wake it. "How may we serve you, esteemed Drago'Sorceri?"

"Light the remaining torches, then leave us."

The two women scurried to do as Nevara bid and left silently, bowing low again as they went.

With lit torches, the circular room's purpose became clearer. Floor-to-ceiling shelves carved into the stone ringed the perimeter. Leather-bound tomes, yellowed scrolls, stacks of parchments, and even jars holding teeth, bone, and scales packed the shelves. In the center of the room, upon a raised stone platform, loomed a dragon skull larger than Vahgrin's. Torchlight danced across the dragon's skull, making it seem alive.

Quen's voice was a hushed whisper. "A dragon skull."

"Not just *a* dragon skull." Nevara moved toward it, Quen on her heels. "That is Ishna, the Winter Dragon. Unceremoniously murdered by Indrasian Kovan."

Every child in Indrasi learned the story of Indrasian, the heroic warrior who ended the dragon scourge and ushered in the new era, Nomo Teplo, the Age of Man. Like most people, Quen had been taught it was more myth than reality. Indrasian was the first ruler to unite all Indrasi, hence first a country, then an entire continent named after him. The Kovans claimed they descended from Indrasian's bloodlines. The enormous skull was from a dragon, but whether it was the dragon Indrasian supposedly killed, Quen couldn't be sure.

Quen circled the platform and inspected the skull. There was a large hollow between the eyes, covered over with lacy bone. As she got to the back, she noticed ridges at the base of the dragon skull. She fingered her neck-ridge as if she could press it back into normal shape. The Nixan spirit within was quiet.

It unnerved her that the shadow soul had abandoned her when she needed it most. Her phantom second heartbeat had annoyed her. But now that it was quiet, Quen realized her shadow soul had supplied strength and courage. *You choose now to be still?* There was no answer. As she stared at the brittle bone, remnants of the body that supposedly once housed her shadow soul, her resolve to destroy Vahgrin waned. Not gone, but the bloodlust was diverted by recent revelations and the unshakeable feeling that as much as Rhoji was Quen's kin, Vahgrin was Ishna's.

"Assuming what you say is true—that this is the last remnant of the dragon Indrasian slew—how did it end up here?"

Nevara's eyes were shiny with emotion, as if she held back tears at seeing the thing. "The Dragos Sol'iberi is an old order, and the Rajani sisterhood ancient. They learned Indrasian hauled Ishna's severed head from her mountain home to a nearby village. There he paraded it like a prize, seeking glory for his villainous deed."

"Glory he got." Indrasian, ancient ancestor to petulant Xa'Vatra. Heat rose in Quen's throat. In her belly roiled fires of anger at what the ruling family had done to her and the poor dragon Indrasian slew. *Why is this making me angry?* Quen shook her head to clear her mind. *I'm being sucked into her story. This dragon was Vahgrin's kin, not yours.*

Nevara's eyes were wide, her pupils so dilated her eyes were two black orbs. "Indrasian's descendants will pay. Oh yes, they will pay." Her laugh was the call of a night bird crackling in cool, dry air. "Soon, all Qülla will pay for Indrasian's crime."

The woman looked positively crazed, her mind a spooked drey running this way and that. But her words sounded familiar. Like what Quen had said after Vahgrin razed Solia and killed her father. She, too, had promised to avenge the loss of someone she loved. *Is that what I looked like?*

Quen's mind was a sea of doubt, and the world around her spun. Pahpi had drilled into her a mantra meant to quiet the wild heart within. *Still Waters. Still Waters.* But it was no use. Enara was out of her reach.

Though Vatra's fires burned strong in her, she wasn't crazed like the Dragos Sol'iberi. *At least not entirely. Not yet.* The Dragos Sol'iberi plan was pure madness.

"Death for death. That is the grand plan?" Quen shook her head. "The Dragos Sol'iberi plans to lay waste to an entire city because one man killed this over a thousand years ago?" She gestured toward the giant skull.

Quen's words broke Nevara's unwavering gaze upon the dragon skull. "You think this is about one life?" Her whole body trembled with emotion. "The Winter Dragon was not just any dragon. She was a Dragos Primeri. One of the original four, and a living god. Dragos Primeri magic fuels all dragons. When Indrasian killed her, he doomed them all. Extinction, or nearly so as far as humans knew. And he gloated about it." Her lips curled into a sneer, as if speaking of him made her mouth taste awful.

Quen pinched the skin between her eyes and took a deep breath. "What in the name of the Three does any of this have to do with me?"

Nevara grabbed Quen's wrist and dragged her to the wall of stone shelves. She didn't bother with a torch, instead conjuring a ball of yellow light that hovered nearby as she searched. Nevara found what she was looking for on a shelf near the bottom. It was the scroll she'd brought to Solia. It was still dusty from being stomped into the dirt by Pahpi.

The Drago'Sorceri took the scroll to a table, lit a table lamp with the flick of a wrist, and extinguished her magical orb of light. The table had several devices, like the one Quen had seen Pelagia use, to unfurl a scroll and hold it for reading. "Here. Read for yourself."

Quen had wanted to see this scroll so badly she'd flung herself into the desert churning with haboobs just for a glimpse. Now it lay unfurled before her, and she was afraid of what it said. She hesitated and stood in the shadows behind Nevara.

The Rajani gestured to the table. "Do not be afraid, Doj'Anira. You have questions, now find the answers. Learn the truth."

What did she say about Vay'Nada? That it showed the truth, but weak people didn't want to see it? *What if I am weak?* Quen forced herself forward to read what her mother had promised to this dark sorcerer so long ago.

The flowery, wordy language was of the kind used in the capital's edicts. *Language meant to obscure truth rather than reveal it.*

She had to read most sentences a few times to fully digest the meaning. The more she understood, the more her stomach felt hollow. Because her father, Santu, was the Consular of Bardivia, it was auspicious that he have three children to mirror the Trinity. It was most auspicious to have a son, another son, and then a daughter. But Quen's mother, Suliam, could not conceive a third child. When severe drought hit Bardivia, the people thought they'd angered the gods. They blamed Suliam's inability to bear a third child. Desperate to appease her husband's people, Suliam bargained with the Dragos Sol'iberi and Nevara specifically to help her conceive.

The scroll said:

> *"And said child will be Dragonborn and promised to the Dragos Sol'iberi. At the time of the Dragonborn's first Promena, to Volenex she must*

go. There, the Rajani of the Dragos Sol'iberi will welcome the Dragonborn with open arms and lovingly attend her metamorphosis with gratitude for her vessel. Praise to Primal Dragos'Madi. We praise the dragon reborn. Praise for the rebirth of our god, Ishna, the Winter Dragon."

Quen's legs quivered, her knees buckled, and she grabbed the table to steady herself. She slumped into a nearby chair. Her body slick with sweat, Quen felt like she was breathing through sand. Her lower lip trembled as tears dripped onto her lap. "No. This cannot be. I thought—Rajani. I had accepted that. To be—like you."

Nevara knelt and took her hands, her lips smiling, her eyes alight with joy. "You, Doj'Anira, are so much more than Rajani. Do you not see? Our entire order has existed for over a thousand years, sustained by a single goal. To bring Ishna back into the world. And you, most blessed among us, are the vessel which carries our god back to us. You, dear Quen, house the soul of the Winter Dragon. You have borne her well, but the time has come to bring Ishna forth—to become all you are destined to be."

"But... how? This isn't possible."

"In a dragon, their primal life-force rests—" Nevara touched the space between her eyes. "Here. My Dragos Sol'iberi sisters of ancient times preserved Ishna's. My sisters of yore didn't know what to do with the vital essence, but over the years since, we perfected our magic. And we used Ishna's primal essence to create—you."

Between the blood rushing in her ears and her brain not wanting to accept this news, Quen heard only a portion of what Nevara said. The scroll didn't answer one crucial question. "Did Pahpi... Did my father know you planted a dragon soul inside me to be harvested in the future?"

"He did not sign the scroll, if that is what you mean."

Quen shook her head. "No, I mean after I was born." Her breaths were shallow. "All my life—'Still Waters, Quen'—did he know?" It was a question as much to Nevara as to the aether.

"I don't see how this matters." Nevara's eyes grew stormy again. "You are Dragonborn, and the time has come for the vessel to bear fruit."

The ground beneath them shook with a tremor. Quen screamed, "It matters to me!" She wiped at a tear, careful not to poke her eye with her talons. "It's the only thing that matters to me."

Nevara sighed. "Of course he knew."

"How do you know for sure?"

A dark shadow of intense anger lit Nevara's eyes like smoldering coals. "He knew because I told him. A foolish thing to do. Prideful. A mistake I have had to atone for all these years. I had expected him to hand you to me, grateful the Rajani would take you away, a burden to him no longer. How could I have known he would steal you away in the night, sneaking across borders like a cut-purse thief? Who knew he would renounce his position as Consular, his financial estate, and subject his family to shame? A human father protecting his Dragonborn child? No, I did not expect that."

What Nevara and the Dragos Sol'iberi had done to her and her entire family was abject horror. Yet within the cruel deed was a kernel of goodness that swelled her heart. *Pahpi knew. He'd always known my truth—a truth I've only recently understood. He knew, and he loved me anyway.*

All those years of drilling lessons about Lumine, Enara, and Still Waters—love drove him, not fear. He didn't want to lose me. Oh, Pahpi.

She didn't want Pahpi's sacrifice for her to be for naught. But the barking-mad Rajani kept referring to her as a 'vessel' and talking about harvesting her shadow soul. Quen wished she could still believe she was merely Rajani, destined to a life in a crater, soaring the night skies as a winged beast of prey. But the words on the scroll made the band of knowing tighten around her middle. The soul within her—the one she'd shared her life with—was Ishna. As much as she'd wanted to deny it, the shadow soul tainted her. *So long as it remains within me, I'm a creature of Vay'Nada.*

Truth is one thing. Rolling over, belly up, and vulnerable is another. Perhaps Nevara and her order of curd-brained sisters expected Quen to be honored that she'd carried Vay'Nada's spawn inside her. Maybe if she'd lived in a hollowed-out crater her whole life like they had, she'd be more up for the task.

But Quen had lived and, more importantly, loved. From Pahpi's wisdom and persistent conviction that he could help still her turbulent waters to Rhoji's brotherly ribbing mixed with friendship. Liodhan would surely recoil from her, devout as he was to Vaya di Solis. He would sooner face death than embrace anything tainted by Vay'Nada. Though Liodhan's feelings for her would likely change, her feelings about him were unaltered. She'd die to protect Lio, Zarate, and wee Lumina from dying by dragon fire. Though she'd known them less time, the Jagaru pod and even Nivi were family.

And what of Aldewin? Her feelings for and about him were complicated, but she couldn't deny her love for him. He was a mystery still awaiting the unraveling. Aldewin might be the love of her life or only the first. She couldn't yet know because her life had only recently truly begun. *I will not slip aside peacefully so these dragon-obsessed sisters can throw a dragomancer party over my corpse.*

"You expect good ole Quen to what? Step aside and let this—thing—take over?" She pulled her hands from Nevara's and kicked the chair behind her. "Well, the joke is on you, Vay'Nada spawn. The Nixan soul in me is fast asleep. Has been for some time now. Whatever dark magic you used on my mother didn't work. I may be Nixan, but I'm no dragon-born. And even if I am, the dragon has decided it doesn't want to come out to play with you."

Nevara rose too, and though Quen towered over her in height, the Drago'Sorceri loomed like a late-day shadow. "Doj'Anira, you speak as though you have a choice—as though you ever had a choice—in any of this."

Quen stood her ground. "And that's another thing. Stop calling me that. I am Quen Tomo Santu di Sulmére, daughter of Santu Inzo Dakon di Sulmére. You cannot cast me aside like a corn husk."

Nevara's face softened. She put her palm on Quen's forehead, between her eyes, and said, "I am sorry, Doj'Anira, but your time is done. The human in you will die. It is all part of Vay'Nada's plan, and we will not disappoint our Lord and Master again." She mumbled an incantation in the ancient Rajani language. She put her other hand to the small of Quen's back to catch her as Quen fell into a magically induced sleep.

CHAPTER 24

Grotesque keening woke Quen from a deep, dreamless sleep. Disoriented, legs unsteady. Aching hunger, empty yet queasy gut. Voices, squawking and high-pitched. Menauld beneath her thrumming. The deep rumble of drums. *Or am I the one quaking the ground?*

Blink eyes open, the world swaying. Black figures. Fire and heat. The odor of burnt flesh. *Is it mine?* Vision fading. A tunnel of darkness threatened to pull her under. *I won't let them take me.* Quen gulped air, forced eyes open. Aware. Listening. Patient. *Only one beat in my chest and one voice in my head. Why are you silent, Ishna?*

Sensing her stir, the Rajanis' melancholy and discordant song grew louder. Hands buttressed her. She wasn't in Vay'Nada, but her legs were as numb and useless as she'd experienced in the Shadow's realm.

Despite fiery columns spewing heat into the already-warm night, Quen shivered. The Dragos Sol'iberi had stripped off her road clothes, garments the Jagaru had cobbled together when they'd escaped Qülla. While under Nevara's sleep spell, the Rajani had clothed her in a form-fitting gown of black silk, as gauzy as the white linen robes worn by the Atyro. Unlike the Atyro, though, she wore no gold-chain girdle or face covering. It was as if a spider's web ensnared her, cocooned like an insect to be devoured.

Hands at her elbows pushed her toward a dais of stone. The sky above was visible but nearly black as Niyadi sought rest below the horizon. She was in the large entry courtyard of Volenex. Her senses returning, her nose wrinkled from the horrid smell of rotten fish, burned flesh, tar, and wet feathers.

A pyre in the center of the courtyard, raging fire. A figure slumped and aflame. Once a woman. *She will sing no more.*

It is better to be numb than a witness to this madness. Calling to the Nixan within. Pleading. Begging it to come forth at least a little to lend her strength. No second thump in her chest. Like a distant song, the once-incessant hum, now barely heard. Silent and still. *Alone.*

The pyre turbulent, flames licking, embers swirling to the Three above. The woman's ashes, taken by Juka's breath, mixed with the sand, salt, and sea. *Will my flesh fuel the pyre next?*

A woman's voice, large and round and loud, intoning and droning, not unlike Dini's at her Pahpi's nilva. Vahgrin's call rumbled in her chest.

Hairs on end, neck ridge hot. Pulsing. There, deep within. *Tharump. Tharump.* Faint as the whisper of a butterfly's flapping wings. *The dragon lives.*

409

It still didn't heed her silent call, but to know it was alive brought unlikely hope. Her Nixan soul. Hated—suppressed—reviled. It was, nonetheless, a part of her. *Am I a part of it?*

Hundreds of figures surround her at the center of the stone platform. The outermost ring of Atyro hovering at the edges like specters, faces upturned beneath gauzy wisps of whisper-thin cloth. In front of them and closer still, row upon row of dark-haired women in black robes trimmed in red. Their hands in the air, ruby-red lips open, chanting. Their voices a low, insistent thrum.

A dozen women surrounded her. Their red outer dresses shone like silk in the firelight, their red-rouged mouths like deep gashes.

Quen scanned the faces and recognized Nevara among the Drago'Sorceri. Amidst others of her kind, Nevara didn't stand out. She was just another Rajani zealot, a cog in the Dragos Sol'iberi's plan to sow chaos by ushering forth Quen's shadow soul. To welcome it like a newborn babe into its parents' loving arms. *To cast me aside like last night's refuse pot.* Her stomach coiled tightly, and bile rose in her throat. *By Lumine's holy light, these crazy Nixan plan to sacrifice me.*

A Drago'Sorceri intoned about the dawn of the new age—of Dragos Teplo—and the renewed supremacy of the Dragos Sol'iberi with dragon-kin at their command. Hundreds of women hollered approval in unison, the volcanic shafts of the caldera echoing their shouts.

An elderly woman came forward, body bowed with age, but her hair a thick mane as black as a raven feather, free of silvery threads of age. The woman cried out to the gathered. "Tonight, sisters, we reunite the two most powerful Primals. Vahgrin, our Dragos'Badi, Keeper of the Flame, and son to Vay'Nada. And we welcome back to our fold Ishna, Dragos'Madi, bearer of the Waters of Life, Sister to us all, and Keeper of the Night."

The women roared their approval, the Atyro in the outer edges of the circle rattling instruments and banging drums. *Lumine, the Goddess, is the Watcher of the Night and Sister to us all.* Not only had they co-opted Lumine's holy name for their twisted purpose, but they falsely believed Ishna could be the bearer of the Waters of Life. *They have it all so wrong.* The words "Keeper of the Flame" and "son of Vay'Nada" echoed. *What will happen to Rhoji, Liodhan, Zarate, and little Lumina if they succeed?* Her face was wet with tears. *And what of Aldewin?*

Quen tried to scream out—to plead with them—but her throat was as dry as the day she'd followed Nevara into a sandstorm outside Solia. The day Vahgrin had taken Pahpi from her and turned her world upside down.

The elder Rajani raised a wrinkled arm to quiet them. "Soon, Sisters, with Ishna by his side, Vahgrin, our Lord Dragon, will raise the other Primeri."

The uproar was nearly deafening. Vahgrin yowled so loudly Quen feared the black spires around them would topple.

Now the speaker raised both arms, urging quiet. It took a few minutes, but finally, she continued. "Oh, Sisters, rejoice! For once our gods have arisen, dragon-kin will sleep no more. Our beloved dragons will rise from every barrow and cave from deep slumber beneath sand and wave. And we, the Dragos Sol'iberi, will take our rightful place at their side. Together to rule over man and beast. We welcome the new Dragos Teplo."

411

The gathered women screamed and shouted their agreement. Vahgrin bellowed, and the drums pounded.

The elder Rajani raised an arm again, and her voice rang out loud and determined. "Anyone who opposes the Dragos Sol'iberi shall know the cleansing fires of our Lord or the chill wind of our Lady's breath."

In answer to this last statement, Rajani danced and gyrated approval. Young Atyro swooned and were caught from falling by their Sisters.

"As for Xa'Vatra—"

The crowd sent up a hiss and murmured low curses, smiting Indrasi's ruler and her family. Their drums pounded.

"The Kovan throne and all who sit on it bear the taint of Indrasian the Murderer. This Xa'Vatra, proclaiming herself to be the daughter of our Lord Vatra." The speaker spat. "The vile usurper is a great pretender, heir to a bloody throne, and a keeper of lies. At long last, my Sisters, the usurper and all her kin will pay for the grievous sins of their forebears."

Like the Dragos Sol'iberi, Quen despised Xa'Vatra for what the woman had put Quen, her brother, and Jagaru friends through. If the Exalted hadn't ordered Kovatha mages to hunt them, Druvna would still be alive. *Xa'Vatra deserves the justice of a Jagaru blade, but an entire city's people shouldn't perish to pay for one woman's crimes.*

The Rajani pressed closer together and moved toward the dais in a frenzy. Quen wanted to back away—to retreat from their lurid gazes and obvious bloodlust. But Rajani arms held her tightly where she stood, her legs still unsteady.

The elder Rajani ended her speech with one last and horrifying call to arms. "We, the Dragos Sol'iberi, Children of the Dragon, will have our time. We, Sisters, will reign over all Menauld!"

Dizziness still plagued Quen. The odor of the poor sacrificial Nixan woman, now ash, made bile rise. The smell reminded her of the day she found Pahpi. Her vision blurred. Fire raining from the sky. Ash and smoke obscured sight. Screams. A child's whimper. A vision. But of the past or future, she didn't know.

Not true.

It was the voice within.

The voice within. The dragon. *Ishna? So you have not abandoned me completely.*

What Ishna whispered into her mind was true. The vision was prophecy, not memory. It was the same vision she'd had when she first met Nevara.

Her eyes found Nevara. The woman was staring at her, her look knowing.

Quen's mind buzzed again with phrases in the ancient dragon language. Ishna spoke to her, and Quen began understanding what the shadow soul said. *Cannot. No Rajani. No control.*

On this, at least, the dragon soul and Quen agreed. Quen couldn't fathom why Ishna would deny herself the opportunity to push Quen aside—to squash the human soul and re-enter the world as a living god. For most of Quen's life, she'd battled this inner beast. It had tried to make itself known at the most unwanted times. *Why remain hidden now?*

What was it Ishna had said? *"No Rajani. No control."* Was Ishna hiding from the Rajani? *Is that why you've been silent?*

Quen didn't need to wait for an answer. She knew it was true as soon as she thought it.

And she knew she couldn't allow herself to take part in whatever ritual this unhinged cult planned for her. The stakes were no longer simply about her or her dearest ones. Her head buzzed with the agonized screams of thousands of tortured souls. It echoed Ishna's past, but it predicted Indrasi's future.

Another wrinkled Rajani came forward and motioned for the women holding Quen to bring her forward. The woman opened a small compact filled with red powder. She smudged Quen's forehead with it, then her cheeks and chin. "Praise to you, blessed Doj'Anira, for housing our Dragos'Madi in the temple of your body."

The gathered women bowed low to Quen, a murmur of whispered praise filling the courtyard.

"We will forever honor your name in the halls of Volenex."

Quen shook her head and gave a scornful laugh. "You expect me to go along with your sacrifice, so I get what? A plaque or a statue? A scroll with my story in your library cave?"

Quen's words dampened their mood, like Yulina telling people she was out of ale.

The elder who'd been speaking glared at her, black eyes wide, her mouth twisted in an angry grimace. It looked as though she wanted to strike Quen. *Maybe she's used to smacking the Atyro around.* But Quen was Doj'Anira, and her body was their god's temple.

414

Are they forbidden from harming me? There was only one way to find out.

Quen studied the rocky outcropping above. Still feeling the lingering effects of the Rajani sleep spell, her legs were unsteady. And the rock ledge was at least thirty spans above, possibly forty, and unreachable. There was an exit, a doorway cut into the stone. But there were hundreds of Rajani between her and freedom. Despite long odds, giving in wasn't an option. *To die fighting—an honorable death for a Jagaru.* Druvna would have approved, and the thought gave her courage.

Quen breathed deeply and searched for Still Waters. Lumine had gone to her rest several hours ago, and Quen wished the Sister was in the sky, a steadfast ally, a comfort in the dark. *What was it that Pahpi always said? "Just because you cannot see her doesn't mean she isn't there. Lumine's loving arms always bathe us in her light, even during the day. She will never abandon you."* Quen said a quick prayer to the Night Sister. *Don't abandon me now, Lumine.* She leaped as high and far as she could.

She cleared the tight throng of Rajani pressed close to the platform. Shouts and alarmed screams rang out behind her. Quen didn't stop to look back. Sprinting, her strides long, the activity awakening, clearing the Rajani webs from her mind. A commotion behind, but Quen pressed forward, coaxing the return of preternatural speed. She vaulted over the stone gate and leaped upon a rocky outcropping.

Boulders loomed, and craggy ledges paved her path. Though her legs had regained strength and solidity, the Brothers slept. It was nearly impossible to see where to land on black volcanic rock that melted into the night.

Quen's foot slipped, and her leg found a hole. Stuck, but only momentarily. Determined. *I will not end like this.* She pushed up, her talons stretching and gripping, pulling and scrabbling from the crevice. She bounded higher and higher until, at last, she was atop the inner caldera.

Below her, a nearly vertical wall, steep but inverted. She was on a ledge about forty spans above the moat's lapping waves. In the dark, she couldn't tell if the water would be only knee-high or deep and swimmable. From the sky, the outer caldera looked closer to the inner, and the moat narrow. But from this position on the ground, she couldn't see the other side of the water ring where it met the far shore.

She wasn't a strong swimmer, having only practiced it for a few weeks during the occasional spring when the Lakmi swelled deep enough for swimming. If she leaped, even if the water was deep enough to absorb her, she could drown before arriving at the other side.

Quen rubbed her fatigued eyes and concentrated on her surroundings, trying to find an alternative path. She stood on a craggy and inhospitable ring of rock. Unless one was atop a dragon, there was only one way out. Jump to the water.

Screeching rang from the courtyard. Flapping wings.

"Suda!" Without further consideration of the consequences, Quen leaped from the caldera's ledge, her legs straight down, her arms tucked at her sides. On the way down, she murmured prayers to Lumine. *Faced with death, I'm as devout as a monk in a Pillar.*

She'd expected the waters to be icy cold. Instead, it was like landing in a warm bath. Her lips tasted of salt. She kicked wildly and stroked her arms as Liodhan had taught her. Quen never enjoyed having her face in the water. She sucked in a deep breath and forced herself to put her head into the warm lake. Stroking evenly, she plowed the water.

Breathing every three to four arm strokes, her ear momentarily out of the water, birds shrieking. *Getting closer.* Quen put her head down and paddled, propelling herself across the caldera channel.

Her foot caught on something. A plant, perhaps, or the top of a reef below. Quen ignored it and pressed on. Hiyadi's first light chased away the gloom of total darkness. She'd never been happier to see Hiyadi rise from his rest. An outline now of the rocky shore on the other side. An even steeper mountain to scale. She would have welcomed dragon wings sprouting from her shoulder blades. Then she could have effortlessly cleared the intimidating cliff ahead.

Again, something clutched her foot. She shook it off, kicking with all her remaining force. Scraping at her ankles. The heat of an open wound. Claws clutching. Wings tearing the air. Shrill birds' cries and guttural croaks. Aggressive clacks of their bills and piercing alarm calls.

Wings flapping, churning up waves around her. Talons grasping, tearing at her flesh. Around her, a circle of oversized birds of prey. Eagles, hawks, and Corvus the raven, Nevara's Nixan soul. Their outstretched talons like a gauntlet of knives ahead and behind, answering her question. *No, they're not opposed to harming me.*

Despite the gauntlet, Quen pressed forward, the shore now visible. The promise of survival. Of being Quen Tomo Santu, at least for a while longer. Her arms were leaden, tired of the fight to remain afloat. Her legs were like two dead thukna strapped to her, threatening to sink her to the bottom of the black abyss. Salty tears met briny sea.

The battle is over. It had just begun.

Talons gently grabbed at her upper arms. They lifted her sodden body from the dark waters.

Her head hanging, her body bloody. Dripping saltwater stung the open gashes. The pain was inconsequential compared to the despair of defeat.

Once again, she stood on the dais. No longer showing deference to her as their honored Doj'Anira, the elderly Rajani Drago'Sorceri, who'd restrained herself before, stepped forward. Her withered hand, small and gnarled, palm open and connecting with the tender flesh of Quen's cheek, already smarting from saltwater in scratches. Her voice was a low hiss of condemnation. "To release Ishna, I will shred the flesh from your bones. Pick you to bits and share your liver with my Sisters." The woman spat at Quen.

Corvus landed, shook the water from its feathers, and immediately morphed into Nevara. Dripping wet, she stormed toward them. "Calm yourself, Sister Tilvani. This Nixan has not yet had her first Promena. The dragon within may die if you stress the host too harshly."

Tilvani eased back. Her eyes were less wild, though she still sneered at Quen.

Another Rajani, a Dragomancer not wearing the red dress of the higher-ranking Drago'Sorceri, came forward. "Set it to the pyre, Sisters. Ishna will not allow herself to die. She'll press this human trash to the side." Her eyes were alight with the fervor of a zealot.

Nevara shook her head and stepped forward, placing herself between Quen and the advancing throng. "What does Vatra fire do to ice or water?" Her eyes blazed with anger as she looked around the circle of women. "The pyre will sear the flesh of the Doj'Anira and destroy the Winter Dragon's heart. I—We—have worked too hard for too long. We cannot obliterate our progress because we lack patience."

Nevara's actions confused Quen. The woman bounced back and forth between wanting to kill Quen and protecting her. If Nevara kept her off the pyre, still smoking from the night's sacrifice, that bought Quen time. *Time is my only ally.*

Another Drago'Sorceri pressed forward. "What then, Nevara, do you suggest?"

"You are right, young Dragomancer. The dragon will not allow herself to be killed. Not if the host remains alive. The ancient rites speak of coaxing the Nixan soul."

"But if not on the pyre, then how?"

Nevara clasped a handful of Quen's hair and yanked her head backward. "Pain."

Murmurs rose from the circle of women surrounding her. Quen jerked away from Nevara, but the woman clenched her in a firm grip.

"Bit by bloody bit, we break it down." Nevara's claw-tipped finger stroked across Quen's forehead. "Lost in a desert of privation, her mind will do the work for us. Illusion. Reality. Will you be able to tell the difference, Doj'Anira?"

Whispers of approval and beaks clacking from the Rajani who remained in Nixan form. Their body heat warmed her back.

"Patience, Sisters. Bring the Doj'Anira to within an inch of death, and I promise you, Ishna will rise. She remains. Oh yes, I feel her." Nevara's silver-claw-tipped fingers pressed into Quen's chest. Her eyes closed, an odd, nearly orgasmic smile on her lips. "It is not our failure, Sisters, but the strength of the Winter Dragon seeping into this Doj'Anira's soul, fueling her defiance."

Shouts of "Praise Dragos'Madi" rang out.

"With reverence to Ishna, we will chip away at the will of this human until she hangs on but by a single breath. Then we will have our Winter Dragon."

Quen licked her lips, her throat tight and dry, and her voice croaked. "I will die before allowing you to control Ishna or me."

Nevara gripped Quen's head even more tightly and laughed. "Oh, I promise you will die. One way or another, the Dragos Sol'iberi will have control of the Winter Dragon."

The Rajani didn't bother using a sleep spell. They dragged Quen from the Volenex courtyard, kicking and screaming.

CHAPTER 25

Obdurate to the end, Quen preferred a slow, painful death to obedient submission to the Dragos Sol'iberi. She begged Ishna, the dragon within, to lend her power. The dragon's strength might have allowed her to break free of the Rajani talons, but Ishna couldn't risk coming to the fore. These dragomancers had a method of controlling dragons. Quen didn't understand how it worked, but Ishna feared their power over her. It took a half-dozen Rajani handlers to subdue Quen, but they dragged her to a cave dug into Volenex's rocky foundation.

Nevara had promised to break Quen, but many hours passed, and Quen remained alone in the dark. They had dressed her in a black silken gown. *Hardly clothing at all.* But now the thin dress hung on her like rags. Despite the blazing heat of the southern suns outside, the walls of her cell were dank and moist with seeping seawater. Wet when they tossed her in the room, she was still damp and shivering. Extreme thirst had cracked her lips, and her hunger made a painful hollow in her belly. *Do they plan to starve me into submission?*

Hour after hour, Quen passed the time on a knife edge of fear, worried the iron gate would open and torture would begin. Sleep was the only respite from hunger and angst about her demise. But every time she drifted off, the sharp agony of starvation jerked her awake.

On the cusp of her twentieth year, Quen hadn't thought about her death. Now accepting she'd never leave Volenex, Quen wanted to weep. She was so dehydrated, though. Tears wouldn't come. She wound into a tight ball to preserve what little warmth remained. Hunger and thirst kept her from forming a coherent train of thought. Instead, memories flitted into her consciousness like golden leaves falling from a kukiri tree in late autumn.

Sitting on Pahpi's knee as he sang the old children's song, "To Bed, To Bed," while clapping her hands. Giggling. His arms were solid and warm.

Liodhan teaching her how to pull a scraper across a hide, shearing off every fiber of hair, making it smooth. "That's it, Quen. Smooth as a newborn babe's bottom that skin'll be, and you can sell it yourself in the spring." He beamed with pride. She drank it in like spring's first rain.

Watching Dini light sage and lift it to the sky, eyes closed, mouth open, performing O'Dishi chants over a sick child. *What was that girl's name? Why I can't remember it?* She'd made fun of the girl behind her back, telling Rhoji the girl smelled like a thukna's arse. The O'Dishi chants weren't enough. The girl died two days later. Guilt was like the layers of silt lining the Lakmi River basin.

Each year the roiling waters brought a new deposit of soil. *Pray Lumine forgive me.*

When she played Ligos with Rhoji, he won every time. A strategy game involving cards and runed stones, Ligos required patience Quen didn't have. He'd always gloated when he won, even though he knew she was no match for him. *Yet.* Once, he found her alone in the meat cellar, curled in a ball and crying. He'd held her in his arms and sang a song to soothe her.

She shivered, and her teeth chattered. *Why didn't I stay with Rhoji?* With shaky fingers, she touched the ridge on her neck. It was cool to the touch now, not hot and tingling. It reminded her why she'd left Rhoji and the rest of the pod. *Did I have a choice? They ousted me, but I cannot blame them.* She'd fought the gnawing beast within her entire life. *But was my battle for naught?* It was—had always been—inevitable that the dragon soul she'd carried would force her into oblivion. They'd all be in danger if she'd remained with Rhoji and the pod—or with Liodhan, Zarate, and little Lumina. *I am the danger.*

A rustling sound. Her vision was bleary, a figure before her. "Rhoji?" Her voice strained, her throat tight from unwept emotion.

A hand on her forehead. Claw-tipped fingers, but the touch gentle. Warmth.

The smell of water. Fresh, not dank, and salty. Cool moisture at her lips.

Drinking. Sweet relief!

"Easy."

She blinked, trying to clear the cobwebs from her mind, the haze from her eyes. A halo of golden light shone behind a figure, its head a round silhouette against the darkness. "Lumine?" *The Watcher of the Night has answered my prayers.*

Pressure, a gentle touch, on her forehead. Words whispered in the ancient Rajani tongue, unintelligible.

She'd hoped it was Lumine guiding her to the Great River to reunite with Pahpi and her mother, Suliam. Hope gone, memory morphed into visions. Past, present, and future as one. Fires raged. The odor of burnt hair and flesh. Screams. A child cries for its mother. Charred corpses, yellow smoke curling to Juka's æther.

And among the rubble and burnt debris of a ruined village, a child's toy. A small stuffed drey made of the smoothest white leather, soft as a newborn's skin. It was familiar. Quen recognized this toy because she had made it—and given it to Lumina the day she left Solia with the Jagaru. The last day she'd seen Liodhan and his young family.

She screamed out, "No! Murderers." Quen slashed at the woman with her hand on Quen's forehead. Vatra's fires roiled in her belly. "I will kill you all."

"Yes, that's it." The woman's voice was a low hiss. "Allow Vatra's fires to kindle your power."

A single tear welled, her voice a strangled cry. "You killed my family. She was a child. Innocent."

"'Tis only a vision of what may be, Doj'Anira. You can prevent this. Step aside. You know Ishna is more powerful than you. Her Promena is inevitable. You hold the key to end your own suffering, Quen."

This Rajani's words echoed the thoughts she'd been having. That her thinking agreed with the Rajani harrowed her.

More cool water at her lips. Quen pulled the skin to her lips and guzzled, unable to deny herself Enara's gift. *The Waters of Life.*

A passage from her favorite story, *The Saga of Ilkay,* came to mind. *"Fear not the beast's fire, Ilkay, for Lumine blessed you with the Waters of Life. Carry them in your heart always, for the Shadow feeds on chaos and fears nothing more than the glassy stillness of calm waters."*

She'd treasured that book, not only because it had been her mother's, but because Ilkay faced the beast with calm assurance. *I've tried to be like Ilkay.* It was also how she'd imagined her mother might have been.

Pahpi had a way of sensing when her gut roiled with Vatra's fires of anger or jealousy. *"Still Waters, Quen,"* he'd say. Pahpi's mantra, repeated so often, it became like a well-trodden path. Knowledge of how to achieve a tranquil heart. Her vitality sapped, Quen doubted she could keep Ishna locked away, but if she was going to die, she wasn't about to leave Menauld with her mind in chaos. She didn't want to end up lost in Vay'Nada for all eternity.

Quen called on the loving light of Lumine, the Sister, to aid her. *I'll answer Rajani chaos with the glassy stillness of an untroubled soul.* Her eyes closed, her breaths shallow but calm. She imagined a pool of tranquil water, still as glass. The second heart was quiet, adding to the peaceful feeling.

Claws scratched at her, dashing the calm. Her cheeks were ablaze with pain, wet and trickling with blood.

The Rajani screamed at Quen. "Stop it, you wretched creature. You're killing our god."

A second voice. "Do not get hysterical, Tilvani."

Quen recognized the slippery quality of the woman's voice. One minute filled with the warmth of Lumine's light, the next cold as the hissing hollowness of Vay'Nada.

Nevara.

"Ishna is with us still, Sister, but barely. Do not fret. I know how to coax this Doj'Anira to Promena."

Fingers at her wrist. "Her heart is weak. She'll last only a day." Tilvani slammed Quen's hand down. "We did as you said before, Nevara. Still, this greedy creature keeps Ishna from us." Tilvani's voice rose into a shrill note of panic.

"Leave it to Vahgrin and me. We will return soon with the key."

A cool breeze as they vacated the tiny space of Quen's cell. As awful as they were, she missed them when they were gone. Life tethers life. Without others to anchor her, Quen feared she wouldn't last the day they'd predicted.

•   •   •

Wet trickled at her temples. Horns had sprouted from her head. She thought it had been a dream. *Was it?* Hand to her face. Wet. Cool. Water, not blood. No horns. *Yet.*

A splash coupled with high-pitched keening. The sound, irritating beyond measure, brought queasiness.

Nevara's voice grated on her nerves as much as the Rajani keening. "Wake, Doj'Anira. I brought you a gift."

A gasp.

It wasn't from her.

A low growl.

It wasn't the dragon.

Through bleary vision, two figures were beyond, outside the narrow doorway of her cell. Firelight dancing, chasing away the shadows. *That stance is familiar.* Tall. Broad shoulders. Hands held in front, bound in chains, as were his ankles. An aura of brackish green surrounded Aldewin, wrapped in the fabric of Vay'Nada.

Her throat was tight, parched, and exhausted. Quen's voice was like the sound of wind sweeping sand. "Aldewin."

Beside him, bound in a similar cage of brackish green, Nivi yowled. He didn't appear injured, but his pained cry rent her heart.

The only word she could manage. "No."

Claw-tipped hands removed her bindings. Strong arms bore her and carried her, slack-legged, from her cell.

"Come, Doj'Anira. I am not heartless. We cannot deny our sacred vessel the opportunity to make peace with this world before eternal sleep. Say goodbye to your lover and pet." Her lips against Quen's ear. "And know if you kill Ishna, so do you kill them."

Quen shivered not just from the bone-chilling cold of the damp dungeon, but with anger and fear for her loved ones. She was powerless to help them. She was ready to give in—to allow Ishna to rise. But the dragon soul was quiet and didn't come to her defense. "It is as I've told you. Ishna doesn't answer my call." Her voice trembling, desperate. "You can kill them. Destroy me. Suda, Nevara, you can murder every soul in Indrasi. You cannot make the Winter Dragon bow to you. She'd rather we all die than submit to your control."

Nevara's claws, savage and angry, swiped at her face. Fresh blood trickled, the wound raw. Nevara dug her claws into Quen's chest, gouging and ripping at the surface flesh. Her face nearly touched Quen's. "You lie." Nevara stood still. Listening. "There," she whispered. "I feel it, as do you." Her eyes grew wide, dark orbs twinkling with delight. "Ishna lives. It is you, vile human, that keeps her from us."

"She was never yours to command."

"We control Vahgrin. Ishna will also submit, and together, dragons and Rajani, side by side, we will rule."

"Rule what?" Quen forced a wry laugh. "Rubble and death? Your plan is madness. You know it is."

Nevara twisted her claws and then released her hold. Blood dripped down Quen's nearly naked stomach. "No, humans built a mad world. A usurper queen exulting herself, acting as though *she* is a god." Spittle shone on Nevara's lower lip. "To fuel their paltry Menaris, humans put the yoke of bondage on any magical creature they can." Nevara's eyes were black as a raven's feather, wide and wild. "And when they can't control a creature like us—oh yes, Quen, do not exempt yourself. You belong to our caste whether or not you like it." She leaned closer, her putrid stench making Quen gag. "Humans hunt creatures like us. Torture us. Kill us. They hate anything unlike themselves. Violence marks Nomo Teplo—the Age of Man." She cackled. "And you call us mad? For wanting to burn it to the foundation and start anew."

"Chaos is not the answer." Quen sighed. "Besides, Ishna hasn't answered me. You spat at humans and complained about their control of magical creatures. Yet listen to yourself, Nevara. Isn't that what you do to Vahgrin? And what you seek to do to Ishna as well." She gave a wry laugh.

Nevara scowled at Quen. "We are nothing like humans," she hissed. Nevara placed her forefinger on Quen's forehead, between her eyes.

Quen feared the Rajani would force upon her another horrific vision, but she didn't.

"The Dragos Sol'iberi revere the Winter Dragon. We carry out her will, what she asked of us nearly a thousand years ago. We have remained faithful servants of the Dragos. And in exchange for being her servants, she will allow us the control we've always had with dragon-kin. You saw the skull. Remember the hollow there." Nevara pressed her fingers into Quen's third eye. "In a living dragon, the dragon's primal life essence fills that hollow. And we, the Dragos Sol'iberi, know how to command it."

A knowing inside told Quen this was true. Ishna feared the Rajani's ability to control her. That fear kept her hidden. But... there was something else. *What did Nevara say in the library?* Quen remembered Ishna's skull, and Nevara's words swirled in her mind. She'd told Quen how the Rajani—how she, Nevara—used the magical liquid they'd preserved from Ishna's skull to... *To create me.*

Barely perceptible, but unmistakable. The phantom heartbeat, a fleeting flutter.

Nevara sensed it, too. The dark scowl of concern gave way to a twinkle of delight. "There. Our Dragos'Madi answers my call. She will tolerate your attempts at suffocation no longer."

The Rajani Drago'Sorceri turned her back on Quen. "To honor the Winter Dragon, allow this Doj'Anira a few moments to say her goodbyes. Then bring them to the courtyard. The Winter Dragon is ready to be reborn."

The two Rajani holding Quen pushed her forward. Quen's knees gave out once they stopped bearing her up, and she fell at Aldewin's feet.

He knelt, and though his wrists were bound, he helped her stand. "Oh, Quen. What have they done to you?" Aldewin kissed her forehead, and his lips came away tinged in her blood. He offered his hands for support. "I would heal you, but they've put me in a binding. I'm cut off from the Corners."

"Healing would be a waste, anyway."

He protested, but she interrupted. "Shh, love, we haven't much time." With trembling fingers, Quen untied the singed leather cord around her neck. The amber pendant, the last remnant of her family. She tied it around Aldewin's neck. "If you survive, take this to Rhoji for me."

Aldewin's lower lip trembled, and red rimmed his eyes. "You will take it to him yourself. You—"

Quen kissed him. His lips were so full of life, she lingered, pulling warmth from him. The memory of his arms around her, the strength of Menauld beneath them, the Brothers overhead. Dreams of a future exploring the world together. *If only we'd gone north to his homeland.* Away from the Dynasty, the Dragos Sol'iberi, and even the Pillars. She was done with people trying to claim her as a prize—or worse, a weapon to be used in petty battles. All she wanted—all she'd ever wanted—was to be Quen. To wake each morning in the arms of someone who saw her and loved her for all she was. She wanted to run toward that dream.

You cannot run from yourself. The thought was Quen's, not Ishna's.

Quen sighed. "My end is inevitable."

"No." Aldewin shook his head. "You mustn't say that. This can't be—"

"How my story ends? Why not? Pahpi's story didn't end happily. Nor did Druvna's."

"Yes, but—"

"But…" Quen moved closer so only Aldewin could hear what she said. "I see a way—maybe. A possibility, anyway. But whatever happens, know this: I love you, Aldewin di Partha."

He kissed her deeply and sighed. "If only we'd had more time. There's so much I wanted to tell you." He wiped his face on his shoulder. "So much to show you."

She forced herself up on shaky legs to whisper in his ear. "I will not die, Aldewin. No matter what you see, know this. Ishna lived within me for twenty years. When she rises, I will remain within her. Together, the dragon and I will find a way to separate our souls. A way for me to, at long last, simply be Quen. Someday." Quen withdrew her lips from his ear and laughed. "Remember when you said you'd love me even if I sprouted hairy spider legs?" She held up her talons. "Can you love a dragon?" She smiled.

He returned a wan smile. "I will love you, Quen Tomo Santu di Sulmére, until the day I go to Lumine's arms." His smile faded, and fresh tears welled.

Quen knelt and wrapped her arms around Nivi, burying her blood-caked face in his fur. "Stay with Aldewin, my friend. He will care for you until we meet again."

They'd brought her to the dungeons, kicking and screaming. She'd been determined to fight their horrific plan to the end. But now she knew. *Ishna is the answer.* The dragon was the only way she would survive—and her only hope of protecting Aldewin, Nivi, Lumina, and all whom she loved. She allowed the Rajani to lead her through the twisting labyrinth of Volenex back to the courtyard.

Again, surrounded by the Dragos Sol'iberi. Vahgrin's voice quivered in her hollow belly. Neck muscles weak, her head bobbed, causing the scene to bounce.

Above her, the Brothers, their warmth a balm to her soul. Dampness receded, heat on her scraped and battered face, restoring a bit of strength as her shivering ceased.

The blood rushing in her ears muted Tilvani's droning, and she warbled as if speaking underwater. Quen was glad Tilvani's words were unintelligible. *I've had enough of the woman's shrill pronouncements. I don't need to listen to know what they intend for me.*

Quen ignored the Rajani and tuned out Vahgrin. She turned inward and searched for Ishna. Though she'd fought against the Nixan her whole life, now the dragon was the only hope for saving her beloveds.

Ishna, I know you remain with me. I've felt your heart.
Silence.
I will die. I see that now. I wasn't meant to survive this.

Quen's eyes were like hot cinders, her throat tight with emotion, choking pain. Rajani sisters, flanked by several Atyro, shuttled Aldewin and Nivi into the courtyard. *To witness my end? How kind of our Dragos Sol'iberi hosts.* Tears shone on Aldewin's cheeks, his mouth set in a pained grimace, his eyes red. Nivi kneeling, paws covering his ears, a low whimper of agony.

Urgency rising. *We have no choice, Ishna. If you die, then not only will you cease to exist, but my family... Everyone I love will perish.* Quen didn't bother wiping her tears. *You can protect them. You must save them.*

A flutter in her chest. The familiar tharump of her phantom heart. Faint and slow, it was unlikely to draw the attention of the frenzied Rajani. *But it's there. Is it horrible that I'm glad to feel you once again?*

I understand now why you fear them. Quen glimpsed Vahgrin, a Rajani handler straddling his back. Two additional Rajani crooned at his side, their red mouths open, but singing in a pitch inaudible to human ears.

I will fill the hollow, Ishna. They will not control you—us.

The phantom heartbeat, clearer. The ridge on her neck burning, tingling. Quen wept with joy. The sensation she'd hated, evidence of her shameful truth, now welcomed like an old friend.

The internal voice, felt but not heard. Like a memory or dream. *Fill the hollow.*

Quen's skull buzzed, and blinding pain shot like an arrow behind her eyes. A vision came to her, floating like a feather wafted on a breeze.

Ishna's skull. The one Nevara had shown her. Between the eyes, an odd hollow space in the bone. The space Quen must occupy. *But I don't know how.*

"*Together as one,*" Ishna thought. "*Our family—humans and dragons—will survive. Trust in me, Quen. Fill the hollow.*"

Quen's neck felt like it had split in two. Searing heat.

Aldewin screamed, "No! Quen, you mustn't. They'll control two dragons. They'll end our world."

Rajani voices sang an eerie chant, intoning Ishna forth. Some shifted to their Nixan form, wings flapping, churning the air.

But it was not Dragos Sol'iberi chanted prayers that urged Ishna forth. The Winter Dragon would not bend to their will. Ishna would be born anew to protect love, not fuel Dragos Sol'iberi ambition.

Occupy the space, Quen. Fill the hollow. You will survive. We will rise together.

Quen wasn't sure how to fill the hollow, but she concentrated on a single thought. *Together.*

Fear and pain receded. Her talons lengthened, and her spine undulated. Quen's nightmare of horns sprouting at her temples coming true. Her eyes burning, teeth falling out. Plink, plink, plink on the stone.

Nivi howled. The sound of Aldewin's tears splashing on stone. His eyelids blink, the flutter of his eyelashes like the breeze of a bee's wings. The amber pendant at his neck, twinkling in the midday light of the Brothers.

Quen's last words were strained and primal. "Go to Rhoji. Give him the amber. Tell him the story of what I've become." A guttural scream, her vocal cords changing, soon unable to speak with a human voice. "Goodbye, sol'dishi."

"No." His only word was both a plea and a regret. It would echo forever in Quen's heart, now the phantom beat within Ishna.

Ishna's spine was limber, undulating like a snake. Her silvery-white scales shimmering reflected shades of teal, glacial blue, and sea green. She unhinged her mighty jaw and showed two rows of razor-sharp teeth to the Rajani. She rose on strong limbs, talons digging into the rock and a long serpent tail whipping behind.

Their shouts of joy were deafening, and their keening enough to rattle the bones. Within the Rajani lament,

434

merely annoying to Quen, a high-pitched tone beyond human ears. This sound, perfected by Rajani dragomancers, quivered in the hollow space between the eyes of a Primal dragon. This empty cavity in a Primal dragon's skull, filled with magical fluid allowing them to create new dragon-kin. The 'Rend,' as the Dragos Sol'iberi called it, caused a Primal dragon such agony it became docile just to end the Rajani torture.

Ishna's rumble was low and deep, echoing off the caldera's stone walls. She took to the sky, her long white mane whipping in the wind. Spiraling upward, testing her new skin and wings. The magic of creation, rippling through the fabric of the æther. Primal Dragons were both tied to and fueled by Menauld's ancient magic. Without access to primal Menaris, the magic of creation, humans must use the intermediary forces of spirits and gods to access magic. A pale copy of the Menaris known to Primal Dragons, such as Ishna and Vahgrin. *And our two other Primal dragon-kin.*

Ishna undulated her lithe form, lean and swift. Hunger pained the hollows of her stomach, but the Rajani Rend didn't cause her to fold. Quen occupied the space in the dragon skull just as she'd said she would. *A human teaching this old dragos new tricks.*

The Dragos Sol'iberi had made two errors, and Ishna smiled at their mistakes. To grow a dragon soul within Quen, the cult had used the magical liquid that normally filled the hollow in Ishna's skull. Without it, their Rend held no sway over Ishna. *And they hadn't counted on Quen's soul filling that cavity, pushing back against their Rend.* Their second error, though, was even more significant. They hadn't counted on a father's unconditional love or the strength of the human, Quen Tomo Santu.

And yes, Quen was with her, entwined within every fiber of her blood, skin, and bone. Filling the hollow in her skull. Like Ishna had been the whole of Quen's life, Quen lived in Ishna's periphery. Not in control, but enmeshed with her. She—Quen—filled the hollow, and together, they were immune to the dragomancer Rend.

Though her human life had been brief, Quen had learned much. And now, all Quen knew, Ishna carried. Ishna had lived thousands of years, but she had learned much from her human life. But it was more than knowledge. Quen's greatest gift to Ishna was the love she'd known.

Quen's love remained, and it was part of Ishna now. To be alive—gloriously alive—after a thousand-year sleep! Ishna roared and shook the foundations of Volenex.

Vahgrin, her brother, was bound by the Rajani keening their Rend song at him. They jangled him into submission. It was no excuse for what he'd done to Quen. And Ishna still harbored resentment, a thousand years in the making, for his role in her original death. After all, it was Vahgrin who led Indrasian to her mountain lair. Without Vahgrin as his guide, the human warrior, Indrasian, could have never found her.

I should ice-burn Vahgrin's traitorous scaly hide until he's nothing but snowy powder.

Quen's voice, deep within but alive. *The heart of Vaya di Solis is forgiveness. Especially for our kin.*

Oh, Sulmére Sister, Vahgrin is unworthy of exoneration. You know not what havoc he has wrought in my world and your own. I promise you this, Quen. His reckoning will come, but not this day.

Vahgrin was one of the original Primal Dragons. Ishna needed him to complete the primal circle. *And we need to produce one more. A deed for another day. Leaving him in Rajani hands is punishment enough — for now.*

Ishna turned downward, her long white whiskers sleeked by the rush of air. Hunger in the pit of her scaly belly drove her down, spiraling. The woman known as Tilvani, her voice grating like the slow drip of water.

Clutching with her great talons, scooping, teeth tearing into the old woman's thin flesh. Warm blood. Waters of Life. The dragon's thirst and hunger was slaked, and Quen's need for revenge returned. The engine of her power roiling.

Rajani loudly keening, attempting with all their might to Rend Ishna. Fear unfurled from them like an oily film. Gauzy white neophytes running, frightened. From the air, they looked like unsheared drey.

Ishna bellowed, cold misty steam turning their bodies to ice. Frozen in space, their eyes forever wide with fright, their hearts stopped by the sudden freeze. Ishna flew close to the ground, scooping up several frozen Dragos Sol'iberi to fuel her insatiable hunger.

Nevara called to Vahgrin. "Zhijnatu, Vahgrin."

Ishna laughed. To human ears, it was a burst of low rumbles. She spoke to Vahgrin in the dragon tongue. "You heard your master, brother. Be still and obey."

Vahgrin's voice, a low thrum in her chest, speaking in the language only four souls understood. *Five, as Quen now joins our fold.* "I killed you once, Sister. I will kill you

437

again." Eons-old jealousy fueled his anger, unabated after all these years. Vahgrin spewed fire at Ishna.

Nevara cursed at him in the Rajani tongue. Two dragomancers in tow, they mounted his back and keened madly, Rending him into submission.

Panic made Nevara's voice shrill. "Don't kill her, Vahgrin. We need her, you fool."

Ishna laughed. The Dragos Sol'iberi unaware of the irony of their words. They'd believed they could control the Winter Dragon. The idea, once worrisome to Ishna, now laughable. That her brother could best her, more comical still. He'd never won a battle against her in over three thousand years. *But these foolish Rajani don't know that. They arrogantly think themselves privy to ancient knowledge.* Ishna laughed, and the entire foundation of Volenex rumbled.

They believe Vatra fires the strongest because Vatra is the Pillar of war. Have they never seen a wave swallow a city or a glacier gobble a mountain?

Ishna hurled an icy volley at Vahgrin, a small showing of what more followed for him if he chased after her. Her freezing breath burned the flesh of his thigh, opening a gash that would pain him but not maim him.

A Drago'Sorceri screamed, "Why is our Rend not working on her?"

Nevara shook her head. "Sing higher."

Another added, "Or lower."

They set about modulating their pitch. The cumulative sound like a tumult of broken bells thrown down a well, sickly pinging.

Ishna laughed, and the deep, robust sound shook Menauld. She spoke then in the Rajani language. "Dear

438

Nevara, Rend in every pitch you can muster. You cannot control me. You wanted the Winter Dragon? Here I am."

She spiraled downward, claws outstretched. Ishna snatched Nevara from Vahgrin's back. He shouted a protest and spewed fire at her, but Ishna swiftly swerved, dodging his assault.

Nevara wriggled and screamed. Gone was her commanding demeanor. She smelled of urine and acrid sweat. Of rotten fish and wet feathers.

The vengeance was Quen's to take, and Ishna searched her feelings for how her human sister wished for justice to be served. Visions flooded Ishna's mind, some of Quen's memories, others of Ishna's own knowing. Memories of a woman posing as a Bruxia, coaxing a desperate Consular's wife to sip a potion filled with the distillate of Ishna's magical soul. A small child—Rhoji—flopped over his dead mother's body, sobbing the silent tears of a loss so great, he wanted to lie on the pyre with her as she burned. A woman posing as a Kovatha, arguing with Quen's father and offering a grim prophecy. Nevara atop Vahgrin's back, laying waste to Solia and ending the life of Quen's beloved Pahpi. From deep within, Quen's anger and hurt fueled Ishna's ire and answered how to mete out justice to the woman who had callously disregarded the lives of so many.

Ishna soared above the caldera's edge.

The calm demeanor of an esteemed sorcerer gone, Nevara begged. "Please, Dragos'Madi. I brought you back to life." Her voice trembled with fear. High in the sky now, the remaining Dragos Sol'iberi below were like specks of bird shite. "I live only to serve you, great dragon. Please spare me, and I will be your humble servant."

Ishna spoke to Nevara in the Rajani tongue. "Quen wants you to know this is justice served for killing her Pahpi."

Nevara whimpered as Ishna flung her into the air. Nevara's face was pale as winter's coldest snow, her expression absolute terror. The woman hung in the sky before descending.

"Nothing burns like the cold." Ishna's icy breath came from deep in her belly and up through her throat. Ishna hurled a torrent of frosty breath on the tumbling Rajani, freezing her into a Nevara icicle.

The solid ice block of Rajani gathered speed as it fell to the courtyard's black stones. The remaining women at first craned to see what was happening above. Once they saw frozen Nevara barreling toward them, the women scattered like black rats jumping from a burning ship.

Nevara struck the ground and shattered, her body now shards of frozen glass reflecting the loving light of the Brothers. In the space between Ishna's eyes, the hollow within the bone, a deep satisfaction.

We have avenged you, Pahpi.

CHAPTER 26

N ascent. It had been over three thousand years since Ishna was born. Aware but imprisoned in the formless existence of Vay'Nada, Ishna had almost given up hope of experiencing life again. Yet here she was, glorious sun on her scales, Juka's breath rippling through her hair and filling her lungs. She longed to fly with her dragon-kin, dance in the sea and air together, laugh, and share stories.

Soon, my brothers and sisters, daughters and sons, cousins and friends. A dragon reunion must wait. I have business to attend to on behalf of my human heart.

Feeding her bottomless hunger could also wait, but she could kill two birds with one stone. The Dragos Sol'iberi had starved Quen. *Only fitting they should now feed the Winter Dragon.*

Ishna would have liked to dine on their flesh for days, filling out her muscle and bone. But she needed some of the Dragos Sol'iberi to live. She wasn't yet ready for her trials with Vahgrin. Until she was, the remaining Dragos Sol'iberi would keep Vahgrin where Ishna knew she could find him.

She gobbled up a half-dozen Rajani and froze several dozen more. By the time Ishna landed in the courtyard, Nevara was already melting. The Rajani's body seeped into the soil of Volenex. *Menauld take you.*

The remaining Dragos Sol'iberi scattered from the courtyard in every direction, some running, others taking to wing and headed to the Lenxofré geyser fields to the northwest. Forgotten by the fleeing cult, Aldewin and Nivi stood where they'd witnessed Ishna's rebirth. Aldewin leaned on his staff, his chin covered in stubble, deep hollows beneath his red-rimmed eyes. A lone glistening tear shone on his cheek.

With grace belying her massive body, Ishna landed. She wiped Aldewin's tear with the pad of her taloned finger. She'd lived with claws for many millennia and was adept at using them to both rip and soothe.

Aldewin turned his face up to her, his words choked. "Your eyes. They are the same." He smiled. "One clear-sky blue. One amber yellow."

Ishna nuzzled him against the snowy-white fur of her beard. With his ear against her chest, he could hear the double thump of her two hearts. Though Aldewin spoke neither the ancient dragon language nor Rajani tongue, he knew the eons-old language used in the Pillars. The language of Vaya di Menaris. Though Ishna had difficulty forming some words, she tried to speak the language of the Pillars as best she could.

"Be easy, Aldewin." Ishna's vowel sounds stretched, and her dragon tongue added clicks. "Quen lives in me."

442

Aldewin wept into her fur, his tears silent, his shoulders heaving. "I know. It's just...."

Nivi roared. He was not frightened, but his eyes drooped.

Ishna put a knuckle under Nivi's chin and ruffled his fur. The giant cat's chest rumbled a contented purr.

"Are you ready to leave Volenex?" Ishna asked.

Aldewin wiped his face and stowed his staff. "I don't want to smell this place again."

Ishna knelt, her belly skimming the stones. Aldewin understood. He grabbed a bit of her hair, pulled himself onto her back, just behind her horns, and wrapped his arms around her.

"What of Nivi? We cannot leave him."

"Worry not, Aldewin."

Ishna scooped the giant tiger in her great talons, careful not to squeeze too hard. They soared high, clearing the inner caldera and its chaos. Up and up she flew, the water below glistening like black jewels.

The air ahead shimmered with heat, and the air smelled of sky-fire. Ishna cared for Vay'Nada no more than Quen did. She'd spent far too much time in its icy chasm. But opening the door to the Shadow's realm was necessary to travel with haste.

"Brace for the Void."

Aldewin gripped more tightly, and Nivi's muscles tensed beneath her talons.

Within Ishna, a whisper. The faintest hint of thought, but not Ishna's. *I thought opening doors to Vay'Nada was a Rajani power.*

Ishna laughed at the thought. *You saw what you wanted to see, dearest Quen.* Or perhaps believed what she feared

443

to know. *It was the dragon within you who knew how to travel the Void. Rajani have no such power.*

Ahead, a clear blue sky of the province of Quen's birth and a vast, temperate forest below. The sky cracked, and a thunderous boom shook Menauld. Then Vay'Nada was a memory.

At their backs, the splendorous peaks of TasūZaj, the Roof of the World. But they'd landed on the western side of the range, not the eastern. The Brothers' light reflected off the glaciers on the highest peaks, sparkling in the midday light. The dense Dajianta Forest spread before them for many leagues. Once through the forest, Aldewin and Nivi still had to journey through farmland and vineyards before reaching Bardivia, the city-state of Quen's birth. Ishna could not risk getting them closer. She had made a promise to Quen, and she intended to keep it. To keep Quen's loved ones and the people of Indrasi safe, Ishna needed to stay away from them. Confrontation between people and dragons always ended in tragedy. *The way it has always been.*

She released Nivi into the lush grass of the meadow. No longer trapped in Ishna's grasp, Nivi roared his appreciation.

Ishna knelt, and Aldewin slid from her back. He teetered on shaky legs, his face the color of a pale moon. "I hope never to do that again."

Ishna smiled and nodded once. Her movements were slow and meant to reassure. She blinked and her long eyelashes fluttered. Ishna scooped her neck, and her great forehead met Aldewin's. His heart quivered, maybe in panic, perhaps excitement. She did not know.

"We will see each other again."

Aldewin nodded. Gone was the nervous quaver in his voice. "I know." He smiled up at her. "Be well, Ishna. And take care of Quen."

She nodded then pointed her snout northwest. Bardivia was a problematic word for her to pronounce, containing 'b' and 'd,' two of the most challenging letters for her dragon mouth to say. Instead, she said, "Rhoji."

He got her meaning. Aldewin clasped the amber pendant, his eyes misting with tears again. "I will find him, Ishna. And give him this, as Quen asked of me." Nivi nuzzled Aldewin's other hand, reminding him of his promise to care for the great cat. Aldewin chuckled. "Yes, yes, and you will come too." Aldewin ruffled Nivi's mane. "It will be a glorious adventure, my friend. We'll meet up with our pod. After being in Volenex, I'm even looking forward to seeing Mishny." He laughed.

Ishna laughed too, her chuckle a low rumble interspersed with tongue clicks.

"Where will you go, Ishna? If you remain in Indrasi, I fear you will not be safe. The Exalted plans to yoke as many dragons as possible to match the threat from the Dragos Sol'iberi control of Vahgrin. Are there others like him? That breathe fire, I mean?"

Ishna nodded. She looked north toward the highest peaks of TasūZaj, where she once lived. *So long ago.* She could hide in the mountains, slumbering in the ice. Her eternal heart would keep her alive while men waged war and eons passed.

Because humans could not long withstand the thin air on TasūZaj's highest peaks, she'd be safe from people there. But even hibernation on the highest peak wouldn't prevent danger from other dragons. Vahgrin took advantage of her slumber once before. Worse still, now that she was fully awake, her dragon-kin would rise. *I need to protect them, too.*

She closed her eyes and listened, not just with her ears, but with the inner ear of knowing. Her feet to the ground, Menauld beneath her whispered knowledge of all the world. *They wake, and it is up to me to protect them from humans. And to protect Quen's human family from my dragon-kin.*

"Tinox," she said at last. "Bídea."

Aldewin tilted his head. "My homeland. That's an odd place to go." He rubbed his chin, his brows furrowed. Then a look of understanding. "Or is it?" He nodded. "Yes, I see now. Yes, to Tinox." He smiled and slapped his thigh. "By gosh, the Bídean Islands. Brilliant." His eyes shone with mirth. "Of course it's brilliant. I mean, you are, what, several thousand years old." He laughed. "My soul's mate, older than civilization."

Ishna laughed, too, and nuzzled his shoulder with her broad nose.

From the mountains behind, a thunderous call shook the ground. And in a range beyond human hearing, a second tone. *A lament.*

"They awake," Ishna said.

"The dragons?"

Ishna nodded. "I must go." She peered north, and though her eyesight was keen, she couldn't yet see the dragon who called. She sensed the life-force of an ancient dragon. *Naja.* Not primal, but no babe either. A winter dragon as well. At home in frigid weather and snowy peaks, this dragon-kin had slumbered amidst the glacial peaks of TasūZaj. *I will take you home,* she thought to it.

Aldewin nuzzled her downy neck one last time. "Goodbye, Ishna. Tell Quen I love her, even as a dragon."

The space between Ishna's eyes buzzed, not unpleasantly, but insistently. "She knows," Ishna said. "Menaris made us, Aldewin. Menaris will separate us."

She knew Aldewin longed for her to remain by his side, but the frozen north called to her, and her dragon-kin needed her guidance. The ground rumbled with their awakening. *I wonder if Aldewin and Nivi feel it?* Menauld carried their rhythm to her, and it synced with the beat of her heart so well she couldn't distinguish between them. The rolling rumble grew more insistent, tugging like an invisible rope pulling her to the sky, urging her to fly.

Ishna thrust her neck up, opened her mouth wide, and sent a plea to the skies. Her voice shook the ground and filled the air with thunder. She swirled above Aldewin and Nivi.

Aldewin waved and shouted, "Goodbye, Quen Tomo Santu di Sulmére." He put two fingers to his heart and lips and then made a crescent sign on his forehead. "May you walk always in the light of the Brothers and know the Sister's loving embrace."

Ishna shook her body, sending a light shower of iridescent scales to the ground around Aldewin and Nivi. It was all she had to give him to remember her by.

Aldewin picked one up, and it changed colors as he moved it. His voice was low, a whisper only a dragon could hear. "Be at peace, sol'dishi."

Ishna flew toward the dragon's call. Another cry, this one a mournful lament. Ishna returned the call and spoke in the dragon tongue. "To me."

On the horizon, a small roan-colored dragon flapped her tiny wings, circling up and into the dragon spiral.

From behind and near the sea, another dragon called. Its voice warbled, making its way from the sea bottom through the waves.

A third, then a tenth, and soon more voices than Ishna could count. She answered them all. "To me, to me."

At first, a half-dozen dragons circled the skies, scales shimmering in most every color. Their wings flapped, creating a wind even Juka couldn't control. There, a brilliant green dragon, black scales upright on his back. His eyes shone red, and Ishna remembered him, even after a thousand-year sleep.

"Owaanir!" Ishna cried. *My friend, how I've missed you.*

A smaller black dragon flew behind, her scales matte black and smooth, pale-green eyes like mossy pools. *Côzhili.* Ishna called to Owaanir and Côzhili, and their return cries gladdened her heart. *We will have ample time for reacquaintances.*

Ishna kept her gaze ahead, not behind. Though her heart swelled with love for the long-lost family she was meeting again, Quen was part of her now. And Ishna feared if she looked back, Quen's heart would break. Instead, Ishna focused on the sky and the growing throng of circling dragons.

Several leagues away, in a massive cave, Niezhan, a great yellow-eyed white dragon had buried himself to await the Awakening. Now, Niezhan pecked his grave's ceiling, eager to breathe fresh air once again and bask in sunlight. Light spilled into the cave coffin, the first light he'd known in millennia, and it urged him on. He drove upward with all his strength, willing himself to be free.

Ishna's primal call was intoxicating to him, like the primordial chord of life itself. Niezhan pushed his sleek-scaled head from the burial chamber.

His piercing call was so loud it shook the village's houses near his burrow. On the road, villagers gaped as Niezhan soared, casting a dark shadow over the village. Desperate to once again be with his own kind, Niezhan strained and pulled strength directly from Menauld. It was a dragos trick Ishna had taught him while he was still a youth. "Ishna, old friend, I am coming." Niezhan's voice shook the villager's houses, and made the people tremble.

In a grass-covered mount at the base of the mountains, villagers had buried alive twin dragons. Shackled to a thick post and left to rot, the dragons not only weren't dead, but hadn't decayed. *Men know not the ways of dragons.* The dragons hibernated while metal and wood deteriorated year after year, melting eventually like a snowball in the Sulmére. For creatures that can live tens of thousands of years, dragons don't dread a thousand in hibernation. The twins with scales of blue and green shut themselves down. "We will wait," one had said to the other. They'd slumbered in a world of dreams, waiting for the Awakening.

Ishna called again, and it awakened the twins. First, Liejala, a dappled blue drowsily blinked open an emerald-colored eye. Liejala's voice was dry and crackly like dried reeds in an arid wind. Her sister opened her eyes the color of deep pools of water.

"It is time," Liejala said.

The chains meant to bind had long ago rusted, and the twin dragons easily broke free of their bindings. They clawed their way out of the mound, their scales once

449

brilliant and shining, now dull and covered in mud. They were initially slow and ambling, using the dewclaws on the aft side of their wings to dig into the soil. Like Niezhan, their pace quickened once they saw first light. Their frenzied wings flapped away the last remnants of the barrow's ceiling, and with a powerful surge, they pushed through and took to the sky.

In caves now buried in shallow waters along the coasts, dragons clawed and pecked their way out of the water. Flapping wings created wind. Their barrows and caves crumbled as if caught in a land quake. Their calls drove fear into the hearts of the peoples of the realm. Humans didn't know what the loud thunderous roars and screeches meant. They worried about dragon fire burning their villages and feared for their lives.

Ishna soared higher and higher. She joined the fray of circling dragons and spiraled through the center of them like a mighty wind. Higher and higher and higher still, wind sleeking back her silvery-white hair.

She called again, a great bellow shaking air and land. A thunderous roar shook Menauld as dragons from across the realm answered her sonorous call.

It was time to leave this land, the only one Quen had known. Time to lead Ishna's large family to a more hospitable place. To the realm where human magic, Menaris, had been born. A place where people respected magical creatures and dragons, not feared them. They would cross the Orju Sea and seek the land of primordial dreams.

Higher and higher into Juka's realm, they climbed. Below, the world was a lifeless mass of land and water. Distance and time obliterated human dramas. The mountains reverberated with Ishna's last cry to the land and people Quen had known. A song of respect for the person Quen had been and for the loves she'd made—and lost. Other dragons added their laments to hers until they filled the air with wails of sorrow and regret. It was their way to mourn and leave these sadnesses in the land of their nascence.

Before long, thermals rose from the Sulmére's scorching sands. They'd coast on these winds, Juka's gift, and soon meet the eastern sea. Ishna smiled and pressed forward. A new Dragos Teplo had begun. *I am going home.*

THE END OF BOOK I

APPENDIX

DRAMATIS PERSONAE
(in alphabetical order)

Aldewin di Partha (AHL-doo-win)
Anu'Bida di Māja Wix (AH-noo BEE-dah dee MAZH-ah WIX)
Caz
Dini (DEE-nee)
Druvna (DROOV-nah)
Eira Nathisen di Suab'hora (EYE-rah)
Hrabke (HRAHB-kee), Prelate of Val'Enara
Imbica di Tikli (im-bee-KAH)
Ishna, The Winter Dragon
Kine, Archon of Val'Enara
Liodhan Tomo di Jima (lee-oh-DAHN)
Lumina Zarate di Jima
Luz
Mishny di Sulmére
Nevara (neh-VAR-ah)
Nivi (nee-vee)
Pelagia (peh-LAY-zhi-ah), Mistress of the Menagerie
Quen Tomo Santu di Sulmére
Rhoji Tomo Santu di Sulmére
Santu Inzo Dakon di Sulmére (SAN-too IN-zoh DAY-kahn)
    (aka **Pahpi** (PAH-pee), formerly Ser Santu Inzo Dakon
    di Vindaô)
Shel di Suab'hora
Tomo Suliam Vindiére di Vindaô (TOH-moh SOO-lee-yahm)
Vahgrin (VAH-grin), The Summer Dragon
Vidar, Prelate of Val'Vatra
Xa'Vatra (ZHAH-vah-tra), Exulted of Indrasi
Zarate Kareth di Jima

GLOSSARY OF TERMS

Altair (ALL-tare): Archon of Val'Qüira. He coined the term Doj'Anira (*see Doj'Anira entry.*)

Archon (AR-kahn): Spiritual leader of a Pillar.

Ascended: The designation after Rising at the Pillars.

Atyro (ah-TYRE-oh): A neophyte in the Drago Sol'iberi at Volenex, they are Nixan girls that have not yet had their first Promena (*see entry for Promena*).

Badi (BAH-dee): A word for father, especially in reference to the "Great Father," the masculine aspect of the Creator godhead.

Bardivia (bar-DIV-ee-ah): A prosperous city-state and capital of Vindaô Province.

Béanju River (bay-AN-joo): River that creates border between Sulmére and Tikli Provinces.

Besha di Tikli (BESH-ah dee TEEK-lee): Trader that carts wool and leather from southern provinces to the capital.

Bídean Archipelago (BEE-day-ahn): Archipelago of islands to the northwest of the continent Tinox.

Bíduan (BEE-do-wahn): An ancient language spoken in the Pillars and by mages for spellwork.

Bivet: Gondola driver in Qülla. Sister of Caz and Luz.

Boy: Mishny's kopek mount.

Brothers: The two suns of Menauld's star system, Hiyadi and Niyadi.

Bruxia *(BROO-zhee-uh):* Usually women, a town's healer and wise woman. Skilled in herblore. May have some knowledge and skill with Menaris, but most do not.

Castor *(CAST-er):* Warehouse owner in Qülla.

Chasm of Nil: The place one must cross to gain entry to the Val'Enara.

Cinwa *(SIN-wah):* Head Reeve of Qülla prison.

Conclave: The inner council of the Kovan Dynasty. Historically comprised of the master of each Māja and the Prelates of each Pillar. Exulted Héru, Xa'Vatra's grandsire, dropped all Pillars from the Conclave except for Vatra Pillar. Later, Surya, Xa'Vatra's father, dropped all but two of the major merchant houses (Māja Neyda and Māja Wix). The current Exulted, Xa'Vatra, kept her husband, Asar, on the Conclave as representative of Māja Neyda (he is her maternal cousin and Xa'Vatra's mother was from Māja Neyda). Xa'Vatra further consolidated power by removing Māja Wix. The current Conclave consists of Xa'Vatra's family (sisters, brothers, husband), and Prelate Vidar representing Vatra Pillar.

Corner: In the dominant theology in Indrasi, there are four elemental Corners, or "Ways" to which people belong. The two most popular are Enara (Water), and Vatra (Fire). The other two are Qüira (Ground/Rock), and Doka (Wood). A person that follows none of these is referred to pejoratively as "Cornerless."

curd head: A derogatory term, referencing a person's brain is like curdled milk.

Dajianta Forest *(dah-ZHEE-ahn-tah):* A dense temperate forest of mixed conifer and deciduous trees in the south/southeastern portion of Vindaô Province. The Dajianta is known to be haunted and cursed, so people rarely go there and the area around it is very sparsely populated. Though people could conceivably travel from Vindaô Province to the Sulmére in the south, the Dajianta Forest, the Lenxofré geyser fields, and Volenex create a nearly impenetrable barrier. Thus all trade between Vindaô and Sulmére goes north through the Suab'hora and Tikli, thus funneling trade through the taxation stations the Dynasty tightly controls.

dar: A unit of Indrasian money, worth ten pits.

darmanitong (dar-MAN-i-tong): A type of Nixan. Ugly, bottom feeding lake and river creatures.

Dauer (DOU-er): Druvna's gaunt old kopek mount.

Djeuthui (ZHOOTH-wey): Xa'Vatra's brother and a member of the Conclave.

Doj'Anira (DOHZH ah-NEAR-ah): "Twice Blessed." A term that refers to people with eyes of two different colors, such as one green eye, one brown. The term originated in the Suab'hora Province, first used by Archon Altair of Val'Qüira Pillar. Originally used as a term of respect for people born with a spirit containing equal parts of two Corners, the terms was co-opted by the Kovan Dynasty and twisted to ugly purpose.

Doj'Badi (DOHZH BAH-dee): "Blessed Father." The masculine aspect of the creator godhead.

Doj'Enara: "Blessed Waters." Not to be confused with Doj'Anira (*see Doj'Anira entry*), Doj'Enara is busy trading port in the southern bay of Bardivia. The name "Blessed Waters" refers not to the literal water in the bay, but to the prized wines from the region.

Doj'Madi (DOHZH MAH-dee): "Blessed Mother." The feminine aspect of the creator godhead.

Doka *(DOH-kah):* One of the four elemental corners, Doka represents wood, but more generally plants, growth, healing, and renewal.

Drago'Sorceri *(DRAGOH sor-SAIR-ee):* A sub-type of Rajani shapeshifter, these Rajani have skill and powers of both sorcery and dragomancing.

dragomancer: A person who can control dragons with a skill known as the Rend. All dragomancers are Rajani, but not all Rajani are dragomancers.

dragos *(DRAG-ohs):* Translates roughly as "of dragons." Can refer to dragons, or anything relating to dragons.

Dragos Sol'iberi *(SOHL-i-bairee):* Dragon cult in Indrasi.

Dragos Teplo: "Age of Dragons."

drey *(DRAY):* A herd animal throughout Indrasi. Dreys have horns like goats, long hair that can be sheered like alpaca, and are squat like sheep. Prized for their meat and milk (used primarily to make cheese), their hides are more supple than thukna hides and often used for clothing items.

Duple di Marc *(DOOP-l dee MARK):* A gambling gamed played with cards and domino-sized tiles. A favorite pastime in Qülla.

Earnôt *(air-NO-eet):* A human trafficker in the Tikli Province.

Embrir *(EM-breer):* Small village in Suab'hora Province, north of the Niri Bridge, on the Trinity road.

Enara *(e-NAIR-ah):* On of the four elemental corners, Enara represents water, ice and steam. Patron goddess is Lumine.

Fano (FAN-oh): A traveling blacksmith and Quen's friend.

Finira (fin-EER-ah): Proprietor of the Exulted Inn in the town of Embrir in the Suab'hora Province.

First Kin: In the Sulmére, the relative responsible for the family. Primarily the father, but if the father is deceased, then the mother, and if she is deceased too, then the oldest child. First Kin make decisions for "unbound" family members, i.e. people who are not bound to a herdclan or have a family of their own. A First Kin could also be named for an incapacitated adult.

gib-rig (jib-rig): Flying gondolas found in the capital.

Ginarli (JIN-ar-lee): Town in northwest portion of Suab'hora Province, near Val'Qüira.

gliniri (glin-EER-ee): A type of reedy grass that grows during wet season along rivers in the Sulmére Province.

Hauké (HOW-kay): Xa'Vatra's brother and a member of the Conclave.

heja (HAY-jah): A smokeable herb used in pipes. Calming. Not a hallucinogen.

Hem: A guard who works for Anu'Bida.

Hiyadi (hee-YAH-dee): The larger sun in Menauld's double star solar system. It is approximately the same size and brightness as Earth's sun.

Hooxaura (who-ZHOR-ah): The guardian spirit that guards the Chasm of Nil and protects the path to Val'Enara.

huson pine (HUSS-on): Not truly a "pine." A reedy plant that grows during the wet season. Prized for its pleasant but strong-smelling oil used to mask the pungent odor of kopeks. The oil is also a powerful anti-bacterial.

Ilkay/Saga of Ilkay: A fictional character. The *Saga of Ilkay* is a popular heroic saga, first an epic poem told by bards, and more recently one of the first books in Indrasi. The story tells of a young woman's heroic battle to rescue her aging father from a dragon's lair.

Indrasian Dakon Kovan: A great warrior, credited with killing the Winter Dragon which ended the first Dragos Teplo and ushered in the Nemo Teplo. He united much of the continent under a common language and rule. Indrasian's reign began what is commonly referred to as the First Era, or Dakon Era (0-1022 NT). Indrasi is now in its third era.

Ishnay ôhmla cureā: A spell to calm a beast or person. The language is ancient Bíduan (*see Bíduan entry*).

Ishnay recine: A spell to still someone or freeze them in place.

Ishtu Era (ISH-too): The second era of the Kovan Dynasty, it lasted from 1022-1267 NT. A proto democracy and loose republic of the four provinces. The Ishtu government proved weak as wealthy merchant families in Qülla and Bardivia had already created dynasties of their own. The result was chaos with varying laws, decrees, and edicts depending on which family ruled a particular area. These dynastic families united and ousted the Ishtu government in 1267 when they installed the Kovan dynastic government (though they did not intend the Kovans to usurp the level of power the family has today).

Jagaru (JAG-ah-roo): Vigilante justice groups that patrol the Sulmére Province.

Jijig (ZHEE-zhig): A dragon.

Jima Clan (JEE-mah): The largest and most prosperous herdclan in the Sulmére. Liodhan bound into this clan.

Juinar (JOO-in-ar): A small village in Tikli Province and on the Trinity Road. Two days south of Tilaj Gate.

Juka (JOO-kah): Goddess of wind, air, and æther. Unlike the other elementals, Juka is unaffiliated with a Corner. Known as a trickster and unpredictable, people should pray to Juka with caution as one never knows how she'll answer prayers. Helpful and antagonistic toward humans in equal measure.

Juka-jod: Jagaru members who use wind magic to track people. Druvna's small Jagaru pod doesn't have a Juka-jod.

kabu stalk *(KAH-boo):* A sugary reed that grows by rivers. Sweet and a powerful stimulant. Jagaru and others suck on the stalk to stave off hunger and given energy on long rides through the Sulmére.

Kensai (KEN-sahy): Designation for a person who has achieved mastery of the novice stage at one of the Pillars (also called Ascended, especially within the Pillars). One can achieve Kensai level without taking vows at a Pillar. All levels after Kensai require vows of commitment to a Pillar.

Kentaro (KEN-tar-oh): A level above Kensai at the Pillars. Kentaros take vows to a Pillar, but some work outside the Pillar (for example, Kovatha mages that work for the Dynasty, most of whom have taken vows at Val'Vatra Pillar.

kopek *(KOH-pek):* The preferred mount animal in the Sulmére Province and unique to the continent of Indrasi. Hairless, skin pigments range from dark tan to nearly black. Like a hairless cross between a horse and camel.

Kovan Dynasty *(KOH-van):* The current ruling Dynasty. The current Exulted, head of the Kovan Dynasty, is Xa'Vatra.

Kovan Era: The current era that began in 1267 NP. The five most powerful Mājas in Suab'hora Province, with the backing of the Mājas in Bardivia, ousted the Ishtu proto democracy. The Kovans, descended from Indrasian Dakon Kovan, first ruler of Indrasi, garnered a vote to install their patriarch as the first Exulted. Notably, Bardivia did not agree to this new arrangement, and has been an independent city-state operating within Kovan Dynasty territory (though treaties manage a tenuous arrangement for Kovan border defenses in exchange for levies). The Cadre became the Conclave, the inner counsel to the Exulted. Raj'jin di Kovan was the first Exulted and is Xa'Vatra's great grandfather. With golden amber eyes, he was said to be blessed by Hiyadi.

Kovar *(KOH-var):* A unit of money. Silver Kovars are a similar unit of measure to a dollar or pound Stirling. Gold Kovars are worth anywhere from five to twenty times a silver Kovar, depending on the area of Indrasi and economy.

Kovatha *(koh-VAH-tha):* Mages that work for the Dynasty as tax collectors and the long arm of the law throughout Indrasi.

Lakmi River *(LAK-mee):* Large river on the eastern edge of Solia.

Lenxofré *(LEN-zhoh-frey):* A region of geysers and sulfurous hot springs in the Vindaô Province, northeast of Volenex and south of the Dajianta Forest.

ligos *(lee-gohs):* A strategy game played with runed stones and molded leather game pieces on a leather "board" (which doubles as the carrying case). A favorite game in the Sulmére. A battle game, the "sides" can be any faction the players choose, such as opposing herdclans, or Bardivia vs Qülla.

Linzaô: A small town in Tikli Province on the coast.

Lumine: The moon in the Menauld solar system. Lumine is part of the Trinity, along with the "Brothers," the two suns (Hiyadi and Niyadi). Lumine is also known as the Sister, and the Watcher of the Night. She is the patron goddess of Enara Pillar/Corner, and is associated with water.

Lyas (LAHY-uhs): A gib-rig operator in Qülla.

Madi (MAH-dee): "Mother," especially in reference to the "Great Mother," the feminine aspect of the Creator godhead.

Māja (MEY-zhah): Merchant houses and guilds found in Qülla, Bardivia, and Partha. Mājas rule the cities Partha and Bardivia, while in Qülla, the Mājas have lost power over the past two generations as the Kovan Dynasty has grown in power.

Māja Wix: One of the oldest Mājas in Qülla, formed at the same time as the Kovan Māja formed (later to become the Kovan Dynasty, ruling family of Indrasi).

Menaris (men-AIR-is): A term for magic, but refers specifically to human magic as mediated through elemental gods and spirits and the planet, Menauld.

Menauld (MEN-ahld): The world on which the story takes place.

Mistress Idaya (AHY-day-ah): Matron of Māja Wix.

Mitosh River (MAHY-tosh): A river that runs southwesterly in the Suab'hora Province.

Morana: Xa'Vatra's sister and a member of the Conclave.

moss-brained squib: An insult, and one of Druvna's favorites for the young members of his Jagaru pod.

Mt. Néru *(NEY-roo):* An odd land formation in the capital resembling a spoon hovering over the city, location of the Palace di Solis.

Nabu *(NA-boo):* Quen's kopek mount.

Naja *(NAH-zhah):* A dragon.

Niezhan *(NEE-zhahn):* A great white dragon with yellow eyes.

Nilva *(NEEL-vah):* Sulmére rite for the dead and pyre.

Niri Bridge *(NEER-ee):* Bridge over the Suab'hora River chasm that spans the border between Tikli and Suab'hora provinces.

Niyadi *(NEE-yah-dee):* The smaller of the two suns in Menauld's solar system. About the size of Earth's moon, when in close Menauld orbit, the same brightness as Earth's moon. Niyadi's orbit, however, is elliptical and it currently is on its journey to the outer Menauld solar system. The full orbit takes two generations. When Niyadi travels to the outer solar system, people believe he goes to Vay'Nada, the shadow realm.

Nojyro *(NOH-zheer-oh):* Nixan shapeshifters and members of the Dragos Sol'iberi cult, but not Rajani (i.e. they do not have dragomancing abilities). Beast form not limited to avian.

Nomo Teplo *(NOH-moh TEP-loh):* "Age of Man." Abbreviated as NP.

nys't *(NIST):* A powerful narcotic and painkiller, derived from the Nystrem plant, a river's edge flower.

Nyx: Xa'Vatra's sister and a member of the Conclave.

O'Dishi/O'Dishi Chants *(OH-DEE-shee):* Healing prayer spells performed by Bruxia.

Orrokan Arts *(OR-oh-kahn):* Martial and defensive training taught at the Pillars, including training in use of weapons such as bow, swords, daggers, and staff. Val'Vatra Pillar focuses almost exclusively on Orrokan teachings, while Val'Enara and Val Doka focus on defense and Orrokan training to strengthen the mind.

Owaanir *(oh-WAHN-eer):* A dragon.

Palace di Solis: The home of the Exulted, ruler of Indrasi and head of the Kovan Dynasty.

Partha: A prosperous city-state in Tinox, across the Straits of Minea from Qülla.

Path of a Thousand Waters: The stone stair path that leads up the mountain to Val'Enara. Guarded by a spirit, Hooxaura.

Phisma Tar Pits *(FISH-mah):* Tar pits south of Val'Vatra Pillar and north of Volenex.

Pillar: The place where people study Vaya di Menaris ("The Way of Magic"), Vaya di Solis ("The Way of the Gods"), and Vaya di Orrokan ("The Way of War"), together known as "The Way." There are four Pillars in Indrasi, one for each elemental Corner, or "Way."

pit: A unit of Indrasian money. A base unit similar to a cent or pence.

prelate: Administrator at a Pillar, second to the Archon.

Promena *(proh-MEE-nah):* A Nixan shapeshifter's first metamorphosis from human to beast form, and when the exact beast form is known. For the Dragos Sol'iberi, time when determined whether the Nixan is gifted with the Rend dragomancing ability.

Quipwi (KEEP-wee): Seasonal village on the Lakmi River, north of The Staves.

Qüira (KOO-EER-ah): Elemental earth, ground, soil, and stone.

Qülla (KOO-lah): Capital of both Suab'hora Province and of all Indrasi. Seat of power for the Kovan Dynasty.

Rajani (rah-JAH-nee): A specific type of Nixan shapeshifter, Rajani always take avian form when they shapeshift, and they have the gift of the "rend," which allows them to control dragons. Some Rajani are blessed with sorcery as well, and they are referred to as Drago'Sorceri (*see Nevara*).

ranju (RAN-joo): Huge tortoise-like creatures in the Sulmére. Herdclan children often ride juvenile ranju as the creatures are docile and well adapted to the desert.

ranka (RANG-kah): A unit of Indrasian money worth twenty-five to thirty pits, depending on region. (*See entry for pits.*)

rend: Ability used by Rajani dragomancers to control dragons.

Rising: A novice at a Pillar. Juveniles from wealthy or noble-born families study at the Pillars, and most go no further than the novice designation. If one chooses to continue study at the Pillar beyond the Rising level, the person is tested and if they pass, will be designated Ascended, also known as Kensai.

Saga of Ilkay: Quen's favorite story, and the only bound book she owned. Her copy had been her mother's.

Santu's Stand: A permanent trading post in the village of Solia in Sulmére Province, and the largest general good store in the Sulmére. Owned by Quen's father, Santu.

sayari ale (sah-YAR-ee): A homebrewed liquor that's not a true ale, but distilled from an agave-like plant. Our nearest equivalent would be a cross between sotol and tequila.

Ser Chervais (SHAIR-vey): Wine merchant from Bardivia.

skins: Dynasty currency is used throughout Indrasi, but in the Sulmére, people largely rely on trade rather than currency. The nomadic herders trade mainly in animal skins, either "raw" (unworked), or tanned/worked skins. People trade other items too, but most count the value of an item in terms of how many "skins" it's worth.

slints: A type of Nixan, or shapeshifter. Slints are feared and reviled and said to take children in the night and eat them. Though Nixan are known to be real creatures, many believe Slints are a type of shapeshifter created in stories to frighten children into not venturing away from their parents/herdclan tents.

sol'dishi (sol-DEE-shee): A term of endearment in the Sulmére.

Solia (soh-LEE-ah): Quen's home village. The unofficial capital of the sparsely populated Sulmére Province.

Soliberian (SOH-li-bair-ee-uhn): Ancient language spoken by the Dragos Sol'iberi dragomancers.

Solis (SOH-lee): 1. Collective term for the two suns in the Menauld solar system. 2. Generally, refers to sun, light of the sun, or the celestial sun gods.

Steps of Infinite Light: Steps leading to the Palace di Solis.

Straits of Minea (min-EY-ah): Narrow sea channel between Partha and Qülla

Suab'hora Province (SOO-ab-HOR-ah): Northernmost province in Indrai, home to both the capital, Qülla, and Val'Doka Pillar.

suda (SOO-dah): A curse word, equivalent to shit or *merde.*

Sulmére Province: Also called the "Sea of Sands," the vast, arid Sulmére is home to nomadic herdclans and Val'Vatra Pillar.

sunginare: A word of the ancient tongue used in the Pillars. The word translates as "blood."

TazūZaj (TAH-zoo-ZAHZH): The vast mountain chain that cuts across the center of Indrasi.

The Staves: A rock formation in the Sulmére, north of Solia.

The Trinity: The three primary celestial gods under Vaya di Solis: Hiyadi, Niyadi, and Lumine.

thukna (THUK-nah): Ubiquitous herd animals in the Sulmére, like a cross between a wildebeest and a buffalo.

Tide di Solis: A Sulmére festival around the time of the longest day of the year and in honor of the Brothers. Marks the end of the spring trading season, and herdclans return to roaming.

Tikli Province (TEEK-lee): Small province in Indrasi, between Sulmére to the south and Suab'hora to the north.

Tilaj Gate (TEE-lahzh): The taxation and guard station near the border of Suab'hora and Tikli Provinces.

Tilvani (til-VAH-nee): A member of the Dragos Sol'iberi.

Timeframe of the Story: The Indrasian calendar begins with year 1 NT, being the year commonly believed that Indrasian Kovan slayed the Winter Dragon and united the continent under a common rule. Season of the Dragon takes place in year 1449 NP, Third Era, and the fifth year Xa'Vatra's rule.

Tinox: Continent to the north of Indrasi.

Val'Doka, Val'Enara, Val'Qüira, and Val'Vatra: See Note below about the Pillars.

Vas O'Nai (VAZ-oh-NAHY): Oft-quoted prophet of Vaya di Solis.

Vatra (VAH-trah): The element of fire. Vatra refers to both the god of fire, and the Menaris school or "way" of fire. Seen as the most aggressive and warlike of the four Corners, Vatra is associated with the Orrokan art of war and defense.

Vay'Nada (VAHY-nah-dah): Vay'Nada is both an entity, the "Shadow," and where the shadow dwells, aka the "Void."

Vaya di Menaris (VAHY-yah dee men-AIR-is): "Way of Magic."

Vaya di Solis: (VAHY-yah dee SOH-lee): "Way of the Two Suns." Vaya di Solis is the "Word" of the "Way," the scripture and religious portion of the Way. *See "A Note About Religion and Magic, below).*

Vindaô Province (VIN-dow): Western province in Indrasi, home to the prosperous city-state of Bardivia, prized vineyards in the Vign Gadon Region, and the desolate, sparsely populated Dajianta Forest and Lenxofré geyser fields in the southeast.

Volenex (VOHL-en-ex): At the southernmost tips of Indrasi in an extinct volcano caldera and home of the Dragos Sol'iberi. Nearly impossible to reach on land due to the Phisma tar pits to the northeast, and the Lenxofré geyser fields and haunted Dajianta forest to the northwest.

Waloo *(WAH-loo):* One of the herdclans in the Sulmére.

Yindril *(YIN-dril):* A magical creature from continent of Tinox, with features of both plant and animal. Though unable to cast spells or manipulate the Menaris, Yindrils are known to enhance the powers of human mages.

Yulina *(yoo-LEE-nah):* Owner of the alehouse in Solia.

Zal Kovan *(ZAL KOH-van):* Xa'Vatra's grandfather.

Zenith: The highest level of study and mastery at the Pillars.

Zhijnatu *(ZHISH-nah-too):* Translates as "be still and obey," from the ancient Soliberian.

Zhishni *(ZHISH-nee):* A root vegetable. Long in shape like a carrot, but with a flavor and texture more like a sweet potato.

Zhongdu Sea *(ZHONG-doo):* A vast sea on the eastern side of Indrasi, said to be home to all manner of fearsome sea creatures.

A Note About Religion and Magic

Vaya di Solis

Vaya di Solis is the main religion in Indrasi. It is often referred to as "the Way." Followers believe in a creator god, "Doj," with both feminine and masculine aspects: Doj'Madi ("Great Mother"), and Doj'Badi ("Great Father"). Followers of the Way believe this dual-aspect godhead created the cosmos. Doj'Madi and Doj'Badi are "hands off" gods, while the Trinity (*see below*), and elemental gods and spirits are considered the intermediaries in human affairs.

The primary gods believed to influence the world are the Trinity: Hiyadi, personified by the larger of the two suns; Niyadi, the smaller sun; and Lumine, the moon. There are ballads, poems, and stories throughout Indrasi about the Trinity. Views differ depending on the region. In the Sulmére, the primary belief is that Hiyadi and Niyadi are warring brothers, fighting for the love of the fair Lumine.

While there are numerous gods and spirits, the elemental gods and spirits are most important to the theology of Vaya di Soli. Each of these elemental gods/spirits rule a "Corner," and people are said to "belong" to a Corner, meaning they pray to that Corner the most, or find the teachings of a particular Corner most relevant to them.

The Corners are:

Enara—Water/Ice—Associated with Winter
Doka—Wood/Plants—Associated with Spring
Vatra—Fire—Associated with Summer
Qüira—Rock/Ground—Associated with Autumn

There is a fifth aspect of Air/Sky, the Æther, ruled by an unpredictable trickster spirit known as Juka. In the lore, it is said that Juka refused to be bound by humanity, and so she does not have a Corner of her own, but rather is omnipresent.

Vaya di Menaris

Vaya di Solis predates humans wielding magic. Once humans began manipulating magical energies—the Menaris—Vaya di Soli brought magic under its wing. Thus, at the Pillars (*see below*), students learn about the teachings of the prophets and scholars of Vaya di Soli as well as learning about Menaris. Thus, in Indrasi, magic is not shameful, shunned or feared, but a vital part of the teachings of religious life.

One might think of mastering Menaris like playing an instrument or other artistic endeavors. Anyone can create notes on a violin (or put paint to canvas), but one becomes adept only through years of daily practice. Even then, no matter how much a person studies and practices, most will never be virtuoso. The same holds true regarding mastery of Menaris arts. So while all people are born with an innate ability to manipulate Menaris energies on at least some level, most are unable to tap into this ability either because of lack of training or simply being unable to open their mind to the possibility.

Additionally, most people have an affinity for one "school" or Corner of magic—Enara, Doka, Vatra, or Qüira. Ascended Masters who study at the Pillars often have a working understanding of all four elements, but mastery of only one. Rarely, a person has natural ability to master multiple Corners. (Though, it should be noted, some believe this is due to how Vaya di Menaris is taught, i.e. spitting up into Corners so that the focus is on one element.)

It is important to note that Menaris is the magic of people, not dragons or magical creatures. From a dragon's perspective,

471

human magic is weak as it relies on the intermediation of gods and spirits, while dragons pull magical energies directly from elemental gods/spirits, from Menauld (the world), or even from the Void (the shadow realm).

THE PILLARS

In Indrasi, the Pillars are the great schools of Vaya di Soli, and where future mages are taught magic, and where future generals and leaders are also taught the Orrokan arts of war, battle, strategy, and martial arts.

Each Pillar has an Archon, the spiritual leader of that Corner not only for the Pillar, but for all Indrasi—like the "pope" of that Corner. To handle the administration of the Pillar, each Archon appoints a Prelate. The Prelate is the "face" of the Pillar, and thus the Corner, to most of the world as Archons often spend much time in quiet study and mediation. An exception to this currently is the Vatra Pillar, where Prelate Vidar sits on the Conclave in the capital leaving the administration of the Pillar to Archon Utu.

There are four Pillars in Indrasi:

Val'Enara

- Location: Tikli Province, nestled in the foothills of the TazuZaj mountain range
- Archon: Kine
- Prelate: Hrabke
- Elemental Corner: Enara (water, ice, steam)
- Associated Season: Winter
- Patron Spirit/God: Lumine
- Known For: Astrology, Astronomy, and deep thinking. The most well-rounded of the Pillars, but also the most

secluded and selective making it the most mysterious of the four.

Val'Doka

- Location: Vindaô Province, southwest of Lac'Azuro
- Archon: Séchen (SAY-shen)
- Prelate: Chigaru (SHEE-gah-roo)
- Elemental Corner: Doka (wood, plants)
- Associated Season: Spring
- Patron Spirit/God: Wopang, a forest spirit
- Known For: Healing arts. Corner favored by farmers and vintners in Vindaô Province.

Val'Vatra

- Location: Sulmére Province, southwest of Solia
- Archon: Utu (OO-too)
- Prelate: Vidar
- Elemental Corner: Vatra (fire, sun energy, heat)
- Associated Season: Summer
- Patron Spirit/God: Hiyadi
- Known For: Orrokan Arts, training of warriors and generals, and training mages in battle magic

Val'Qüira

- Location: Suab'hora Province, the northern rocky coast
- Archon: Altair
- Prelate: Vesia
- Elemental Corner: Qüira (earth, soil, ground, rock)
- Associated Season: Autumn
- Patron Spirit/God: Ben-dry'naia, a spirit of stone

- Known For: Favored by miners and smiths. Also trains heavily in Orrokan arts, though not as much as Vatra Pillar.

ACKNOWLEDGMENTS

Gratitude to early readers and editors including Jane Friedman, Ann Kroeker, Lindsay Ribar, and especially to Dario Ciriello. A huge thank you to Adam Bassett for designing the amazing maps of Menauld and Indrasi. Thank you to @DrawBraken (Ivoa) for the fabulous cover art, and to Streetlight Graphics for designing the covers, and thank you to Irene S. at RedAdept for final proofreading.

A huge thank you to my pal and podcasting partner, Robyn Dabney. There's no one else I'd rather be in the trenches with than you. Thank you for being a sounding board for both ideas and rants, for being an unmitigated force of tenacity, and an inspiration to both write—and live—to my fullest.

Thank you to all the readers who have hung in there with me waiting for this new release. A special shoutout to Ngtasha and Elisa. You ladies never fail to show support and encouragement, and it is so appreciated.

As always, thanks to my boys. To my sounding board, partner in life, and patron of my art, JRF; and to the light of my life and my favorite muse, FF.

ABOUT THE AUTHOR

Natalie is an award-winning author of fantasy and science fiction novels and short stories for young adult and adult audiences. She is also a judge in the NYC Midnight international short story writing contest.

Natalie frequently appears on panels for fiction writers and fans at book festivals and conventions across the United States. Her first novel, written for young adults, was featured by popular online site Wattpad and has been read over 2.1 million times worldwide. Her most recent short story was included in a short-story anthology, *25 Servings of SOOP, vol. ii* (Nov. 2021).

Natalie also co-hosts a popular SFF podcast, "Tipsy Nerds Book Club: The best of Science Fiction & Fantasy—with a Twist." The show focuses on reviewing and discussing both the classics of SFF genre fiction and recently published books. Natalie also enjoys international travel, hiking in the desert, cooking French food, and playing fantasy RPGs for Xbox. She lives with her husband and two cat overlords in Arizona, and visits her college-age son in NYC often.

BOOKS BY NATALIE WRIGHT

H.A.L.F.: *The Deep Beneath* © 2015

Book One of Natalie's award-winning young adult Sci-Fi series: When high school senior Erika helps an alien-human hybrid escape black ops forces, she unknowingly starts the countdown to an inter-galactic war.

H.A.L.F.: *The Makers* © 2016

A new alien threat arises as Erika, Tex, and the rest battle to save humanity. Learn what's really behind the Roswell while new realtionships blossom, and old friendships are strained.

H.A.L.F.: *ORIGINS* © 2017

Erika, Tex, and crew have fought to save themselves. Now, with alien threats on two fronts, they battle to save us all. And in the final climax, the ORIGIN is revealed.

The exciting conclusion to Natalie's epic Sci-Fi trilogy.

Printed in the USA
CPSIA information can be obtained
at www.ICGtesting.com
LVHW041042141023
760904LV00005B/502